RISE OF THE DRAGON RIDERS

Dragon Tongue

Dragon Scales

Dragon Fire

Dragon Plague

Dragon Crystals

Dragon Wars

Ava Richardson is a pen name created by Relay Publishing for co-authored Fantasy projects. Relay Publishing works with incredible teams of writers and editors to collaboratively create the very best stories for our readers.

Cover Design by Joemel Requeza.

www.relaypub.com

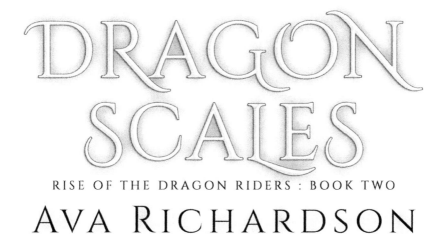

DRAGON SCALES

RISE OF THE DRAGON RIDERS : BOOK TWO

Ava Richardson

BLURB

Will dragons defend a kingdom founded on lies?

Novice dragon rider Cora and her dragon Alaric are determined to rescue their families from the king's fortress, but after her first attempt at infiltration, Cora is captured! Panic turns to hope, though, when she realizes her captors are antiroyalists. Maybe she won't have to face Onyx alone…and maybe she and Alaric can have help with their training when a mysterious woman who helped her before is revealed to be the only surviving dragon rider.

But rumors of a new dragon rider are spreading in the Tenegard kingdom, making Cora's training even more dangerous. And she and Alaric have yet to harness the full power of their mystical bond…a power they desperately need, if they are to have any chance of defeating King Onyx and rescuing their loved ones.

On their own, Cora and Alaric are no match for the powerful sorcerer king. But will other dragons rally to their cause, after a century of lies sent them fleeing from humans? Even as they struggle to form this new alliance, Onyx's forces are closing in on Cora and Alaric.

And a darkness beyond their imagination looms on the horizon…

MAILING LIST

Thank you for purchasing *Dragon Scales*
(Rise of the Dragon Riders Book Two)

If you would like to hear more about what I am up to, or continue to follow the stories set in this world with these characters—then please take a look at:

AvaRichardsonBooks.com

You can also find me on me on
www.facebook.com/AvaRichardsonBooks

Or sign up to my mailing list:
AvaRichardsonBooks.com/mailing-list

CONTENTS

Chapter 1	1
Chapter 2	14
Chapter 3	30
Chapter 4	42
Chapter 5	52
Chapter 6	61
Chapter 7	73
Chapter 8	81
Chapter 9	88
Chapter 10	96
Chapter 11	102
Chapter 12	115
Chapter 13	125
Chapter 14	137
Chapter 15	148
Chapter 16	163
Chapter 17	174
Chapter 18	185
Chapter 19	194
Chapter 20	202
Chapter 21	215
Chapter 22	225
Chapter 23	238
Chapter 24	251
Chapter 25	262
Chapter 26	274
Chapter 27	282
Chapter 28	291
Chapter 29	305
Chapter 30	317
Chapter 31	326
Chapter 32	336

End of Dragon Scales   339
Thank you!   341
About Ava   343
Sneak Peek: Dragon Fire   345
Sneak Peek: The Dragon King's Egg   353
Also by Ava   355
Want More?   365

CHAPTER 1

There was nothing particularly intimidating about the entrance to the fortress. It was as normal as a gate could be: a worn lattice grille made of wood pieces connected together with steel bolts. But the guard standing in front of the gate was another matter entirely. With his broad shoulders, square jaw, and a neck that was as thick as his bulging bicep muscles, it was perfectly plain to see that nothing was getting past him—which was irritating, since that was exactly what seventeen-year-old Cora Hart had spent the entire day trying to do.

Sighing, Cora slumped further into the alleyway where she was hiding and she reached out mentally to her bonded dragon, Alaric. *It's no use,* she said through their telepathic bond. *That guard is as unmovable as the Therma Mountains.*

Alaric's voice came back instantly. *He cannot stand guard around the clock, correct? You humans are not designed to work longer than a span of hours before needing rest. Eventually, someone will come to relieve him. Perhaps you can sneak through during the changing of the guard.*

Before responding, Cora couldn't help but marvel at how easy it was to hear and speak to Alaric. When they'd first met, communication had been difficult. Well, to be honest, when they'd first met, she'd been so terrified at the approach of an angry dragon that sitting down and having a chat had been the last thing on her mind. But if she *had* known it was possible for them to chat, she would have definitely tried.

Dragon Tongue, the magic that allowed humans and dragons to talk to one another, had long been forgotten by the humans. And so had the bond that humans and dragons used to share, allowing for the dragon riders of myth and legend, who protected the realm. But myths and legends were all that remained, and no one believed those old stories anymore—except for Cora's grandmother. She was the one who had brought Cora to the cave where Cora had been able to learn the first elements of Dragon Tongue—just enough that, when she encountered Alaric for the first time, they'd both been surprised when they could understand each other. Not perfectly, not completely, but enough to serve as a starting point.

Together, they had managed to master Dragon Tongue enough to have whole conversations, though the connection had often felt like she was trying to communicate through a thick wall where she could only catch part of the conversation. Now that the bond had snapped into place between them, communication was as easy and as natural as breathing. They could even speak to one another mind to mind— something that Cora still found absolutely fascinating.

Yeah, but if this guy is any indicator, it will probably be another mountain of a guard, Cora grumbled. *And if I got caught, there's no way I'd be able to get past both of them.* She was honestly lucky that she'd been able to go this long without attracting any attention, despite the way her rough, rural clothes stood out next to the crisp, neat fashions of the city. Hanging around and just hoping that she'd find an opening didn't seem like a workable, long-term plan…but it wasn't like she had a better one.

You should eat something, Alaric encouraged. *You are far more optimistic on a full stomach.*

I'm not hun— She was interrupted by a gurgling sound as her stomach rolled over. *Okay, fine. Maybe I am a little hungry. But you know the second I leave this spot, some opportunity to get inside will pop up and I'll miss it.* She let out a low sigh.

I wish I could help you, Alaric replied, his own voice laced with the same frustration Cora could feel burning through their bond. *I do not like being stuck out here, hiding, while you are in there by yourself.*

Cora softened slightly at this. *I know. We're a much better team than we are separate, but we have to be careful. We're the first bonded dragon pair in a century, and King Onyx is looking for us.*

King Onyx the Deathless—the man who had slaughtered all the dragon riders of old through treachery and betrayal. A foreign king who had taken Tenegard by force and used magic to convince the native people that he was their savior, saving them from a famine that he himself had created. What was worse, he had used his authority and position of power to wipe away the native, genante culture as well as any belief in the stories of the dragon riders or the relationship humans had once had with the dragons. But Cora and Alaric knew the truth.

What was scarier was that King Onyx now knew of their existence, and he would stop at nothing to destroy them. The good news was that Onyx did not know the specifics of Cora's identity or which dragon she was bonded to. The bad news? Comparative anonymity hadn't kept their loved ones safe. Inside that fortress—the same one Cora was desperately seeking to enter—were both Cora's father and Alaric's mother. Viren had been arrested on trumped-up charges by an official who had a grudge against him, while Raksha had been taken by mistake. The gods only knew how much danger they were in, and the knowledge that there was nothing she could do to help them ate at Cora far worse than any hunger.

But rushing in and getting herself arrested or Alaric caught wouldn't help anything, either.

We can't risk anyone seeing you or seeing us together, she reminded Alaric.

Another burst of frustration came spiraling down the bond. *I know, and I will stay here, as we discussed. But that does not mean that I have to like it.*

No, Cora snorted. *You don't. But if we've any hope of freeing Raksha and my father, this is what we must do.*

You are right, of course. It is just so strange that they would bring my mother here. I have yet to determine what is so special about this place. Wouldn't it have made more sense to transport her to Onyx in the capital city?

It was something they'd been wondering about since the moment Onyx's forces had mistakenly taken Raksha from the Therma Mountains. The reasons why she had been targeted were clear enough. Someone had seen Cora and Alaric flying together—though not well enough to clearly identify them—and Raksha, who shared Alaric's coloring, had been captured under the suspicion that *she* was the newly bonded dragon. In Cora's deadly confrontation with Secare, one of Onyx's top generals, she had learned that Onyx wanted the new dragon rider pair captured. It had been his intention to experiment on them and make sure that the magic he'd worked so hard to bury would stay hidden.

When Cora and Alaric had finally managed to conjure Dragon Fire, killing Secare and allowing them to evade capture, they'd thought they were safe. They hadn't realized until Raksha had been reported missing that Secare's men had found and captured her, bringing her here—along with other prisoners, including Viren—to the fortress smack in the heart of the bustling city of Llys.

It is strange, Cora agreed. *You'd think Onyx would want her brought straight to him in the capital. Do you think they've realized she's not a bonded dragon? Maybe they're hoping to use her as bait to draw you out.*

Alaric growled at that. *I do not like the idea of my mother being used as bait for anything.*

Cora thought of her own father, likely locked away in some jail cell. "I know," she said, sighing again. "Trust me, I understand."

The clattering sound of wagon wheels on the cobblestone streets filled the air and Cora straightened up, leaning forward to continue spying on the fortress gate. She could tell from the white uniform of the driver that this was a butcher's wagon, come to deliver a shipment of meat products to the soldiers. The driver lifted a hand to the guard before pulling something out of his pocket, something gold that glinted slightly in the sunlight.

Cora squinted, leaning even farther out from her hiding spot, attempting to get a better look. *Well, this is new,* she said to Alaric, watching carefully as the driver flashed the gold item in his hand at the guard. The guard nodded once and stepped back to pound on the gate three times. It opened instantly and the butcher's wagon was waved inside.

What? What's going on? Alaric asked.

Cora sent him a mental picture of what she'd seen. *I think the driver was showing the guard a seal of some kind. I remember my father telling me about them once. We didn't use such a thing in Barcroft because the community was so small. There was no sense in choosing someone as the official vendor for the fortress. The town only had one butcher, so of course he was the one who brought the meat deliveries. Here in the bigger cities, vendors must go through a vetting process. The government seal shows that they've been approved to enter the fortress without having to go through additional security checks.*

And that means that if they show that seal, they can come and go as they please? The guards do not stop them at all?

Cora eyed the gate of the fortress. *It certainly looks that way. The guard barely gave the wagon a second glance. Once he saw the seal, he just waved them right in.*

We need to get one of those seals.

Yes, we do, Cora said, standing to full height. *Any idea on how to do that?*

I'm afraid I cannot assist you there, especially not from where I'm hiding.

Cora nodded. She knew Alaric hated being away from the action, unable to help, but him showing up would do nothing but cause panic. Dragons were feared and loathed by the whole populace, thanks to Onyx, and if he showed up at the fortress, the soldiers would be sure to attack. They'd actually considered that as a way to sneak Cora in— taking advantage of the chaos—but they'd decided against it. One dragon couldn't stand up to a fortress full of well-armed soldiers. There was always Dragon Fire, but given its power, it would be difficult to control. And with a marketplace full of people right outside the gates, the likelihood of injuring innocent people was high. Cora and Alaric had already agreed to fight their way into the fortress if need be —even if that ultimately meant using Dragon Fire—but only if the situation was truly dire. They wanted to exhaust every other possible option first. Using one of those seals was the best possibility they'd come across so far…but first she'd have to get one.

"Come on, Cora, think," she urged herself. "Think, think!"

Scanning the market square, her eyes fell on one particular building. There wasn't anything ornate or special about it, but the thick plume that rose steadily from its chimney and the rhythmic *ting ting* coming from within was so familiar to Cora that she felt as if her heart had been caught in a fist that was squeezing it tightly enough to steal her breath. The blacksmithing forge. It was exactly like the one she and her father had owned and operated back in Barcroft. She had seen it when she'd first arrived in the square, but she hadn't given it much thought other than to view it as a painful reminder of her father and everything they'd lost. But now, an idea had begun percolating in her mind.

Cora had spent nearly every day of her life with her father in his forge; she knew the ins and outs of smithing like the back of her hand —and in this case, that knowledge might just come in handy. This was the only forge she'd seen so far in Llys, and given its proximity to the fortress, there was a good chance that the blacksmith provided weapons and other services to the fortress. If so, then he had access to one of those golden seals.

I think I have an idea, she said to Alaric, her feet already carrying her across the square. She sent him a mental image of her destination and approval surged towards her through their bond.

The door to the forge was shut, so Cora lifted a fist and knocked firmly, hoping the pounding of her heart wasn't audible.

"Come in," a low, gruff voice called out, and Cora pushed open the door, stepping into the thick heat of the forge.

A man wearing a long, leather apron stood near the hearth, working a molten piece of steel on an anvil. His hammer was clutched in one hand, and he used the other to wipe at the sheen of sweat on his forehead. "Can I help you?"

Cora's mouth was dry, and the words seemed to stick in her throat. The man's hair, dark and starting to streak with silver, was cropped short in the typical hairstyle of the Athelians—Onyx's people.

When he had conquered Tenegard, swarms of people from his homeland of Athelia had come to settle there. Many years had passed since then, but the Athelians—known as malhos—had remained, even if they'd never truly assimilated. Cora's main experience with them had been courtesy of Captain Daggett back in Barcroft: a petty, vain, arrogant tyrant who'd taken pleasure in grinding down the genante townspeople and crushing their culture and traditions wherever he could. As far as she was concerned, malhos were to be avoided as much as possible. If this blacksmith was one of them, then it was almost certain she wouldn't find any help here.

She looked desperately for any sign that she might be mistaken, that he might be genante after all…but in addition to the Athelian hairstyle, the silver rings in his ears were a dead giveaway.

"Can I help you?" the blacksmith repeated, narrowing his eyes.

It can't hurt to ask, Cora reasoned with herself. *For Papa and for Raksha. Besides, it would look even stranger—and draw even more unwanted attention onto me—if I came in here and then just turned around and ran back out.* Swallowing her inhibitions, she cleared her throat. "Hello, sir. I've come to inquire about a job."

"A job?" The blacksmith's bushy brows lifted. "You have smithing experience?"

Cora nodded. "I do, sir. My father is a smith, and I grew up in his forge. I know the trade, and I'm a good assistant. I was hoping you might hire me. I'm a hard worker, and I'm willing to do whatever you need done. Take care of chores around the shop, run errands, make deliveries."

"You're not from here, are you?" It was a simple, seemingly casual question, but Cora noticed the way the smith's eyes swept over her— quick and measuring—before returning to his project. She didn't take offense at the minimal attention he gave her—she knew that hot metal worked on its own timetable, and she never would have expected any smith worth his salt to halt a project midway through. But a quick scan likely meant he hadn't had a chance to notice much more than the basics: her rough, country clothing and likely her accent. If she could have, she would have shown him the callouses on her hands, the strength in her arms, the healed burns from years of assisting in the forge. She would have shown him all the signs a blacksmith would recognize of someone who knows the trade. But he didn't look long enough for that.

"Um," she swallowed. "No, sir. I'm new to town. But like I said, I'm a hard worker, and I'm willing to do whatever needs to be done."

The deep V between the smith's brows deepened. "Hmmm." He tilted his head, considering. "No," he finally answered. "I'm sorry, girl, but I'm not looking to take anyone on at the moment. Check back with me in a few months' time."

Cora's heart sank. "Wait!" she cried out, refusing to let him dismiss her so easily. "Please, sir, I…I really need this job."

She let the desperation she felt seep into her tone and her face. And she truly *did* feel desperate—that part wasn't an act or a con. If she couldn't make this work, if she couldn't get a job with the blacksmith that would gain her access to the fortress, then she didn't know what she would do. The blacksmith must have sensed her sincerity because he visibly softened. A few more strokes of the hammer put his current project at a point where he could step aside for a moment, and once that was done, he set the hammer down and moved from out behind the anvil. "Your family? Have they traveled here to Llys as well?" His voice was gentle and there was kindness shining in his eyes.

Cora swallowed. It was a little strange seeing a malhos reacting so kindly. The blacksmith seemed reasonable and understanding—not the cold, self-seeking attitude that she had expected. She didn't want to lie to him, but telling him the truth certainly wasn't an option. Well…telling him the *whole* truth wasn't an option. Maybe she could pick some pieces of the truth that would serve.

"No, sir. It's just me. My father and I were separated. His health has been so poor lately, and I…I'm so worried about him. You have no idea. I don't even remember my mother—she died when I was a baby. My father is all I've got—the only family I have left. I'm just trying to get back to him." Her voice broke on the last word, and the smith let out a deep sigh.

"Please, sir," Cora continued, hoping against all hope that the blacksmith would be amenable. "Give me a chance."

The blacksmith let out another sigh, his shoulders slumping in resignation. "Very well. I suppose there are a few things I could use some help with. I have a large order for the fortress that I need to deliver next month, and if you really are qualified, then I could use your hands. But you'll need to prove yourself first."

Cora's heart lifted. The blacksmith had all but confirmed that he was a supplier for the fortress—which meant, if her suspicions were correct, he had one of the golden seals that she needed. "I can do that." She beamed. "I promise you, sir. Whatever you need me to do, I can do it." She held up her hands so that he could see the marks of experience on them. He nodded in approval at the sight.

"Right, then. How about this: If you prove yourself useful to me over the next few days, I'd be willing to officially take you on as my apprentice. But we'll need to conduct a trial period first to make sure that we're able to work well together. If we turn out to be a good match, then we can discuss you taking on even more responsibilities. Does that sound fair?"

Cora had no real intention of taking up the apprenticeship—at least, not for any longer than it took for her to get her hands on the seal—but she couldn't help but feel gratitude for the offer. It was a kindness she had not expected, especially from a malhos.

"Oh yes, that sounds perfect. Thank you so much, sir."

"Bram," the blacksmith said, pressing a hand to his chest, indicating himself. "You can call me Bram."

"Bram," Cora repeated. "Thank you. My name is Cora."

"Right." Bram reached into his pocket and pulled out two coins. "Take this as an advance on your wages. You look like you could use a decent meal."

Cora's eyes widened slightly as he plunked the coins into her palm. Another unexpected kindness. "Oh, um…thank you, sir."

Bram nodded, returning his focus to his anvil. "I'll see you tomorrow, then, Cora. Be here early."

Cora nodded and then dashed out of the forge before Bram changed his mind about the job.

It worked, Cora reached out to Alaric. *I can't believe it, but it actually worked. He's going to give me a job.*

Ah, finally we have a bit of luck, Alaric replied. *It was much needed.*

Cora let out a breath, shared relief pulsating through their bond. *It was. And this means we're one step closer to getting one of those golden seals and one step closer to Papa and Raksha. Though I do feel sort of bad. The blacksmith was kind to offer me an apprenticeship. I hate to feel like I've deceived him.*

You did what must be done. You cannot feel bad for that.

I know. I guess I sort of wish that my situation really was as simple as just needing a job. That seems a whole lot easier than what we're attempting to do.

Yes, Alaric agreed. *Much easier.*

Back out in the square, Cora scurried around the stalls and vendor stands, stopping only long enough to use the coins Bram had given her to purchase a roasted turkey leg before heading out of the city. It was the first real meal she'd had in a while, given that she had been stuck with what they could forage up to now, and her stomach seemed to happily accept it. Cora licked the grease from her fingers as she headed out of the city, nearly skipping at the day's good fortune.

Outside the city walls, there wasn't a lot of foot traffic, just the occasional merchants and their wagons traveling to and fro. Still, Cora was extra careful to ensure that no one was paying her any attention before she slipped into the darkness of the forest that bordered Llys.

The thicket where Alaric was hiding was dense with trees and thick foliage, so Cora didn't have to worry about someone seeing him, especially now with night falling.

"Welcome back," Alaric greeted her, and she released a breath of relief when Alaric's blue scales came into view. She'd kept in touch with him all day through the bond, but still she felt much more secure when they were together.

"Thanks," Cora replied, hurrying over. There was a chill in the air, but it was too risky to light a fire. Instead, she tossed her shoulder bag to the side and snuggled up next to Alaric, yawning widely. His body heat was more than warm enough to evade the crispness of the evening air.

"Tomorrow is one step closer," she murmured. "Soon, we'll find Papa and your mother and then…" she trailed off.

"Indeed," Alaric replied. "Soon we'll find them and set them free."

But Cora could feel the unease churning through their bond. Because even if they did manage to get into the fortress and find their parents, they had no idea how they would be able to release them. Raksha was a fierce and powerful dragon—what kind of restraints would be able to hold her in check? And how would Cora be able to overcome them?

You'll figure something out, Cora told herself, sinking into the warmth of Alaric's side. *One way or another, you'll figure it out.*

We will figure it out, Alaric added, his voice soft. *Together.*

"Together," Cora whispered. And with that, she let her drowsy eyelids close.

CHAPTER 2

The heat from the forge was stifling. The back of Cora's tunic was nearly soaked through with sweat, but she didn't complain. She and Bram had managed to forge a tenuous…well, not friendship exactly, but at least a good working relationship. And despite the anxiety Cora felt about freeing her father and Raksha, there was something comforting about spending the long days in the forge. It reminded her of home, of the time she'd spent at her father's side. It was the motivation she needed to stay her course.

On the first day she had arrived to work for him, Bram had seemed hesitant to let her do more than just the most basic of chores, but Cora had quickly shown him just how trained she was, and now, nearly a week later, Bram didn't hover over her every move or watch her out of the corner of his eye. If anything, he seemed pleased to have stumbled upon such a willing and competent apprentice. He had started giving her more difficult tasks and even hummed appreciatively when she did something particularly well. Everything was going according to plan—except for the seal.

Cora had managed to figure out where Bram kept his seal, but the drawer of the wooden desk in the back of the forge was always locked. And Bram kept the only key on a ring in his pocket. A ring that he always carried with him.

Cora swiped at the droplets of sweat that rolled down her temple. Her long hair was tied back in a braid, but there were still errant strands that had come free that stuck to her neck and the sides of her face. Sucking down a mouthful of the thick, hot air, she leaned against a metal rack of tools to catch her breath. It wasn't all that late in the afternoon, but Cora was already imagining curling up next to Alaric and going to sleep. The days of grueling work in the forge coupled with all the travel she and Alaric had done prior to arriving were starting to catch up with her.

A warm burst of energy came cascading down the bond, filling Cora's body. The refreshing effect was immediate. *You didn't have to do that,* she said to Alaric, moving over to the hearth to stoke the fire.

It is not as if I require the strength for anything of note, Alaric replied. *Lying low requires hardly any energy at all. So I might as well share. Besides, you are no good to any of us if you keel over from exhaustion.*

Cora snorted. *Yes, I suppose that's true. Want to switch places? You can come work in the forge, and I'll curl up and nap all day long.*

Indeed. Do you think the blacksmith would notice if we were to swap? We do share a striking resemblance, after all.

His tone was light, but even though Cora could tell that he was doing his best to keep her spirits up, he was clearly also battling frustration. He hated being stuck in his hiding place, unable to do anything to rescue his mother or protect Cora. He itched to do something more helpful, but they both knew that was impossible.

Maybe if we got you a bonnet of some kind, Cora continued, smiling as she imagined a massive bonnet atop Alaric's head. *And then we could get a—*

"Cora, come here." Bram's voice broke through her conversation with Alaric, and Cora jumped slightly.

"Coming," she called out, hurrying over to where he stood next to his desk in the corner of the forge that served as his office. "Yes, sir?" she asked, wiping her grimy hands on the front of her apron.

"I need you to do something for me," Bram said, as he hunched over the desk, scripting something hastily on a piece of cream-colored parchment.

Cora waited as he finished his message and signed his name with a flourish. Once it was folded and sealed, he straightened and handed it to Cora. "I need you to take this missive to the fortress arms master."

"Me?" Cora squeaked.

"Do I have another apprentice that I should know about?" Bram looked about the forge before giving Cora a small smile. "In truth, I usually deliver these myself, but the officer is a terrible grump when it comes to dealing with anyone who is taller than him. He always tries to puff himself up around me, but maybe he'll skip the nonsense with you. And if not, at least I won't be the one who'll have to deal with that today."

Cora chuckled, hoping he wouldn't be able to tell that it was forced. "Well, I'm happy to deliver the letter. The arms master's office is within the fortress?"

"It is," Bram confirmed, and Cora's heart began to thump.

"But how will I get inside?" she asked, playing innocent. "I'm new to Llys, but even I know that they won't let just anybody inside the fortress."

"No, you're right about that," Bram said, removing the ring of keys from his pocket and unlocking the drawer of his desk. "But this," he plucked up the golden seal from within the depths of the drawer, "should get you in and out without too many questions." He held out his hand.

Cora took the seal, running her hand over its golden face. "It's so pretty," she murmured to distract him from noticing the way her hand was trembling. He'd seen her work—he knew she had steady hands. But they were far from steady now.

"Yes, well, it is important that you do not lose it, aye? It would be quite a nuisance trying to explain to the fortress officials why I need a replacement."

"I won't lose it," Cora assured him, tucking the seal safely in the pocket of her tunic along with the letter. "I will deliver the letter and be back shortly."

"Very well," Bram said, nodding at the door. "See that you do."

With his dismissal, Cora removed her apron, turned on her heels, and headed for the door, reminding herself not to rush, not to look excited, when all she wanted was to jump for joy.

Alaric! Can you believe it? Cora practically screamed down the bond. She quickly relayed the blacksmith's instructions. *After days of waiting for an opportunity to steal the seal, he just handed it right to me.*

I certainly was not expecting this, but I will happily accept any stroke of luck that comes our way, Alaric responded.

Cora couldn't agree more. She hurried through the square and over to the north gate of the fortress. The burly guard she'd seen a few days prior wasn't on duty, but in his place was another guard who seemed just as burly and no-nonsense. If anything, he seemed even *less* accommodating, his face seemed etched in a permanent sneer. His eyes narrowed on Cora as she approached.

"Um…hello," she said, pulling out both the seal and the letter from her pocket. "I'm here to deliver a message to the arms master."

The guard studied the seal in her hand for a moment before running his eyes over Cora's face and then down at her clothes. She knew she looked a mess, and her fingers tugged at the hem of her tunic, as if to straighten it.

"I've never seen you before," the guard finally grunted, not an ounce of friendliness on his face. "This seal belongs to the blacksmith, Bram. Where is he?"

"He's back at the forge," Cora replied, trying not to let the annoyance she felt churning in her gut show. "I am his apprentice and he sent me to deliver this message in his place."

"You? His apprentice?" The guard's face split into a wide grin as a booming laugh shook his torso. "A little pipsqueak like you, training to be a blacksmith? Now I've seen it all. If you even tried to lift his hammer, you'd probably fall over."

Heat rushed up the back of Cora's neck and warmed her cheeks. "I'll have you know, sir, that I am stronger than I look—and more than capable of doing the job."

This only made the guard laugh even harder.

This wasn't the first time someone had questioned Cora's strength or competence, but the guard's laughter rocketed through Cora, sending waves of aggravation through her body. She wasn't used to having her abilities treated so dismissively. Back in Barcroft, everyone had seen her working her father's forge for practically her entire life. Even those who disliked her or her father—such as Daggett—had held some respect for their skill and craftsmanship. In this town, where the population was dominated by malhos, respect and common courtesy such as she received from Bram seemed to be the exception rather than the rule.

I do not eat humans, Alaric's voice was low and growly, *but for this human, I will make an exception.*

You will do no such thing, Cora responded quickly, though it did make her feel better to know that Alaric was as offended by the man's attitude as she was. *He's an ignorant fool, that's all.* Antagonizing him wouldn't do her any favors—nor would it get her into the fortress any faster. Cora forced herself to swallow her frustration and speak politely.

"Please, sir, if you'll let me pass, I have a message to deliver."

The guard continued to guffaw, and Cora was contemplating whether she'd be able to get away with just shoving past him when another guard appeared.

This guard wore his midnight black hair cropped short on the sides in the malhos fashion, but the top was a bit longer than usual, with a thick curl swirling just above his forehead. His clear, deep blue eyes landed on Cora.

Cora braced herself for more laughter as the newly arrived guard clamped a hand down on the other guard's shoulder.

"Mattius, what in the gods' names is so funny? Because it sounds as if you're giving this young woman a difficult time." Surprise rippled through Cora at the bite to his words that Cora hadn't expected. She'd assumed the guards would be on the same side—united in looking down on her. She certainly hadn't expected anyone to come to her defense.

"I'm just having a bit of fun, Faron," the laughing guard replied, though he straightened up and did his best to look more serious. "The girl's claiming to be an apprentice to the blacksmith, if you can believe that."

"And have you got Bram's seal as proof?" Faron asked, turning to Cora.

Cora lifted the seal, showing it to him. He gave it a quick glance, then nodded.

"It looks to me like it's a fact, not a claim," Faron pointed out to Mattius.

"But…but you can't really believe she's a blacksmith's apprentice," Mattius blustered. "No little girl could do a job like that."

"Right now, her job seemed to be to…deliver a message, yes?" Faron said, eyeing the parchment in her hand. She nodded. "Well, then," Faron said, turning back to Mattius. "I'd say that at the moment, she's handling her work with no difficulty at all. Your job, on the other hand, is to let in people who show the proper authorization. She's doing her job, so isn't it high time you started doing yours?"

Mattius had no response to that other than to gape unattractively before slamming his mouth shut. His scowl made it abundantly clear that she had not made a friend in him today.

Faron, on the other hand, shot her a wink and stepped around the other man, gesturing towards the gate. "Right, then. If you'll just follow me."

Cora let him lead her through the gate.

"Thank you," Cora said, once the gate had been closed firmly behind him. "I don't know what his problem was."

"Oh, I know exactly what his problem was," Faron replied, clasping his hands behind his back. "Mattius's brain is the size of a walnut and stars bless him, it has left him physically incapable of being anything other than an arse. It is our duty to pity him this misfortune and treat his impairment with compassion—after all, he can't help being absolutely intolerable." He said this with such a perfectly straight face that Cora couldn't stop the chuckle that bubbled up her throat. She pressed her lips together, for fear of offending Faron, but then he laughed too.

"I really am sorry about him. We're trained better than that, I assure you." He pointed down the walkway. "You've got a letter to deliver?"

"Yes, to the arms master from the blacksmith."

"I am happy to show you to the armory if you wish."

"Oh no!" Cora replied hastily. "I think I can manage. I'm sure you have other guardly duties to attend to, right?"

Faron dipped his head. "That I do. And if you're sure you can find your own way, then?"

"Quite sure, thank you." She returned the gesture with a smile and headed in the direction Faron had pointed. In truth, she wasn't sure where the armory was located—but nor did she particularly care. It wasn't the arms master she'd spent so many days desperate to see. And her odds of finding either her father or Raksha would increase dramatically if she could do some poking around on her own.

"Wait, one second," Faron called after her.

Cora froze. Had she said something wrong? Did he suspect that she was up to something? She turned around. "Yes?"

"Your name," he replied. "I didn't catch your name."

"Oh, um… it's Cora," she answered.

"Faron," he replied, placing a hand on his chest to indicate himself. "Well met, Cora." He lifted a hand, giving her a small wave.

"And you," Cora replied before turning back around and resuming her walk.

That was interesting, Alaric piped up, having been monitoring the situation through Cora's thoughts.

It was, Cora agreed. Faron wasn't at all like she had expected. She'd never have imagined a malhos coming to her rescue like that. Most were too arrogant to put their necks out for anyone. And one like Faron—a guard in a position of power...and ridiculously handsome, at that, which surely was even more cause to be arrogant—she'd have expected to ignore her completely or join the other man in putting her down. *He was...intriguing.*

Shoving the thoughts of Faron aside, Cora refocused on her task, glancing over her shoulder to make sure she was alone. When she saw that she wasn't being followed by anyone, she took the first turn she came to, hurrying along the walkways as she searched for any clue as to where Viren and Raksha were being kept. She knew there was a dungeon within the fortress confines, but she wasn't sure where it was located.

She moved quickly, doing her best not to appear suspicious. When she turned the corner and found herself in a wide-open courtyard, she almost swore under her breath. She had thought the prisoners' keep might be in the center of the fortress, in the most protected part of the compound—but either she'd been completely wrong, or the containment cells were located underground, accessible by some staircase that she hadn't yet found.

Then she spotted them. A work crew of raggedy-looking men and women working on repairs to the inner fortress wall. They were also tending the lush garden that sat at the center of the courtyard. All of these individuals looked worn and tired, their clothes shabby and faded. They also looked like they hadn't had a decent meal in a while. Their faces and hands were covered in a layer of grime, and their eyes were glassy in a way that spoke of ongoing hardship.

"Prisoners," Cora murmured, realizing what she was seeing. "They're prisoners who have been sentenced to work detail for their crimes."

The words had no sooner left her lips than a hacking wheeze of a wet cough—a painfully *familiar* sounding cough—echoed across the courtyard, drawing her attention to a man with hair the color of her own and a profile that Cora would know anywhere.

Papa! She wanted to scream the words, but she kept them inside, not wanting to draw attention to him or to herself. There were a handful of guards that looked as if they were supposed to be watching the work crew, but they were several feet away engaging in what looked like a card game of sorts. She could only hope their distraction would last.

Your father? Alaric piped up, reading her emotions through the bond. *You've found the dungeons?*

No, but I did find him. She told Alaric about the work crew. *I'm going to see if I can talk to him.*

And my mother?

No sign of her yet, but don't worry. I'll find her.

Cora walked silently along the perimeter of the garden at the center of the courtyard, inching her way towards the work crew. When she was close enough, she parked herself on one of the benches that lined the garden, putting her back to the workers. If anyone saw her, she hoped they would assume she was resting or taking in a bit of air. But after glancing at the guards to make sure they weren't paying attention, she twisted around and hissed, "Papa! Papa, over here!"

Viren Hart jerked when he heard Cora's voice, his eyes going wide when he spotted her.

"Cora?" he rasped, hobbling over to her. "Cora, what are you doing here?"

"I came to find you," Cora answered, her eyes filling with tears.

"Oh my sweet girl." Viren's eyes also welled up as he threw his arms around her. Several of the other prisoners had noticed the exchange and moved closer. Cora tensed, thinking that they were about to sound the alarm, but then one of them gave her an encouraging smile and she realized they were forming a human barrier between them and the guards, giving them time to talk without getting caught.

Cora mouthed a thank you and turned back to her father who had begun coughing again, his entire body shaking as he gasped for air.

"Oh, Papa, that sounds awful," she said, pounding on his back. "You're getting worse out here. You should be inside resting. Don't they know you're ill?"

Viren gave her a wry smile. "Do you really think that matters to them? I'm a prisoner, Cora. As long as I am able to stand and work, that's all they care about."

"But you shouldn't even be here. You were wrongfully accused."

"That may be so, little lark. But I have already been tried, convicted, and sentenced."

Cora paled. "Sentenced?"

Viren nodded. "Yes. Eighteen months of hard labor to pay my debts. Then I should be able to return home."

"Eighteen months?" Cora blanched, feeling as if someone had just punched her in the gut. Her eyes ran over her father's frame. Already he looked more feeble than he had the last time she'd seen him. Thinner too. And from the wet rasp of his cough, it was obvious that his illness was ongoing. If things continued in this manner, the likelihood of Viren even living to complete his sentence was slim.

Swallowing her fear and worry, Cora reached for her father's hand, squeezing it gently. "Oh, Papa, I'm so sorry this happened to you. But don't worry. I'm going to get you out of here."

At this, her father looked alarmed, his grip on her hand tightening. "No, lark. You can't do that. If they catch you, you'll end up out here next to me, and I can't abide the thought of that. You must leave Llys and return home to Barcroft. Find a job and keep your head down until I return. There are plenty of good people there, and I know they will help look after you and keep you safe. You need to get as far away from here as possible."

Cora shook her head. "I'm not just going to leave you in here to die, Papa. I'm going to get you out of here." Lowering her voice, she whispered. "I have a dragon that's going to help me."

Viren stared at Cora, as if struggling to understand what she'd just said. But then his eyes seemed to cloud over strangely—almost unnaturally. "A dragon? No, Cora. You mustn't go anywhere near the dragons. It is illegal to even approach them, and for good reason. They're dangerous."

Cora felt her frustration surge. She had tried before to tell him about the dragons, to explain the friendship she'd built with Alaric, but her father refused to even consider the idea. It was as if he had some sort of mental block around the very idea of a bond between humans and dragons, refusing to see them as anything other than wild and dangerous.

"And I would know," Viren continued, "because there is a dragon here at the fortress that arrived the same time I did. Nasty thing that looked as if it would eat anyone who got close enough. I was grateful that the guards had the beast muzzled and bound in chains."

"Wait, you saw a dragon here?" *Raksha!* "Where, Papa? Can you tell me where the dragon is? Is she in the dungeon?"

Viren's eyes were still strangely unfocused. "You mustn't go looking for it. Dragons are vicious and you could get hurt."

"You don't have to tell me—I know how you feel about dragons, Papa," Cora replied. "But I need to know—where are they keeping the dragon?" Deciding to try another tack, she said, "You want me to avoid it, right? Well, how can I avoid it if I don't know where it is? Don't you think you should tell me?"

Viren looked as if he was weighing that idea. For a moment, she thought he was going to refuse her again, but then he nodded. "Very well. I don't know for sure, but I think it's—"

"Hey!" A voice called out from across the garden. "What's going on over here? Why are none of you at your workstations?"

The prisoners all scattered, including Viren who hurried away from Cora as fast as his feeble frame would allow.

"Cora, is that you?" Faron strode towards Cora, his brows furrowed.

"Faron," Cora lifted a shaky hand. "Hello again."

The friendliness she had seen on his face earlier was gone, replaced by a hard line of suspicion. "What are you doing here?" he demanded. "I thought you were here to deliver a letter to the arms master."

"I am, I just—"

"What were you doing talking to those prisoners?"

"I…I…" Cora stammered over her words, her heart hammering. "I'm sorry, I got lost and so I stopped to get a sense of my bearings and… and I thought the prisoners might know the way to the armory. I don't want to get them into trouble or anything. I didn't know that I wasn't supposed to speak to them. I'm sorry." She blurted out the words.

Faron softened slightly, though her excuse didn't completely erase the mistrust in his eyes. "Come with me, then. I'll take you to the armory myself."

"Of course, thank you." Cora leaped from the bench, following Faron out of the courtyard. She didn't dare turn back or glance over her shoulder to give her father one last look, but her heart seized at the thought of leaving him there, and the ache was sharp as it radiated through her. She tried not to resent Faron for interrupting their time together—he was just doing his job, after all—but she couldn't quite swallow down her annoyance. She only hoped it didn't come through in her tone.

"I really am sorry," Cora said to Faron as they walked. "The fortress is much larger than I thought."

His eyes cut over to her for a moment, studying her. "Yes, it is easy to get turned around at times," he said at last. He still wasn't nearly as friendly as he had been at their initial meeting, but he seemed to have bought her story. She let out a breath.

As they headed down a corridor, a loud commotion met them. Several guards rushed back and forth, calling out to one another something about how someone had arrived. They passed a window and Cora snuck a peek outside, trying to see what was going on. Her eyes lit immediately on a massive black carriage—far and away the grandest she'd ever seen. On its side was a golden crest. While that carriage was the largest and the fanciest, there was quite an entourage before and after it. Whoever was inside the carriage was clearly important. Cora tried to see inside, but there were too many people scurrying around outside and blocking her view. All she caught was a glimpse of a girl her age. A girl with golden hair and a wide-eyed expression.

Before she could discern anything else, Faron pulled her away from the window. He pointed down the corridor. "I apologize—I can't accompany you after all. Keep walking this way and take a left. The armory will be right in front of you. You can't miss it."

He didn't wait for a response before he hurried towards the gate.

Cora, not wanting to press her luck, followed his directions to the armory. However, when she arrived, the armory appeared to be just as much a flurry of activity as the rest of the fortress.

A man who appeared to be the arms master stood in the center of the room, barking orders at half a dozen or so of the soldiers assigned to him. His face was bright red, and he looked rather frenzied.

"Sir?" She approached. "Sir, are you the arms master?"

The arms master waved a hand in front of Cora's face. "Be gone, girl. I am busy."

"But, sir, I have a message for you," Cora held up both the parchment from Bram and the golden seal. "It's from Master Bram. I'm his new apprentice, and he sent me to deliver this to—"

"I said be gone, girl," the arms master snapped, shoving Cora's hand away. "Do not bother me with this right now. Can't you see there are more pressing matters?" With a shake of his head, he shoved past her, yelling at two apprentices to Cora's left.

Cora watched him for a second, clutching the letter and the seal. *What on earth is causing all this chaos?*

"Hey, what's going on?" she asked one of the soldiers, a boy who was hastily organizing daggers on a shelf. "Why is everyone scurrying around like this?"

The apprentice stopped long enough to give Cora a strange look. "You didn't hear?"

Cora shook her head. "No, I have no idea what you're talking about. Hear what?"

"The king and his retinue have just arrived at the fortress."

CHAPTER 3
OCTAVIA

O ctavia fought the urge to fiddle with her blonde hair or fidget in her seat as she stared out the carriage's window. She knew that a young lady of her position—the adopted ward of the king, groomed for most of her life to one day ascend to the throne—was not supposed to do anything as undignified as bounce in her seat, but she couldn't stop the excitement that coursed through her. After several long days of travel, they had finally arrived at the fortress in Llys.

It wasn't often that she was allowed to leave the castle to accompany the king on matters of state, so she was determined to make this trip as memorable as possible.

It was only when she saw the way King Onyx's eye zeroed in on her skirts that she realized that her knee was bouncing up and down. She flushed and stilled. The king's response was to arch one brow. "I expect you to act in a manner benefiting the crown."

His voice was high for a man's, but there was nothing feminine about it. "Piercing" would be a better word for it. Or maybe "dangerous." He did not shout, ever. He did not have to. He could speak at the lowest of tones and everyone around him—from the highest courtiers to the roughest soldiers—would immediately fall silent to hear him, waiting to learn if those razor-sharp words would be directed at them.

"Yes, sire," she said softly, feeling the king's stare on her like a physical weight. She did not look up to meet his piercing brown eyes.

"Remember, this is not a pleasure excursion. You are here for a purpose—to compose a report on the military resources of Llys and the surrounding areas. You are eighteen now, and the time has come for you to take a more active role in my plans for Tenegard. Your studies *should* have prepared you to formulate a thorough, accurate report, presented without bias or sentimentality. Was I wrong to think you were ready for such a task?"

She *did* look up at that, fighting the urge to flinch at the cool, assessing expression that met her. It wasn't as if she expected to see affection in his eyes. Not when it had never been there before. He was the closest thing she had to a parent, having raised her since the loss of her mother and father when she was quite young, and yet there was no element of warmth in her relationship with the king. Though he saw to her care and education, she was under no illusions that he loved her. She had long since stopped trying to love him. These days, she focused on her duty—to her king, to their people, and to the country she'd one day be expected to lead. It wasn't a substitute for love, but it was better than nothing. At least it gave her life a feeling of purpose.

"I am well-suited to the task, Your Majesty. The report will be prepared to your specifications."

"Hmm," he said, seeming to weigh the matter, still pinning her under his stare. Then he turned back to the window and made a dismissive gesture. "See that it is."

"Of course, Your Majesty," she replied, keeping her voice low and soft, trying not to demonstrate visible relief at losing the king's unnerving attention. Onyx wasn't looking in her direction anymore, but that didn't mean she had the freedom to slouch. After all, they weren't the only ones in the carriage.

Next to her on the velvet bench, Ismenia, the king's soothsayer, began to hum under her breath. It wasn't a pretty melody—it was more like the woman was sustaining a single dissonant note, to the point where Octavia felt as if it was vibrating in her very bones. A shiver crawled down her spine.

Ismenia's eyes, which always seemed to be permanently clouded over, landed on Octavia. Ismenia's long silver hair swished free around her shoulders as she cocked her head. She never bound it back, something Octavia had learned was common for genante women above a certain age, especially if those women practiced the strange, mystical art of soothsaying—a type of genante magic that still made absolutely no sense to Octavia. She wondered if all soothsayers were so unsettling to be around. She doubted it. It mostly seemed like Ismenia went out of her way to rattle everyone. Maybe it was how she amused herself.

"Interesting," Ismenia murmured.

Octavia could never be sure if Ismenia was speaking to her or just in general, but she managed to find her voice enough to whisper, "What is?"

Ismenia did not move or respond for several seconds before finally murmuring, "*Very* interesting." She turned away then, and Octavia hugged her side of the bench, hoping not to draw the soothsayer's eye again. She didn't like being in the same room as Ismenia, much less sitting next to her, but seeing as she had no choice in the matter, Octavia did her best not to garner any more of her attention.

Fortunately, Ismenia rarely bothered to pay her any mind. The soothsayer was Onyx's creature, through and through, using all the fortune-telling instruments at her disposal to warn him of any threats to the kingdom or to the security of his rule. The king's Athelian-style magic was ferociously powerful, to be sure, but it didn't include precognition. That was almost exclusively a Tenegardian gift. And while he had multiple soothsayers under his protection—for some reason, the locals didn't seem to know how to deal with women born with the power of visions, meaning they all had to come to the capital to be trained—Ismenia was far and away the most powerful and the most trusted.

By Onyx, anyway. *Octavia* didn't trust her as far as she could throw her, but the king did not consult her opinion on such matters. And if Octavia had tried to complain about Ismenia's presence on this journey, she had no doubt that the king would have chosen for Ismenia to join him and Octavia to be left behind—so she had kept her mouth shut. As usual.

Steering her thoughts away from Ismenia, Octavia peered out the window of the carriage as it rolled down the pathway towards the front gates of the fortress, marking every detail that stood out to her. The tall stone walls, the dozens of guards that rushed around, and the wooden lattice gates. She opened the notebook in her hand and jotted down a few of the details, even free-handing a few rough sketches of the fortress itself. She already had a dozen questions, but the carriage was silent, and she knew better than to speak first.

"The fortress is currently under construction with plans to expand it," a low voice spoke up from the other side of the carriage, addressing the king. "I believe the plans are to complete the project within a few months."

Valaine, Onyx's main advisor, did not sound pleased or disappointed about the news that she was sharing. But then, she never really seemed pleased or disappointed—or happy or sad or angry or hopeful or anything at all. If she experienced emotion at all, you could not prove it by her. It was as if her cold, unfeeling features were etched from granite, her aura entirely void of anything expressive. Though Octavia could see the slight pulsing movement in Valaine's throat—evidence of her mortality—she seemed like an undead creature, disconnected from vivid, emotional life.

Onyx nodded at her, acknowledging the information. "And have they made arrangements as we instructed?"

"Yes, my king, I believe so."

Octavia wanted to ask what arrangements he was referring to, but she knew Onyx hated when she questioned him, seeing it as a challenge to authority. He didn't seem to understand that Octavia was simply very curious and wanted to learn as much as possible. But she had learned the hard way that if the king wanted her to know something, he would tell her. So, despite the fact that she hated to speak to Valaine, she looked to her with her questions. Perhaps the king would object less to her questions if he was not the one expected to answer them.

"Excuse me, Valaine? I was wondering if I could ask you a few questions?" She held up her notebook. "For my report."

Valaine blinked twice and then let out a grunt, which Octavia took as a sign of agreement. So, she inquired about the fortress and its population, as well as the specifics of the city itself. Valaine answered her questions in the same monotone voice she used for everything else, and Octavia carefully jotted the answers down in her notebook.

"What of the special matter we discussed?" Onyx asked, and this piqued Octavia's attention. "Have all the necessary accommodations been prepared for the…project that I came here to pursue?"

"I believe that everything is in readiness for your work, my king. The specimen has been entirely secured and all is prepared for your experimentation."

Specimen? Experimentation? Octavia knew that Onyx was a scholar as well as a warrior, particularly in the field of magic. His studies were what allowed him to extend his lifespan to hold his position as protector of the realm for so many years—over a century—and what allowed him to save the kingdom from that historic famine in the first place. But what specimens would he need to collect from all the way out here?

Valaine responded, "All should be ready for your inspection, my king."

"Yes, but you must be careful," Ismenia murmured. "Considering what the bones had decreed, I urge you to take heed."

Curiouser and curiouser. Whatever the experiment was, Ismenia seemed to be against it—and Octavia had never known the king to ignore her advice. What experiment could be so important that he'd take such a risk?

"We've gone over this before, Ismenia," Onyx replied, rubbing at the bridge of his nose. "The potential danger is precisely why we must take the necessary steps. We cannot have security in the future if we do not gather the necessary knowledge here and now."

Security? Was the kingdom under some kind of threat? Was the king himself at risk? But no, the very thought was absurd. What could endanger Onyx? He had a strong army, a loyal populace, and the power and experience accumulated over one hundred and eighty years of life to prepare him to face any threats. What could possibly be strong enough to harm him?

"Very well," Ismenia said, her voice sounding as though she were far away. "Just let me remind you, my king, the bones do not lie, so take heed you must."

Onyx responded only with a slight nod.

The carriage rolled to a stop in front of the main gate, effectively ending the conversation. Octavia's heart began to hum in her chest, but she wasn't sure if it was from nerves or excitement.

Guards from within the fortress rushed outside to attend to the carriage and soon they were ushered inside, where an entourage of the highest-ranking officers was waiting to greet them.

"Welcome to the fortress at Llys, Your Majesty," a tall, balding man with brass at his shoulders called out. Octavia gathered that he was the commander of the fortress. He bowed low at the waist, along with the rest of the assembled crowd.

Onyx dipped his head in acknowledgment. "Thank you, Commander. It was a long journey, but we are glad to be here." He gave the necessary pleasantries, and Octavia did her best, as always, to take note of his interactions; how he spoke and dealt with people. Though he was not a tall man, his presence filled every room he entered, drawing every eye and making every back straighten. Octavia knew that one day she would be expected to do the same—to command attention and compel respect—but she had not yet learned the trick of it. On the contrary, while a soldier had courteously stepped forward to hand her down from the carriage, as soon as her feet touched the ground, everyone seemed to mostly forget that she was there. Well, at least it meant that she could focus on her observations and note-taking without any difficulty. There was no one attempting to make any conversation with her, so there was no one she risked offending by focusing on her notepad.

The rest of the retinue joined them from the other carriages, creating a moment of bustle and confusion. Altogether, there were more than a dozen additional members of their group, including several of Onyx's generals, a few advisors, the king's private secretary, and everyone's personal servants. The generals clustered around Onyx protectively, as usual, and it took another minute or two before the passageway quieted down enough to allow the commander to launch into introductions, presenting several of his officers to the king before beginning a tour of the fortress. Walking behind the king with her hands clasped demurely in front of her, Octavia took in all the details of the fortress, taking careful notes of everything that might be useful for her report. Despite being an old military facility, it was still beautifully crafted, and she admired the stonework.

"And up ahead, we have the armory," the commander was saying, sweeping his arm out as they neared a large opening in the corridor. The armory was a flurry of activity, with people bustling to and fro—right up until the group from the palace entered—after which everyone froze in place before bowing low.

But then Octavia's eyes fell on one person who was *not* bowing. A girl. A girl around her age with long brown hair that had been pulled back into a genante braid. She stood to the side, half of her body hidden behind a large metal rack of daggers. She wore a simple tunic and trousers, and she looked as though she might be an apprentice of some kind. The lack of a bow was surprising, but Octavia's first thought was that the girl had been too surprised or flustered to react properly. That was a common enough response. Then she saw the expression on her face. Her eyes were wide, but it wasn't awe or respect that she saw shining in them. It was pure, naked fear, as if she had seen her worst nightmare brought to life.

For a split second, Octavia and the girl made direct eye contact before she slowly slid out of sight, tucking herself completely behind the rack of daggers. It was an odd reaction, and Octavia cocked her head, trying to puzzle it out. What had made the girl look like that?

Perhaps it was nerves. He is the king, after all, she reasoned. *She must have been intimidated by him.* But the depth of her fear…that stood out. Octavia had always been told that the people of Tenegard universally adored Onyx. Every history book painted him as the great

37

hero who had saved the country. And no, she wasn't naïve enough to believe that the history books always told the whole truth, but still. Onyx was a good king, was he not? The people were safe and prosperous. Onyx was not a warm man, but he was a fair and honorable one, surely. What reason would this girl have to fear him?

Octavia waited, watching the rack for any glimpse of the girl, but she did not reappear. Octavia's shoulders slumped. She stepped forward, closer to the rack of daggers with some half-formed thought of approaching the girl and trying to talk to her. Her steps brought her closer to the king and Valaine—close enough to hear the whispered conversation between them.

"—yes, I definitely smell it," Valaine murmured. "There's no doubt, sire. The magic is here."

Onyx pursed his lips. "Well, of course. Given the nature of our... guest, I'd be surprised if the scent *wasn't* present." He seemed rather smug about something, but Octavia hadn't the slightest clue what it was. "There is no time like the present," he continued. "I wish to begin my experimentation as soon as possible. The bond is something that should not exist, that must not be *allowed* to exist. Not ever again. And I intend to get to the bottom of how this came to be, and how I can ensure it never happens again."

Frustration zipped through her. She was the king's heir, and it was her job to learn the ropes of running a country, but there were so many things that he couldn't be bothered to discuss with her. This, for example, seemed like a serious issue—and yet she had no idea what he was talking about. Couldn't even begin to formulate a guess. What bond? Who was bonded? Why was a bond dangerous? And what did it have to do with the king's experimentation?

Just ask him, a small voice whispered in her head. *You're his protegee. You have a right to know.*

Octavia straightened her shoulders. If she could just work up the courage—

"Octavia." Onyx turned to her, his eyes narrowing on her face. "I know you must be tired after such a long journey."

She wasn't at all tired, but she knew what this was: A very clear dismissal. And if she didn't act accordingly, there would be trouble. For a moment, she wanted to protest. But she knew it wouldn't do any good. "Yes, Your Majesty," she agreed quietly. "I am, indeed, very tired." Tired of being pushed to the side. Tired of being shut out of important matters. Tired of being treated like an encumbrance when all she wanted was to be useful. It was certainly no lie to say that she was tired.

Onyx held up a hand to stop the commander. "I'm afraid Octavia is rather exhausted from all of our travel. Might it be possible to show her to her quarters here at the fortress?"

"Of course, my king," the commander replied, snapping his fingers at one of the soldiers. "Take Lady Octavia and her maidservants to her quarters immediately."

"Yes, commander," the man replied, hurrying over to Octavia's side and bowing respectfully. "If you'll just follow me, milady."

Octavia let out a sigh, but nodded, falling into step beside the man. Behind her, she could hear the two maids she had brought with her from the castle falling in step a few paces back as they headed down the corridor.

She glanced over her shoulder once, but the commander had already moved the entourage past the armory and further out of view. Onyx had not spared another word or even a parting glance at Octavia as she left.

Disappointment churned low in her gut, and she wondered again what the king was up to. What experiment was he off to perform? What specimen had been prepared for him? What bond did he need to study or break or understand? And would he ever share anything about it with her, ever truly train her to understand the matters of greatest import to the kingdom? He had said that this trip would be the first step in her taking on more royal duties and she had hoped... Well, it was foolish of her to have hoped at all.

It had been clear to her for some time that King Onyx was actually quite indifferent to her, that he cared very little about whether or not she succeeded in becoming the exacting political mind he claimed he wanted for his heir. No, if anything, she was starting to think that he never intended her to take over the throne at all. He had already extended his life to an astonishing extent—and yet, he did not seem aged in the slightest. Though his hair was gray, his face was unlined and he seemed as active and agile as a man in his prime. Why would he hand over the throne? Why step down when he could just stay in power forever? Why bother with an heir—except to keep up appearances? What purpose did she serve other than to be paraded in front of the public as a reminder of his generosity and goodwill towards poor little orphans?

You mustn't think like that, she chided herself. *No good can come from that line of thinking.*

But still, she couldn't shake the feeling that her suspicions were correct. And she wasn't sure just what to do with that.

The soldier stayed silent as he led her through the fortress until finally depositing Octavia in one of the guest rooms. It wasn't as grand as she was accustomed to, but from what she had seen, she was sure that it was likely one of the nicest rooms in the entire fortress.

The women got to work, making a fire in the fireplace and pulling down the heavy duvet that covered the bed. They also assisted

40

Octavia out of her traveling clothes and into a long linen nightgown. A tray of meat and cheese, as well as a pitcher of water, were brought up from the kitchens, and Octavia helped herself as her maids finished unpacking her trunk.

"Is there anything else that we can assist you with, Lady Octavia?" One of the women, Ruth, asked kindly.

"No, that will be all," Octavia said with a smile, as she crawled into bed.

The women scurried from the room, leaving Octavia alone, with only the crackling fire for company.

"What am I doing here?" she mused out loud, snuggling farther under the covers of the bed.

But of course, no one answered back.

CHAPTER 4

Cora's heart felt like it was going to beat right out of her body. Pressing a palm to her chest, she forced herself to inhale deeply and then slowly release the breath. She did this several times until she finally felt her heart begin to slow.

She was hidden in a small alcove just outside the armory, still reeling from the sight of King Onyx in the flesh. *The king has just arrived at the fortress.* The apprentice's words had stunned her, like a bucket of cold water, and she'd only had a few minutes of processing time before the commander of the garrison had led the king himself practically right in front of her.

The sight of him had been one of the most chilling experiences of her life. He wore traveling clothes made of luxurious charcoal fabric and a long black cape that seemed to swirl around him like a thunder cloud. He hadn't looked at all how she'd expected, but still, there was a chilling presence about him that had made her shudder. She had half expected him to notice her immediately, to draw his sword, and demand her arrest. But the king had not noticed her at all. No one in his entourage had paid her any attention, save for the blonde-haired girl she'd seen standing further back behind Onyx and his advisors.

Cora had managed to gather her wits enough to duck fully behind the rack of daggers, hiding herself from view, but her whole body remained tense and poised to run as she listened to the king order someone to take the girl—Octavia was her name—to her rooms. After that, Onyx and the rest of the entourage had been whisked down the hallway away from the armory.

Once she was sure they were gone, Cora stumbled her way out the door and into the first alcove she saw. It was here that she allowed the weight of the moment to fully fall on her shoulders. That had been a tremendously close call. She, a newly bonded dragon rider, had been only a few feet from the most powerful, deadly sorcerer on the entire continent—the same sorcerer who had *slaughtered* all the previous dragon riders before covering up any proof that they had ever existed at all—and yet she had lived to tell the tale.

For now, at least.

She was beyond grateful that the experience hadn't ended differently, but with the shock of the moment finally letting up, she couldn't help but wonder why. How was it possible that Onyx hadn't noticed her?

Did you know that Dragon magic has a certain...smell? Few would know it or recognize it, but it's quite distinct. The memory of General Secare's words floated back to the front of her mind. She didn't doubt that Secare was telling the truth, that dragon magic had some sort of unmistakable scent to it. After all, it was how Secare had been able to find her and figure out that she'd been in communication with the dragon, even before the bond had fully snapped into place. She'd been given an amulet that had allowed her to hide the magic long enough to put him off for a little while—but the amulet was long gone now. And since the magic should be even more noticeable now, then shouldn't Onyx have been able to smell *her?*

Cora shook her head. It didn't make sense. Still, she was grateful to be alone in this alcove, rather than on her way to a jail cell or worse. She knew that there was no way her punishment for daring to dragon bond would be manual labor like her father. In fact, she was certain that Onyx would have much worse planned for her should he ever capture her. Cora considered fleeing the fortress— she wanted nothing more than to put as much distance as possible between her and Onyx— but she had yet to find Raksha, and she hated to think of returning to Alaric with no news as to her whereabouts.

No, I must keep searching. I owe it to Alaric. And to Raksha, herself.

On the other hand, Cora knew that she also needed to be careful. She had no idea where the king or his retinue had gone, but she'd heard enough to know that they'd be staying in the fortress for a while. Even though she'd managed to avoid drawing his notice once, she didn't want to find out if her luck would hold if they were to have a second encounter. She needed more intel on the king's whereabouts before she went wandering around.

Slipping out of the alcove, she swallowed down one last mouthful of air and hurried back to the armory. The arms master was deep in conversation with a handful of soldiers, and Cora didn't want to inter- rupt or draw attention to herself, so she plunked down on an over- turned crate and waited for him. She couldn't very well go back to Bram's forge without having delivered his message, lest he become suspicious. And either the arms master or one of his apprentices would hopefully know where the king had gone, so that she could be sure to avoid him as she continued her search.

Alaric? She reached out to the dragon through their bond, needing the comfort of their connection to soothe her strained nerves. Besides, he deserved an update.

I am here. His response was immediate, and Cora nearly teared up at the relief she felt when she heard his voice. Seeing Onyx had rattled her greatly, but knowing she wasn't alone helped a bit.

She let out a deep breath. *I still can't believe it myself, but…Alaric, he's here.*

Your father? But weren't you aware of that already? You found him earlier, did you not?

No, not my father—Onyx. The king and his entourage just arrived at the fortress.

Where are you? Alaric growled.

I'm still in the fortress. But don't worry, I am safe for now. He didn't notice me.

Cora felt Alaric's relief at her words. *What is he doing in Llys? Did anyone say?*

No, at least not to me. It's strange though, she continued. *I thought for sure that he would be able to sense our magic, like Secare did, but he walked right past me without giving me a second glance.*

That is strange, indeed, Alaric agreed. *Although, now that I am thinking about it, perhaps it is not strange at all.*

What do you mean?

Well, is it not possible that any smell of dragon magic that Onyx may have encountered would be attributed to my mother?

Cora hadn't thought of this, but it made sense. *Oh, I bet you're right— especially if he still thinks she is the newly bonded dragon. If I'd run into him anywhere else, then he might have been suspicious, but since it happened here, Raksha was the perfect camouflage. Onyx had no idea that the dragon rider he seeks was actually right in front of his very nose.* Cora couldn't help but smile at that. But when she thought of the danger that Raksha faced as the focus of the ruthless king's attention, the smile faded as quickly as it had come. What would he do when he found out that Raksha wasn't the bonded dragon after all? Would she become disposable to him then?

We need to find your mother and find a way to get her out of here. And quickly. They knew the extremes to which Onyx was willing to go—the scores of dragons he'd slaughtered in the past. And Raksha was captive, bound. Helpless. The thought of leaving her at Onyx's mercy was intolerable.

Yes, Alaric's tone was resolute. *The sooner we are able to do so, the better.*

Cora quickly filled the dragon in on the conversation she'd had with her father and everything that had occurred from the time she'd left the courtyard until now. *I'm going to do a little more looking around,* she told him. *Who knows when Bram will send me back to the fortress. I don't want to leave until I have at least some idea of where they're keeping Raksha.*

Alaric groaned, frustration spiking through the bond. *Not being able to speak with her is driving me mad. Were our link intact, we would not have to waste time searching the fortress by foot. I could just ask her outright.*

Telepathic communication was the gift of all dragons. Magic played into it when the communication passed between dragons and humans, but from dragon to dragon, reaching out mind to mind was as automatic and instinctive as it was for a human child to reach out to take her mother's hand. With dragons, though, proximity was not a requirement. Dragons could communicate with their minds over sizable distances. But from the moment Raksha had been taken, Alaric had been unable to reach her. The bond was still there—intact enough to leave him certain that she was alive. But it was closed—no, *blocked*—as it had never been before in his life.

Cora sighed, sympathy blooming in her chest for Alaric. Seeing her own father and being able to speak to him had given her such relief. Despite the condition he was in, knowing that Viren wasn't completely lost to her, being able to hear his voice and relish his hug, had been like inhaling a deep breath of fresh air. But Alaric had yet to experience such, and the whereabouts and condition of his mother were still unknown—which troubled the dragon greatly.

I can't remember a time in my life when I could not speak to my mother, Alaric continued. *No matter how far away I was, no matter where in the world I happened to be, if I needed her, she was always there. A comforting presence in my thoughts. Now, it is like a void. I do not like it.*

I know. Cora wished she had some words of comfort for Alaric or a solution to offer him, but all they really had was speculation and guesswork. *As soon as we find her, we'll figure out a way to get the muzzle off her.*

The muzzle—the one Secare had threatened Alaric with. It was the only thing that made sense, the one thing they could come up with as a possible cause of the block in the telepathic link. If the contraption had magical properties, then it would make sense why Alaric wasn't able to reach his mother through telepathy.

But they had no way of knowing for sure. Speculation and guesswork. Cora wished for something more concrete, but the only way to get that was to keep searching the castle until she was able to find out something more. There was no one to help her, no one she could trust to turn to, aside from Alaric—who was, sadly, of little use in this situation. So that meant it was all on her.

Just be careful, Alaric warned. *And get out of there as soon as you can.*

I will, Cora promised. *Don't worry.*

Not likely. Just do what needs to be done and leave.

Cora nodded, cutting off the conversation as it looked like the arms master was finally finishing up. As she watched him shake hands with the soldiers, her eyes fell on something she hadn't noticed initially. Staked against the wall were several large crates. Their wooden lids leaned against the sides, so Cora could see easily enough what was inside. Shiny, unused weapons lay at the heart of each crate, stacked on top of one another and full to the brim. There were dozens of dozens of weapons in each box and more boxes than Cora could count.

What in the world, she thought, eyeing the crates. She expected to see weaponry in the fortress, but she'd spent days scoping out this particular fortress and had a fairly good sense for how many soldiers this compound held. The number of weapons she saw in those crates dwarfed the number of soldiers. The amount of surplus didn't make any sense to her. She couldn't dwell on it further, though, because the arms master, having finished his conversation with the soldiers, stalked past her perch. Cora leaped to him and practically thrust Bram's message into his hand.

"That's from Master Bram," she all but shouted at him, scooting out of the way so he couldn't yell at her or return the message.

The arms master seemed far less frenzied now that Onyx's visit was over, though he still looked so frazzled that Cora thought he might do well with a bit of wine and some rest. He narrowed his eyes at her, but said nothing as he continued past, Bram's message clutched in his hand. She had no idea if he'd actually read it…but her job had only been to deliver it, and she'd done exactly that.

Cora let out a breath. Now it was time to see what information she could find that would help lead her to Raksha—and avoid the king.

Cora spotted the soldier she'd spoken to earlier, the one who'd told her of Onyx's arrival.

"Hey," she called out, hurrying over to him. "I can't believe King Onyx is here." She tried to sound excited and in awe, even though the words tasted like ash on her tongue. "Do you happen to know where he went? I'd love to catch another glimpse of him. I admit I was a bit shocked when he appeared out of nowhere like that. I couldn't pull myself together fast enough to react before he stepped away again, but I'd love to shake his hand if possible." She was a terrible liar, but she hoped that the nervous tension she felt would be enough to convince him that she was just worked up and overwhelmed.

The soldier stopped long enough to shrug. "I don't know, probably the training courtyard."

"The one with the gardens?" Cora asked, fear pulsing through her at the thought of her father and Onyx being in the same place. There was no reason to think that Onyx was a direct threat to her father—not when Onyx had been just a few steps away from her and hadn't noticed her at all—but panic was rarely rational.

"No," the soldier shook his head. "The one further south. The one where they're keeping the dragon."

Cora's blood ran cold. "The dragon?"

"Yeah, big blue thing. I saw it myself the day they brought it inside. I heard someone say that it had been captured on the king's orders."

"They're keeping a dragon in the courtyard," Cora repeated, not quite sure if she had heard correctly. She had expected them to have Raksha locked in a dungeon of some kind, not out in the open.

The soldier seemed to think her shock was a sign of fear or dismay. "Just between you and me, I think it's mad, myself. Who'd want to keep a dragon captive? Kill 'em or drive 'em off, that's what I say. No good comes from having a dragon around, am I right? But the king is a learned man and all. He must have some use for the creature, though devils claim me if I know what it could be. If all he wanted were scales, then there are scavengers for that. Let them take the chances with their lives, out there near the wilds where the dragons nest, yeah? Why bring something like that into town?"

"Yeah, it's…surprising," Cora replied. "There's really a dragon just… out there, in the courtyard? But…" Cora struggled to find the words. "But how is that possible? Dragons can fly. How are they keeping her…I mean, *it* contained?"

The soldier lifted a shoulder and then let it drop. "They've rigged up some sort of chain mail netting over it to keep the dragon from flying away. Quite inventive, really. I had my doubts when I first saw it, but it seems to be doing the job. Still that element of danger, though, of course. Couldn't pay me enough to be the one responsible for seeing the beast fed every day. Not a job for volunteers, right? The commander's using it as a punishment detail. Screw up bad enough, and it's out to the courtyard with you." The soldier gave her a wink, and it was a sudden shock to realize that he was *flirting* with her. Trying to make her laugh by joking about a dragon being chained down, kept from the sky. The very thought turned her stomach.

Cora resisted the urge to pull back her arm and sock the soldier in the face. "Right," she said through gritted teeth. "Well, thanks for that. If I'm going to see the king again, I better head on over to the courtyard, then."

Cora scooted past the soldier, leaving the armory in the hurry. "Oh, Raksha," she murmured, leaning against the stone wall. She hated the thought of leaving without seeing the dragon, but if there was any chance that the king was there, then she couldn't risk going to the courtyard. She'd have to be content with knowing where Raksha could be found.

Not that there was any contentment to be found in that. All Cora felt was frustration and fear. Frustration over her failure to help her father or Alaric's mother. And fear over what Onyx's presence could mean for them all. She and Alaric had struggled to survive against just one of the king's generals. But he'd been surrounded by an entire retinue when she'd seen him earlier, and every one of them seemed dangerous. How could she get her loved ones out of harm's way? How could she keep *herself* from falling into the king's hands?

There were just too many ways all of this could go disastrously wrong —and she couldn't seem to think of a single way that it would end well.

CHAPTER 5

Hurrying out of the fortress, Cora kept her head down and didn't look up again until she was safely back out into the square and right outside of Bram's forge. Breathless, she pushed open the wooden door and stepped inside. The heat of the forge smacked into her, wrapping around her like a thick blanket. It was so familiar and comforting, that tears welled up in her eyes.

"I see you're finally returned," a deep voice called out, shaking her out of her thoughts. Bram stood next to his anvil, a hammer clutched loosely in his hand. "I thought for a moment that perhaps you had sprouted wings and flown far away."

She was relieved to hear his joking tone, but the mention of wings still started Cora, making her jump slightly—especially since her bonded dragon sat just outside the city walls.

"Oh…um, no. Definitely not." Cora straightened her tunic. "I'm so sorry I've been gone so long. The arms master had no time for me when I first got there because the fortress was in a tizzy over the king's arrival."

Bram lifted a bushy eyebrow. "King Onyx has arrived in Llys?"

"Yes," Cora confirmed. "I saw him myself. Some kind of inspection of the fortress or something? I'm not sure, but his visit had the arms master quite unraveled. It wasn't until after the king had come and gone from the armory that I was able to pass along your message."

Bram waved a hand. "The arms master is a skittering fool, that one. The king is nothing but a man. A powerful one, beyond a doubt—but a man, nonetheless. And no freer of fault than anyone else. His magic has made him long-lived, but it hasn't made him a god, no matter how some people choose to behave."

Cora stared. She'd never really heard anyone speaking of Onyx in such a way before, and she certainly never would have expected it from a malhos. They—or at least their ancestors from a few generations back—had come to Tenegard to follow Onyx, to live in his kingdom. She had assumed their loyalty was absolute. "It...sounds like you don't think very highly of him." It was a baited question, and there was some risk that she might offend him if she'd read too much into what he'd said, but she was curious enough to press the point.

Bram let out a sigh. "What I don't think highly of is all the problems Onyx's decrees have created in the supply chains."

Cora's eyebrows shot up. "What's the matter with the supply chains?" In Barcroft, there always seemed to be issues with getting materials, but Cora had always assumed that was due to the remote location and Captain Daggett's greediness, reserving the lion's share of every supply wagon for himself and his men, even if it left the townspeople with not enough to get by. It had never occurred to her that a larger issue was at hand.

"He's soaking up all the resources—metalwork, woodwork, foodstuff, clothing. All of it is being taken off the market, tucked away into his fortresses and keeps. What little is left for everyone else isn't enough to go around, and high demand is pushing the prices far beyond what many people can afford," Bram explained, his tone filling with frustration. "He claims it is for the good of the people, but how can depriving the people of basic necessities be good?"

"It isn't," Cora responded, slightly awed by the vehemence of Bram's response.

"Think of it like this," Bram continued. "Entire villages have been tasked with taking up production of charcoal. The supply should be enormous, yet you can't find it for sale except at the highest of prices. Come winter, what are people supposed to use to keep warm? What am I supposed to use to fire my kiln? What is the silversmith to use, or the apothecary? And those who produce the charcoal, you might ask, are they benefiting? No, they are not. The fruits of their labor are seized with nothing more than a pittance for payment, forfeit to the needs of the crown."

He was getting worked up now, pacing back and forth. Cora was a little in awe. In Barcroft, the people were too cowed to speak their mind this way. Was everyone in Llys as free with their words as Bram? Or was he unique in seeing things this way? "But why would Onyx do that?" she asked, egging him on. "Wouldn't he want to keep his people well-supplied?"

Bram shrugged. "One would think, yet that is not the case. And there are many people in the kingdom who are unhappy about it."

So it wasn't just him. "Many, you say?" she asked softly. She had to swallow against a lump in her throat. Ever since she'd learned of the way he'd betrayed the dragon riders of old, Cora had known that it was her place to stand against Onyx. There was no other route she could take and still respect herself at the end of the day. And yet, she'd felt so very alone in her opposition to the all-powerful king. It was deeply heartening to hear that there were others who saw past his grand, hollow reputation. It didn't mean that anyone else was ready to embrace the idea of dragons as allies instead of enemies, but it was still *something*. Something important. Something that meant she and Alaric weren't entirely on their own after all.

"Aye, there are many antiroyalists here and elsewhere." Bram gave a curt nod. "Though we'd both do well not to speak of them further."

Cora wanted to ask Bram if he was one of the antiroyalists, but she sensed that would be going too far. He'd been far more open with her than she'd ever expected, but they were still mostly strangers. There would be limits to how much he was willing to reveal. And given how many secrets of her own she was hiding, she couldn't exactly blame him. She chose to redirect the conversation instead. "You know, I saw several crates in the armory, all of them filled to the brim with new, unused weapons. Do you think…is that Onyx's doing as well?"

"It is. In the last eighteen months alone, the fortress has been demanding that I make more and more arms for them. They have yet to give me a reason why such a number is required. As far as I can tell, it doesn't appear as if they actually need the weapons for anything. I wouldn't complain about such a steady stream of work, especially given that I get paid either way, but it just doesn't sit right with me. It feels like a waste of my time and also good iron-making products that aren't getting used. Especially when there's regular folks queuing up to order household goods that I haven't the time or materials to make for them. They have needs right now—but there's nothing I can do for them because our king seems to be supplying himself for a war that we aren't even in. Not yet, anyway."

"Do you think he plans to go to war?" Cora asked, shocked by the notion. There hadn't been war in Tenegard for many, many years. The soldiers were kept at readiness at all times, of course, but no one expected them to actually be *used*. Not in actual battle. The garrisons in most towns acted as peacekeepers, enforcing the laws and maintaining order. Back in Barcroft, the worst the soldiers had ever had to face had been breaking up a rowdy night at the local tavern.

"I think he's behaving like a king who wants to *start* a war," Bram replied curtly. "And gods protect all of us if that should happen, because it's not the king who'll be going to the battlefield. It'll be ordinary people, conscripted as soldiers to fill in the ranks."

"But we have soldiers already," Cora argued.

"Enough soldiers for peace," Bram retorted. "But nowhere near enough for war. Those crates of weapons? Our fortresses don't hold enough men to use them all. More soldiers will need to be found or worse—he'll conscript civilians who have no business fighting. I fear for the future they will face."

So did she. She thought of the men and boys she had known back in Barcroft—imagined them sent off into a war at the whim of a king who showed no concern for his people. It was a horrible thought. "Is there nothing that can be done?" she asked.

"Like what? He is king after all, and that means he can do as he wishes. Who is there to stop him?"

Me, she thought—then shook the thought away. Who was she to believe that she could fight the king? She was terrified just at the thought of facing him again.

"Right," Cora replied, pulling the golden seal from her pocket. "I should return this back to you."

Bram took the seal with a grunt before turning back to his anvil, evidently done with conversing. That was fine with Cora. There were plenty of things to mull over while she worked the rest of her day. Alaric, sensing her mood through the bond, left her alone mostly other than to check in a few times. There was much that she wanted to tell him—much that she'd love to get his thoughts on—but it would be easier to talk once she returned to the thicket after nightfall.

Cora moved around the forge automatically, completing her tasks and chores, all while her mind whirled, struggling to process the idea that the nation might be headed towards war. It seemed profoundly unfair that one man would make a decision like that which would impact the whole nation, and that no one would have a chance to say a word against it. But on the other hand, what power did anyone have to stop him? Even if the antiroyalists tried to protest, what could they really do? As Bram had said, Onyx was the king. So even though there were people who disagreed with his methods, what could they actually do about it?

Cora sighed, shaking her head. She couldn't think about this anymore. She had her own problems to contend with, starting with freeing both her father and Alaric's mother. Now that she knew where they were being held, it made things a little easier, but only just. She and Alaric still needed to work out some sort of plan for freeing them—and given the presence of the king and some of his generals, that would likely be more complicated than they'd expected. On top of that, Viren's declining health and Onyx's direct interest in Raksha added an element of dire urgency to the situation. She and Alaric would need to work quickly.

As soon as Bram dismissed her for the day, Cora hastened to clean up her workspace and hang up her apron before hurrying out into the crisp night air. She was eager to get back to Alaric and out of the city for a few hours. The streets were bustling with people, yet there wasn't a lot of friendly conversation among them. Most of the city dwellers passed each other without a word, intent on carrying out their own business. That was the way of city life, Cora had assumed. Surprisingly enough, the more time she spent in Llys, the more she was eager to leave it. Everything within the city walls still felt strange, and the way of life here was entirely different from what she'd known in Barcroft. She'd always felt out of sorts in her tiny mountain township, but that isolation was nothing like the alienation she felt here. She hadn't really been close to the others in Barcroft, but at least she had *known* them, had felt safe with them. It was strange to be in such a large city, surrounded by people, and still feel so entirely alone.

Except for Alaric, of course, Cora reminded herself, picking up her pace. But just as she did so, a peculiar feeling of unease washed over her. It felt as if someone was watching her. And more specifically, following her.

"No," she mumbled under her breath. "You're just being paranoid." And after what she'd experienced at the fortress, who could blame her? She'd feared catching Onyx's eye so strongly that it was no wonder she'd tricked herself into believing she was being observed now. She kept walking, expecting the feeling to diminish, but it didn't. If anything, it intensified. Could it be that there was someone on her trail after all?

Thinking on her feet, Cora stopped next to a glassworks vendor and bent down, pretending to adjust the strap of her boot. While she did so, she carefully peered behind her. There were dozens of city folk milling about and several street vendors, but no one looked out of place and there wasn't anyone who looked suspicious in any way. The feeling persisted, though. And the city was full of dark corners—there was always the possibility that someone was watching her while hidden out of sight.

Alaric, I can't be sure, but I think someone may be following me.

His response was low and gravelly as she felt his alarm through the bond. *Someone from the fortress?*

I don't know. Maybe? Or it's possible that it's all in my head. It's been a rather strange day and I have all these thoughts running wild. I'm probably just being paranoid.

That may be so, but I also believe our instincts are what promote survival. If yours are telling you that something isn't right, it would be prudent to heed them.

He was right, of course.

Yes, Cora agreed, standing up. She glanced behind her again, but still saw no one of interest, so she started walking again, taking an unexpected right turn. *I do think it's probably all in my head, but you're right. We can't be too careful. I'm going to take a different route back to the front gates. If there is someone following me, I can't risk leading them to you.*

It is dark enough. Perhaps if I fly, I could come to your aid, in case—

No. Cora cut him off. *No one can see you, Alaric. Even with the cover of darkness, there is still a chance someone could spot you. If they did, it would cause a panic. And with Onyx here, it's too much of a risk. I can't lose you, too. Stay where you are.*

If you are in danger, Cora, I will do what I must to ensure your safety.

I know, but I won't have you risk your life unnecessarily. I'm still not sure there's even anyone there. It's probably just nerves or something. I'll take a different route to be on the safe side and then once I make it back to the thicket, we'll figure all of this out and laugh over how silly I'm being.

I feel so helpless out here among the trees.

Just promise me you'll stay put. She could feel the dragon's hesitancy, but a few moments later, he grumbled his acquiescence. *Fine,* he replied, *but may your feet be swift, Cora.*

Cora picked up her pace at that, taking as many turns as she could. If she was being followed by a simple pickpocket or cutpurse, hopefully they'd decide that she was too much trouble to target. The strange feeling of eyes on her back was still there, but the more she deviated from her normal path, the more she began to think that maybe she'd been imagining it after all.

Still, a breath of relief escaped her lips when the front gates came into view. The corners of her mouth lifted in a smile.

Almost there, she said to Alaric through the bond, sending him an image of the gates. *Just a few more—*

She didn't get to finish her sentence as someone grabbed her from behind, yanking some sort of rough fabric over her head and face.

Cora yelped and immediately started swinging, but then there was a brief jolt of pain against the back of her head and everything went black.

CHAPTER 6

The first thing Cora noticed when she came to was the feel of coarse fabric scratching at her cheeks and nose.

She blinked, trying not to jostle her aching head, but even though her vision was clearing, she still couldn't see much. Whatever fabric barrier her assailant had pulled over her head was still there. A burlap sack, maybe? She wasn't sure. Nor did she know where she was or why she had been taken. All she could be sure of was that this hadn't been the work of a thief. A thief might have knocked her out, but then she'd have been left on the side of the road—not taken away to… wherever she was.

With her heart hammering in her head, she quickly took stock of her body. Aside from the headache, she didn't seem to be injured anywhere other than her head, though she couldn't move much. She seemed to be sitting in a wooden chair, with her arms and legs bound —and, of course, her vision blocked by whatever was covering her head. She wouldn't be able to see anyone approaching, didn't even know if there was anyone else in the room with her at the moment. Realizing how vulnerable she was made the breath hitch in Cora's throat and hot tears prick her eyes, but she blinked them away and reached for the bond between her and Alaric.

Alaric?

Cora! What happened? Where are you? You were talking to me and then I felt a rush of alarm and then you went silent. I expected you back a while ago, but I have not been able to reach you. Are you all right? Where are you? I will come get you!

The dragon fired question after question at her, his anxiety over the situation clear in his tone.

I don't know where I am, Cora answered honestly. *But it turns out that someone actually was following me.*

Alaric's growl echoed in Cora's mind, making her wince. *Are you hurt?*

Not really. They knocked me out to bring me to wherever I am now, so I have a bit of a headache, but I'm fine otherwise.

And you don't know where you are or who took you?

No. A lump formed in Cora's throat. *No, I don't.*

Alaric, who must have felt Cora's fear and anxiety, let out another growl. *I will find you, Cora. If I have to tear the city apart piece by piece, I will come for you.*

The fierceness of his words and the absolute conviction that rang in them made Cora feel a little better. Her situation was precarious, but it helped to know she wasn't completely alone. But just as he was protective of her, she was protective of him, in turn. As they had said from the start when it came to saving their parents, Alaric flying into the city was an absolute last resort, and she didn't want him to forget that. *I know you'd rescue me if I needed you to. But hopefully it won't come to that. I—*

"I believe she's awake," a deep, unfamiliar voice cut through the silence of the room. "I saw her stirring a few moments ago."

Cora held her breath at the sound of footsteps getting louder as they approached.

"What is your name, girl?"

Cora started a little at the sound, for this voice was different from the one who had spoken before. It was softer, though there was still a steel-edge to the question. This voice belonged to a woman. Just how many people were in the room with her?

"You ask my name without supplying yours," Cora responded to buy herself some time. She had no idea if she should answer these people's questions or not.

"Aye," the woman responded plainly. "That I did. And I'll ask you again, girl. What is your name?" Cora recognized this tone. It was a tone that meant business and said that the speaker was not to be trifled with.

"Cora. My name is Cora Hart."

There was a beat of silence and then, "And what, Cora Hart, were you doing inside the fortress today?"

This caught Cora by surprise. She had assumed that whoever had kidnapped her must have known about her and Alaric. It was the biggest secret she had, the one she was most desperate to protect, so it was where her thoughts went first. This question had her scrambling mentally, trying to figure out what this was really about. Why would anyone care that she went to the fortress? She'd seen dozens of people come and go in the days she'd spent watching the gate. There shouldn't have been anything suspicious about her visit.

"I work as an apprentice for Master Bram, the blacksmith," she replied, trying to keep her voice even. Her captors probably already knew that, given that they'd been following her since she'd left the forge, but it was the simplest, most straightforward answer she had. And anyway, it happened to be true, even if it wasn't the *whole* truth. "There was a message that he asked me to deliver to the master of arms."

"Yes, we know all of that," the woman replied. Cora couldn't see her, but she imagined from the inflection of the woman's words that they were delivered with an eye roll. "Yet you were seen in the courtyard. So I'm going to ask again, what were you doing in the fortress today?"

Cora had no idea how to respond. She certainly couldn't tell them about her attempts to find Raksha. They either wouldn't believe her, thinking that no one would be reckless or foolish enough to seek out a dragon…or they *would* believe her, and the rest of her secret would be exposed. "I told you…" she stammered. "I was there to deliver a message from Bram to the arms master."

"She is lying." This time it was the man who responded, his voice gruff with annoyance.

"Perhaps she needs a little *motivation,*" another voice said, a new voice this time. Another man. And the threat in his words was plain.

"Just tell us, girl." And yet another new voice. A woman.

Cora's head swam at the proof of how outnumbered and helpless she was. She realized that these were likely Onyx's people. Who else would capture a woman off a public street with such impunity? But her past experience with Onyx's emissaries just made her fear grow. Would this group be as ruthless as Secare? He had tried to trap her as well—to cage her and send her away for the king's cruel experiments. Was that what her future held? Terror swept through her, rising like bile in her throat, but she swallowed it down. She couldn't fall apart at the seams. She had to keep it together if she was going to survive this.

She decided to tell the truth, at least some of it. The least dangerous part of it. Maybe it would be enough to throw them off the scent.

"Fine. You're right, I wasn't just there to deliver a message. The reason I went to the courtyard was because I was seeking out my father."

"Your father?" The woman in front of her repeated. "Your father is inside the fortress?"

"Yes," Cora replied, a little more confidently. "We come from a township in the mountains. My father was accused of a crime he didn't commit and sentenced to a work detail here in Llys. I went to find him so that I could talk to him and see if there was a way to have him released. He's in poor health, and I was worried about him. I haven't seen or spoken to him since he was taken away."

The group of captors took a minute to process this, their whispered voices blending together and making it impossible to discern individual words.

"There is still something that doesn't feel quite right about your story," the first male voice growled. "I find it hard to believe that on the same day the king appears in Llys, there's also a strange girl from the country snooping around the fortress."

Cora's brows lifted. She couldn't see the faces of her abductors, but the way the man had chewed on the word "king" made his opinions of Onyx clear enough. So…these *weren't* Onyx's men? The thought held some relief, but it only added to her confusion. If they weren't working for Onyx, then who *were* they working for?

"We know the king came to the armory to inspect something. What is it he wanted to inspect? If you were there to deliver a message to the arms master as you claimed, then you would have been in the armory —you would have seen the king arrive."

Well, they definitely weren't working for Onyx, then. If they were, they wouldn't have needed her to fill them in on what their boss was doing.

"Yes, I did see the king, but I couldn't tell you what he came to inspect. I didn't hear him say anything specific. I could see him talking with someone—his advisor, I think—but I wasn't close enough to hear what they said. To be honest, I found his presence a little intimidating, so I hid."

"You hid?"

"Yes, behind a rack of weaponry in the armory."

One of the captors let out a deep sigh, while the others seemed to have gone back to murmuring to one another. It gave Cora time to think, to wonder how they got their information—that Onyx was inspecting the armory, that she'd been there at the time, even that she'd gone wandering in the fortress and had been seen in the courtyard.

They must have eyes inside the fortress, she realized. And her thoughts immediately went to Faron. He definitely knew that she'd been wandering where she wasn't supposed to be. At the time, she'd thought that he was just doing his job as a soldier and guard of the fortress, but maybe he was working for whoever it was that had snatched her off the street.

They don't work for Onyx, Cora passed the information along to Alaric. *I still don't know who they are, but of that much, I am pretty certain. I'm not sure if that means I can trust them, though. Just because we have a common enemy doesn't mean that we're on the same side.*

I do not care who they are—they have kidnapped and harmed my rider. Cora could tell that Alaric was getting particularly antsy, and his worry for her wasn't helping. *I will not feel at ease until you are safe, Cora.*

I know, but we can't do anything rash. Maybe they just want information out of me. It's possible they'll let me go soon. Just sit tight for now, okay?

Alaric didn't respond, though a grumbling burst of agreement rolled down the bond.

Cora refocused on the room, on the whispered murmurings of her captors.

In short order, they began to question her again, demanding more and more information about anything she had noticed about the king's behavior in the fortress. Cora answered their questions as best she could, giving them as many details as she could remember. It seemed, at least for now, that they were willing to trust her to be honest. To her relief, there were no more threats to compel answers out of her by force.

"He had an entourage with him," she said. "I didn't recognize them, of course, but I believe there were several who were either advisors to him or perhaps generals in his army. And then there was a girl with him—she looked to be about my age. His heir, the Lady Octavia, maybe? He sent her away to her rooms."

"Generals?" one of the voices asked, to which another responded. "Secare?"

Thinking the question was for her, Cora shook her head and replied, "No, not Secare. He's gone."

The room grew instantly silent.

"What?" one of the men barked out, his voice sharp. "Gone? What do you mean?"

"I...I..." Cora stammered. She and Alaric had left town not long after the confrontation, so she hadn't had a chance to find out whatever official story Daggett and his men had given to explain why Secare hadn't returned from the mountain, but surely they would have told the people *something*. Maybe not that the general was dead—he'd been reduced to ash by the fire she and Alaric had used, leaving no body behind, so it was possible people just thought he was missing—but the situation would have needed some kind of explanation… wouldn't it? She thought everyone at least knew that he wasn't around anymore. Had the information been kept secret? How was that possible?

"And furthermore," the same man continued, "how does a girl from the country know anything about the king's generals? How would you even know that name?"

The blood drained from Cora's face and for a split second, she was glad the burlap sack was still covering her face. She had messed up, revealing information they hadn't known to question her about until she'd let too much slip. How could she possibly explain what had happened to Secare without revealing her most important secret?

"Oh, um…he came to my village…for some reason. He held an inspection of the garrison. There…there isn't much to do in my town, so everyone came out to see it." It happened to be true, but she was working so hard to not say anything incriminating that she could hear how it sounded like a lie, her stumbling over the words like she was hiding something…because she was.

"Do you think us fools, girl?" the man barked, crossing the floor to lean in over Cora. She could see his shadow looming over her. "We won't tolerate anything but the truth from you!"

Cora recoiled slightly from the feel of his hot breath through the sack.

"Now, let's try this again. How do you know it wasn't Secare in the fortress with the king?"

Her brain whirled as Cora tried to come up with some sort of excuse, but she was drawing a blank.

"Answer me!" the man roared.

Panicked, Cora blurted out, "Because Secare is dead!"

The words fell over the room like a blanket, thick and stifling.

"Dead?" The woman nearest her sucked in a breath. "How do you know this, child? Tell us at once!"

The hair on the back of Cora's neck rose. She should have stuck with "gone." She could justify knowing that Secare was gone. But how could she explain how she knew for certain that he was dead when apparently that was something that no one else knew?

Stupid, Cora! She chided herself. *If you're going to get out of this alive, you have to be much smarter!*

She quickly backtracked. "A-as I said, he was visiting my village. One afternoon, he went up into the mountains and did not return. The mountains can be treacherous this time of year, even for those who travel them frequently. A scouting party was sent when the garrison realized that he had not returned, but General Secare's body was never recovered. It was assumed that he had fallen prey to some misfortune up in the stone hills."

"And what mountains are these?" one of her captors asked.

"The Therma Mountains," Cora replied. "I come from the township of Barcroft. Our village sits at the base of the tallest peak."

"Barcroft," The gruff man seemed interested in the name. "Why does that sound so familiar? I'm sure I've never been there myself, but that name sticks out in my mind for some reason."

"Yes, I too—oh! I know! The Crow," the woman captor replied. "I believe the Crow has mentioned it."

Cora wasn't sure who this Crow person was, and she wanted desperately to interrupt the conversation to ask, but she knew the abductors likely wouldn't respond. Besides, she didn't want to draw their attention back to herself. She'd learn more by listening. So, that's what she did.

"The Crow, yes, I think you're right." The man let out a deep sigh. "Come, we should consult the others."

There was a rush of movement as her captors left the room. She wondered if someone would be left to stand guard over her, but she heard all four sets of footsteps head out the door. Unless there was someone else in the room who had remained still and silent all this time, they had left Cora alone.

"Hello?" she called out, just in case. "You can let me go now," she yelled, her voice echoing back to her across the empty room. She didn't hold out much hope that her captors would let her loose, but if they were still in town, then there was a chance someone else might overhear and come to her aid. She waited hopefully for one minute… then two…but nothing happened. All right, then—on to plan B. Squirming, she tried to free her hands from the bonds wrapped tightly around her wrists, but it was no use. The knots were too tight. Time for plan C—which meant that she'd have to figure out what that plan was. Maybe her dragon would have some ideas.

Well, she reached out to Alaric. *I'm pretty sure at this point that these people do not work for Onyx, but I still don't know who they are.* She quickly relayed their conversation. *They mentioned someone named the Crow and then they just left.*

Did they say anything else? Are they planning to release you?

The lump was back, rising again in Cora's throat. *No, they said nothing. I called after them, but there was no response. I tried to get around the bonds, but they're too tight.*

I am coming to get you.

You can't. I don't even know where I am.

I will find you, Cora.

Alarm welled up in Cora at the thought of Alaric searching for her. The search would be a slow process since she had nothing she could share to lead him in the right direction. He'd have to fly low and slow to have any chance of locating her—and that would leave him incredibly vulnerable. He would surely be seen. He would likely be attacked. He might even be killed. She knew that Alaric would stop at nothing to find her, but Cora couldn't allow him to do so, not when it put his own safety at risk. So, she swallowed down her panic and forced her tone into the neutral voice of reason.

I know you will, but let's wait for a bit, see if I can figure out some idea of where I am. I'm not saying no, I'm just saying it would be rash to just fly in without any sort of direction. You can't take on the entire city of Llys on your own, Alaric.

No, but I can try.

Cora wanted to hug him for that. *Just stay put, my friend. I'm okay for now. They're not harming me in any way, other than keeping me against my will. I can sit tight for a while longer. Who knows—I may end up learning something useful.*

Alaric huffed, clearly seeing the reason in this, but hating it all the same.

Fine, but if things get worse, if they try to harm you, let me know immediately and I will come. And not even you will be able to stop me.

Tears welled up in Cora's eyes and she sent a burst of warmth down the bond. *Very well. It's a deal.* She shifted in her seat, trying to get comfortable. She had no idea when or if her captors were planning to return, so she settled in for a long night. *But until then? Will you keep me company?*

Of course.

Good. Now, tell me a story.

A story?

Yes, something adventurous with a happy ending. That is…if you know of one? Do dragons even tell stories?

Alaric chuckled, the sound deep and throaty. *Do dragons know stories?* He scoffed. *We are excellent raconteurs, I will have you know.* As if to prove his point, he did what Cora requested and began to tell a story.

And as he spoke, the minutes passed them by, and Cora's worry and fear faded away. She knew they weren't gone for good, but Alaric's voice soothed her, his words like a balm to all her ailments.

As his story came to a close, Cora drifted off to sleep.

CHAPTER 7
OCTAVIA

The pages of her notebook were filled with lines of neat script and columns of calculations. Yet, as Octavia scanned the words and numbers she had carefully printed on the pages over the last several days spent in the fortress, she couldn't help the feeling of frustration that coiled low in her gut. She wanted to prove that she was useful and that she was intelligent, but despite all of her efforts, Octavia felt less like the heir of a king and more like a fancy ornament that one might sit on a shelf. Something pretty and useless, easily forgotten and left to gather dust. It wasn't a feeling she relished.

Her bedchamber was bathed in a hazy orange glow from the roaring fire in the fireplace, and the heat from the flames wrapped around her, warding against the general chill in the air. Were she here for a recreational visit, she imagined herself walking the streets of the city, exploring all the nooks and crannies and exploring all the shops and street cart vendors selling their wares. In her mind, she could see herself out there, among the people, learning about their lives and gaining new experiences—but instead, she was stuck inside, forbidden to step even a toe outside the gates of the fortress.

She had done all that had been asked of her. She had busied herself with noting all things related to military prep at the fortress so that she could include them in her report. She had sat in all of Onyx's meetings with the commander, discussing troop movements and efforts to expand resources for the war to come. She had taken copious notes during these meetings and had also accompanied Onyx as he, his generals, and the fortress commander had inspected the fortress and discussed the various items that had been ordered or commissioned and were scheduled to arrive soon—more blades, more cannons, more barrels of gunpowder, more dried foods, more uniforms, more crates, more horses…the list went on and on. Everything must be in readiness for the invasion of Athelia.

Athelia, Onyx's home country. The country Octavia's ancestors had come from as well, a hundred years or so ago. It had always seemed so far away—a place of no consequence, really. Her family, and the others who had come from there, had brought much of their cultural and personal practices with them to Tenegard—but if they had had any loyalty to Athelia, then they wouldn't have left in the first place. Tenegard was where they had seen their future, under the leadership of Onyx, the newly crowned king. But now, with the king planning to return to his home—return and invade—Octavia tried to understand his motives.

"Athelia is not unlike what Tenegard used to be before I arrived on these shores," he'd explained to her once. "The people there are suffering under short-sighted political chaos with no one powerful enough to ensure the nation's smooth running. If the country is going to survive, it will need new, stronger leadership."

"And by that, you mean your leadership," Octavia had responded.

"Precisely," Onyx had replied, giving her a rare smile. "I have the exact thing Athelia needs."

A dozen questions had buzzed in Octavia's mind at that, but she had kept her mouth closed. Onyx did not like it when she questioned his motives or his meanings. Those doubts had continued to circulate in her mind, though. Something about the way he had laid out the situation didn't quite add up. She wasn't convinced that invasion was the solution Athelia needed. If people were already struggling under chaos and instability, then surely war would just make things worse. But there was no way she could voice that without causing trouble for herself. Besides, Onyx was king, not her. And he knew best. After all, he was the one who helped save Tenegard from self-destruction so long ago, when poor leadership had brought famine to the land. No, life under Onyx's rule was better than the alternative, Octavia had decided.

Yet, as she sat alone with only her notebook and the crackling flames for company, she wondered if perhaps there wasn't something more to life than following orders. She knew she was lucky to be in her position. Still, she wished she weren't so lonely all the time. Onyx ensured that she had all the necessities. Food, clothing, education— she never lacked for any of it, and it was all of the highest quality. But companionship or friendship were not, it seemed, things that he deemed necessary, so she had always had to do without. The only people she spent any noticeable amount of time with were her tutors and her maids, and they were all too aware of the gulf between their positions to treat her with warmth or familiarity. When it came to her rank, the only one who came close was Onyx, and he never took the time to connect with her on a personal level, not even to educate her on any matters of court politics or the running of his kingdom.

It was the same here in Llys. She had hoped that he might take more interest in tutoring her while in residence at the fortress, but so far, that was not the case. Instead, Onyx spent most of his time in the armory with Valaine and two other generals, Nedra and Lanius.

Octavia wasn't allowed to attend these inspections, though she did note that after every one, the king's mood was noticeably sour—a rarity, since he prided himself on keeping his emotions under wraps. She wasn't sure what to make of it. Everyone at the fortress had fallen all over themselves to attend to his every whim. What could he possibly be seeing or doing that would upset him to such an extent?

The previous day, she had managed to creep down to the armory without being seen, to conduct an inspection of her own. However, the vast hall of weapons and armory looked exactly as she expected it to. There was nothing new or noteworthy within the walls, nothing that would warrant multiple inspections—certainly nothing that would explain the king's frustration. It was beyond perplexing, and when she'd asked Onyx about the inspections, he had sneered at her and reminded her that the reason for her inclusion in the trip was so she could compile her report, and he'd advised her to focus on that.

So that's exactly what she'd done, and her notebook was nearly full from all the information she had accumulated. She'd be able to compile a very thorough report with everything she had learned. She should feel satisfied and proud of her work, but she wasn't. She still didn't know what the *real* reason was for her inclusion on the trip, but she was smart enough to know busy work when she saw it.

A knock on the door broke through her thoughts and she snapped her notebook shut. "Come in."

Helda, one of her maidservants, popped her head in the door. "Hello, milady, I've come to help you prepare for dinner."

"Of course," Octavia said with a smile. She would not say that she and Helda were friends, but the woman had been one of her maids for the past several years, and she had always been kind.

Helda returned the smile and stepped fully into the room, returning Octavia's smile. "What would you like to wear tonight? I think the green silk would look lovely."

"Then green silk it is," Octavia replied. The truth was, she didn't care at all what gown she wore to dinner. No one paid her much attention, so it really didn't matter. However, she knew Helda loved marveling over the fabric of her gowns, so she tried to be a good sport. "I think I'd prefer a good pair of trousers," Octavia murmured under her breath, "not that anyone asked me."

"What was that, milady?" Helda came over with the chosen gown across her arms.

"Oh nothing," Octavia said, waving a hand. "Just going over some calculations in my head for the king."

Helda nodded, carrying the dress over to the bed, where she laid it out carefully so as not to wrinkle the fabric. "Shall I do your hair?"

Octavia let out a sigh and sat down in a chair by the fireplace. Helda's hands were gentle as they combed through Octavia's long tresses, arranging them into a lovely, braided knot at the back of her head.

Once her hair was finished, Octavia donned the gown that Helda had chosen for her and made her way to the dining chamber, a large open room full of long, wooden tables. Her place was, of course, at the head table where the king sat. She walked with her back straight and her chin lifted as she passed the troops already seated.

When she reached the head table, a steward indicated her seat, pulling out the chair for her. The chair was three spaces down from where Onyx already sat, a wine goblet in his hand. Between them were two of his generals. Octavia found herself directly next to Lanius. She fought back a grimace and forced her lips up into a small smile as she allowed the steward to push her chair in for her. Next to her, Lanius did not bother to greet her. Nedra, on his other side, did not either—

which was fine by Octavia. She didn't entirely know why, but the two generals had always made her uncomfortable. They were…well, creepy. Each in their own way. She couldn't explain why, but it always felt as if Nedra was watching her when she wasn't looking, sneaking around and appearing when she wasn't expecting it. And she had seen glimpses of how Lanius enjoyed violence for violence's sake. It was unnerving to say the least, and if she had her pick of dinner companions, these two generals would be the last on her list.

Reaching for her water goblet, Octavia straightened her back and tried to think about nothing but serene thoughts as she quietly ate her meal, counting down the minutes until dinner would be over and she would be dismissed back to her rooms. As much as she craved company, dinners like this left her feeling lonelier. The presence of other people wasn't the same as *company* when none of the ones surrounding her had any interest in making conversation with her or hearing what she had to say. Besides, she hated the way all the eyes in the room seemed to land on her. If it was because she was the heir to the throne or a girl in a room almost entirely composed of men, she wasn't sure. But both notions made her slightly uncomfortable.

Finally, as the last of the dinner dishes were being cleared away, Onyx rose from his seat and clapped his hands together. The room instantly fell silent. "I want to thank the commander for his hospitality," Onyx said in a clear, quiet voice. "This visit to the fortress has been illuminating, to say the least. I must announce, however, that I will be leaving in the morning. My plan is to travel west in order to seek out some information I require."

Octavia's heart leaped. She hadn't expected this announcement, but the news was rather interesting. She was more than eager to leave the walls of the fortress, to travel to a new place and experience something other than the stiff routines of the military encampment. It didn't even bother her that Onyx had failed to mention their new plans to her. All that mattered was that they were leaving, and she couldn't help but feel excited about it. If necessary, she would stay up all night to get her trunks packed and ready for their departure.

"I will return as soon as my business has concluded. Until then, do not forget that the ever-watchful eye of Princess Octavia will be on you in my stead."

The soldiers applauded as Onyx took his seat, but Octavia sat frozen in her chair. Under her watchful eye? That could only mean one thing: she was staying at the fortress and not accompanying the king westward. She hated the disappointment that swirled through her at being left behind and overlooked yet again. She tried to cheer herself up with the reminder that Onyx needed someone he trusted to stay behind and keep an eye on the things occurring here at the fortress, but as her heart pumped faster and tears welled up in her eyes, she knew deep down that it was less about needing to leave someone competent behind and more about her being an afterthought to the king, someone not sufficiently worthy to take with him.

She waited until it was acceptable to excuse herself and then did so quickly, nodding at Onyx as she passed. He did not nod back.

It had taken a long time for sleep to come that night, but when she did drop off, she slept hard. It wasn't until the morning sun streamed through her window that she woke. Octavia rolled over and rubbed the sleep from her eyes. They felt achy, and she knew they were likely red after nearly crying herself to sleep, but she did feel a little better. One of her nurses had always told her that it was better to let strong emotion out than to keep it in and let it rule you. The woman had been right. Giving herself permission to cry her feelings into her pillow had actually made the news from the previous night a bit easier to handle.

Throwing off the covers, she crossed over to the wash basin and splashed water on her face. Then, with new resolve and the help of one of her maids, she changed out of her nightclothes and into a day dress. It was one of her simpler fashions. The twill skirt was cut close to her legs and the tunic she wore was a soft green fabric that she'd always thought brought out the emerald hue of her eyes. Onyx preferred she dress in her fancier fashions—as befitting of her station, he claimed—but she'd never cared for the way the fussy dresses hampered her movements and made her feel constrained. Since Onyx and his entourage had likely left before dawn, Octavia decided on comfort instead of fashion.

It still chaffed a little what the king had done, but she was determined to make the most of this opportunity to enjoy her time free from the cloud of Onyx's disapproval. She smiled at the thought of being able to spend the next few days doing just as she pleased. And as a bonus, Onyx had likely taken his generals with him, so if nothing else, she would be free of Lanius and Nedra's leering glances for a while. That in itself was a reason to celebrate.

Besides, it had occurred to her last night that without Onyx around watching her every move, perhaps she might finally have the opportunity to seek out her own answers to questions that had been plaguing her. If he wasn't going to fill her in, then she would simply have to find the answers on her own.

CHAPTER 8

C ora let out a deep sigh, trying to ignore the persistent ache in her back, located directly between her shoulder blades. Her entire body felt achy, but it was her back that bothered her the most— probably due to spending so much of her time over the past few days sitting on a cold, stone floor.

It had been four days since she'd been snatched off the streets, but she was still no closer to understanding who her captors were or why she was taken in the first place. At least they had removed the sack from her head and untied her, but she had been confined to the same small room for the entirety of her captivity—and once they had freed her hands and feet, they had taken away the chair, seeming to think that she might use it as a weapon against them.

To be fair, she probably would have, if it meant that she had a chance to get away. But her captors were far too careful to permit that. As a result, her room held nothing that could be turned into a weapon— which meant that it held nothing at all, aside from herself. She was fed regularly, but the food never came with utensils—restricted to items that she could eat with her hands or drink out of a bowl or cup.

She was also watched carefully as she ate to keep her from smashing any plate or cup and attempting to keep any of the shards. She was allowed a few breaks to go to the bathroom, but she was guarded the entire time, and afterward, she was always returned to her room—or her cell, as she had come to think of it.

She eyed the tall, lanky man who stood guard near the door. He looked about as bored as she was, though he didn't relax his position. A thick piece of black fabric covered the lower half of his face, leaving only his eyes visible. Cora thought this was a little silly, especially given that she wasn't from Llys and knew literally no one other than the blacksmith, Bram, but still her captors seemed determined to disguise their identities. They also refused to answer any of her questions, which caused a whole separate level of frustration.

Picking up a small pebble from off the floor, Cora rolled it around in her palm before flicking it across the room. It hit the guard's shin. He didn't react, but the sight of it hitting him was so satisfying to Cora that she nearly laughed out loud. She picked up another pebble, doing the same thing. This one also hit the guard, and Cora instantly chuckled. She reached for another pebble and flicked it. Another direct hit.

"Cut that out, will you?" the guard growled indignantly.

Cora smirked at finally having cracked through his silence. "If you're going to keep me in here without even so much as a book for company, you cannot fault me for seeking out my own entertainment," Cora fired back. She knew she was behaving childishly, but she couldn't bring herself to care. After four long days, she'd lost her patience with her captors. It was obvious that they didn't work for Onyx, and so far they had made no move to hurt her, which was a good thing, yet they'd also made no obvious plans to release her. So Cora let the sarcasm drip from her tone. It was the least she could do. "Or better yet, why don't you release me? Then I'll be out of your hair for good."

The guard grunted. "Sorry, I can't do that."

"All of you keep saying that," Cora practically yelled, "but no one will tell me why. You snatched me off the streets and you're holding me captive for no reason. If you think I'm someone worth all this attention, then why won't you *talk to me* and let me know what's going on—why you captured me, what you want, what all of this is *for*. Because it all feels to me like an enormous waste of my time." The words, angry and direct, poured out of her. It felt good to let some of her frustration out, even though she knew it wouldn't amount to anything. The guards weren't going to budge, no matter how much she yelled at him.

This is why you should let me burn the city to the ground, Alaric said bitterly in her mind. They'd stayed in constant contact through the bond, and Cora was certain that being able to talk to him was the only thing preventing her from completely going mad. But Alaric was as miserable as Cora was, and his frustration and anger over what was happening burned as hotly as Cora's own.

We both know that's a horrible idea, Cora said back, replaying the familiar argument. *One, a lot of innocent people would die, and two, I still have no idea where in the city I'm being held. If you raze the entire place, you'll likely be cooking me alive along with it.*

Perhaps if I fly closer to the city, I will be able to sense you through the bond. It is worth trying, is it not? We are so newly bonded, and there has been no one to teach us the extent of what we can accomplish together. I imagine there are quite a few abilities we are capable of even if we are not fully aware of them yet.

Cora sighed. *I'm not saying it's not possible, but Alaric, I won't have you risk your life for a mere possibility. Besides, I really don't think I'm in danger here. No one has tried to harm me. Soon enough, one of these guards will slip up and say something useful. Or they'll grow tired of me and dump me back out on the streets. Until then, we both have to be patient.*

It was the same thing she'd been saying for days now, but Alaric still wasn't thrilled with that response. Cora wasn't either, and deep down, she worried about how all of this would end. Whatever her fate, she knew she had to protect Alaric, even if that meant protecting him from himself by keeping him away from the city.

I do not think I am capable of much more patience, Alaric growled.

Well, that makes two of us. But we don't have a lot of options right now, so sit tight. Cora hated how sharp her words sounded, but she was tired and achy and frustrated, and her ability to hide all of that had long since disappeared. Alaric, able to read her emotions through the bond, didn't argue or call her out on her grumpiness. A kindness she knew she'd have to thank him for later. She knew that when things got bleak, it was all too easy to take your frustrations out on the people who cared about you, the ones closest to you. That seemed to be true now. Cora hadn't meant to snap at Alaric—it wasn't him she was angry with—but it was hard staying positive. She let out a low groan.

"Look," the guard said, drawing Cora's attention away from the conversation in her head. "Once the Crow arrives, then we'll know what to do with you. It shouldn't be long now, okay?"

Cora narrowed her eyes. The Crow. She had heard mention of this person several times, but they never mentioned any specifics around her. She didn't even know if the Crow was male or female, though Cora was smart enough to realize that the Crow was someone they highly respected. Maybe this highly respectable person would tell the others that they should let her go immediately, and that would be that. Of course, she didn't consider that very likely.

She glared at the guard. "You make it sound as if I am some sort of rabid animal that needs to be put out of its misery. Tell me, does this Crow person plan to exterminate me? Spear me like one of the wild hogs who roam the shadow woods?"

The guard scoffed. "What? No. Of course not. The Crow would never condone such violence."

Cora leveled her gaze at the guard. "Oh, but kidnapping? The Crow is fine with that, huh?"

The guard returned her glare with one of his own. "You know nothing of the Crow. Perhaps you should not speak of things you do not know."

"Yeah, well, perhaps you shouldn't abduct random girls from off the streets," Cora grumbled, all the fight leaking out of her like hot air. There was no point in arguing further with the guard—she'd tried arguing, cajoling, begging, bargaining…none of it made any difference. Her fate would not be decided until the Crow arrived, whenever that would be. Until then, she might as well save her breath. So, she slumped against the wall and closed her eyes. She was tired and had slept very poorly since she'd been taken captive. She doubted deep sleep would find her now, but her body could do with a bit of rest at least, so she settled in for that, trying to still her mind.

An hour or two later, there was a commotion outside the door to her room. The guard at the door jerked upright from his perch against the wall and flung the door open. He hurried out into the hallway and slammed the door behind him, leaving Cora alone. She heard the key click in the lock before footsteps echoed down the hall, scurrying away.

Alaric, she said, reaching out to the dragon. *Something is happening.*

Alaric's response was instantaneous. *Are they letting you go?*

No, but there's a lot of noise outside my room. The guard just left in a hurry.

I don't like the sound of that. A burst of worry flooded through Cora from the bond. *Will you consent to letting me storm the city now? I cannot sit back and wait any longer. Especially if whatever is outside that door will cause harm to you.*

No, stay where you are until I know what's going on. There is no need to overreact. Just...stand by.

Alaric harrumphed at that, but didn't argue. Cora strained her ears to see if she could make out any discernable sounds outside. She could tell there were many people talking, but the voices were too muffled for her to make out any words.

The conversation outside lasted for several minutes more before the voices cut off and gave way to the sound of footfalls coming down the hall. Cora only had time to suck in half a breath when the door to her room burst open and four figures who she recognized as her guards stepped into the room. There was a fifth person behind them, and when she stepped fully into the room, Cora gasped.

The woman, with her long dark hair and dark eyes, was familiar. In fact, her memory of their original meeting was still crystal clear in Cora's mind.

The woman standing in front of her was the same stranger she'd first seen in the Barcroft tavern not long after she'd first started communicating with Alaric—the one who had warned her to stay away from the dragons. Cora didn't think much of the woman's advice, seeing as her bond with Alaric was the best thing in her life, but the woman had been genuinely useful in a different way: She had given Cora a protective pendant that had helped shield her from the likes of Secare, somehow hiding or dampening the traces of dragon magic on her so that he couldn't detect it. At least, until she lost it.

Cora's brain immediately pulled up the memory of their first meeting and the words the woman had said: *"I know that I am a stranger to you and that you have no reason to trust me, but you must. I am trying to protect you, to keep you alive. Trust me, some things are just not worth the risk. You must stay away from the dragons."*

"Who are you?" Cora demanded. The woman's words had struck a chord within Cora, but not in a good way. Unease slithered across her skin, and she shivered. "You can't just come here, practically kidnap me, and then expect me to listen to what you're saying. I don't know you."

The woman stared, her features softening as she exhaled slowly. "You don't want to know me, girl," she breathed out, her voice low. "I know that you have no reason to trust me, but what I've told you is true. If you continue crossing the line, you or your loved ones will get hurt. Stay away from the mountains, and stay as far away as you can from the dragons."

In the time since then, Cora had frequently thought of the encounter with the stranger from the tavern. She had wished she could talk to her again. Her list of questions had only grown longer since their first encounter. It was more than a little odd to see her again—especially given the circumstances.

The woman's eyes landed on Cora and widened. "Wait," she demanded. "*This* is the girl you summoned me about?"

CHAPTER 9

"Aye," one of the guards responded, shaking his head. "This is the one."

Cora watched as the woman lifted her eyes skyward and swore. "You're a bunch of paranoid idiots, the whole lot of you!" She threw up her hands. "I can tell you without a shadow of a doubt that *this* girl is definitely not working with Onyx. She is no threat to us."

"Now, wait just a minute. You can't possibly know that," one of the other guards protested. "This girl was in the fortress when the king arrived, and her behavior was more than a little suspicious. Not only that, but she claimed that General Secare is dead—shouted it out as if it was a fact that she knew for sure. But no one else has any clue what has happened to him. If he really is gone, how could she have found that out?"

The woman's brows arched slightly at that but then she let out a deep sigh. "Clear the room. I wish to speak to the girl alone."

"Now wait just a minute," the guard who had been keeping Cora company all day spoke up. "This girl is our captive. And if you're going to question her, then we need to be present for the interrogation. We have a right to any information she shares with you."

"I have made my position among you quite clear," the woman argued, looking down her nose at the guard. "You know I can be trusted. If I find out any information that is relevant to you, I will be sure to pass it along."

The man begrudgingly nodded. "Fine, but don't take too long." He waved his hand and he and the rest of the guards filed out, shutting the door behind them.

The woman waited until she heard the sound of retreating footsteps, before letting out another sigh and plopping herself down on the floor across from Cora.

"So," Cora said. "You're the Crow?"

The woman nodded. "Yes."

"And you're in charge of this group?"

"No, I'm not in charge, but I do work closely with them."

"And who's 'them'?" Cora demanded. "Why are they doing this? I was just walking down the street when someone jerked a bag over my head, and I was kidnapped. I've been here for days, and no one will tell me anything about where I am or why I'm being held prisoner." She was yelling by the time she finished her sentence, all the frustration of the last few days pouring out of her.

The Crow held up a hand. "I know you've been through a lot and that you have more questions than answers, but if you'll allow me, I can try to explain a few things."

"Just start talking," Cora growled, done with pleasantries.

The Crow nodded. Leaning back against the wall, she stretched her legs out, and then cleared her throat and began to speak again. "First of all, I can tell you that the people who grabbed you and have kept you here are a part of a faction of antiroyalist rebels working to destabilize the king's rule. The king's visit has gotten them very worried. Onyx rarely frequents the area, and this visit came with little warning —a factor that has the rebels very concerned. You just got caught in the midst of it all by being in the wrong place at the wrong time."

Cora took a moment to process the information. Antiroyalists looking to destabilize Onyx's rule. When Bram had mentioned the movement, it had seemed so abstract. But here they were: the men and women right here in this building. To know that there were people in Tenegard actively working against Onyx was both a shock and a relief. Perhaps, she and Alaric wouldn't have to face him completely alone.

"Right, and…who are you?" Cora asked. "It was strange enough when you appeared out of nowhere in Barcroft, and now you're here and nothing makes sense. I don't know anything about you, and yet here you are. Again."

"I understand. They call me the Crow, as you know. You may call me that as well."

Cora shook her head. "That's not your name."

The woman pressed her lips together. "No, it's not. But you're the first person in a long time that's dared to ask for my name."

"Are they afraid of you?"

"They respect me—but I guess in some ways it's the same thing." She ran a hand down her face. "It's Tamsin," she said after a moment. "My name is Tamsin. But I'd prefer it if you kept that between the two of us for now."

Tamsin. Cora committed the name to her memory. "Of course. And… if you're not the leader of this merry band of rebels, then what *is* your connection to them?" Cora's ability to try to remain polite left her days ago. Now, all she wanted was answers and to get out of here. "You say you're not in charge, yet they sent for you to deal with me. They kept me waiting *for days* so that you could be the one to decide what should be done. They defer to you on some things, it seems."

Tamsin gave a small half smile. "You're intelligent and very observant. That's good. You'll need both of those things."

"For what exactly?"

Tamsin just gave Cora a knowing look. "They trust me because they know that our interests are aligned. But the reason why they look to me for guidance is because I employ some of them. I guess paying their salaries gives me a bit of authority. I like to use their network of spies to keep an eye on the movements of Onyx's shadow soldiers."

"Shadow soldiers?" Cora had never heard the term before. "Who are they?"

Tamsin's eyes darkened. "An abomination and one of Onyx's strongest weapons."

"That sounds rather terrifying," Cora said with a swallow.

"There is much to fear from them," Tamsin practically growled. "The shadow soldiers are a group of cursed men and women. Onyx made a deal with them decades ago. He extended their lives indefinitely and made them impervious to pain, but in return, they had to swear a magically binding oath of loyalty to him. From my understanding, the pull of that loyalty is nearly the only thing they feel anymore. The same magic that keeps them from feeling pain has also dulled their senses. They rarely show emotion—I'm not even sure they're capable of it anymore. It's made them brutal and merciless fighters. Nothing seems to be able to hurt them, and there are very, very few things in this world that can kill them."

A chill skipped down Cora's spine and she shuddered, remembering the cold, unfeeling gaze behind General Secare's eyes. The only emotion she had seen him show was an odd, muted sort of joy when she and Alaric had used the Dragon Fire on him. He had smiled in those final moments and had looked relieved, even as the flames of Dragon Fire ate away at him. The memory still made Cora uneasy, though it also made a lot more sense now. Tamsin said their lives had been extended. Just how long had he been alive…but incapable of feeling? No wonder he'd been relieved to finally have it come to an end.

"The Shadow Soldiers," Tamsin continued, "are all highly skilled in combat and have the ability to sense magic as a means of better hunting their targets. I believe you've already come into contact with one of them."

"Yes." Cora nodded. "General Secare."

Tamsin leaned forward at the mention of his name. "Cora, I need to know what happened to Secare. Can you tell me?"

Cora chewed the inside of her cheek. A small part of her warned her that she should keep her mouth shut about the Dragon Fire—but the larger part recalled the pendant that Tamsin had gifted her in Barcroft. It had protected her. If Tamsin had wanted harm to come to her, why give her the pendant in the tavern? No, she had done it to keep Cora safe. If there was anyone that Cora could speak of Secare with, it was her.

"I'll tell you, but I want to know one thing first."

Tamsin held out a hand. "Go on."

"I want to know about the pendant. The one you gave me in the tavern. You knew it had protective qualities and that it would protect me from him, from General Secare, right?"

"Yes," Tamsin answered plainly. "It's why I gave it to you. The amulet had been mine for a long time, but I could tell that you needed the protection more than I did."

Cora nodded, taking a moment to soak in this answer and its implications. It seemed that Tamsin knew genante magic of old. How else would she have been able to recognize the signs of dragon magic on Cora when there had been no dragon magic in Tenegard for nearly a hundred and thirty years? How else had she known about the cave—the one that Tamsin had referred to as a temple? There was so much that Cora and Alaric were having to figure out by stumbling along on their own, trying to find answers that had vanished years ago. It was clear that this woman knew more. Much more. There was so much that Cora could learn from Tamsin, but it would require Cora to be honest first.

There were a dozen reasons to trust her and only one thing holding her back. But it was the most important thing imaginable to her.

Alaric.

In order to tell the whole story, she would have to speak of Alaric and explain that they had bonded—and Cora wasn't sure if she was ready to do that. Revealing the nature of her relationship with Alaric could put them both in great danger.

As if Tamsin understood her conflict, she let out a breath. "I know what you're thinking, but don't worry. I already know that you didn't stay away from the dragons as I warned. I also know that you've bonded with one."

Cora grimaced. She'd been afraid of that. Tamsin had been aware of her connection to the dragons before. It wasn't that surprising to learn that she could recognize the bond, too.

Tamsin continued, "You know, having a bond like that makes you dangerous to the king. You'll need to make sure your magic is under control, or you risk being hunted down by Onyx. If he gets anywhere near you, you're done for."

Cora perked up at this, despite the shock still percolating through her. "I saw him at the fortress."

She grimaced. "The others mentioned that you and the king were at the fortress at the same time. It's what had them so suspicious of you. But are you saying that you actually saw him? What happened? Was he off at a distance?"

"No, he was only a few paces away. I was inside the armory when he was brought in to perform an inspection," Cora explained. "I hid behind a rack of weapons, but he was quite close by—maybe as far as from here to the wall," she said, gesturing.

Tamsin stared at her in shock. "He was that close? But…how is that possible? How did you manage to escape? From that close, he should have noticed the dragon magic on you. Unless…were you wearing the amulet then?"

"I wasn't," Cora admitted. "I lost it back in Barcroft. But while he may have sensed dragon magic, he didn't seem to think it came from me."

"Who else could it have come from?"

"From the dragon he's holding captive in the south courtyard," Cora replied. When Tamsin just stared at her, Cora began to explain about Raksha and how she had been mistaken for the bonded dragon and captured in Alaric's stead. "So when Onyx found traces of dragon magic when he arrived in the fortress, he had no reason to search for me. He thought he already knew where it was coming from."

Tamsin shook her head, clearly rattled. "I can't believe the king is holding a dragon captive in the fortress. He hates dragons—loathes them. For him to be near one, he must be truly desperate for answers. Tell me of General Secare. Could that be what spooked Onyx?"

Cora sucked in a breath. "Right. General Secare." She felt in her gut that she could trust Tamsin, but she didn't particularly like reliving the memory of that day. Still, she knew it was necessary. So, taking a deep breath, she quickly recounted what had happened between her, Secare, and Alaric up in the mountains. "There you have it," she finished with a shrug. "Alaric and I killed him using Dragon Fire."

Tamsin looked slightly awed at this, but she gathered herself quickly. "You and your dragon are very brave, Cora. I know it is never easy to take a life, but you did what you had to do. And you should be proud of what you managed to accomplish, working with your dragon like that. Very few riders and dragons have been able to master Dragon Fire."

"How do you know that?" Cora couldn't help but ask. "You speak of the dragons and the dragon riders as if you know with certainty that they existed, but everyone I've come across acts as though the dragon riders were never real."

"Oh, they were real enough, all right," Tamsin said, a trace of bitterness in her voice.

"Yes, but how do you know that?" Cora demanded. "What makes you such an expert of the dragons and the dragon riders of old? And how did you know that I had bonded with a dragon?"

Tamsin swallowed. "I know because..." She paused, inhaling deeply. "I know because I could sense the magic of your bond. And I know about the dragon riders of old because...I was one."

CHAPTER 10

OCTAVIA

For the last few days, Octavia had vacillated between playing the role of spoiled princess and serving as an extension of King Onyx. Both left a sour taste in her mouth, but the performance had served its purpose. The majority of the fortress inhabitants now paid little attention to her. Rising early this morning, she felt restless.

Flinging open the door, Octavia marched purposefully out into the corridor. It was breakfast time and nearly everyone was in the dining hall, so the passageways were mostly quiet. With her stomach rumbling, Octavia thought to head down in that direction herself, but another idea struck her. The armory. It would be deserted this time of day and perhaps that would give her the chance to inspect it again, properly this time, without prying eyes watching her every move.

She made for the armory and smiled to herself when she saw just how empty it was. She moved through the space, looking for anything that might explain the king's frequent inspections—and his frustration in the aftermath—but as far as she could tell, there was nothing to justify his behavior.

"I don't understand," Octavia said out loud, eyeing a suit of armor that stood erect against the wall. "Why would Onyx insist on frequenting this place? There's nothing of interest here."

But no sooner had the words come out of her mouth than she spotted a corridor that she hadn't noticed before. It branched off from the armory leading towards the back of the fortress. Most of the guest rooms and meeting spaces were housed in the front of the fortress, so Octavia hadn't yet been to the back side yet. She hadn't had a reason to.

"Maybe…" she considered, "maybe it wasn't the armory itself that Onyx was frequenting." For a moment, she considered turning back. She had no idea what she might face. Perhaps she'd been kept away because it was dangerous. Maybe she would be better off approaching someone else for information rather than going to seek it out directly. That would surely be the safer course.

But today, she didn't feel like being safe. Octavia swept past the armory door and down the long, dimly lit corridor.

There were a few soldiers standing guard along the way. They looked nervous when Octavia approached, but she lifted her chin and gave them her best imperious stare, continuing to charge forward as if she had every right to be there, and they backed down immediately.

The corridor was long, and Octavia was beginning to think it would just continue on forever when it finally opened up into what appeared to be a small courtyard.

It was more brightly lit than the hallway…but somehow, not as bright as she had been expecting. The sun had been shining brilliantly moments before, so why…? Octavia's eyes scanned upward and immediately saw what was blocking a portion of the sunlight, casting odd shadows on the ground. There was a massive net made of what looked like chainmail that had been strung over the entirety of the courtyard, cutting off all access to the sky. It was the oddest thing, and Octavia couldn't fathom why such a thing would be needed. Was it for some sort of training exercise?

She stepped further into the courtyard, scanning the net and mulling over its potential uses. But then a massive shape moved out from the shadows and Octavia jumped back, startled. At first she couldn't make sense of what she was seeing, but then her hand flew to her mouth. Because there, moving slowly towards her, was a dragon.

Despite everyone's insistence that dragons were vile, dangerous creatures, Octavia had always been fascinated by them. When she was little, her nurse used to read to her from books filled with legends of the dragon riders of old, and she'd been utterly enthralled. "Fantasy nonsense," her tutor had scoffed when she'd asked about it. "Meant to amuse gullible children. Actual dragons are nothing more than beasts —incapable of speech or understanding." Still, the idea wouldn't let her go. What if dragons *could* be more than just beasts? She knew she wasn't the only one to believe such a thing was possible because she'd found several dusty artifacts in the bowels of the castle that seemed to be designed with dragon riders in mind: a saddle that could only fit a dragon, beautiful swords with dragons engraved into the hilt… She didn't know who had created the items, but she liked to think that it had been someone else who had believed that the myths could be made true, that magic could form a bond between a human and a dragon somehow, someday. She'd hidden the items in her room, and they were there still. Her own trove of secrets.

"By the stars," Octavia breathed, unable to take her eyes off the creature. Its scales were light blue, and it was bigger than she would have expected. She had seen many images of dragons in books, but dragons lived in the mountains and there weren't any colonies near the lowlands of the capital city. She couldn't help but admire the way the filtered sunlight glinted off the creature's scales.

But her awe gave way to dismay when she realized that something wasn't right about the dragon's face. A muzzle, made from thick bands of leather, was strapped to its snout. Something about the muzzle seemed...odd. It didn't close off the dragon's mouth completely—in fact, Octavia was relatively sure that it could still eat with the muzzle on—and yet the muzzle seemed to be paining it, as if it had been fastened too tightly. As Octavia stared deep into its eyes, her throat began to ache. This dragon's eyes were filled with sorrow and the sight of it made Octavia stumble forwards.

"Oh," she said, holding out her hand. "Here, please. Let me help you." She took a step towards the dragon, slow and measured, and then another.

She had watched the stable master work with wild horses back in the capital, and he had always told her that it was important not to make sudden movements that could startle the horses. She assumed that the same principle would also apply to dragons.

"I'm not going to hurt you," she said softly, trying to convey as much gentleness and kindness as she could in her tone. She didn't expect the animal to understand her words, but perhaps it could sense her intentions in other ways.

She took another step towards the dragon and then another. The dragon did not move away, but its large eyes followed Octavia's every step.

Octavia kept her hand out in front of her. "It's okay," she murmured again. "I don't want to hurt you." She took one last step until she was close enough to touch the dragon's snout. She inched her fingers out, ready to snatch back her hand at any second if the dragon began to thrash or charge at her, but to her shock and surprise, the dragon lowered its head and slowly, so very slowly, tapped its snout on her outstretched hand.

"You poor thing," Octavia murmured, pulling her hand back. "What are you doing here?"

Of course, she knew the creature couldn't answer back. Still, she continued to speak softly to it, trying to give it whatever comfort she could.

The dragon watched her every move, its eyes still full of such profound sadness that it made it hard for Octavia to look it in the eyes for long. She examined the muzzle the creature wore. She wanted so badly to remove it, even if just for a little while to give the dragon some respite, but she knew she couldn't. There would be no way to hide that she was the one who had done it, given that the guards had seen her go in, and while Onyx had no time to spare for her when she was well behaved, she was under no illusions that she would have his full attention if she stepped out of line. The thought scared her. He had never raised a hand to her, nor had she ever seen him strike anyone else, but still…the fear came automatically, an instinct she couldn't ignore. It was why she had never acted out in a bid for attention before. As lonely as she was, there were some kinds of attention she would much rather avoid.

"What has he done to you?" she murmured, continuing to stroke the dragon's snout. "All those visits to 'the armory.' Obviously, it was you that he came to see. But why? What is he after? What is it he wants from you?" Because there must be some reason why he had chosen to trap a dragon when he'd always said they were strictly to be avoided. There was clearly something he wanted from this one—and judging from his obvious displeasure, he hadn't gotten it yet.

She mulled it over for a bit, content to stand near the dragon as long as possible, but as the sun continued to rise in the sky and no answers came to her, she knew she needed to clear the courtyard. At some point, whoever was in charge of feeding and tending to the dragon would come back, and she didn't want to have to explain her presence.

"I have to go," she said to the dragon, feeling the need to explain herself even though she knew the dragon couldn't understand her. "I must get back before someone comes looking for me. I assume I'm not supposed to know about you."

She turned on her heel and started to head for the door, but her heart ached at the thought of leaving the sad dragon alone—especially since she knew quite a bit about being lonely and sad herself.

"Don't worry," she promised. "I'll come back and visit you, okay? I won't stay gone long."

The dragon only stared at her.

"You can trust me," Octavia said again, willing her meaning to be clear. "I know you're probably scared, and you've been taken from your home. I don't know why, but I'll see if I can find out. And I promise you, I *will* come back."

There wasn't anything left to say, but still Octavia hated to leave. With a heavy heart, she crossed the courtyard and stepped into the corridor. She glanced over her shoulder one last time. The dragon stood in the exact same spot, staring after her.

Octavia lifted a hand and waved. Hurrying back down the corridor, she tried not to let the guilt she felt swimming inside overwhelm her. *It's just a dragon,* she tried to remind herself. *It's not like it will miss you.*

Still, the tug on her heartstrings was strong. *I'll be back,* she said to the dragon in her mind. *I promise.*

And she intended to keep that promise.

CHAPTER 11

Cora stared at Tamsin, feeling as if the wind had been sucked right out of her lungs. "What?"

Tilting her head back against the wall, Tamsin stared up at the ceiling. "I was a dragon rider." Her voice got quiet, as she whispered, "A long time ago."

"But…but that can't be true. All of the dragon riders were executed by Onyx. It's not possible…" Cora argued, searching Tamsin's face. "Is it?"

Tamsin held out a hand. "I can show you if you like. I understand why it might be difficult to believe, but I have proof if you wish to see it."

Cora eyed the outstretched hand. "All I see is your hand."

Tamsin's lips twitched a bit at that. "I'd like to show you something with magic if you'll let me. All you have to do is touch my hand."

Cora wasn't sure whether she liked the idea. She didn't think Tamsin would hurt her, but magic on the whole was still such a mystery to her. Among the genante population, it had barely existed for decades, present only in soothsayers who were just as likely as not to be driven mad by the magic behind their visions. The only other magic users were the malhos, and chief among them was Onyx himself. Could anyone blame her for being scared? There was so much she didn't know, didn't understand…but maybe this was how she'd finally get some answers. She reached out her hand and gently placed her palm down atop Tamsin's.

Instantly, Cora felt as if she had been sucked out of her body. An image appeared in Cora's mind, playing out as if she was actually there, seeing it happen. It was Tamsin, unsaddling a massive, burgundy-colored dragon. The two of them were murmuring to each other—too softly for Cora to hear what was said—but then the dragon said something that made Tamsin laugh out loud, bright and joyous and miles away from the serious, almost haunted woman whose hand Cora had taken. Cora marveled at the sight the two of them made, the details that she knew could only come from real life experience. But there was something else too. Despite the joy of Tamsin and her dragon, visible in everything from their relaxed, comfortable stances to their warm expressions, there was an immense sadness that seemed to hang over the image that Cora didn't understand. She opened her mouth to ask questions, but Tamsin pulled her hand away and the image disappeared completely.

"How did you do that?" Cora asked. It was the easiest of her questions.

"The bond that we riders have with our dragons makes us capable of sharing limited connections with other riders too. My dragon is no longer with me, but I can still access the magic."

Her words were laced with the same sadness that Cora felt when viewing the image. Pain was such a personal thing, and although a dozen questions bubbled in her mind, she had the sense that it would be wise not to press Tamsin further where her dragon was concerned.

Still, her curious nature was running wild. She had a million questions, and she said so to Tamsin.

"I know there is much to discuss," Tamsin replied, "but before we talk further, we should take a break. I have come a long way, and I am quite hungry. And you look like you could do with getting out of this room."

Cora's heart leaped at that. "You mean, I can go free?" Immediately, she thought of Alaric.

"Of course. There is no reason to keep you prisoner here, and I will see to it that the rebels do not hinder you further. Do you trust me enough to vouch for you among the rebels?"

It seemed a silly thing to ask, considering all that had been revealed between them, but still Cora nodded. "Yes, I trust you."

"You have to promise not to flee as soon as we let you out, however. There is still much to say between us, and I don't have the time to waste chasing you down."

"You have my word. I won't flee."

"Good." Tamsin rose to her feet. "Then let's see about getting you out of here."

Leaping to her feet, Cora followed Tamsin out into the hall. Now that she wasn't confined to her room, she got a better sense of where she was. The building wasn't much to look at, but it had the appearance of a personal residence. In the main living area, a group of people sat around a worn looking table. There were no masks on their faces this time, but Cora recognized them by their body types and the clothes they were wearing. These were her captors. She tried not to glare at them as she stepped a little closer to Tamsin's side, for fear that they might try to imprison her again.

"As I said before, the girl is no threat to you," Tamsin addressed the rebels. "There is no need to hold her any longer. She is willing to cooperate and tell us what she knows."

"And you're sure of this?" A man with dark hair asked, leaning forward.

"Yes," Tamsin answered. "She is an ally to us."

"Very well then," the man answered, his tone significantly lighter. "Who's hungry?"

Could it really be as simple as that? Cora wanted to scream in frustration but didn't want to risk getting locked in that room again. She snapped her mouth shut as no one offered a word of protest as Cora was ushered to a chair and provided with a serving of dinner.

Cora gripped her spoon, eyeing the wooden bowl of stew before her. It looked hearty enough and it smelled even better, but it felt odd to be sitting at a table, having a family style dinner with the same people who had kidnapped her and held her against her will.

She lifted her head and slid her gaze across the table. The man who'd been her main guard sat there, shoveling mouthfuls of stew into his mouth. There were tiny specks of gravy in his beard. She hadn't even known he'd had a beard due to the mask he always wore. Seeing him now, decorated with those specks of gravy, he seemed to transform from threatening captor to...well, something else. Not a friend, certainly, but maybe someone she could work with, if they had a common goal.

Her other guards were there too. A woman named Shila and a man named Tyberon, according to the conversations happening quietly around her. Shila was older than Cora by at least twenty years. A hard twenty years, Cora would guess, based not just on the gray streaks in her hair but the eyes that bespoke of more than her share of trials and loss. Tyberon appeared to be just a few years older than Cora with shaggy blond hair and a jawline covered in stubble. There were about half a dozen other rebels sitting at the table as well. They paid her little mind, which suited Cora just fine, as she tried to take it all in. It was clear from the way the rebels conversed with one another that they were a tight-knit group. They reminded her of Strida and the team of scale scavengers back in Barcroft, and for a split second, a pang of homesickness shot through Cora. But it was gone as quickly as it had come—especially with thoughts of Viren and Raksha burning in the back of her mind. There were those in Barcroft who had been kind to her—but no one mattered as much to her as family, and she couldn't even consider going home until she knew her father and Raksha were safe and away from that horrible fortress.

I do not know what to make of all this, Alaric's deep voice rose up, echoing in her ears. Using the bond, Cora had caught him up on what was going on, and he seemed torn between being pleased that she was now free and being worried that it was somehow all a trap. *They kidnap you and now you are dining with them like an old friend?* The dragon let out a snort. *I still feel tempted to storm the city, tearing down every single wall until you are returned safely to me.*

The corners of Cora's mouth lifted slightly. The dragon's concern for her was touching. He was also saying the very thing that Cora herself was thinking. Well, not the part about tearing down walls, but the rest of it? Feeling like the change was too abrupt? Yes, she understood those feelings very well. *I know what you mean*, she responded through the bond. *One minute I was a prisoner and now I'm a guest. It's...strange. But now that Tamsin has vouched for me, they apparently see me as a potential ally. So no need to burn down the city, okay? I am well and they are treating me kindly. I don't think they would do anything to go against Tamsin's word.*

Alaric let out another snort. *And Tamsin, are we sure we can trust her?*

Cora mulled this over for a moment. She understood Alaric's hesitation, but Tamsin's actions thus far had proved that she could be trusted and that she only wanted to help Cora and Alaric. And she was a dragon rider. The only other one in existence that she knew of. That wasn't something they could just ignore.

She's a rider, or at least, she used to be. If there's anyone we can truly trust, I think it's her. The image she showed me, of her dragon, it felt so real, and the emotions attached to it? I'm not sure anyone could have faked that. No, I think we can trust her.

Very well, but I will feel much better when we are together once more.

Me too, friend. Cora let out a deep sigh. She'd never been away from her dragon for this long since they bonded, and it had long since started to wear on them both. *Me too.*

"You better eat that," someone said from the seat beside her. "It's fine now, but it's not as good if you let it get stone cold." The voice seemed a little familiar.

Cora turned her head and let out a gasp. "You!"

The guard from the fortress, the one who had helped her get past the gate guard, now sat beside her. His name, she remembered, was Faron. He gave her a half smile, his own bowl of stew in hand.

"Me," he replied with a nod, picking up his spoon and gulping down a mouthful.

"What are you doing here?" Cora had already figured out that the rebels must have had someone on the inside stationed at the fortress—how else would they have known about her or her movements within its walls?—but it was still a bit shocking to see Faron in the seat beside her.

"Eating dinner." Faron lifted a shoulder and let it drop. "Same as you." But the side of his mouth quirked upward again. "You're surprised to see me again, I guess?"

"Yes," Cora answered honestly. "I am."

"Admittedly, I'm surprised to see you again too," Faron replied, and there was something in his expression that made Cora's cheeks burn slightly—though she wasn't sure why.

She opened her mouth to ask another question, but two loud voices at the other end of the table rose in volume and all heads swiveled in their direction.

Tamsin and a stout man sat beside one another, their faces inches apart as they glared at one another. The man's clenched fists slammed against the top of the table with a loud thud. "We have to do something," he was saying. "All of our reports indicate that Onyx is gearing up for war. He has already done so much harm to this country —are we going to stand back and let him drag us into armed conflict, as well?"

These words seemed to draw all the other rebels' attention, as if it were the opening statements of some kind of formal business meeting. All at once they began to discuss people and missions that Cora had no prior knowledge, including the recruitment drives among some of the garrisons in the Llys region.

Tamsin listened attentively and added her thoughts when asked, but she mostly held back, listening more than she spoke and letting others take the lead. Cora was surprised by this—she was even more surprised that the rebels continued to call her the Crow. No one used her name, which made her wonder if they even knew it or knew that she was a dragon rider.

When her stew was gone and her bowl scraped clean, Cora found herself torn over what came next. She was desperate to reunite with

Alaric…but at the same time, there was still so much she needed to talk over with Tamsin. Things that she didn't dare bring up when the others were around. It was a relief when the meal concluded, and Tamsin led her to a private room in the house.

Tamsin gave her a half smile as she settled in one of the wooden chairs near the hearth of the fireplace. "There are many things I would like to ask you, but I'm sure you have a whole list of questions for me. Go ahead, then." She held out a hand and motioned for Cora to proceed.

"I guess I'm still in shock over the fact that you're a dragon rider," Cora admitted. "I thought Onyx killed all the riders?"

Tamsin pressed her lips in a line for a second, breathing deeply, before she answered. "The short answer is that he did. He would have killed me too, but I managed to escape before that happened. It was actually here in Llys. I was being held in the fortress. I was lucky, that's all. All of the other riders…well, they were not so lucky."

The words speared into Cora like an arrow, and she winced slightly at the pain in them. Tamsin's voice was soft, but there was so much emotion packed into it. It was clear that she deeply mourned the riders and their dragons. It occurred to Cora that the other riders had been her team, her friends. The loss must have been devastating. Not to mention the loss of her dragon. That particular thought was too terrible to even contemplate. "I'm sorry."

Tamsin shook her head. "It was a long time ago."

Cora knew from personal experience that time didn't necessarily dull the pain of grief, but she didn't press. Casting around for something else they could discuss, a new thought struck her. "Wait, you said you were imprisoned here at the fortress but escaped? By the stars, that's amazing!"

Tamsin's eyebrows shot straight up.

"Oh no, sorry," Cora hurried to explain. "I didn't mean that the way it came out. I just meant that if you escaped the fortress, then you can help me break out my father and Raksha."

"No, I don't think I can do that."

"What? Why not?"

Tamsin let out a sigh. "It's not that I don't want to, Cora. I would help you if I could. But the circumstances are very different now. Onyx will be expecting you to come after Raksha. In all likelihood, the reason that he had her brought here instead of to the capital, where he could contain her much more securely, is because he's using her as bait to draw out the dragon rider—draw you out. I have no idea what kind of traps he might have laid in place for you. You can't risk going near the fortress again."

"I have to save my father and Raksha," Cora replied. "Whatever Onyx is hoping, it doesn't change that fact."

"Think of it, Cora. Right now, no one but the two of us knows who the new rider is, but Onyx will figure it out eventually. And once he discovers your father's link to you—he'll have even more leverage to use against you. Especially if you try to break out your father and fail. Even contacting him the way you did before is too dangerous now. It's better for your father if you stay away from him. Raksha too."

Cora stared at Tamsin, unable to fully believe the words the older woman had spoken. "No," she finally uttered, shaking her head. "That's not going to happen. I'm not going to get caught. Especially if you help me."

"You got lucky last time you were in the fortress, Cora." Tamsin's face hardened slightly. "The fact that you were feet away from Onyx and are still standing in front of me right now is a testament to just how lucky you truly are. How long do you think it's going to take for Onyx to realize that the dragon magic he sensed wasn't coming from

Raksha? By now, it's likely that he's already figured that out. Raksha carries the *potential* for dragon magic, but she doesn't have a bond. The energy she gives off is very different from what Onyx would sense from you or Alaric. In the days since you've been gone, don't you think he's noticed the difference? Onyx is a horrifically brilliant man—it won't take him long to figure out what happened. The moment you step foot in that fortress, Onyx and the shadow soldiers will be on you and that will be the end of it."

The words struck Cora like a physical blow, but before she could say anything in reply, Tamsin continued.

"I know your heart, Cora, and I know that it's devastating to consider leaving your father and your dragon's mother behind, but you have to be smart. Being a rider does not make you invincible. I trained for years with my dragon in combat and magical skills and look what it got me." She lifted her shirt to show a long, jagged scar that ran from her upper arm all the way done to her hip. "One of the shadow soldiers nearly killed me. I got lucky too. But luck will only take you so far. It's not worth the risk—not when the chances of success are so low. The best thing you can do for your father and Raksha, as well as you and your bonded dragon is to stay out of sight—and train."

"Train?"

"Yes. You and Alaric need to know how to protect each other and defend yourself. You need to be trained in the ways of the dragon riders. I can't help you break into the fortress, but training you is something I *can* do."

Cora took a moment to process this. There was a side of her that wanted to refuse, to go her own way, but in spite of herself, she couldn't help but see the logic in Tamsin's words. Returning to the fortress wouldn't rescue her father or Raksha—it would only result in her becoming captive alongside them. And if that happened, nothing she said would stop Alaric from charging in after her; she didn't see any way that that would end well. And the crux of the matter was truly that she and Alaric *did* need training. They'd been able to successfully conjure Dragon Fire against Secare, but that had been one time against a single opponent. Cora wasn't sure if they could even do it again—and if they could, would they even be able to control it? They couldn't exactly charge into the fortress and set fire to things in the middle of a densely populated city. Innocent people would be killed.

Dragon Fire was, so far, the only magical weapon in their defensive arsenal, and it wasn't one they could fully control or trust yet. There was bound to be so much more that they could learn from Tamsin. About magic, yes, but also about self-defense and combat. She shivered at the memory of Secare charging her with the sword, stabbing her. She pressed her hand to the freshly healed wound. She had been lucky that it wasn't a deep puncture and that somehow the magic between her and Alaric had sped up the healing process. But it still twinged from time to time. And Cora never wanted to be in that position, to feel that helpless again.

"Okay," she finally replied, "but there's one thing I need to know before I agree."

Tamsin arched a brow. "All right, what's that?"

"If I agree to train with you, Alaric as well, will you help me plan and rescue my father and Raksha?"

"Cora, I told you—"

Cora held up her hand. "I heard what you said, but I can't and won't abandon them. I understand that it's too dangerous to rush in without a solid plan and without a better understanding of what Alaric and I can do together. If we train and learn to defend ourselves, though, I think we'll be able to find a way. Especially with your knowledge of the fortress. I know it's a risk, but I have to do this. I'm certain Alaric feels the same. If you really think the best thing for us is to train with you, then we'll do it. But only on the condition that once we are ready, you will help us free our family."

Tamsin ran a hand down her face and let out a huff. "Fine," she finally said, sounding aggravated. "Once your training is finished, I'll do what I can to help you free your father and the other dragon."

"Good." Cora beamed. "I was hoping you'd say that. But now that I've had a second to think about it, there's one more thing."

"Another?" Tamsin barked. "And what by the stars could that be?"

"I know how I feel and the deal we've struck, but I can't officially agree to anything without discussing this with someone else first." She smiled. "Alaric. We're a team, and if we're going to do this, it has to be something we both agree on."

Tamsin softened slightly at that. "Of course, I understand completely." She gathered up a spare change of clothes. "I'm going to go freshen up for bed. We'll leave in the morning."

Cora startled at that. "Leave? You mean we won't be staying here?"

"No, some of the training will need to take place in the air. It wouldn't be safe here—there are too many people and too much risk of being seen."

It felt wrong to leave, as if they were running away…but Tamsin's reasoning made sense. Slowly, Cora nodded. "Where will we go, then?"

"West of the city, to my home. We won't be disturbed there. Now, get some rest. Tomorrow will be a long day." She turned on her heel then and swept out the door without waiting for a reply.

Cora sank down on the bed and let out a long exhale. "Well, okay then," she murmured. *Alaric?* She reached for the bond.

I am here.

There's something we need to discuss.

That sounds serious.

Cora snickered, but sobered almost immediately. *It is. I've been talking with Tamsin, and we've worked out a deal. But I told her I couldn't officially agree to it without speaking to you first.*

Very well. What are the parameters of this deal?

Cora took a breath and told him.

CHAPTER 12

The next morning, Cora's entire body hummed with energy. She couldn't wait to finally be reunited with Alaric, and knowing that they would soon begin training with Tamsin added a little extra pep in her step. She'd grown up listening to Nana Livi's stories about the dragon riders, and now with Tamsin's help, she and Alaric were on their way to becoming exactly like the bonded pairs in the stories.

As always, Cora felt a gentle twinge in her heart at the memory of her beloved grandmother. It was Nana Livi who had not only taught her about dragons and the true history of Tenegard, but who had also taught her to be brave, to follow her heart, and to believe in herself. None of the things she'd achieved over the past several months would have been possible without the lessons she had learned from her grandmother, and it was always a little heartbreaking to remember that she wasn't around anymore to show her pride in all that Cora had achieved. But while she couldn't share her triumphs with her grandmother anymore, she could continue to strive to live a life that would honor her memory. And today, that included starting her training to shape herself fully into one of the dragon riders she and her grandmother had admired.

There were moments when Cora still couldn't wrap her head around everything that had happened, but as she felt the tug of the bond between her and Alaric, she couldn't help but feel tremendous gratitude. Whatever it was that brought them together, she was more than thankful for it. And more than ready to see just what they could be able to accomplish together.

Standing outside the house that served as the meeting place for the rebels—which, after all her wondering, Cora now found to be on a nondescript street not far from the town gate in Llys—Cora bounced up and down on the balls of her feet. She was more than ready to be on their way, but she had to wait for Tamsin to finish up her business with the rebels. Several of them stood outside talking among themselves, waiting to see them off. To anyone passing, it would look like nothing more than a group of friends seeing off another friend on a trip. No one would guess that all of these men and women were actually antiroyalists involved in a conspiracy against the king.

It made Cora wonder just how many others there were within the city walls and in Llys who shared their feelings about the monarch. Bram had mentioned the antiroyalists, and it was clear from the look on his face when he spoke of Onyx that he was no huge fan of the king. Was it possible Bram was also part of the organization—in fact or even just in spirit? And what about outside the city walls? The more time Cora spent with Tamsin and the rebels, the more questions she had. She just hoped that eventually she would get the answers.

"I still have some things I need to finish up around here," Tamsin announced, checking all of their gear for a second time. "But there's no need for you to be around for all of it. In fact, before we head out, I need you to do something for me."

Cora nodded. "Of course. What is it?"

Tamsin nodded to where one of the rebels was leading over her horse. The horse was a gelding the color of ground powder. Tamsin gave it a soft smile and ran her hand along its neck. "This is Grainger. I bought him on short notice after receiving the rebels' message about you. But," she lowered her voice so that only Cora could hear, "by the time we meet up with Alaric, we'll no longer be needing a horse. I want you to take him to the market and see if you can sell him."

Cora scrunched her nose. "The market? That's right outside the fortress. I thought you wanted me to stay away from there."

Tamsin nodded. "Yes, but the section of the market that deals with livestock is several blocks further east than the fortress itself. It's far enough away that I think you will be safe. Only those who are interested in buying and selling animals frequent there. There's little to no reason why Onyx or his shadow generals would be there, and they are the only ones you need to be sure to avoid. Anyone else from the fortress would have no cause to give you a second glance."

Cora nodded, agreeing that that made sense. "All right, then," she said. "But I don't know very much about horses. Are you sure you want to trust me with this?" She knew how to ride, of course, but she and her father had never actually owned their own horse—they had been too expensive to feed and shelter. On the rare occasion when one was needed, for a delivery from the forge that was especially large or that required them to go especially far, they would rent a horse temporarily from the livery. She hadn't the faintest idea what kind of price she should ask for at the market.

"I'm sure you're up to the task," Tamsin replied. "Anyway, it needs to be done before we leave, and I can't do it myself—I really need to meet with Gavril and Shila one last time before we leave. There are a few loose ends to tie up." She then gave Cora a quick overview of the horse—how old it was, what selling points she should bring up when talking to a buyer, and the bare-minimum price she should accept.

"Okay, I think I've got it all," Cora confirmed when Tamsin was done. "What's the best way to get to the market from here?"

"I could show you if you want?" Faron, who had been standing beside the other rebels, stepped forward, having obviously overheard their conversation. "To the livestock market, I mean." He dipped his head. "Sorry, I wasn't eavesdropping or anything, but I'm headed in that direction anyway, and I'd be happy to show you the way."

Cora narrowed her eyes, unsure how she felt about spending any more time with him. On the one hand, it was thanks to him that she'd been able to get into the fortress and see her father. But she was pretty sure that it was *also* thanks to him that her behavior had been reported to the other antiroyalists, leading to her capture. And then just as an added issue, Faron was distractingly handsome, and with everything that was going on in her life at the moment, she really didn't need any more distractions. She was about to open her mouth and turn down his offer when Tamsin spoke up.

"Thank you, Faron," she said. "I expect you to see Cora to the livestock market. Keep an eye out for her while you're there, won't you? I don't *expect* her to run into anyone problematic from the fortress, but it never hurts to be careful—and I'd feel better if she had someone watching her back."

"Of course." Faron dipped his head again.

Tamsin nodded at them both and then disappeared back inside the house.

Seeing as she had no other option, Cora let out a sigh and fell into step beside Faron, who led Grainger by the reins.

They didn't speak for several minutes, until finally Cora broke the silence by asking, "So…you work at the fortress. Undercover."

"Yes. I got the job so that I'd be in a good position to report back anything of interest to the rebels." He made it all sound very matter-of-fact, though his eyes told a different story. It was clear from his fierce expression that he had strong opinions about Onyx. She wondered what was behind that. She had always believed that all malhos firmly supported Onyx. If there was any sign of rebellion against the king, she would have expected it to come from the genante —the conquered people rising up against the man who had invaded their country and erased their culture. But when she'd finally seen the other antiroyalists at dinner the previous night, it had been easy to see that they were an even mix of genante and malhos. It wasn't at all what she would have expected.

"It was you who told the rebels about me, wasn't it? It's your fault I was kidnapped off the street." She didn't bother to hide her anger or annoyance.

Faron chuckled, rubbing at the back of his neck with the hand that wasn't holding Grainger's reins. "Yes, that was me. I could say that I'm sorry…but it wouldn't really be true. You have to understand my position. It's my job to report anything that could be potentially dangerous to the rebels. It was obvious that there was something more behind your visit than what you were claiming. I wasn't sure what you were up to, so I had to take whatever steps were necessary to protect my friends."

"Did you really think they needed protection from me?" she shot back. "Did I look like that much of a threat?"

"No, but that wasn't my call to make. It's up to the leaders of our group to decide what is and what is not a threat. My job is to report back if anything seems strange. And let's be honest, you weren't exactly acting normal in there."

"I was too!" Cora scoffed. "I was acting completely normal."

"You were acting like a rabbit in a fox hole," Faron replied dryly. "I'm not sorry for reporting you, but I am sorry about the way you were held and interrogated for so long. I didn't agree with that—especially after you mentioned your father. With that piece of the puzzle, your strange behavior made a lot more sense. Your father's on the work detail crew, isn't he?"

Cora nodded. "He got into hot water with the garrison commander in our hometown, just because he was trying to stand up for himself and our neighbors. After that, Captain Daggett never stopped looking for ways to make our lives harder and to find some leverage he could use against my father. When he couldn't find something legitimate to charge him with, he made something up. The result was that he was taken from our home and dragged all the way here to be put through a mockery of a trial where the sentencing was already a foregone conclusion. All for a crime that he never actually committed. He's innocent."

"I'm sorry. I know that happens a lot. It shouldn't, but it does." Faron frowned. "Our group tries to aid the innocent when we can, but our hands are mostly tied with Onyx's dogs watching everything going on. There are many rebels within the fortress, but the majority are loyal to the crown—or too cowed to stand up against it. We have to tread carefully."

"My father's been ill the last few months, and I worry that the treatment he'll get as part of the work crew—poor housing, limited food, too much labor with no time to rest—will only make it worse," Cora's voice cracked on the last word. She quickly swallowed down the lump that rose in her throat. "He's stubborn, he always has been but…" She sighed. "I just wish I could do something."

"I understand. I see a lot of things within those walls that aren't right or just. It takes everything I have not to speak out about them, but I'm only a guard. My job is to do what I'm told and keep my mouth shut."

"What's it like?" Cora asked. "There's so much I'm still trying to figure out. Is it all like it was back in Barcroft with Commander

Daggett—small, petty men taking out their power on everyone else? Because while that's horrible, I'm starting to think that's not the real danger. Learning more about Onyx, about the things he did when he came to power…" She didn't know how much Faron knew about the truth behind the myth of the dragon riders, so she redirected. "And now, from the things everyone was saying last night, it sounds as if he's leading the nation into war. It's more than just power plays, isn't it?"

"A lot more," Faron agreed solemnly. "Some of the people in charge —at the fortress and elsewhere in Tenegard—are like the captain from your town. They're greedy and self-important, and they cause a lot of trouble for anyone who challenges them, but their ambitions are on a small scale. I think the king deliberately picks people like that to put in positions of power because they'll be so focused on themselves that they won't realize what's really going on or what the king is actually planning. Onyx's goals are far grander…and far more damaging. He needs to be stopped. It's why I joined the antiroyalists. I'm just glad there are others who feel the same way I do. Gives me hope, at least, for change."

Cora stared. She knew Faron wasn't much older than she was, but he spoke with a degree of conviction that she hadn't seen in anyone else her age. It made her feel like she could trust him.

"Faron, can I ask you a favor? Do you think you could keep an eye on my father? I'm not sure when I'll be back this way, and it would make me feel better knowing that someone was watching out for him."

Faron smiled. "Of course. When the prisoners aren't working in the courtyards, they keep them in the south dungeon. I pass it when I make my usual rounds. I'll keep an eye on your father, and if I can help him at all, I will. I swear it."

The words were sincere. Cora could tell from his tone, but also the look on his face. "Really?"

"Sure, why wouldn't I?"

Cora shrugged. "We barely know each other, and yet you'd still be willing to look after my father? Just like that?"

Faron cocked his head. "You act as though you've asked me to do something impossible instead of something that should be part of my job anyway. The prisoners deserve better treatment than what they get. Why would I mind doing the right thing?"

Cora's heart leaped at that. She'd never met anyone like Faron before.

"Thank you, Faron. That means a lot to me."

"It's no trouble. I'll make sure your father is waiting for you—as strong and healthy as I can get him—whenever you return to Llys, however long that may take."

Cora had to swallow the lump again.

"I do have to say, though," Faron said, indicating Grainger, "on the topic of your journey away, I find it quite odd that we're selling off the Crow's horse instead of buying an additional one." He looked sideways at Cora. "I mean, you're traveling together, no? Won't you both need horses? I can't imagine that you'll be walking to your destination."

Cora chuckled. She could well understand that the situation must seem more than a bit strange from the outside looking in, but there was no way that she could tell Faron about Alaric, no matter how kind he was. For now, there were some secrets that were safer to keep.

"What?" she teased. "Do you have some sort of aversion to walking?"

Faron laughed. "No, not at all. I am quite fond of walking, actually. Especially with such pleasant company."

Cora's cheeks flushed and she quickly looked away, pretending to look into one of the storefronts. That smile of his made her heart speed up, and she wasn't sure what to do with that.

"I guess I find it a bit curious," Faron continued. If he'd noticed the effect he was having on Cora, he didn't give any sign of it. "Although, if I've learned anything from my time with the antiroyalists, it's that you never can tell what the Crow is up to. I've learned not to question her."

"Probably wise," Cora agreed with a smile.

They arrived at the market, a bustling area of town full of livestock for sale and trade. Faron led Cora and Grainger over to the stables where a squat, balding man haggled with them for a few minutes before they all settled on what Faron assured her was a fair price.

She had assumed that he was headed this way to get to the fortress or to the market for his own errands and that they would part ways after she had finished with the sale, but to her surprise, he joined her on the walk back to the rebels' headquarters. Maybe he hadn't been "headed in that direction anyway" after all—maybe he'd simply wanted to walk with her. The thought made her flush.

The walk back felt as if it took less than the walk to the market, and when it was over, Cora felt a pang of disappointment burrow in her chest.

"Well," Faron said, stuffing his hands in his pockets. "I'm not sure when we'll see each other again, but until then, I wish you well, Cora." Her name rolled off his tongue as if they were old friends, and that familiar flush crept up the back of Cora's neck.

She nodded once at him, giving him a half smile. "And I you, Faron."

He returned her smile and lifted his hand to give a little wave before sauntering away into the rebel base. Tamsin emerged half a second later, her long cloak secured around her shoulders. "Very well," she said. "Everything seems to be in order here, so if you're ready, we can get moving."

The words were like water to the thirsty.

Cora beamed, thinking of Alaric. "I'm ready."

CHAPTER 13

C ora's cheeks ached, but she still couldn't seem to stop grinning. The closer she and Tamsin got to the thicket where Alaric waited for them, the more excitement built up inside her, like a geyser just waiting to explode.

Tamsin, who walked beside her, glanced over at Cora and chuckled. "Someone's excited."

"Of course I am. It's been days since I've seen Alaric and…well, you know how it is."

Tamsin smiled, though her expression looked to be a little tight around her eyes, and nodded. "Yes, I do. If anyone can understand the bond between you and Alaric, it's me. I know you're anxious to get back to him, and he's likely just as anxious to see you again. It's never easy for a dragon and a rider to be separated." Tamsin's voice cracked slightly on the last word, and she swallowed hard. "How do you think he'll feel about training?" she asked, keeping her eyes focused on the road ahead.

A swell of sympathy bloomed in Cora's chest. She didn't even want to imagine what it would feel like to lose Alaric, so she respected Tamsin's need to quickly re-route the conversation.

She shrugged. "I'm not sure. I know he's not going to be happy about our plan to leave while my father and his mother are still being held at the fortress. It will be very difficult for him to leave before freeing her, but I think together we'll be able to convince him that this is the right course of action." This time, it was Cora who swallowed. She didn't like the idea of leaving her father behind either, but doing so was the only way for her and Alaric to truly prepare them for whatever was coming. It was the best opportunity they had to give all of them a fighting chance against King Onyx and whatever he could throw at them. She let out a slow exhale. "He and I both know that this is something we must do. Inevitably, it will come down to a fight and we need to be ready for that."

"I'm sorry to say that I agree," Tamsin said. "I wish that weren't the case, but now that Onyx knows of your existence, and that he hasn't succeeded in stamping out dragon magic for good, he'll do everything in his power to find you. He won't hesitate to destroy what he feels is a threat to him."

"And Alaric and I are a threat," Cora finished, the words bitter and metallic on her tongue.

"Yes," Tamsin said solemnly. "You are. That's why you need to be ready."

Cora dropped her shoulders and rolled them against the tension that never seemed to leave her muscles. "It's all overwhelming."

Tamsin nodded, her face softening a bit. "I know," she said, "but I'll do what I can to help you. I'll teach you all that I know. I'll train you and Alaric as best I can. If I can help prevent a tragedy like the destruction of the dragon riders from happening again…" She trailed off. The look on her face was one of absolute devastation. One that spoke of deep, personal loss. Cora's heart tugged at the sight of it.

"Thank you, Tamsin," she said. "For helping us."

Tamsin's head snapped to Cora, her eyes blazing as they found Cora's. "Don't thank me." Her tone was sharp. Not angry, but a bit intense, and Cora started a little at the sound of it. "I don't deserve thanks."

Cora didn't understand, but she somehow knew whatever had sparked that reaction wasn't about her—not entirely anyway. She decided it would be wiser not to question it. And before she could spare more thought on it, the trees began to thin out and open, indicating that the clearing where Alaric waited was close.

Cora picked up her pace, leaving Tamsin behind as she practically sprinted towards the clearing. She cleared the last of the foliage and stepped into the open space.

Alaric was there, pacing back and forth, but the second his eyes landed on Cora, she no longer felt the ground under her feet.

Alaric!

She threw her arms around the dragon as he made soft, affectionate chuffing sounds. The relief pouring out of Cora was so strong it brought tears to her eyes. She buried her face in Alaric's scales, sighing at the feel of them against her cheeks.

Oh Cora, I am so glad you have returned, Alaric said through the bond. *I must be honest. I was quite worried that I would never see you again.*

I know, Cora said, already feeling more grounded than she had in days. She pulled away and looked up into Alaric's wide, familiar eyes. *I was worried about that too, but I'm here now. And if I have anything to say about it, we won't be separated like that again.*

Alaric let out a grunt of approval. *If we* have anything to say about it.

Cora laughed. *Of course, we're a team, you and me.* She hugged the dragon again, joy filling her at finally being reunited with her friend.

And I'm guessing this is her? Alaric had noticed Tamsin standing quietly at the edge of the clearing, observing their reunion. Her hands were clasped in front of her in a casual way, but Cora could see the emotion swimming in her eyes.

"Alaric." Cora stepped back and motioned for Tamsin to come closer. "This is Tamsin, she's the dragon rider I told you about."

"Hello, Alaric," Tamsin said, holding out her hand. "It's an honor to meet you."

Alaric's head, which he'd been leaning forward to sniff Tamsin's palm, jerked upright. "I can understand you!" To any other person, it would have sounded like nothing more than a series of discordant sounds, similar to a grunt or a growl. But Cora understood him completely—her brain instantly translating the words thanks to the magic of Dragon Tongue. Tamsin also had no problem understanding Alaric, and she tossed her head back and laughed.

"Yes," she said, her face breaking into the first real smile Cora had seen from her outside of the vision she had shown Cora the previous night. It made her face look far less severe and much younger than Cora thought her to be. "I have been without my own dragon for quite some time now, but I still recall how to use Dragon Tongue. It's still instinctual for me."

Alaric cocked his head, studying Tamsin with his large eyes. He was curious about Tamsin—Cora could feel that surging through their bond—but there was also a bit of hesitation there too. "I should have expected that," he said. "But it still came as a surprise. I am not used to being able to communicate with any human other than my rider. And according to her, you are here to offer us aid?"

Tamsin nodded. "I am," and then because she must have noticed Alaric's hesitation, she said, "I know that trust does not come instantly—especially for dragons—but I want you to know that I have no intention of harming you or Cora. I only want to help prepare you both for what is coming. Onyx will stop at nothing until he destroys you. I want to help prevent that from happening." She crossed her right arm across her chest, her fist resting against her heart. "You have my word, Alaric. I only want to help."

Alaric studied Tamsin for a few more seconds before speaking to Cora through the bond. *And you're sure she's trustworthy?*

I am, Cora answered honestly. *I mean, she helped me back in Barcroft by giving me that pendant. She didn't know me at all, but still she tried to protect me from Secare. Plus, she's right. We do need training, and she is the only one with knowledge of how to do that.*

Alaric dipped his head. *I see your point, and I agree. There's just something about her, a feeling that I have…*

Cora frowned. *A feeling? What sort of feeling?*

I cannot explain it—and I do not know whether it is good or bad. But there is definitely more than we know to the story of Tamsin the dragon rider.

Cora considered this. *Do you think we should try to find help elsewhere? If you are not comfortable, then I won't—*

No, I do not feel as if the secrets put us in any danger. But let us just be cautious as we move ahead.

Cora reached out and put a hand on Alaric's side. *Of course.*

Alaric refocused on Tamsin. "So tell me, Tamsin, dragon rider, what would this training consist of?"

"Working to control your magic, mostly," Tamsin responded. "You need to be able to defend yourself against Onyx's magic. He's a very powerful sorcerer."

Alaric seemed to accept this, but there was still one part of the plan that Cora knew he wouldn't like. She steeled herself for his response. "Alaric, in order for us to complete the training Tamsin has in mind, we'll need to leave Llys."

Alaric let out a deep sound. It was a mix of a growl and some sort of surprised chortle. "Leave Llys? What of Viren? What of my mother?"

The vice around Cora's heart squeezed. She felt Alaric's panic keenly through the bond—it mirrored her own when she thought of leaving her father behind. But as strong as the panic was, the sense of purpose she felt was even stronger. "We have to leave them behind for now. We can't practice magic so close to the city walls. Someone would see us. Or worse, sense us."

Alaric's nostrils flared. "I understand that, but Cora, how can you ask me to leave my mother here, alone and unprotected? Your father is unknown to Onyx, but my mother cannot hide behind anonymity. He will destroy her if he thinks it will bring him closer to the bonded dragon from his soothsayer's vision, to *me*. I cannot allow that to happen." There was such fierce pain in Alaric's tone that Cora almost winced from it.

"But Alaric, this is exactly why we have to go. We can't protect your mother from Onyx or free her or my father until we learn how to defend ourselves. We are no good to either of them if we strike before we are truly ready. That would end with us in the king's clutches right along with them without any means of fighting back."

"She's right," Tamsin said softly. "Without training, you're no match for Onyx and his forces. And once he manages to capture you, he will not be merciful. I know what it is to leave someone you love behind, especially when they are behind enemy lines. It is a painful endeavor. I will not lie and claim that it gets easier—it doesn't. But if leaving now means finding a way to free them in the end, then isn't it worth that agony?"

Cora eyed Tamsin. Her face was earnest, as was the understanding shining in her eyes. Alaric must have seen it too, for he let out a deep exhale and lowered his head.

"I understand, though I do not like it. I will go with you, and I will train. But as soon as it is within my power to free my mother, I will return here and do so. I will not leave her to suffer and perish at the hands of the mad king."

Cora sent a surge of comfort down the bond. "We will return together, Alaric. We will free them both."

Tamsin nodded, letting out her own deep breath. "Good, now that's been settled, we should all get some rest. We leave at nightfall."

When the last rays of golden sunlight had been snuffed out by the inky blackness of the night, Alaric unfurled his wings and leaped into the air, Tamsin and Cora perched on his back, with Tamsin directing him which way to go.

It was the first time he'd left the thicket since their arrival in Llys, and the joy he felt at flying through the open space of the skies flooded through the bond, making Cora smile. Despite the misgivings they both felt about leaving their loved ones behind, there was something exciting about traveling to a new place, especially with the prospect of learning and training ahead of them. Cora's own anticipation bubbled through her entire body.

Tamsin, who sat beside her on Alaric's wide back, had a look of contentment on her face, but there was also sadness in her eyes. It was a combination that was quickly becoming familiar to Cora. It made sense—Cora imagined that while Tamsin was eager to help her and Alaric, every moment spent with them must be a reminder of what she had lost. Cora thought of Alaric, of how close they had become. The bond between them was new, but it was strong, and Cora already couldn't imagine what she would do without it. There's nothing she wouldn't do to protect Alaric.

"How far away is your home?" Cora asked after a while, breaking the comfortable silence.

"We should be there before the sun comes up," Tamsin replied, her face serene. "Though only just."

"And where exactly is that?" Cora pressed. She'd come to notice that Tamsin rarely offered more than one tidbit of information at a time, but her curiosity was strong.

Tamsin gave her a half smile. "A place you've likely heard of, the Meldona Forest."

Cora's mouth dropped open. She had indeed heard of it. She'd wager that everyone in Tenegard had. "The Meldona Forest? But…but everyone says that it is cursed, that anyone who dares travel there never returns."

Tamsin pressed her lips together as though suppressing a laugh. "Aye, that's the place."

"And you live there?" Cora continued. "Like actually *live* there?"

"I do," Tamsin said, "though it's hardly a place of nightmares as so many have come to believe."

Cora still couldn't believe that was their destination. "I've grown up hearing stories of the wild woods and of the fearsome creatures that dwell within it. They say there are beasts that feast upon the bones of travelers."

"I have lived there for some time now, and I can assure you, I have never noticed anything beyond the usual flora and fauna. My bones have never even been nibbled."

"But the stories—"

"Are just stories," Tamsin finished with a smile. "Though I do admit the forest is a bit unusual and can be quite intimidating at times, I have never felt unsafe within its depths. In fact, its reputation is what allows me to live there with any sense of security at all. The reputation of the woods keeps most travelers and curious adventure seekers at bay—which is exactly what I prefer. And it's a good thing too given what we will be doing once we get there."

"So the forest truly isn't cursed, then?"

Tamsin chuckled. "No. At least I do not believe it so. Over the years, it has become quite famous for its mysteriousness, which, as you know, has bred quite the collection of lore, but I think it's driven more by a fear of the unknown instead of actual evidence. The land is largely uncharted save for a few small villages that border the edge of the woods. The greatest danger comes from the fact that the terrain is quite rugged and not easily traveled. The trees hide steep ravines and narrow ridges that even horses and donkeys can rarely handle. It's not ravaging beasts that cause people to disappear but insufficient caution on difficult paths—but of course, that makes for a less exciting story to tell at the tavern late at night. But whether they are driven by superstition or common sense, most travelers circumvent the forest entirely rather than try to traverse it by horse or on foot. The terrain and the mystery of the forest make it a place that no one wants to be—which is also what makes it the perfect hiding spot."

Cora nodded, though she still felt slightly dumbfounded.

Alaric, who had been listening to the conversation, spoke to her through their bond. *I imagine humans think dragons are just dumb brutes who liked to eat humans for breakfast.*

Cora snorted at that, understanding his point. *Not everything is as it seems or as I've been told, I know that. I'm just surprised, is all.*

Alaric laughed, the sound making his torso rumble. Tamsin lifted an eyebrow, to which Cora waved a hand. "Alaric finds my belief in the lore of the wild woods a bit ironic."

Tamsin let out her own laugh, the sound light and melodic. It was such a rare sound coming from Tamsin that it made Cora feel a little proud to have accomplished it.

Well, technically, it was my joke that made her laugh, Alaric countered, reading her mind—to which Cora rolled her eyes.

The open air gave her mind the opportunity to wander to all the things she hoped to learn from Tamsin. A few times, she tried asking Tamsin about the olden days, but every time she did, Tamsin's face would harden and her eyes would tighten, and she wouldn't really answer the question beyond some vague tidbit. She knew Tamsin's hesitation to elaborate on the past was likely due to the grief she still felt over losing all her friends and her dragon, and she didn't want to hurt her further—but how was she supposed to learn if she couldn't ask questions? Surely the history of what came before would help her understand the extent of what she and Alaric could achieve. And yet, each question seemed to button Tamsin up even tighter. Clearly, she wasn't going to get any answers this way.

Therefore, she switched tactics. "Tamsin," she said, coming up with a new direction for her questions. "Can you tell me about the magic side of being a rider? I want to make sure I understand how it works, how Alaric and I will be able to use it."

At this, Tamsin inclined her head slightly. She seemed much more willing to expound on this topic. And that was fine with Cora.

"Well, for starters, it's important to understand that the magic itself comes from the power of the bond between the dragon and rider," Tamsin explained. "The stronger the bond, the more powerful your capabilities, because the magic must be fueled and directed by you both."

Cora thought back to her faceoff with Secare in the Therma Mountains. She had tried to summon Dragon Fire on her own, but only with Alaric's help had she achieved it. She listened closely as Tamsin talked, amazed at everything she didn't know. The scope of what was possible was much greater than she'd previously imagined.

"Back before, the rider pairs could manipulate the elements," Tamsin said, pointing to the open skies around them. "Wind, water, fire, even the land itself responded." She smiled. "All thanks to the dragon bond, of course."

"And what would the riders do with that?" Cora asked. "I imagine that would be helpful in a battle, but what about in times of peace?"

"Well, the riders weren't just knights and soldiers. We were also people who helped nurture the community." Tamsin gave a soft smile. "We considered ourselves not only protectors of the people, but also helpers. And we did what we could to make the people's lives better. We would use our abilities to assist in the building of dams, for example, or we might help the farmers ensure their harvests were bountiful."

"That's really wonderful," Cora said wistfully. "You put others before yourselves."

"Yes," Tamsin agreed, though that familiar shadow of hers crept over her face once more. "We did."

Cora continued to pepper Tamsin with questions, listening to her stories until weariness began to pull at her eyelids, making them feel as if they weighed a hundred pounds.

"You should get some rest," Tamsin said, eyeing Cora as she yawned widely. "We'll begin training almost immediately after we arrive. Time is of the essence, I'm afraid, so you had better get some rest while you still can."

She's right, Alaric agreed. *I can feel your exhaustion through the bond.*

Cora yawned again. *What about you? I know you're probably getting sleepy from flying all night long.*

Do not worry about me. I am well enough, and my stamina is not the same as that of a human. Rest, Cora, and when you wake, we learn how to challenge the king.

CHAPTER 14

Cora rubbed at her eyes, trying to wipe away the lingering remnants of sleep. She had a vague memory of them landing a few hours earlier, setting down on the ground. She had woken up for long enough to stumble off of Alaric's back and had then curled up against his side and immediately gone to sleep again, ignoring the amused chuckles from Tamsin as she gave up on convincing her to come inside the house. The house, she had decided before sleep took over, could wait until daylight when she was less likely to stumble into things.

But now, daylight had arrived. The sun was rising steadily in the sky, and it was already shaping up to be a warm day. As Cora sat up and looked around, she saw that a few feet away, Tamsin stoked the flames of an outdoor pit, where she was cooking breakfast. Alaric was curled up like a cat next to Cora, still sleeping.

Behind them sat Tamsin's house. The structure itself wasn't very large. The door stood open, letting in fresh air and allowing Cora a view of the interior. She saw that it was more or less a cabin-style home with a single room that served as both the living and sleeping quarters. It was fairly open and airy, especially with the wide windows that gave a view to the forest, and the earthy wooden paneling on the outside helped the house blend in among the tree giants that surrounded it. It wasn't a grand building, but it had a coziness to it that Cora hadn't expected, especially nestled in the heart of the wild wood. And the atmosphere of the place was calm and peaceful. So far, the Meldona Forest had proved to be quiet and unassuming —just like Tamsin had assured her it would be. If the worst this place had to offer was rough roads, then that would be just fine by Cora. It wasn't as if she planned to traverse those roads anyway as long as she had the option of flying instead.

"Here." Tamsin walked over and handed Cora a tin mug of steaming coffee. The fresh aroma wafted towards Cora's nose, and she inhaled deeply, feeling more alert just from the scent, even before her first taste. She'd never been much of a coffee drinker, but the smell reminded her of her father, and she had a feeling she'd need the extra boost of energy, so she eagerly took a sip. The warmth of it spread from her throat and through her body, warding off the last of the chilliness that had lingered from their long flight, in spite of Alaric's warmth at her side.

"Thank you," she said to Tamsin, who nodded.

"You're welcome."

Alaric lifted his head and sniffed the air.

"It's coffee," Cora said, indicating her mug. "Not for dragons, I'm afraid."

Very well, Alaric replied, *but the smell is rather divine.*

Cora snorted at that. "It is, isn't it?" She grinned at him and took another sip. "I'm surprised you're awake. Considering that you flew all night long, I expected you to be out for much longer."

"I was hungry, so I was up early to hunt. Besides, I had plenty of rest back in the thicket, days and days of it," Alaric responded dryly. Cora knew he still wasn't completely over his disgruntlement from having to sit helplessly while she was held captive by the rebels. "I'm well enough—ready to begin our training."

"Good," Tamsin, who'd walked over with a bowl for Cora, said, having heard the conversation. "We should get started soon."

Cora shoveled a spoonful of the warm oatmeal into her mouth. She swallowed and asked, "And what exactly will we be doing?" She knew the overall goal of the training was to build her skills, but she had no idea where they would begin.

"Well, first, I need to get a feel for where you and Alaric are with your magic," Tamsin said in between bites of her own breakfast. "Aside from the Dragon Fire that you were able to conjure, have you been able to tap into any of your other magical abilities?"

"No," Cora said as Alaric shook his head. "We haven't exactly tried to, though. We didn't really know what we should be trying *for*. It's not as if there's a manual to tell us what was possible for us. Besides which, we were worried about something going wrong and drawing attention to ourselves."

"That was smart, actually. It's always better to err on the side of caution if you're unsure of yourselves or of the safety of your environment. Magic can be unpredictable. Although most dragons and dragon riders do have a keen awareness of it. Have either of you felt the pull of magic since you bonded?"

It was Alaric who asked, "The pull?"

"Yes, it's similar to the bond you feel with Cora," Tamsin explained. "It's an awareness or a sense of connection that you might have felt beyond your tie to one another."

Cora started to shake her head, but then she recalled something, a moment where she and Alaric had been so in sync that something magical had happened. "Well, there was a time or two before. In the cave up in the Therma Mountains, at the tomb of the Dragon Rider. I always felt a strong presence in the cave. I assumed it had something to do with my grandmother, but now you've got me thinking maybe it was more than that."

She turned to Alaric. "You felt it too, remember? When we were trying to open the lines of communication between us more. We were looking at those scores and scores of carvings, and we both picked the same symbol on the wall."

The dragon dipped his head. "I remember."

Tamsin looked pleased at this. "Good, that's good. Then you both have the sensitivity for magic. Beyond that, it's just a matter of tapping into it and learning to both wield and control it."

Cora chewed on her bottom lip for a moment. "Yeah, but that's the problem—we don't know how."

"Which is exactly why you're here." Tamsin smiled at her. She stood up and dusted off her hands. "Are you finished?" She indicated Cora's nearly empty breakfast bowl.

Cora scooped the last mouthful into her mouth before relinquishing the bowl. Tamsin took it and walked back towards the house. "I think I know what I want you to do first." She called over her shoulder as she walked over to the side of the house where a shovel leaned against the wall. She grabbed it and headed over to the garden where she scooped up a big pile of dirt, balancing it to stay in place on the mouth of the shovel. She walked it back over to where Alaric and Cora sat watching her with confused expressions on their faces.

"There," Tamsin said, pouring the dirt into a mound in front of them and tossing the empty shovel to the side. She pointed to the mound. "This is your first test."

"It's a pile of dirt," Cora pointed out, not entirely sure how this was part of the training regime. Through their bond, she could also feel Alaric's confusion mirroring her own.

"Yes, it is," Tamsin replied matter-of-factly, "and for your task, I want you and Alaric to use your magic to separate this pile of dirt into two separate piles."

"Okay, but how do we do that?"

"Remember what I told you while we were flying, about how dragon riders could control the elements? You're perfectly capable of connecting with this dirt—and then controlling it enough to separate it into two piles."

"Yes, but…how?" Cora pressed.

Tamsin shook her head. "I'm not going to give you any further instructions. Not right now. Let's just see what you can work out on your own."

That didn't sound entirely fair. "I thought you brought us out here to teach us," Cora argued.

Tamsin looked amused. "I did. And right now, I'm teaching you to listen to your instincts and get in touch with what feels right to you. Better get started." And with that, she walked away.

Cora looked to Alaric. "Ready to try this?"

As ready as I think I can be.

Cora switched from speaking out loud to speaking through the bond. *So, where do you think we should start?*

Alaric cocked his head. *I do not know. I imagine magic is intrinsic, something that is natural and organic. As Tamsin said, it is something that we should be able to tap into without overthinking or trying to force it. Like when we conjured the Dragon Fire. So we need to approach this attempt not as if we are doing something that is impossible but as something that is plausible, achievable. The earth can shift and settle on its own—the potential is there. All we need is to tap into it.*

Cora nodded. That made sense. The magic wasn't something they could create—it already existed, and they just needed to find a way to draw upon it.

I think we should try visualization like what we did in the cave. It helped us with learning how to improve our communication, so maybe it will help us with this.

It is worth a shot.

Cora closed her eyes and did her best to focus her mind's eye on the pile of dirt. She imagined it splitting into two separate piles upon her and Alaric's command. When she felt like she had a strong visual, she opened her eyes. *Are you ready?* she asked Alaric.

The dragon's eyes found hers, and he nodded. *I am ready.*

Good. On the count of three. One…two…three.

Both Cora and Alaric zeroed in on the pile of dirt, giving it their full attention and concentration…but absolutely nothing happened. After several seconds, Cora blinked and pulled back her gaze. "Hmmm… well, that obviously didn't work."

No, it did not. Shall we give it another try?

Yes. On three again? One…two…three…

Still, the pile of dirt remained the same. They tried again several more times, but they were not able to successfully move or manipulate the pile of dirt in any way.

Frustration sparked to life in Cora's gut, but she tried to ignore it. Conjuring Dragon Fire hadn't exactly been easy either, nor had they accomplished it on the first try. The important thing to remember was that in the moment of their greatest need, they *had* achieved it. Tapping into elemental forces *was* possible for them. But still, this felt much more challenging than that, and Cora couldn't understand why.

Finally, after an hour or more of trying, Cora looked over to Tamsin, who had come back to join them at some point and was now sitting near the fire pit, sipping coffee and watching them with casual eyes.

"This is impossible," Cora said to her, exasperation leaking through her tone.

"No," Tamsin replied. "Not impossible."

"It feels that way," Cora argued. "And it just doesn't make sense. How is it possible that Alaric and I were able to call forth the immense power of Dragon Fire before, but now we can't even get a single speck of dirt to move from the pile?"

"It does seem as though we are missing something," Alaric added, plopping down next to Cora. "I assumed that using magic would be more instinctive and natural, but it feels rather like slogging through a swamp, doesn't it? And worst of all—getting nowhere, despite all our efforts."

Tamsin gave a soft half smile. "It feels that way right now, but it won't always be so. There are just a few things you need to under-stand to unlock that part of your mind and your magic. You're not entirely wrong, Alaric. The bond that exists between a dragon and a rider is more powerful than you realize. It's absolute power, completely pure. So, the Dragon Fire—untamed and indiscriminate—

is actually the easiest element for a dragon rider pair to conjure together. You can call upon it practically on instinct. But the smaller tasks, the ones that require focus and control? Those are the ones that can be the most challenging to achieve. It's as if the power in your grasp is a mighty river. Unleashing it all is easier than releasing just a trickle and making it go precisely where you wish. It's that control that I want you to learn. Once you have mastered directing a trickle, directing the whole river becomes possible. That is the power of dragon magic."

A thought struck Cora. "What about Onyx? He's not a dragon rider, so where does his power come from?"

Tamsin's face darkened. "Magic does not only come from dragons. It is a power and a force in the world just as much as sunlight or air. The trick is to figure out how to use it. Dragons are naturally closer to nature, which is why they are more in tune with its resonance. Bonding with a dragon lets you share that attunement and connect with the elements. Then there are soothsayers who have visions of the future brought to them by magic. They have no choice in the matter—they are born with a sensitivity to the magic that is so strong that it resonates with them whether they wish it to or not."

"I've never met a soothsayer," Cora said. "But Nana Livi told me of one who lived in our village before I was born. They say she went mad."

Tamsin nodded sadly. "That is often their fate, if they do not learn how to control their powers. With training, they learn to direct their visions by casting bones, reading entrails, observing tea leaves. With this, they can focus their powers so that the visions don't take over their lives, leaving them unsure of the line between the future and the present. These days, most are sent to the capital as soon as they show signs of visions. It is the only place where they can be trained—but the training comes from Onyx, who uses them for his own ends." The disgust in her tone was palpable.

"So Onyx's magic is like a soothsayer's?" Cora asked, trying to puzzle it all together.

"No, not at all," Tamsin replied. "He covets and collects them because he is not capable of reading the future himself. His power takes a different direction, as is the Athelian way. Years ago, the Athelians decided that they disliked having so many barriers to magic, given the way it required either a bond with a dragon or a sensitivity that came only through nature and could not be forced. Their scholars got to work on finding and creating instruments that allowed anyone who wished to tap into magic. They can manipulate magic and control it for their own purposes—to an extent. But the kind of magic that can be performed this way has limits."

"What sort of limits?" Alaric asked.

"Because they do not have the strength of dragons, the power of the elements is too mighty for them to control," Tamsin explained. "And because they do not have the natural sensitivity of soothsayers, visions of the future are closed to them. But they have extraordinary abilities when it comes to the manipulation of the human body. They can heal injuries or diseases that would otherwise be fatal or disfiguring. If someone has lost themselves to grief or fear after a traumatic event, Athelian magic can heal the damage to their mind or spirit. But there is a dark side to it, as well. Do you see what that would be?"

"If they can change the way someone feels or thinks, then they can redirect their mind in other ways," Cora said, stomach sinking as the implications sank in. "Manipulation, control—to the mind and the body. Like the shadow generals you mentioned, who have forgotten how to feel not just pain but everything else, as well."

Tamsin nodded approvingly. "Exactly. Onyx honed those abilities and used them to his advantage, especially during his stint as a sorcerer general back in Athelia."

Cora was surprised by this. "And did the people know what he was doing?"

"They did, but by that point, it was too late. Onyx took the worst of what his magic could do and ran with it." She proceeded to tell Cora and Alaric more about all of Onyx's shadow soldiers, naming them each one by one and describing them so that Cora would be able to recognize them if they ever crossed her path. Although after hearing their descriptions, Cora hoped that they never would.

"I don't want you to underestimate the terrible danger of Athelian magic," Tamsin said. "But the two of you have a magic that holds just as much extraordinary potential. All you have to do is figure out how to handle it. Achieving balance and control in your magic is going to be a process that you and Alaric will need to go through. It won't come easily, and it won't happen all at once, but with time, you'll get it."

Cora sighed. She had known that their training likely wouldn't be a quick process, but she had at least hoped for some initial progress given what she and Alaric had already accomplished together. Unfortunately, that wasn't looking to be the case. Alaric let out his own deep huff.

Don't worry, she said to him through the bond. *We'll get it. We just have to keep trying.*

I know. I was just hoping for more rapid progress. I keep thinking of my mother and what Onyx's men are doing to her. I hate to leave her there a moment longer than is necessary. I fear even a moment too long will spell the difference between saving her and losing her forever.

Cora frowned. *You can't think like that. Your mother is strong, and Onyx's men won't kill her, not if he thinks he can use her to get to you and me. And the sooner we master this, the sooner we can return to Llys and free her and my father. We can do this.*

Alaric's head dipped. *I believe that, Cora. I do.*

Good. Then I say we try again.

Together, they faced the pile of dirt. Tamsin watched from her place by the fire pit, an amused smile on her face.

Cora took a breath, reaching out to place her hand on Alaric's side. *Are you ready?*

I am ready.

On the count of three, then. One…two…three…

Not a single speck of dirt moved from the pile.

Again?

Alaric shook his head. *Again.*

CHAPTER 15

Cora gripped the wooden sword in her hand, making sure her feet were planted and her weight evenly distributed. The practice weapon wasn't exactly heavy, but after hours of training, her back and arm muscles burned from exertion, and beads of sweat rolled down her temples.

I can do this, she told herself, eyeing Tamsin across the small clearing they'd been using as a practice area for sparring. Tamsin's lips were quirked in a smirk, clearly amused by Cora's attempts to hold strong. "Of course you are," Cora grumbled under her breath. They had been practicing swordplay for nearly two hours and she had yet to disarm her opponent.

Do not be so hard on yourself, Alaric murmured through the bond. He was lounging underneath the shade of several large trees, watching the training session. *You have not been at this as long as Tamsin.*

Cora huffed. She knew the dragon was just trying to encourage her, to offer her support with his words, but his attempts did little to quell the frustration and pent-up annoyance that swirled like a cyclone in her chest.

It had been nearly two weeks since Cora and Alaric had arrived at Tamsin's home in the Meldona Forest, and every single day from sunup to sundown, they trained. In magic, combat, flight—every single skill that Tamsin deemed necessary. Hand-to-hand combat was one of Cora's least favorite lessons, but her body was covered in bruises showcasing her dedication—or her lack of skill. She knew it was important that she be able to defend herself and Alaric, so she took it quite seriously—which is why she was gripping the wooden sword so tightly that tiny slivers of wood bit into the palms of her hands.

"You hesitated in that last attack," Tamsin called out. "When you should have stepped forward and thrust your sword upward at me, you held back. Just for a split second, but it cost you."

Cora chewed the inside of her bottom lip. Tamsin was right, of course. She *had* hesitated, and then, after she'd realized her error, she had darted forward with too much force, overcompensating and leaving herself open for a blow that had knocked her off course, sending her sword into thin air rather than into her opponent. She'd very nearly run the end of her blade into one of the tall trees that surrounded the training area.

"You mustn't ever hesitate," Tamsin went on to say. "That single pause is enough time for your opponent to run you through with a blade. It only takes that one moment for you to lose the fight, and likely your life. You must always think ahead, be ready, and plan the moves before you make them. Before your opponent does. You must anticipate everything, choosing a course of action and sticking to it without taking the time in the heat of the action to stop and consider. If you don't figure out your plan of attack, and you miss your moment, you *will* die."

"Right," Cora said, nodding to show that she understood Tamsin's correction. "That's what—I mean, I've been trying to do that. I don't know what happened that time."

"Well, you hesitated," Tamsin replied dryly, and Cora fought the urge to roll her eyes.

"Yeah, I did."

"Don't do that again," Tamsin said, her words so nonchalant that she could have been remarking on the weather.

This time Cora did roll her eyes. She swung the sword out, taking a practice swing, and then readjusted her stance. The defensive position of her body was just as important as the blade in her hand, and she checked to make sure she could easily shift in any direction. "Okay," she said, breathing deeply to focus her mind. "Let's go again."

Tamsin lifted her own wooden sword and settled into her fighting stance. Cora eyed the way she shifted her weight, trying to anticipate which way she might strike. Her eyes were focused on Cora, but there was the tiniest flick of movement—the briefest glance to the left that caught Cora's eye.

She's going left, Cora concluded, though her mind quickly amended the thought. *No! She's going to pretend like she's going left when she's planning to attack me from the right.*

She didn't wait for Tamsin to make the first move.

Cora darted forward, thrusting forward and swinging her body so that she came at Tamsin from the right.

Tamsin was ready for her, lunging forward in a move that was graceful and strong. She easily blocked Cora's blow and thrust her sword out to land her own strike.

Cora spun out of the way, only narrowly missing the blow. She parried quickly, her sword whistling as it sliced through the air. Tamsin blocked again, using her sword to shove against Cora's, knocking her off balance. Cora stumbled a step or two, but swiftly regained her footing.

Her body hummed with adrenaline and anticipation as they danced around each other, striking and blocking, their wooden swords connecting each time with a loud *thwack!* that echoed off the trees. Back and forth, they came at each other, until finally, Cora saw an opening. Dodging underneath Tamsin's arm, she whirled around and swiped her sword against Tamsin's shins. The older woman yelped, automatically disengaging for a moment.

It was all Cora needed. She lunged forward, knocked Tamsin's sword out of her hands, and pointed her blade at the center of Tamsin's chest.

Both stood still, chests heaving, for several seconds before Tamsin's face lit up with a smile. "Well done, Cora," she breathed out.

Whooping, Cora dropped her sword and did a little dance. "Did you see that?" She skipped over to Alaric. "I finally beat her!"

"Did you?" Alaric asked. "I must have missed it. I was partaking in a much-needed nap." He opened his mouth, feigning a yawn.

"Alaric!" Cora groaned.

The dragon let out a low rumble of a laugh. "I am only teasing you, Cora. Of course, I saw. You were brilliant."

Cora beamed at the praise. "Thank you."

"You did well," Tamsin called over her shoulder, "but it was one victory. Do not let it go to your head." She bent over to pick up her wooden sword. "Especially since we were only using these. Fighting with real blades is another matter entirely."

Cora blanched slightly at this. She wanted to revel in her victory, but Tamsin made a very good point. Fighting with wooden swords was only part of the process. The real test would be when she held an actual blade in her hand—and when she stood against a foe who actually meant her harm. She shouldn't be celebrating yet. Not when there was still so much to learn.

Fighting against a deadly opponent…that was a problem she would face when the moment called for it. For now, it was easier to focus on the mechanics. What *would* it be like to fight with a real sword rather than a wooden one? "The blade will be heavier," Cora concluded, drawing upon her knowledge of working in a blacksmith forge her whole life. "And the balance will be different."

Tamsin nodded. "Yes. And it's not just the balance of the blade, but also your own body. Here." She held up a hand. "I have something for you. Wait here."

Cora waited as Tamsin disappeared inside her house, returning several minutes later with a long parcel in her hand. It was wrapped in burlap.

"Here." She handed the bundle to Cora. "I've been waiting to give you this when the time was right."

Cora carefully unwrapped the outer covering to reveal a sword sheathed in a leather scabbard. Cora's eyes went wide as she took in the familiar-looking crystals laid into the hilt of the sword. She carefully pulled the sword from its sheath. It was perfectly balanced and exceptionally sharp. There wasn't a single blemish on the steel, and a slim vine of tiny leaves had been engraved down the center of the blade. It was feminine *and* powerful, and despite her time spent in her father's forge and Bram's, she wasn't sure she had ever seen a lovelier sword.

"I want you to have that," Tamsin said as Cora continued to assess the weapon.

"What?" Cora looked up, startled. "I can't take this."

"You can," Tamsin said more firmly.

"But this weapon is too nice, and it was clearly meant for someone far more important than me. It must—" Cora stopped, realization slamming into her. "Tamsin, was this…*your* sword? From your days as a rider?"

Tamsin blinked. "It was."

"Then I definitely cannot take it."

"I'm giving it to you."

"I know, but I don't think I can accept it. This sword was meant—"

"For a dragon rider," Tamsin interrupted, her gaze hard. "Are you or are you not a dragon rider, Cora Hart?"

"I am," Cora hurried to answer, "but—"

"But nothing. You're a dragon rider, and you need a sword befitting the role you must now fill. I want you to have it." Tamsin paused, letting her words sink in. "Besides, as I am no longer a dragon rider, I have little use for it."

Cora opened her mouth to object, but the resolute look on Tamsin's face stopped her. She also couldn't help but think about the sword she'd taken from the tomb of the last dragon rider in the mountains. She had brought it with her on their journey, but it was much larger and heavier than this blade. It would be far more difficult for Cora to wield. So if for nothing other than practicality's sake, she decided to accept the gift.

"Thank you, Tamsin."

The older woman gave a curt nod and then pointed to the crystals in the hilt. "See these? They have protective qualities. They are the same as the ones in the tomb—and in the amulet I gave you." Tamsin's brows pushed closer together. "The one that you lost."

Cora's cheeks burned. "It was an accident. I had it in my pocket, but then the pocket tore, and it fell out without me noticing. I didn't realize at the time how special it was. That was how Secare figured out who I was. Without the amulet, he smelled the magic on me."

Tamsin stared for a moment before running a hand down her face. "You must be more careful, Cora. If things had turned out differently—"

"I know," Cora said, eager to change the subject. "Trust me, I know."

Tamsin narrowed her eyes as though the urge to keep lecturing Cora was still there, but she redirected her focus to the crystals. "Like I was saying, the crystals have protective qualities. As long as you have this sword on your person, it should keep the shadow soldiers from sensing your magic. You got lucky with Onyx in the fortress, but you can't count on there being other sources of dragon magic around to throw others off your scent. Your anonymity is something that we must protect, Cora. As it stands, Onyx doesn't know who you are. He only knows that you exist. We need to keep it that way."

"Right," Cora agreed, "I understand."

"Good. Let's break for lunch. We'll start training with real blades after we eat, so you can get used to using it in combat." She stalked towards the house without another word.

Cora let out a breath, watching her retreating back, before walking over to where Alaric rested, his large eyes following as she went.

It's lovely, Alaric complimented after Cora showed him the intricate details on the blade.

"It is. I feel bad about taking it."

"You shouldn't. Tamsin is right. You're a dragon rider and this is a dragon rider's blade. You need it—not just for the blade itself, but for the crystals in the hilt. Even if you went to another blacksmith to commission a sword, or made one yourself, it would not have the protective crystals that you need."

"I know. But it was hers first, and I just think her whole story—what we know of it anyway—is sad."

"I cannot fathom her pain," Alaric said, dipping his nose. "If it is anything close to the worry and agony I felt when you were taken hostage in Llys and I could do nothing to stop it, then I would not wish it upon any other."

Cora sighed. "I wish there was some way we could help her."

"Maybe you are," Alaric replied thoughtfully. "Maybe training you and me is the path of healing for her, a way to reclaim some of what she has lost."

This gave Cora a bit of hope. "Yeah, maybe." She gave the dragon a smile and then, gripping the new sword, followed the path Tamsin had taken towards the house. Her stomach was rumbling, and they still had several hours of daylight ahead.

Tamsin had prepared a meal of root vegetables and slices of thick cheese, which they ate outside under the shade of the trees while Alaric went hunting for his own meal.

"Can I ask you something?" Cora said about halfway through the meal.

Tamsin looked up from her plate and lifted a brow, as if to say, "go on."

Cora leaned forward. "Where did you learn all of this stuff? I mean, I know you were a rider, but what was this whole process like for you? Did you have a mentor?"

Tamsin took a bite of her food and swallowed before answering. "Yes and no. I didn't have a single dedicated instructor just working with me, but I did have several teachers, if you will—along with other trainees that I learned both with and from. There was a school for new riders. I trained there."

"There was a whole school dedicated for dragon riders?" The idea made Cora smile.

"There was. It feels like a million years ago now, but yes. Times were…" Tamsin's eyes darkened slightly. "Well, they were a lot different then."

"Do you mean before the malhos came?" Cora pushed the last of her vegetables back and forth across her plate. Her stomach turned over at the word. "They destroyed everything when they arrived, right? That's why the genante culture is nearly gone."

Tamsin cocked her head. "You're mistaken, Cora." She frowned. "It was Onyx who came to Tenegard and destroyed our entire way of life. Not anyone else."

Cora pressed her lips together. That certainly wasn't how she saw it.

Tamsin studied her face. "You disagree?"

"I don't know. I mean, I understand that Onyx is the root of the problem. But that doesn't mean that he's the only one making life more difficult for the genante. You don't know what it was like in Barcroft —the way the malhos treated the rest of us, looking down on us like it was a given that they were better than us. Most of the malhos I know are greedy and selfish individuals who only think of themselves."

She knew there were exceptions—Bram, Faron, the other malhos among the rebels. But a handful of outliers didn't change the facts. There were far more than she'd encountered in Barcroft and in Llys who had held true to all her worst opinions. And there was no denying that genante culture had been suppressed to a stifling extent. That never would have happened if another culture hadn't come in and taken over. "Onyx may be the one who initiated everything, but he brought the malhos here and they're just as bad as he is."

Tamsin took another bite of her food, chewing slowly. Cora was beginning to understand that the older woman never spoke without carefully considering her response. "I see," she finally said. "But may I ask you a question?"

Cora nodded.

"Are there no greedy or cruel people among the genante?"

Cora could already see where this was going, but she couldn't bring herself to be dishonest. Besides, Tamsin already knew the answer. "Oh…um…well, no, there are many," Cora admitted.

"Does that make the entire genante people bad?" Tamsin posed the question, leaning forward. This time, Cora chose not to answer. Tamsin just nodded, as if the silence was answer enough. "I know it's difficult to think beyond our own perspectives, but it's been a long time since Onyx rose to power," Tamsin continued. "The culture that existed back then likely would have shifted and changed in the years since, whether the malhos were here or not. Culture isn't a fixed point —it grows and develops in response to what's happening to society. What's happening right now is that more and more people are opposing Onyx—and those rebels are not exclusively among the genante. You saw that for yourself back in Llys, for example. Half of the rebels you met were malhos."

Cora's mind flitted to one of the rebels in particular, her mind conjuring a near-perfect image of Faron. Heat rushed to her cheeks, and she immediately shook her head, clearing the image from her thoughts.

Alaric, who was still lounging a few feet away but clearly keeping tabs on the conversation, snorted.

Mind your own business, Cora snapped at him through the bond.

He responded with another snort, though he did send a burst of soothing warmth back towards her.

"I see your point," Cora said, refocusing on Tamsin. "But I have to admit I'm a little surprised that you would be the one making it. You have a better reason to hold a grudge than anyone. I mean, it was the malhos who killed all your friends and your dragon, right?"

Tamsin's face paled slightly, and Cora instantly regretted her words. She scrambled for something else to say that would shift the conversation in a less painful direction. "It's just…everything bad that's ever happened to me has happened because of the malhos," Cora tried to explain. "I know it's not fair to blame every single person who fits into that category, but it's all I've known." She quickly began to tell Tamsin her own stories about her experiences in the past with the garrison in Barcroft and the malhos soldiers there. She told her of the cruelty she and her father experienced at the hands of Daggett. "He was in charge of our whole township, but he didn't care about us at all. He did nothing for the townspeople. And the unwarranted grudge he formed against my father is the reason he's locked up as a prisoner in Llys."

"I can understand your point of view," Tamsin replied when she was done. "And I honestly can't blame you for feeling the way you do, but I think it's important that you realize just how much Tenegardian society has changed since the initial invasion. Our culture is not purely genante any longer, but it is not solely malhos either. There's some value in building a new culture together, I think. There's so much we can learn from those who are different from ourselves. Don't you agree?"

Cora sighed. "Yes, I suppose so. It's just really hard to stop feeling the way I've felt my whole life, to learn a new way of seeing them."

"Difficult, yes. But not impossible."

"No, not impossible."

"Besides, I don't think the Athelian people who came here quite knew what they were getting into with Onyx. There was a civil war raging in their land, and all they wanted was to raise their families somewhere peaceful. They didn't ask too many questions—they were too grateful that Onyx had given them somewhere to go. Besides, with the military successes that he had under his belt by then, he seemed like an exciting new leader to many of the people in Athelia."

"So they didn't know what he would turn out to be then?"

"Of course not—how could they? Only soothsayers know the future, and many of their predictions are vague or confusing and only become clear in hindsight. For those of us trying to make decisions at the time, all we had was the evidence of his past to judge what shape his future would take. The reports that we gathered on him here in Tenegard showed that he was liked and admired by the Athelian people. They believed that he would be their protector, a savior of sorts. He held on to that reputation when he came here, even after he overthrew the ruling family and made himself king. As far as most of the population is concerned, he brought the people of Tenegard out of famine."

"A famine that he created for his own manipulative purposes," Cora pointed out, her frustration rising.

"Yes, but like I said, few know the truth."

Cora sighed. She had more questions, but she felt as if she needed time to process everything they had discussed before she could ask them. And frankly, she wasn't comfortable with how the discussion had gone. She knew Tamsin had some fair points, but it felt a little bit like she was scolding Cora, and that wasn't a feeling she relished.

Tamsin set down her bowl. "Look, all I'm saying is to keep an open mind. Not everyone is what they seem. Okay?"

Cora nodded. "Okay." The word came out short and with a bit of a snap.

Tamsin stood up and dusted off her pants. "I'll say this one last thing and then I think it best that we cut the talking and get back to the training."

Cora braced herself for whatever was coming next.

"If you're to be successful in your training, you're going to have to learn to curb your anger."

A flush of heat lanced through Cora, but she pressed her lips together and nodded. She wanted so badly to retort, to point out that her anger was justified, but she knew that would only prove Tamsin's point. So, she switched gears.

"I understand. I'll keep myself in check, I promise."

"Good."

"Do you think we'll be ready to return to the fortress soon?" Thoughts of her father and Raksha had been weighing heavily on her mind. She knew they weighed on Alaric too.

"We'll return to the fortress when you're ready, Cora. Not until then. You and Alaric aren't fully capable of defending yourselves yet. There is still a lot to learn." She reached down and picked up the empty dishes. "I'm going to take these inside and then we can begin again, yes?"

Cora dipped her chin, watching as Tamsin disappeared inside her house. It was only then that she let out the deep breath she'd been holding in. Dragging her feet, she shuffled over to Alaric.

"I know you might not want to hear this at the moment," Alaric said, straightening as Cora plopped down beside him, "but I don't believe she was trying to reprimand you. Her intent was more to educate you on a new way of thinking."

"I know," Cora grumbled. "I know she's right, but it's never easy when someone points out your own backward way of thinking. Especially when all I've heard my entire life is how different life is compared to what it used to be, and that the malhos were to blame."

"That is understandable," Alaric replied. "But perhaps it is not too late to change your mind."

Cora mulled this over. It was possible, she supposed, to think about the malhos in a more nuanced way. Most of the blame for Tenegard's troubles could be laid at Onyx's door. In a way, the malhos people had been manipulated just like the genante. And when she thought about it like that, it was hard to view them so negatively. Sure, there were bad apples among the bunch. But that didn't mean the entire bushel was rotten.

"I guess not," she answered Alaric as Tamsin re-emerged from her house and began to walk towards them. "People are not always what they seem, right?"

She didn't wait for a response from the dragon. Instead, Cora rose to her feet and hurried to meet Tamsin in the middle of the training ground. "You're right," she said. "I need to be open-minded, and I need to do better about letting my emotions control me. I'm sorry about my frustration."

Tamsin waved a hand. "There's no need to apologize. I understand how you feel. I had to learn the same lessons, you see."

"But now you're old and wise?" Cora quipped.

This made Tamsin snort. "Something like that. Now, come on, let's get back to training."

CHAPTER 16

OCTAVIA

Octavia paced the floor in her bedroom. It was after lunchtime, and she was supposed to be taking a nap—at least that's what she told her ladies' maids that she was doing—but she couldn't seem to turn her mind off enough to get any rest. It had been like that for two weeks now. Ever since she had discovered the dragon in the courtyard, it was all she'd been able to think about.

She knew it was foolish to think about the creature so much. If she had told any of her tutors, they would have reminded her that nothing good ever came from such curiosity. But she couldn't help herself. Whether she was asleep or awake, her thoughts always seemed to stray to the dragon. And the sad look she had seen in the creature's eyes haunted her. "It's just a dragon," she muttered out loud, throwing her hands in the air. "It's just an animal. A wild and dangerous creature that would likely rip my head off if it had the opportunity. I need to stop wasting my time!" But even as she said the words, she knew deep down in her core that they were hollow. And that was what kept her pacing, wringing her hands as she tried to sort through all her jumbled thoughts.

No, it didn't matter how many times she tried to convince herself otherwise—there was something special about that dragon, something that nagged at Octavia like an itch that she couldn't scratch no matter how hard she tried.

She had been told her whole life that dragons were brainless brutes with vicious tendencies. But after seeing that dragon in the courtyard that first time, she could no longer believe that. The dragon had made no attempt to harm Octavia. It had not lunged at her or bared its teeth. In fact, it had behaved as the exact opposite of a savage beast. And there was a sadness in its eyes that spoke of real feeling and understanding that would be beyond the capacity of a mere mindless beast. Octavia could not reconcile what she had seen with her own eyes with all that she had been told. It didn't make sense.

Letting out a long sigh, she plopped down on her bed and flipped her long hair over her shoulder, wracking her brain for anything that might be helpful. She recalled the stories her nurse used to read to her —stories where dragons were magical creatures that could talk to people and perform amazing feats. They had only ever seemed like fairy tales. Until now.

"But what if there's some truth to them?" she whispered to her empty room. She wished she still had the book, but it and the nurse who had read it to her had been gone from her life for years now. But it occurred to her that there was one other resource…

Leaping off the bed, she crossed the length of the floor and reached for the wicker basket that sat beside the vanity. In it were her journals, the dozens and dozens of notebooks that she'd kept since she was a child. She'd always used scribbling in her notebook as a way to process the world around her. Whether it was her deepest thoughts, an interesting tidbit from a library book, or a lovely piece of dialogue stolen from an overheard conversation, she was always writing something. She knew the servants at the palace had probably thought her mad to reserve part of her trunk space in her luggage to bring the whole collection of notebooks with her to the fortress, but she had insisted. Her journals were like her friends, always there to listen to her innermost thoughts. Even the ones from years ago were precious to her, and she often referred back to things that she had written. She couldn't bear to be parted from them. And as she shuffled through them, Octavia was grateful for that. Because if she was remembering correctly, she might already have some information on dragons.

She finally found the journal she was looking for. The cover was worn and the edges creased, but on the inside printed in her own neat script was Octavia's name and the date range the journal covered. This particular one had been the one she kept when she was thirteen. Flipping it open, Octavia thumbed through the pages, eagerly scanning them. It was towards the back of the journal that she found the pages she was looking for, the ones detailing the time she had first come across her treasure trove—the artifacts that she had discovered in the bowels of the palace. At the time, she had thought they were the product of a fanciful imagination, of someone wondering—as she had, after hearing the stories from her nurse—what it would be like if humans and dragons could actually work together and form a bond. But now, she started to wonder. Could there be a deeper meaning? Had the artisan who'd created the pieces seen the potential for dragons to be *more,* the same way she did? Maybe the sigils and symbols she had seen on the items had some greater significance than she had realized.

The items themselves were still hidden away in her chambers in the palace…but the symbols had been painstakingly replicated in her notebooks, where she had spent many hours trying to determine their meaning.

There were several pages of notes regarding her thoughts on the artifacts and the symbols, and so Octavia returned to her bed to read and refresh her memory. After a minute or two, though, an idea struck her. She was desperate to see the dragon in the courtyard again, and she could use a bit of fresh air anyway. So tucking the journal into the deep pocket of her skirt, Octavia hurried over to the door, unlatched it, and poked her head out into the hallway.

It was empty, which was a relief to Octavia.

Walking with purpose, she kept her head focused forward and hurried towards the corridor that would lead her to the back courtyard. She did pass a soldier or two on her way, but just as with the first time she had visited the dragon, she kept her head up as if she expected to be allowed through with no questions...and it worked. No one stopped her.

Octavia took a breath and stepped into the muted light of the courtyard. Specks of brilliant sunlight glinted off the netting that had been rigged up to keep the dragon from being able to fly away, and Octavia frowned at it as she stepped deeper into the courtyard. She herself had been stuck inside the fortress ever since King Onyx had left to attend to business and as far as she was concerned, no creature, human or scaled alike, deserved to be kept in a cage.

It wasn't hard to spot the dragon. Its blue scales also glinted in the light, like hundreds of gemstones that sparkled and gleamed. Octavia's heart leaped in her throat as she took in the dragon's form. It was curled into a ball near the center of the courtyard, its wings tucked in tight. At first glance, Octavia thought the creature might be sleeping, but then she found a pair of large eyes watching her as she moved closer.

Taking a deep breath, Octavia moved towards the benches off to one side of the courtyard. They were close enough to where the dragon was laying that Octavia would be able to get a closer look at the creature, but not close enough to where either of them might feel threatened, hopefully. In truth, Octavia was more worried about the idea that the dragon might feel threatened than the thought that she, herself, was at risk. It was strange, but she couldn't bring herself to think that the dragon presented any danger to her.

"Hello," she called out softly. "I'm just going to come and sit down near you," she said, hoping her gentle tone would ease any worry the dragon might have at her approach. "I don't want to hurt you or anything, I just thought you might like the company."

The dragon did not move or acknowledge her in any way—not that she expected it to. "Silly girl," she muttered to herself. "Talking to a dragon." And yet, people talked to animals all the time, didn't they? Dogs, cats, horses… Maybe it was normal to want to feel like you could build a connection with another living thing, whether it could understand your speech or not. Dragons weren't tame, weren't domesticated like dogs or horses, but they were still living things. They still counted. She took another step, adding, "Like I said, I just want to sit near you. I won't hurt you, okay? I felt like I needed company, and I thought you might appreciate some too."

She knew the dragon couldn't understand her, but she hoped the dragon might be able to find some comfort in the softness of her voice, or at least see her careful approach as proof that she didn't mean the dragon any harm. She had seen one of the stable hands back at the palace earn an injured horse's trust that way. The poor creature had broken its leg and wouldn't let anyone near it to render it care. But the stable hand had seemed to understand what the mare needed, taking it slowly and speaking to her very gently, explaining every move he made before he made it. It had taken a while, all while Octavia had watched, absolutely fascinated by the process, but eventually the stable hand was able to get close enough to the horse to care for her. The dragon didn't need anything from Octavia, as far as she could see, but surely it must be lonely, even for a dragon, to be cooped up like this. Octavia didn't know if the dragon minded her company or not, but she hoped it didn't.

Scooping up her skirt so she could sit down without wrinkling the expensive, impractical material, Octavia settled herself on the bench. The dragon continued to lay to her right, unmoving, though its large eyes still seemed entirely focused on her.

"My name is Octavia. I'm…well, it doesn't really matter who I am. I'm just going to sit here and read a book, if that's all right with you." She reached into her pocket and pulled out her journal. "It's more of a journal, really. There are things in it that made me think of you, which is part of the reason why I decided to come out here for a visit."

She opened the journal to the correct page and began to read through all of her notes. There wasn't much to go on. Most of it was just the musings of a thirteen-year-old, but Octavia still read each detail carefully, hoping she might have copied down something that would help her understand why this dragon was so different from what she'd always believed dragons to be.

She looked over to the dragon, who still watched her. Those eyes, so full of awareness, could hardly be described as anything but intelligent. Octavia let out a breath. She had seen creatures in books who were depicted as truly wild, creatures who reacted on pure instinct and nothing else. In the illustrations, she could always see that wildness in their eyes, so chaotic and unfocused. But these eyes, these eyes bespoke of so much more than just pure predatory instinct. No, there was something quite profound in those eyes, Octavia thought to herself.

"You know, I think you are far more than what I have always been told. I don't know you well at all, but I like to think we could have been friends. Perhaps in another life, in another world where you and I were both free of our cages. Perhaps we could fly and see the world together." She let out a little laugh, amazed at how much the silly notion lifted her spirits. But her smile faded almost as instantly.

"Sorry," she said, "I shouldn't say such things. It's not fair, given the situation you're in. We may both be in cages, but that doesn't mean our circumstances are the same. After all," she admitted, "even if they opened the bars for me and told me that I was free…where would I go? I don't have any home, any family, other than what the king has given me. Do you have a family?" she wondered. "Do you miss them? I'm sure they miss you."

The dragon still made no movement.

"Well, at least you don't seem put off by my being here." Octavia gave the creature a soft smile. "Shall I read to you, then? You won't understand, but we can pretend."

She returned to the journal and began to read the entry. Octavia found herself stopping every few sentences to chuckle at her thirteen-year-old self's vernacular and when she got to the end of the page, she held it out so that the dragon could see her drawing of one of the shields.

"See this? This is a shield I found among the dragon artifacts. And these symbols? Well, I don't know what they mean, but they're beautiful, aren't they? So detailed, as if they really mean something." Octavia looked from the page to the dragon and was surprised to see that the dragon had lifted its head, showing a genuine spark of interest.

"Oh!" Octavia said, a little surprised. "You like it?"

The dragon made no additional movement, but it looked as though it was hanging on every word Octavia said.

"No," she murmured, "that's not possible." She went back to her journal, reading the next entry. This one was specifically devoted to the strange symbols, and there were dozens of them scribbled along the page.

"I wish I knew what these meant," Octavia mused out loud. "Assuming they mean anything at all." They looked like something that belonged in a fairy tale—like they were a secret code that would unlock a magical spell. It was a silly thought, of course. Magic was scarcely practiced at all in Tenegard, except for soothsayers. And they didn't use symbols like this, nor did their magic allow them to impact other people in the way true Athelian magic did. The magic of a soothsayer only affected the woman herself, giving her visions that were usually more confusing than helpful.

As far as Octavia knew, there was no such thing as a kind of magic that could be shared between a human and a dragon. Not outside of children's stories, that is. But then, it was only in those children's stories that dragons were shown as intelligent and calm, rather than as savage animals. The dragon at her side—who was not attacking her or showing any sign of aggression—clearly served to demonstrate that such a seemingly outlandish idea wasn't a fairy tale after all.

"Here," she said, holding out the journal again, the symbols visible to the dragon. "Perhaps these mean something to you."

Almost as if in response, the dragon let out a low grumble. It wasn't a growl and Octavia did not feel threatened in any way, but the tiny hairs all over her body lifted upward, as if someone had traced a cold finger along her spine. Because it had almost seemed as if the dragon had tried to respond to her question.

"Did you just…no." She shook her head. "That's not possible." *Is it?*

She eyed the symbols on the page, trying to make sense of them. What was it about them that had caused the dragon to react? Was it just because many of the symbols showed dragons?

"Do you know what these mean?" she asked the dragon, knowing full well that the dragon couldn't answer back. To her shock, the dragon moved its body, almost as if it wanted to move closer, wanted to be able to understand and answer her.

These have to mean something. Octavia returned again to the symbols, desperate to understand whatever it was the dragon was trying to tell her. "Maybe they're words or maybe spells of some kind?" she mused out loud, imagining in her mind what word each symbol might indicate or what spell it could be used for.

One in particular drew her eye. The symbol depicted two figures, one human and one dragon. The hearts in their chests had been magnified and outlined. There was something about the image, something that made Octavia's entire body hum with energy. It reminded her of something she'd always wanted, but never really had.

"Friendship," she whispered, and the warm energy intensified. Octavia looked up from the notebook in her hand, eyeing the dragon. "That's probably not its true meaning," she said. "But that's what it means to me. It's beautiful, don't you think?" She pointed to the page. "Even though they're different, their hearts are exactly the same."

The dragon let out another low sound and as it floated towards Octavia on the wind, she could have sworn the deep grumble morphed into words, words that sounded very much like, *Yes, keep reading.*

She jumped a little, dropping the journal into her lap. "Oh!" she said, her hand flying to her mouth. "Did you just? Did I…" She shook her head back and forth. "No, that's not possible. I'm so lonely that I'm turning a dragon into my imaginary friend."

The dragon inclined its head as if to say, "Pick up the book! Don't stop reading!"

Octavia's hand moved before her mind even had time to catch up, flipping back to the page full of symbols. She studied the symbols again, returning to trying to decipher their meaning, all the while that strange, warm energy pooled in her chest.

She looked up, making direct eye contact with the dragon who was watching her so intently, Octavia felt as if its stare might burn a hole right through her. "I don't know what's happening right now. But it's as if you're understanding me. Maybe not entirely, but there's something about these symbols, something almost magical about them. Am I right?"

The dragon opened its mouth and grunted. The short, discordant sound shouldn't have sounded very pleasant, except as it landed in Octavia's ears, she once again made sense of it. It was absolutely preposterous, but it sounded as if the dragon has responded with a yes.

Her eyes darted back and forth between the page of symbols and the dragon, gasping as she did so.

"By the stars," she breathed, as the dragon leaned a little closer. She had no idea what to make of it, but there was no denying that something was happening between her and the dragon. And it filled Octavia with both excitement and sheer terror.

Is this really happening? Is this really possible? What do I do? Her heart sped up and she tried to figure out what came next. But it seemed like there was only one option for her.

Octavia chose a symbol randomly from the page, fixing it in her mind. Her entire body felt electrified, warmth filling her. Then she looked the dragon square in the eye and asked with a shaky voice. "Can you understand me?"

It took a moment, but the dragon dipped its massive head and then emitted a series of sounds.

To the naked ear, they were exactly the type of sounds one might expect a dragon to make—nothing more intelligible than the grunts and growls of any animal—but Octavia's heart nearly jumped from her chest, because to her, the words sounded like that of her own native tongue.

And the dragon had responded with "Yes, girl. I understand."

CHAPTER 17

Cora tossed the rusty, broken door hinge into a cast iron bowl and sucked in a mouthful of the crisp morning air, letting it fill her lungs. She continued to inhale and exhale several more times, letting the slow, rhythmic breathing guide her energy and put her in touch with her magic. When she felt ready, she opened her eyes and sank to the ground in front of the bowl. *I can do this. I can do this.*

Reaching deep inside of herself, she reached for the bond she had formed with Alaric. The connection between them seemed to hum and glow as she touched it, and Cora couldn't help but smile. Warm energy flowed through her as she drew it up from the bond, and Cora opened her eyes and zeroed in on the door hinge. The edges of the hinge began to distort, their solid state growing softer.

It both was and wasn't anything like a forge, when the temperatures in the room soared as fires blazed to get metal melted enough to be pliable. There was no physical fire here, no all-encompassing heat. In fact, she could still feel a cool breeze brushing up against her cheek. The only fire was in her magic, heating the metal not from the outside in but from the inside out until it changed, shifted, reformed out of its solid shape. Because she told it to. A burst of excitement flooded through Cora, but she forced it down, doing her best to stay focused and in control of her power.

Six weeks had passed since she and Alaric had left Llys behind and arrived at Tamsin's home for training. Six long weeks of daily drills, practice fights, and training sessions. And they were finally starting to pay off. Together, she and Alaric had been able to perform several bits of complex magic under Tamsin's tutelage. It was becoming easier and easier to influence and manipulate environmental factors—earth, water, and air.

Tamsin leaned against a tree a few paces away and watched her work on the metal hinge. Alaric had gone off hunting in the forest, but she could feel his awareness through the bond, lending his strength to her efforts.

I can do this. I can do this.

"I can do this," she mumbled out loud, pulling more energy from the bond. The bottom of the door hinge was definitely distorting now, its solid shape beginning to morph and change as Cora's magic heated the metal to an incredibly high temperature, hot enough to make the air around it shimmer.

Cora's arms and legs started trembling, and she knew she was expending quite a bit of energy trying to melt the metal. She had to be very careful, as Tamsin has explained, about not pushing past her limits—it would do her no good in battle if she made a grand show of magic to defeat one enemy only to have a dozen more sneak up and catch her too drained to fight—but she was determined to see this task through. The only way to extend her limits was to keep pushing at them. Tamsin had explained that training to use magic was a lot like training the physical body to be more agile or powerful. It took time and practice to build up stamina and strength.

So even though she felt her body beginning to show signs that she was reaching her limit, she drew even more power from the bond.

She could smell the metal melting, a scent so familiar that she'd know it anywhere. It smelled like home, like her father's forge. Like her entire childhood, standing by her father's side and watching as he turned lumps of metal into works of art. Her father's face floated to the forefront of her thoughts, and Cora felt her heart twinge at the memory of his kind eyes and the smile he always reserved for her alone. She'd never been away from her father for more than a few days, and she missed him terribly. It didn't help to think of him as a captive, slaving away on the labor force.

Hot tears began to well up in Cora's eyes, but she quickly blinked them away. Her father's health had been deteriorating even before he had been taken away as a prisoner, and she couldn't imagine that he was receiving any kind of medical care while he was in the prison. Faron had promised to look out for him, but how much could the guard really do? It would look too suspicious to the others if he showed up with medicine for a prisoner, or demanded that Viren be allowed to rest when he was supposed to be working. In the time since Cora had last seen him, his cough could have gotten much worse, or…

A terrifying thought took hold of Cora and she froze, the energy fueling her magic fizzling out. The door hinged began to solidify again as it cooled.

What if he's dead? The thought was so utterly devastating that Cora couldn't breathe. Her chest burned, and she could feel panic and pain creeping over her like a shadow. She reached out to Alaric, those four awful words tumbling down the bond along with her devastation.

No, Cora, Alaric's voice came through loud and clear. *You mustn't allow yourself to think that way. Your father is not dead, I know it.*

But how can you know that? Cora wailed in her mind. *He was so sick before and now…I don't even know if he's getting enough food and water. And I…I'm so worried about him, Alaric.*

I know. But you and your father have a strong bond. The connection between a parent and a child is unlike any other. If your father had perished, I do think you would have felt it. Try to reach out through that connection now. Do you truly believe that your father is gone, or is he there on the other end, still alive and waiting for you?

Cora considered this, closing her eyes and picturing her father's face once again. She could still recall every single detail clearly. Focusing on the image, she allowed herself to open up to the prospect of her father truly being dead…but her body vehemently rejected the idea. The response was immediate and strong.

No, she said to Alaric, as relief swept through her. *I don't think he's dead. I think you're right, I would have felt it. Still, there's no telling what condition he's in. Which is all the more reason to get back to Llys as soon as we possibly can.*

We will. Trust me, I, too, long to return to the fortress. I dream of my mother nearly every night, and I am anxious to see her freed. But to reach that goal, we must focus on the training. As soon as we're ready, Tamsin will tell us, and we will return and free them both.

Cora sighed. Alaric was right, there was really only one thing to do if she wanted to return. So, she cleared her mind as best she could and refocused on the rusty door hinge. Pulling from the power of her bond with Alaric and using the image of her father's shackles as motivation, she returned to her task.

To her surprise, the metal began to respond immediately. In a matter of seconds, the door hinge had completely melted into a pool of silver liquid.

Relief and pride shot through Cora like an arrow, and she let out a whoop, jumping to her feet.

"Did you see that?" she called out to Tamsin, who hadn't moved from her spot by the tree. "I did it."

Tamsin walked over and examined the contents of the pan. "It's a good start," she said, "but it's *only* a start—you understand that, right? This is just stage one, where you learn how to push power into something until it does what you want. The true measure of success will be when you've learned control—how to use just enough magic and concentration to get the job done. You're throwing too much at each task now, using up your reserves too quickly. You'll never get through a battle that way—you'll tire too quickly. We need to return to our practice of trying to conjure while fighting."

Cora groaned at the words. This particular feat of multitasking had previously proven to be quite difficult for Cora. She had vastly improved with hand-to-hand combat, and she had even grown to be quite proficient at swordplay. Tamsin's years of experience meant that the odds stayed very firmly in her favor, but Cora was getting better and better at landing blows of her own and blocking the ones coming from Tamsin. But casting magic while also swinging a sword and dodging someone else's blows was another thing entirely. She could mostly handle each task separately, but trying to combine them felt like trying to balance herself on a ball while juggling live chickens. There was just too much for her to process at once. Tamsin insisted that she'd be able to handle it if she could stay totally calm and focused—but the idea of that felt just as impossible. Centered stillness was a challenge for her at any time, and it was all the harder to reach when she was fighting someone, with both adrenaline and aggression coursing through her.

"You'll never get better if you we don't continue to practice," Tamsin reminded her.

"I know, it just feels like I'll never get there."

"You will," Tamsin replied. "With practice. Like I said."

Cora wanted to roll her eyes, but she didn't. "Fine," she said with a huff. "Let's practice, then."

They were only two moves into the fight when Tamsin sent a breeze at her, catching her completely off guard and knocking her over into a puddle that remained from the previous night's rain. Cora knew better than to complain aloud, but her expression must have said enough for her because Tamsin laughed. "Are you that bothered by a little mud?" she taunted. "If your senses were open as they should be, you'd have felt it coming. Then you could have blocked that breeze—or simply dodged out of its way. If you're wet, you have no one to blame but yourself. Now concentrate. Try to do the same to me."

Cora conjured up a blast of air, but while she was fixated on that, Tamsin slipped around out of its way—and got her sword in under Cora's guard, smacking her on the ribs with the flat of the blade, hard enough to leave bruises. Growling a little in frustration, Cora turned on Tamsin and they exchanged a few strikes while Cora frantically tried to think of what she could cast next. It was so hard to formulate any kind of plan, though, when Tamsin kept up a flurry of swordplay, giving her no time to think or collect herself.

"Slow," Tamsin tsked. "Sloppy. You're thinking about your magic but not using it—and using your sword but not thinking about it, so you're not doing either one as well as you should. Wake up and get out of your own way." She punctuated her words with a wave of her free hand...which lifted one of the puddles off the ground and smacked Cora in the face with it. She could feel rivulets of muddy water dripping down her forehead, along her nose, under the neckline of her tunic, and she snarled, filled with frustration as she glared at her teacher.

"Is that meant to scare me?" Tamsin goaded. "Do you think a shadow general is going to be intimidated by a pouty little girl with mud in her hair?"

"I'm not pouting, I'm *angry*," Cora argued, trying to rush Tamsin, only to get beaten back with some quick strikes and another blow from the flat of the sword, this time against her leg.

"And your anger is making you uncoordinated—fogging your mind, slowing your responses, blinding you to openings of attack." Tamsin proceeded to prove that *she* was not similarly blinded, demonstrating everywhere Cora wasn't shielding herself properly with scrapes from the tip of her blade. None of the injuries went deep, but they all drew stinging trails of blood—as if Tamsin was drawing evidence of Cora's incompetence on her skin.

"What will you do if you're up against Nedra, the king's spy general?" Tamsin pressed, her attacks unrelenting. "She's cunning, clever, and absolutely ruthless. You think she won't know what taunts to use to get you too rattled to fight effectively? Your thoughts might as well be written all over your face. Do you even know how easy that makes you to manipulate?"

"She won't be able to use plants to snare me," Cora grumbled, kicking aside a vine that had wrapped itself around her ankle, waiting to trip her.

"She'll use everything she has, which means you need to do the same," Tamsin shot back. "I'm trying to show you what *you* should be capable of—the tools that you'll bring to a battle. You think the only weapon you have is that sword in your hand? The *whole world* is your weapon, so *use* it!"

Cora concentrated hard and made the ground stir under Tamsin's feet, hoping to throw her off balance. But all she did was raise a disdainful eyebrow. "I've fought from the back of a dragon, little girl. Do you think a little rumble like that could rattle me? And if you were up against the king's executioner, Lanius, I doubt he'd even feel it. The man's a beast—he's built like a bull, and he prides himself on the extent of his brutality. The king is the one who picks his targets, but Lanius doesn't kill because he's ordered to—he does it for *fun*. When you're up against a man like that, your only chance of survival is to call on something that can truly stop your enemy in his tracks. If Lanius gets within five feet of you, you're dead. How would you stop him? Show me how you'd stop him!"

"I don't know," Cora muttered, feeling like she was at the end of her rope, trying to keep from crying. What could she use? What could she do?

"Find something," Tamsin snarled, coming in for another series of blows. "This isn't a game. Lives are at stake! Try harder. *Fight* harder. You have to survive, don't you understand that? You're either the first dragon rider of a new age or you're the *last* this world will ever see, and everything that ever mattered to me will die right along with you. So pull yourself together and *fight,* do you hear me? *Survive,* no matter what it takes."

The look on Tamsin's face was fierce, and Cora's stomach turned over. She hated feeling so weak. Drawing hard on her magic, she shoved it towards the other woman, hearing Tamsin let out a surprised gasp as the hilt of the sword in her hand heated until it was scorchingly hot. Cora heard the sword hit the ground as Tamsin dropped it.

Cora let out a sigh of relief now that the fight was over, her eyes slipping shut against a sudden wave of dizziness as she fought to stay on her feet. She'd pulled too hard, burned through too much magic with that last move on top of the training she'd done earlier with the hinge. It had left her exhausted, but she could only be glad that it had worked.

"That was good," Tamsin said, her voice sounding a bit calmer now. Some tension relaxed out of Cora's shoulders—only to return with a vengeance when she felt the sharp edge of a blade press against her neck. Her eyes flew open in shock as she realized that Tamsin had drawn out a dagger and had circled behind her, giving her nowhere to retreat as she held the knife to Cora's throat. "But not good enough," Tamsin whispered right into her ear. "*Never* assume a fight is over unless your enemy is either restrained or dead. Otherwise, *you'll* be the one who dies."

Cora swallowed hard, feeling the edge of the knife kiss her skin at the movement, and that last thing piled on top of all her emotional turmoil made the floodgates open. She burst into tears.

Instantly, the blade was removed. "Oh, stars," Tamsin muttered, reaching out and awkwardly patting Cora's arm. "I...I'm sorry," she said after a minute or so. "I went too far. I shouldn't have pushed you like that."

"It was all true, though, wasn't it?" Cora said with a sniffle. The tears were slowing now. She tried to wipe them away, but her hands and her face were both muddy, so she was pretty sure that all she did was smear the mess around. "The things you said about the shadow generals...if I meet them in combat, I'll need to be prepared to fight with everything I've got."

"It's all true, yes," Tamsin admitted. "But that fight you're thinking about isn't happening today. You've got time to figure this out. I know you want to get to Llys as soon as you can, but taking this time to fully train yourself is going to pay off for you in the end. This *will* get easier. You just have to keep working at it. Everyone struggles at first."

Cora eyed her. "Did you?"

Tamsin nodded. "Yes, like you, I was always a bit of a hot head and let aggression rule me. I was like you—I wanted to charge in and start swinging, either with a sword or with my fists. But, also like you, I had to find a way to center my mind, even in the midst of combat. It's not an easy skill to master. To be able to not only anticipate your opponent's next move but to also be calm and focused enough to draw upon your magic and use it strategically, making your attacks more powerful and your defenses more robust. But Cora, with practice, you will get there."

"You keep saying that, and I know it's true, it just feels as though it is taking forever."

"We've been focusing on it a lot—perhaps too much," Tamsin mused. "Maybe what you need now is to take a step back, work on something else to clear your head. Look, why don't we change course for today. Why don't you practice a more large-scale reading?"

Reading was one of the new skills Tamsin had taught them. It consisted of using their abilities to sense other living things in a particular area. It was a variation on the ability to manipulate air, actually, since she could use a breeze to capture the visual aspect of an area in her mind and see what objects and creatures the air touched. They were able to read what kind of wildlife was present in a tree, for example, or how many rabbits might be burrowed together in a single hole. This was a skill that would be useful in sensing the approach of and hiding from any enemies. She could only imagine how helpful it would be when they finally returned to attack the fortress. Given how likely it was that Onyx would try to spring a trap on them, having forewarning as to what was lying in wait for her could mean the difference between life and death. It was definitely a skill she wanted to practice.

"What did you have in mind?"

"Let me show you." Tamsin walked over to her workbench and pulled out a large roll of parchment. "For the past few years, I've been trying to map out the forest. Without a dragon, mapping it has been a long, slow process."

Behind her, Cora both felt and heard Alaric land, having just returned from his hunting trip. He quickly joined Cora.

Are you well? he asked Cora through the bond.

Cora nodded, knowing that he must have felt some of the emotional upheaval from her training session with Tamsin. *I'm fine.*

You are not weak, Cora, Alaric replied, his voice gentle. *No matter what you think, it is not true. You have a brave heart. Do not let anything convince you otherwise.*

Warmth spread through Cora's chest at the dragon's encouragement. The training session with Tamsin had shaken her a bit, but Alaric's words soothed the ragged edges of the experience, making her feel better. She offered him a small smile and refocused on Tamsin as she finished explaining the task she had in mind.

"I know there is at least one herd of dragons to the north of here. I think it's important for us to know where the dragons are in this area. Why don't you and Alaric fly over the forest to read the area and see what you find? It'll be useful for you to get practice reading all the different kinds of species present here in the forest—and you might discover more than one colony of dragons after all."

"And what do we do if we find them?" Cora asked.

Tamsin smiled. "Well, you're a dragon rider, aren't you? So, introduce yourself."

CHAPTER 18

T he forest below was a patchwork of green hues. From her
vantage point on Alaric's back, Cora couldn't help but chuckle
a bit when she thought of her earlier misgivings about training in the
notorious forest that so many believed to be haunted or populated by
monsters. The lore surrounding the place had given it quite the reputation, but Cora had come to realize the forest wasn't at all what
everyone believed it to be.

The Meldona Forest, despite its rocky terrain, was a quiet, peaceful
place. Cora had learned to appreciate its stillness. Being on Alaric's
back, flying above the trees with the wind in her face, felt wonderfully
liberating. There was a contentment that flying always provided her,
and she allowed herself to enjoy it.

I am not sensing anything other than the usual animals, Alaric's voice
came through her thoughts.

Cora inhaled deeply and let her senses push beyond her to read the
terrain. *Nor I. I think there were some bears a few miles back, but
nothing bigger, and certainly not a dragon herd.*

Reading an area had quickly become second nature to Cora and Alaric. It was one of the few skills that they'd been able to pick up almost immediately once Tamsin had taught them the basics. Now, Cora found herself doing it constantly. It gave her a sense of security to always have an awareness of the things that lived and moved around her.

They continued their trek northward, reading the forest below for signs of the dragons and enjoying their peaceful time together up in the air. Back in Barcroft, they'd had limited opportunities to fly together, always worried about being seen, but here, there were no people for miles, giving them the freedom to relax and enjoy the flight. As Cora felt the tension unwind from her shoulders, she realized how right Tamsin had been to think this would be good for her. Whether they found other dragons or not, this was the perfect chance to give her mind and magic a chance to recenter and reset.

Wait, Alaric said a while later. *I think I'm getting something.*

Cora straightened her back, her senses tingling and humming with energy that pulsed through their bond. *I feel it too. Over there.* She pointed. *There's more than one of them. I'm not positive they're dragons...but they're certainly bigger than anything I've "read" before, except for you.* Given her connection to Alaric, reading him wasn't quite like reading any other creature—but up until this point, she hadn't been entirely sure how much of what she sensed of him in the reading was different from other animals because he was a dragon as opposed to different because he was *her* dragon.

I believe there are at least a dozen or so of them, Alaric confirmed. *And they seem to me to be the right size and shape for dragons.*

Cora could sense this too. *It must be the colony Tamsin spoke of.*

A spike of curiosity trickled down the bond and grabbed Cora's attention. *What are you thinking?* she asked.

I suppose I was just wondering if perhaps they knew Dragon Tongue? There was a strange twinge of longing and excitement laced in Alaric's words.

Cora considered this. They had no way of knowing for sure whether the other dragons would be friendly, especially to a human in their midst. On the other hand, she could tell that Alaric wanted to at least see the dragons with his own eyes. And speak with them if at all possible. He never said it, but Cora knew that along with missing his mother, Alaric was also missing his herd. Dragons were not meant to be solitary creatures and as much as Cora knew he was happy to be with her, he felt a certain loneliness over being away from his own kind. And she understood that completely.

We should land and go find out. Admittedly, Cora was curious too. The only dragons she had spoken to had been from Alaric's herd—and even then, she'd only spoken to a handful. She wondered what these new dragons would be like.

Alaric immediately banked left, heading towards an open break in the tree line that would allow him to land. Excitement zipped through the bond, making Cora laugh.

We'll have to be careful, though, Alaric said. *They may be alarmed when they see you with me. Humans and dragons have not been close for many years. I cannot be certain whether any here will even remember what it used to be like. But do not fear, I will not let them hurt you in any way.*

Cora reached over and gave Alaric's neck a pat. *I know I'm safe with you. And who knows? If they don't know Dragon Tongue, maybe we can bring the knowledge back to them.*

Cora recalled what Raksha had said about the effects of Onyx's magic and the loss of Dragon Tongue on the herds:

You see, not only did Onyx destroy the dragon riders, he set out to make sure that no one could ever become one again—or even speak Dragon Tongue at all. He destroyed every bastion of rider knowledge. He rewrote the history books and did everything in his power to wipe the relationship between the dragons and the dragon riders from the very culture of the Tenegard people. Soon, all that had once existed between dragons and humans was reduced to nothing more than myths or stories told to children. And without the Dragon Tongue to spark our magic and protect our minds, our herd began to lose some of our mental strength. We forgot our old friendships with humans, forgot our history and traditions. We grew closer and closer to becoming the wild, dangerous beasts Onyx wanted us to be.

Another burst of excitement came barreling towards Cora from Alaric, and she could tell that the idea of helping the dragons regain what was stolen from them was more than a little exhilarating to him. It was to her too.

Once they had landed safely, Alaric and Cora began to move slowly towards the herd's territory. They did not bother trying to camouflage the noise of their steps—on the contrary, they did their best to make noise. They didn't want to sneak up on the herd and cause alarm. They hoped that their noisy approach would convey their friendly intentions.

The first dragon that appeared through the trees was a large male with deep orange scales. He reminded Cora of a sunset, and his large eyes immediately swiveled back and forth between Cora's face and Alaric with curiosity and a bit of wariness.

"Peace, friend," Alaric spoke out loud to the dragon. Cora chose not to say anything herself until they were sure the dragons were friendly.

"My name is Alaric, and this is my friend and rider, Cora," Alaric explained, to which the orange dragon jerked its head back, snorting.

"Rider!" The dragon's voice was much deeper than Alaric's. Cora had no issue understanding him—not like in those early days when she'd first started communicating with Alaric. Back then, it felt like only a small portion of what they tried to say to each other was actually intelligible. Her knowledge of Dragon Tongue was much stronger now and focusing on the symbols that allowed the magic to work had become second nature. It felt a little odd to hear a dragon other than Alaric speak—she'd gotten so used to only communicating with him, where she had the bond to convey mental images and feelings as well as words—but at least comprehension wouldn't be a problem. She would never cease to be amazed by the power of Dragon Tongue.

"Yes, my rider," Alaric confirmed. "We are bonded, she and I."

"You and this girl have bonded? Like in the days of old?" The orange dragon dropped his head to inspect Cora more closely.

"Yes," Alaric answered plainly. "She is my *bonded* rider." There was pride in his voice that made Cora's heart swell just a bit. She smiled at Alaric and then turned her attention to the orange dragon. "Hello," she said, lifting a hand in greeting. "My name is Cora. What's yours?"

The orange dragon lowered his head so that his eyes were level with Cora's. "Hello, rider. My name is Aspen."

Cora's lips split into a wide grin. "It's nice to meet you, Aspen. I have to ask, if you don't mind, how is it that you understand me? I mean, I know *how,* but I guess I'm surprised that you have retained your ability to use and understand Dragon Tongue without dragon riders around to keep the magic intact."

Aspen cocked his head. "I'm not sure how to answer that question, but understand you, I can."

"It's strange, though," Cora went on to explain. "We were told that many of the dragon herds had lost their ability to understand and communicate with humans after the dragon riders were wiped out."

Alaric nodded. "Have you encountered another human before Cora?"

"No," Aspen responded. "Not directly. My herd tends to steer clear of the errant travelers that come through here. Although, I believe there is a human who lives south of here. She has never proven a threat to us, nor has she sought us out, so the herd pays her no mind."

"That's Tamsin," Cora said. "She's also a dragon rider."

"Another dragon rider?" Aspen's eyes widened.

"Yes, but her dragon was lost," Cora explained, her tone softening with sympathy for the older rider. "It is just her living in the forest."

"I see," Aspen said, his own eyes darkening slightly. "Well then, will you come with me and speak with the chief elder of my herd? He is the oldest among us, and I know he would be interested in talking with the two of you. He may also have the answers that will help us unravel this mystery."

Alaric spoke up quickly. "We would like to, but I have to ensure my rider's safety. There are none in your herd who might view Cora as a threat, are there?"

Once again, Cora's heart swelled. The friendship and bond between her and Alaric was only growing stronger with each day, and it still amazed her that they had gotten lucky enough to forge such a connection.

Aspen was quick to assure Alaric. "There are none who will make a move against Cora. I can tell you that with certainty. There will be many who are curious, but no one will harm her. You have my word on that."

"Very well," Alaric replied. "Then lead the way."

Cora fell into step beside the large dragons, quickening her pace to keep up with them. Aspen walked them deeper into the forest where the tree line thickened before finally opening into a wide space where over a hundred dragons were gathered.

"My brothers and sisters," Aspen called out. "We have guests. I would like you to meet my new friends. This is Alaric and his *bonded rider*, Cora."

There was an audible reaction from the dragons, several of whom hurried over for a closer look. Although Cora felt no sense of threat from the curious creatures, she still took a step closer to Alaric and put a hand on his side, needing that physical reminder of his closeness.

Do not worry, he immediately said to her in her mind. *I do not believe we are in any kind of danger here. Should that change, I will remove you from here immediately. Rest assured, I will not let anyone harm you.*

I know. I trust you completely.

And I you, Cora. Nothing will ever get close to you without facing my wrath. Although, I daresay with all the training you've been doing with Tamsin, it would be foolhardy for anyone—man or dragon—to make a threat against you. You are quite formidable with or without me.

Yes, but I much prefer us together as a team.

As do I, rider. As do I.

The conversation had settled Cora a bit, and she gingerly lifted a hand and waved to the newcomers. "Hello," she said to them. "I'm Cora."

"I can understand her!" a young, green dragon exclaimed, nearly leaping in the air with excitement. "I did not know I could speak to humans!"

Cora giggled at the young dragon's words, while several of the other dragons also seemed to marvel at this revelation.

"You can understand her because she is using the magic of Dragon Tongue to communicate," a deep voice full of experience and wisdom spoke over the murmurings of the crowd.

Almost on instinct, the crowd of dragons parted, making way for one of the largest dragons Cora had ever seen. His scales were a deep brown color, and they sagged a bit against his body, reminding her of the wrinkles on the face of an elderly human where the skin had lost some of its elasticity. While she knew that dragons could live for hundreds of years, this was the first dragon Cora had ever seen that actually appeared to be old. Her eyes widened.

"Hello there," the older dragon said gently, stopping in front of Cora and Alaric. He turned to Aspen. "Please make the introductions, young one."

"Cora and Alaric, this is Elian," Aspen said. "He is the oldest dragon in our herd and is our chief elder."

Elian bowed his head formally. "I welcome you to our territory, Cora and Alaric." He turned back to Aspen. "And where exactly did you find our guests?"

"I found them just beyond our eastern border. They were heading our way, as though they were coming to find us."

"Well, that's because we *were*," Cora piped up, "coming to find you, that is." She quickly explained the reading task that Tamsin had given them. "We were curious if you had knowledge of Dragon Tongue, and so we stopped to see."

"And clearly, you do," Alaric added, "though we are curious as to how that came to be, if you have been cut off from humans since the end of the earlier dragon riders."

"I believe the answer to that lies with the human who lives just south of here."

"That's Tamsin," Cora told him. "She's a dragon rider, though her dragon was lost long ago."

Elian dipped his snout. "That would explain it, then. We have known of her since she moved into the forest, and I have always suspected that she carried a dragon bond."

"Elian was alive during the time of the riders," Aspen explained. "If there is anyone in our herd who would know of such things, it would be him."

"I never bonded with a human myself, but many in our herd at that time did. And it was through them that I learned Dragon Tongue. Once the riders were destroyed, however, many from our herds and from others nearby lost the ability to speak with humans." Elian's eyes darkened. "I do not know why exactly, though I can speculate. But it seems as if the old ways have simply been forgotten. And there are some—even within this forest—who have forgotten more than that. Civility itself seems to be fading among some of the more distant herds."

Cora's eyes got bigger as what Elian said sunk in. "Do you mean they've...gone wild?"

CHAPTER 19

"Yes." Elian's tone grew grave. "There is a herd much farther north where the dragons have become nearly feral. Their way of life is more aggressive, more fueled by some deep, basic primal instinct instead of the logic and reasoning that has always served as the foundation of a dragon community. Even more than just forgetting speech, it is as if they have forgotten what it used to mean to be a dragon."

Alaric made a low sound of distress in his throat at this, which Cora immediately understood. It was more than a little unnerving to think of any dragons, as majestic and intelligent as they were, devolving into nothing more than mindless beasts. She imagined it was even harder and more painful for Alaric to imagine.

"It's the effects of King Onyx's decrees," she tried to explain, remembering all that Raksha had told her. "When he rose to power, he defeated the dragon riders with trickery and then used all of his power and influence to change the way that history was written throughout Tenegard. I guess the people who were alive and knew the truth were too scared to speak up…and then the silence just continued until everyone accepted that the dragon riders had been nothing more than a myth. No one was allowed to post or share the symbols that are the basis of Dragon Tongue, and the magic was just…forgotten."

"Yet, we retain our knowledge because of the human—Tamsin, you said?"

"That must be it," Cora replied, putting all the pieces together. "Your proximity to Tamsin meant that you stayed close enough to magic for your senses to connect with it, keeping the memory alive for you. Her magic protected you and your herd from rewilding. That other herd you spoke of, they must be too far away for the magic to reach them."

Elian let out a deep sigh. "And because of that, they are lost to us. Reduced to mere beasts of the woods."

Cora's heart seized at the pain in his voice. Though it was an entirely different herd, Elian clearly felt great sympathy for the wild herd.

"No, not lost," Cora said, trying to comfort him. "Or at least not lost forever. The magic of Dragon Tongue can be restored."

"She's right," Alaric spoke up. "My own herd was protected somehow, but much of our history was forgotten until Cora and I met. Cora brought the magic of Dragon Tongue back to us and in doing so, all that was lost returned to us."

Elian's large eyes widened slightly. "Is that so? Well, then, for the sake of our northern brethren, I hope that is indeed the case."

As Elian was talking, Cora noticed a clump of three or so dragons who were eying her and Alaric. Unlike the others, these did not seem at all excited about her and Alaric's presence.

What do you think their problem is? she asked Alaric through the bond. He threw a quick glance over his shoulder and snorted. *Oh, I would not worry about them. We dragons can be a fussy sort, and in any circumstance, there will always be naysayers who are unhappy with the turn of events.*

But why *would they be unhappy? We're not here to hurt the herd or scavenge scales or anything like that. We just want to talk.*

Yes, but we represent a change to the world as they have always known it. Before today, they would have said that all dragon riders were gone. Now they know that is no longer true, and that is more than enough to make us feel like a threat.

But isn't the return of dragon riders a good thing?

It is to me, Alaric confirmed, *but they may think otherwise, and it is unlikely that anything you or I could say to them would change their minds. Many do not trust humans, and since I am bonded to you, they are likely to trust me even less.*

Cora scrunched up her nose. She didn't like the sound of that, but she tried not to let it get to her as she refocused on Elian.

The little green dragon who had spoken out earlier wormed its way up to Cora. "So how did the two of you become bonded? I am dying to know!"

Cora chuckled at the way the little dragon practically bounced with every word. Elian also chuckled, as did Aspen. "My apologies," Aspen said, indicating the smaller dragon. "This is Vesper, my brother. He is still quite young, and he forgets himself sometimes."

Cora waved a hand. "No, it's all right. It's a tale I don't mind recounting." So that's exactly what she did, detailed for the gathered dragons about how she'd grown up listening to stories about the dragons and the dragon riders from her Nana Livi. She told them about the cave where she had explored the symbols of Dragon Tongue without knowing what they meant, and about how she had joined the scale scavengers and seen Alaric for the first time. Alaric piped up, filling in details from his side of the story, and by the time they were finished with their tale, the other dragons were listening with rapt attention.

Contentment hummed through the bond, and Cora knew it was both her and Alaric's shared emotions that warmed her. *I sure wish Nana Livi could see this,* she thought to herself, and she imagined her grandmother standing next to her, marveling over all the different dragons.

"And what are your plans now?" a deep rose-colored dragon asked, her voice bright.

"Our plans?" Cora asked, her brows scrunching.

"Yes. What do you plan to do to restore what has been lost?"

"Oh! Do you mean the other herd? Well, as I told Elian, the power of Dragon Tongue can be—"

"No, rider," the rose dragon interrupted kindly, "that is not what I mean. What are you and your dragon's plan for all of the other dragons of Tenegard—and for the humans who hold the potential to bond with them?"

Cora stared at the dragon. "Um…"

"Surely now that Tenegard has a new dragon rider," the rose-colored dragon continued, "you will set about resurrecting the practice of dragon and human bonding, correct? I assume that you will be working towards creating enough dragon rider pairs to overthrow and remove Onyx the Deathless from power so that his tyranny towards his citizens and his persecution of dragons can come to an end."

Cora's mouth nearly dropped open. While she and Alaric *had* discussed those things, they hadn't exactly discussed any logistics. Fighting Onyx directly, or training other dragon rider pairs, had been lower on their list, given how focused they were on freeing their parents before anything else. She had no idea how to respond. Thankfully, Alaric stepped in.

"Cora and I are completely aware that being the first bonded pair in over a century comes with a lot of…responsibility. And we have discussed how we intend to manage those responsibilities. But in all honesty, our priorities have lain elsewhere as of late."

"Elsewhere?" A pewter-colored dragon grumbled. "What could possibly be more pressing?" This dragon was one of what Alaric had called the naysayers. He seemed to be a particularly grumpy sort. Cora did her best not to wrinkle her nose at him.

"Onyx must be stopped," Alaric went on to say, "and we fully understand that doing so is a matter of great importance. But we cannot strike a concentrated blow against Onyx while he holds leverage against us. Both of our parents were kidnapped by Onyx's forces. We must rescue them before we can do anything else. Otherwise, any attack against Onyx could lead to retaliation against my mother and Cora's father."

The pewter dragon snorted and rolled his eyes, a gesture that made the back of Cora's neck flush. She had a bit of temper, but she knew it would not serve her well to argue with the dragon, so she kept quiet. Still, she did not like his reaction.

Pay him no mind, Alaric said to her through the bond.

Oh, I won't. But it's hard to ignore what an old grump he is. I don't see him rushing to volunteer to take on Onyx, but he expects us to.

As I said, pay him no mind.

"Alaric." It was Elian who spoke now, and his tone was kind, even as the pewter dragon and his comrades began to whisper furiously to each other. "It is understandable that you and Cora would focus on freeing your parents. Anyone who values family would choose the same. But I do wonder if perhaps you should be thinking more of your long-term plans in regards to Onyx. Even if you are not in a position to attack him now, it would be wise to begin the preparations, would it not? Action is needed, I think."

"It is not that we do not plan to take action," Alaric replied, his tone taking on a slightly more steely edge. "But Cora and I need to complete our training before we even attempt to do what you are implying."

"And this Tamsin," Elian leaned forward. "She is the one training you how to defeat Onyx?"

"She is training us in combat so that we will be able to fight physically and with magic to defend ourselves against any threats," Cora clarified. "Although, yes, those are the skills that we will be using when the time comes to face Onyx."

The pewter dragon let out a loud snort. "You speak of the woman that has stayed hidden in the woods all these years?" He shook his massive head. "If she is the one training you, then I am doubtful that we well ever truly see the rise of the dragons and their riders again. I would not be surprised if you," his large eyes landed on Cora, "hide away in the woods too as she has done for all these years—once your father is returned to you."

Cora's cheeks burned and her entire body hummed with indignation. She wanted to open her mouth and argue, but she couldn't get a word in edgewise as the grumpy old dragon continued his tirade.

"The humans destroyed Tenegard by betraying the riders and bowing to Onyx—or have you all forgotten that?" The pewter dragon sneered. "And they have not lifted a finger to change things since." He narrowed his eyes at Alaric and Cora. "Why should the two of you be any different? You may be a bonded pair, but that means nothing if you do not use your bond to accomplish things for anyone but yourselves. If anything, I think perhaps the dragons would be better off without humans entirely." And with that, he whipped his body around and stormed off, followed by several other of the naysayer dragons.

As for Cora, shock and hurt swirled around inside her like a storm. She hadn't expected such resistance from the dragon, and she certainly didn't understand his animosity.

He is old and bitter, Cora, Alaric growled through the bond. *He lashes out because he is angry and does not care if his words are hurtful. But you cannot let them get inside your head. You must not give him power over you.*

Cora swallowed, trying to keep the tears that were threatening at bay. *It just hurt my feelings to be the target of that kind of bile, is all. Unfairly, I might add. And, ironically enough, he wouldn't have remembered any of that were it not for Tamsin being so close. Her proximity is what kept this herd from going completely wild. But he's probably too stubborn to even consider or admit that.*

We dragons have been known from time to time for being as unyielding as stone. But not every dragon feels the way that one does. Look at Elian, for example.

Cora looked to Elian, whose snout was slightly scrunched as he watched the pewter dragon retreat. The look in his eyes was one of frustration and also embarrassment.

"I must apologize for Galio. He is…well, he has his opinions."

"Yes," Cora said, not really sure what to say. "That he does."

Alaric let out a low sound that was a mix of a growl and a sigh. Cora knew he felt the same as she did. "We should probably head back now," he said to Elian and the rest of the gathered dragons. "We have to return to our training."

Elian, Aspen, and the remaining dragons all seemed to accept this. Given the awkwardness created by Galio, they did not try to counter it. "I think I can speak for most of us when I say good luck to you both," Aspen spoke up. "I hope you get your parents back."

"Thank you," Cora said, giving him a smile.

"It was a pleasure to meet you Cora," Elian said. "And you, Alaric. Like Aspen, I wish you both luck, but I do hope that once you have been safely reunited with your parents that you will consider turning your attentions towards the rest of Tenegard. There are many others who—like you parents—also need rescuing. The sooner the better, in fact, if what we have seen happening with the other herd is any indication of the way the wind is blowing."

Cora and Alaric bid the dragons a good day and become airborne again, all the while discussing the encounter.

"It's a little ironic," Cora remarked, "that pewter dragon, Galio—he accused Tamsin of hiding away from Onyx in the forest even though he is doing the same. I mean, it's not like the dragons are doing anything to fight Onyx. They're hiding in the forest too. I know they can't use magic unless they're bonded to a human, but they knew where Tamsin was; they suspected she was a rider. They could have gone to her and asked for help bonding to humans. But they didn't."

"No," Alaric said, "They didn't. They stayed in the forest and waited to see what others would do. But we will show them, Cora. As soon as out training is over, we'll leave here. And once our parents are safe, we will figure out what we can do to challenge Onyx and bring an end to all the damage that he has done."

"I know," Cora replied, taking the words to heart. "I hope we won't be too late."

CHAPTER 20

After that, Cora didn't feel much like talking anymore. When she and Alaric had first landed to speak with the dragons, she had felt so much hope and excitement. But some of the attitudes and expectations of the dragons had left a bad taste in her mouth. So, as she and Alaric continued with the mapping task Tamsin had set for them, Cora reverted to silence.

Alaric, who always understood her so well, didn't question her mood and left her to stew as he banked east.

Below, the forest was full of life—nothing as large as the dragons they had just encountered, but plenty of other animals that Cora was able to "read" even from her position high above them. Everything from the snails that crept lazily across the bark of the trees, to the fish that swam upstream, to the deer that walked the meadows. It was an incredible thing, this ability to sense life, and as the visit with the dragons faded into the background of her thoughts, Cora felt a smile tug at her cheeks.

But then, just as she settled deeper into the saddle, relaxing into the smooth, worn leather, she felt something wrong, off to the east along the border of the forest. It was an area Cora had planned to read only from a distance, not wanting to risk her and Alaric being seen by any of the people who might live near the edge of the forest—but what she was feeling wasn't something she could ignore. This needed a closer look to explain why, in a forest otherwise teeming with life, a swath of land just felt…empty. There were a few sparks of life, but so much fewer and weaker than there should have been.

Alaric must have felt it too because a shudder ran through his body and reverberated through Cora's. Without a word needed between them, he banked, heading towards the troubling blank spot to see what was going on.

When they got close enough to see, Cora's jaw dropped with shock at the devastating sight. Down below, the forest floor was no longer a sea of green from the thick trees. It was a barren wasteland, a black stain against the earth. Cora gasped, trying to understand what it was she was seeing. It looked as if someone had taken a massive scythe and harvested the trees as though they were nothing more than flimsy stalks of grain to be gathered during harvest season. Or perhaps more gruesomely, it looked as if the earth had a giant gaping wound, with all of its vitality stripped away. It brought tears to her eyes.

It wasn't as if she'd never seen trees harvested for lumber before. That was normal and natural. Barcroft was located in a wooded area, and the townspeople benefited from easy access to lumber. But there were always limits to how much the villagers were allowed to chop down. The forest had to be maintained, had to be kept strong and healthy—never allowed to overgrow into the town, but also never allowed to die off or get pushed too far back. As in all things, there was a need for balance to ensure that there would always be enough resources to go around, not just in the present day, but for years to come. This…this swathe of destruction was unlike anything she'd ever seen. It would take decades for this area to regrow—if it managed to do so at all.

What happened here? Alaric's shock and alarm shot through the bond, mixing with Cora's.

I don't know. Cora scanned the area, trying to discern a cause for the destruction. *Can you get a little closer? Maybe there's something that will help us understand what happened and why.*

But what if we are seen? Alaric pointed out. *I do not want a repeat of Barcroft, where someone saw us flying together. It would put us in danger—and Tamsin, too—if Onyx were to learn that we were here and send someone after us, the way he did with Secare.*

Cora shuddered at the thought. As much as she was looking forward to the day when her training would end and she could actually go *accomplish* something with her magic and newly acquired combat skills, she knew that day had not yet come. And the last thing she wanted was for her and Alaric to be hunted by Onyx's generals or even Onyx himself. No, she couldn't risk their safety if there were other people in the area. Reaching out with her senses, she stretched her "reading" as far as it would go, trying to sense if there was a settlement nearby, with people who might see her and Alaric if they flew into view.

She expected to feel the presence of a sizable number of people—a whole community, setting up a village near the border of the forest. Who else could put to immediate use that much wood? But instead, she was only able to find one. Just one. Nothing about this made sense.

Is it possible? Alaric said, clearly picking up on the same thing as her. *Is there really just one man who has done all of this?*

I don't know if he did it all himself, Cora replied, *but he's definitely the only human that I feel anywhere near here now. I need to talk to him. How about you land here and wait for me, and I'll walk closer to talk to him?*

She could instantly feel Alaric's displeasure with the suggestion. *A man who could cause devastation like this is a considerable threat,* he argued. *Would you really expect me to leave you to face such a man alone?*

We still don't know if he did all this, Cora pointed out. *And besides— he's just one man. I'm armed, I'm trained, and you'll only be a minute away, if the situation really does get out of hand. I'll be fine, Alaric. Truly. And this will protect us from Onyx learning where the dragon rider pair has disappeared to.*

Alaric's only response was a series of unspoken grumbles running through his thoughts. Cora caught snippets of "stubborn" and "reckless," but he didn't actually make any further arguments as he started to decrease his altitude and speed so that they glided downward towards the tops of the trees in the area where she had indicated— close enough that she could walk to the man she'd sensed within a quarter-hour, but not so close that there was much risk of him having seen her on Alaric's back.

"You will wait here?" she asked as she dismounted.

"You alert me the moment you feel you are in the slightest danger so that I can come to your aid?"

She smiled, warmed as always by his protectiveness. "Yes," she promised.

He nodded regally. "Then my answer is yes, as well. Be careful, Cora."

She headed off into the trees, and it did not take long for her to reach the particular patch of former forest that was her target. The devastation was unlike anything Cora had ever seen before. Every single tree had been razed and the whole area had been cleared. It broke Cora's heart to think of all the old, majestic trees that had once stood in this spot that were now gone. And worse, the destruction seemed so senseless. There was no indication that the land was being cleared to be used for farms or homes. It was just stripped, as if someone had come in and grabbed all the things that could be deemed valuable in some way, and then left without a backward glance.

"It's all just…ravaged," Cora said through the link to Alaric, staring down at the pile of wooden scraps, long dried branches, and chunks of tree bark that were all that remained. "Why would they do this?"

She didn't even realize she'd also spoken aloud until someone answered.

"Not they," a deep voice said from behind her. "*He.*"

Cora whirled around, heart jumping into her throat. She'd been so taken aback by the devastation that she'd let her reading drop and hadn't realized that the sole human in the area was that close. She turned to face him, hand on the hilt of her sword, but hesitated before drawing the blade. This man didn't seem like a threat. He just seemed ordinary—a lanky man with worn clothing and a cap sitting low on his brow. His face was grimy, as though it was covered in a thin layer of soot from the fireplace, but his eyes were clear.

"Did…did you do all this?" she asked, gesturing around them.

His eyes widened. "*This*? Ach, no. D'ya think me some kind of wizard, lass, to tear down scores of trees all by meself? Nay, there were teams of men who came to take down the trees. But they left when that work was done. I'm the only one here now—the only one needed."

"Needed for what?"

"Needed for me work, of course." He gestured off to the side, and she looked over to see a carefully arranged piles of wood. It was covered by a layer of material and through the thin spaces between the logs, Cora could see the golden glow of fire.

"You're a charcoal-burner?" she asked.

"Aye, that I am. Javid is my name," he said, giving her a little bow. Cora returned the gesture, even as her mind raced to try to make sense of this all.

"I'm Cora," she said. "So all these trees…" she waved a hand to indicate the devastated spread of land, "will be converted into charcoal?"

"Not just 'will be,' lass. Most of them already have been. I've been here for weeks already, ye understand. Most of me work is already done. There's only that pile of lumber left," he said, indicating a stack of wood that she hadn't noticed before, just beyond the kiln, "and then I'll be off to find work again. Unless the king decides to chop down more, o' course."

"The king? So he was the one who ordered these trees cleared?"

Javid wiped a hand down his face. "Aye, that he did. It's a right shame if you ask me, but no one ever does."

Cora's stomach flipped over at the mention of Onyx. They knew, of course, that he was planning something for Tenegard—she had heard that much back in Barcroft. She also recalled what Bram had said about him creating supply chain issues for the merchants and traders. But seeing the destruction of this patch of forest only made things more real.

"I don't understand, though. Why would Onyx want to destroy the forest? Was he looking for something?" She thought of the dragons, wondering if this was some ploy to draw out the ones that dwelled in the forest.

"Not looking, per se, more like found. The king saw the available resources here and what a king wants, a king takes. He has a need for charcoal to burn to make iron, to make steel, to make black powder.

This was all part of his push for expanding his armies and their resources."

"So he stripped the land bare all in the name of warmongering," Cora spit out, the words bitter on her tongue.

"Aye," Javid confirmed, "And it's not limited to this stretch of forest. North of here, whole families have been evicted. They had a village just inside the forest, y'see—a cluster of houses in a clearing. This area is known for its storms, don't ya know, and the trees gave them some protection. But all those trees are gone now, and all the homes, too. The king's soldiers seized the land they've occupied for generations, all so the king's soldiers could harvest the trees in the name of the crown."

Cora's stomach somersaulted and she felt sick. Onyx was building up his armies and destroying the country—along with people's homes and lives—to do so. It was enough to make the contents of her stomach pitch and roll.

"I figured some good might as well come from this, so here I am." Javid gave a little shrug. "The work has to be done. It does no one any good to just leave the wood here to rot."

Cora nodded. "Of course. Well, I'll let you get back to your work. Thank you for telling me what happened here."

During the short walk back to Alaric's side, she filled him in on what she had learned.

It is a shame, what the king is doing to the land, Alaric said. *An absolute shame.*

Cora couldn't agree more. The damage Onyx was doing to Tenegard hurt her as much as if he were actually there attacking her personally. She had never been a fan of the king, even before she learned what he had done to the dragon riders. But this…it made her feel physically ill to think of all the lives harmed, all the damage done, just to satisfy one man's ambition and greed. There had been no attacks, no incursions. There was no *reason* for them to go to war—no reason other than Onyx wanted to, no matter what he had to do to anyone or anything that got in his way.

With a heavy heart and muddled mind, Cora made her way back to Alaric, where she silently climbed onto his back. They said nothing as they made their way back south towards Tamsin's home.

By the time they arrived, dusk had fallen, and the sky was beginning to darken. Tamsin stood in front of her house with her hands on her hips.

"Well?" she asked them, as Cora dismounted. "How did it go?" But the casual expression on her face faded as she took in Cora's slumped shoulders. "What is it? Did something happen?"

Cora let out a deep breath. She needed to tell Tamsin about the dragon herd they'd spoken with, but she couldn't get the conversation with Javid out of her mind.

"Onyx is harvesting the land for materials to go to war," she blurted out, just needing to get the words out into the open. "It is…so much worse than anything I've seen before. Worse than anything I imagined." Cora quickly filled her in on what they'd seen and what the charcoal-burner had relayed. Tamsin stood stoically, her back ramrod straight as Cora described in detail the patch of land at the eastern edge of the forest and how it had been ravaged and stripped of all valuable materials and resources.

"It's concerning," Tamsin agreed once Cora was finished. "But sadly, not surprising. His efforts to gather supplies for war have only been growing. They touch the nation in a thousand destructive ways. This was not the first, nor will it be the last."

"There's something that I just can't puzzle out," Cora said. "How is Onyx going to justify this war? There's no reason for it. And yet he's cutting down forests and kicking people off their land and hoarding all the food and cloth and iron and steel that everyday people need. Doesn't he worry that the people will grow angry and rebel?"

"I think he is relying on the fact that most people still see him as the savior of Tenegard," Tamsin answered. "Despite all the evidence in front of their eyes, many people will not see him as anything other than a hero. Sooner or later, he will announce his reason for going to war—or he will simply announce that we *are* going to war, and everyone will assume that he must have had a good reason for it."

Frustration spiked in Cora's chest, and she clenched her fists at her side. "He's poaching from the land, creating issues of supply for those in Llys and likely elsewhere too, and yet still, the people are blind to the damage of his reign."

Tamsin offered a small half smile. "Not all people. There's you and me, for example. And the rebels, of course. There are many who can see past Onyx's false reputation, many who see him for what he truly is."

"Well, there's that," Cora said, though she still felt frustrated. She didn't understand how everyone had been so completely taken in to believe that Onyx was some kind of protector of the people he clearly couldn't care less about. It all traced back to the famine: the one that Onyx supposedly saved Tenegard from, leading to a grateful nation naming him their king. Raksha had told her the truth of the story. There really *had* been a famine—but Onyx was the one who had started it with his magic. Then he somehow managed to get all the credit for fixing a problem that he had created.

But whenever anyone spoke of the famine, it was only to praise Onyx. His magic, his strength, and his leadership were touted as the reasons why Tenegard was able to survive. There was also the pervasive threat that if Onyx ever *wasn't* there, if he ever were to leave Tenegard, the famine would return, and the country would be devastated. After all, the incantations that Onyx performed, with the dragon scales that he had collected, were what ended the famine and kept it from returning. The spell had to be constantly renewed, which was why teams worked all around the country to fill the quotas and provide Onyx with all the dragon scales he needed.

Or at least, that was the story everyone was told. Which…raised another question. Cora could understand Onyx hoarding lumber, charcoal, weapons, foodstuffs, textiles…but just what was he doing with all those dragon scales?

Cora's brows scrunched together. "Tamsin, I'm curious about something. The scale scavenging—is that legit? Onyx has let the people of Tenegard believe that the scales are part of the magic that keeps the famine from occurring again. Clearly that's a lie, since he started the famine himself, but what about the scales? What does he use them for?"

Tamin's face twisted with disgust. "Nothing, as far as I can tell. I do not believe he uses those scales for anything other than deception."

Cora suspected as much, though it was still slightly shocking to hear it confirmed. "But why would Onyx go through all the trouble of establishing the scale scavengers in the villages near dragon colonies and having the quotas be set and enforced if he's not actually using the scales for anything?"

Tamsin lifted her shoulders and then let them drop. "I have often wondered that myself. I don't have anything concrete to go on, but my theory is this: I think it's all part of Onyx's plan to make sure that humans and dragons revile each other. Alaric has told you why dragons line their nests with scales, hasn't he?"

Cora nodded. The scales were needed to nurture the eggs in the nest. Apparently, minerals in the scales were essential to the growth and development of the eggs—and to provide physical protection from the elements.

"Dragons are extremely protective of their young," Tamsin pointed out. "Potentially harming the eggs by removing the scales is a guaranteed way to make dragons hate humans. And because humans don't understand the severity of what they're doing, and only see dragons behaving violently, they hate dragons, as well. By pitting them against each other in this way, it helps to make sure that humans and dragons remain divided, lessening the risk that they will join forces to oppose him as they did in the past."

"And the scales?" Alaric piped up. "What do they do with them once they're gathered?"

Tamsin shrugged again. "Like I said, I cannot prove it, but I'd imagine they destroy the scales the moment they're collected in the big cities. I think they're unloaded off the carts and wagons that bring them in and then reloaded directly into the mouth of an incinerator."

Alaric's top lip pulled back into a growl. "I find that quite despicable."

"As do I."

"But wait…" Cora held up a hand. "Scale scavengers get paid quite handsomely. It's the whole reason I wanted to become one in the first place. Why would Onyx be willing to pay so much for something that he just throws away? Why go to all the trouble of creating such demand and then handing over a bunch of money to fund it? Do you think it's possible that maybe Onyx truly is using the scales, but for some secret purpose?"

"That seems highly unlikely," Tamsin said resolutely. "Simply because the material in question is dragon scales." She said this as if her point was obvious.

"I don't understand," Cora said, looking to Alaric, who shook his head, indicating that he hadn't understood either.

"Remember what I told you about Athelian magic? Athelian magic and genante dragon magic just don't mix," Tamsin clarified. "Dragon scales have dragon magic in them—even dragons without Dragon Tongue or a bond. It's that bit of magic that allows them to form the herd link and communicate telepathically. And when a scale is discarded, it carries some of the 'memory' of the dragon that carried it, including that dragon's magic. It's why dragons line their nests with the discarded scales—the magic helps protect the young who haven't magic of their own yet."

"I thought the scales were there to give the eggs minerals," Cora said, turning to Alaric. It was the explanation he had given her, back in Barcroft.

He looked as confused as she felt, and they both turned back to Tamsin. "The scales provide minerals, too," she said with a shrug. "I suppose that if a herd of dragons had mostly forgotten about magic, then the minerals would be the reason they'd focus on for using the scales. But the fact remains that dragon scales remember."

"But…how can a scale remember?" Cora asked. "It doesn't have a mind, a body. What is there for it to remember?"

Tamsin chuckled a bit and asked, "Alaric, would you mind if I took one of your scales?

"Not at all."

Tamsin walked over to where Alaric's tail rested on the ground and plucked a loose scale from near the end of his tail.

"Even though I am not bonded with Alaric, I can still tap into the magic of his scale." She looked to Cora. "It's a lot like when you do a reading of the landscape. It's all about knowing how to look for the magic and how to connect with it." Tamsin covered the scale with both of her hands and closed her eyes, concentrating. "Magic is energy, and once you find the energy encompassed in the scale, you'll be able to reach the memory held within it. Keep in mind, there are only traces of memory, but there should be enough to allow you to glean bits of information."

She opened her eyes and looked to Alaric. "For example, I can tell you what Alaric ate for breakfast. Elk was it?"

Alaric chortled. "Indeed."

"That's amazing," Cora said, eying the scale. "Simply amazing."

"It is, but that is why Onyx can't use them. His magic isn't compatible. As to why he pays so much money for them? My best guess is that he's willing to pay anything to keep the people of Tenegard under his thumb."

Tamsin's words sank like a stone in Cora's stomach. It was beyond sickening—the notion of the king abusing his power so badly. But what could they do about it?

That is the question, Alaric responded through the bond.

That was the question, indeed.

CHAPTER 21

The following day, Cora and Alaric headed back out, flying east until they reached the area where the deforestation was occurring at the edge of the Meldona Forest. This time, they went further north, to the area that Javid had told her about where the village had been wiped out. There were no people around—even the charcoal-burner assigned to this area seemed to have finished his work—so all that was left was the debris of the stolen trees…and some debris from the torn-down homes. Cora found a half-broken plate wedged in a dirt. The remnants of a bedframe. The stones of a chimney. A child's discarded doll. It was all so heartbreaking.

They practiced using their magic to replenish some of the trees that had been cut down, manipulating the earth so that the seeds buried within it would sprout new growth. Unfortunately, since it was only the two of them, they didn't have a hope of keeping up with the rate of destruction. Not if Onyx continued reaping from the land without consequence. Besides, the trees that had been cut down had grown for decades or longer. Even with replanting and careful tending, it would take many, many years for the land to come anywhere close to what it had been before.

They did their best, spending the majority of the day at the northern blight—as Cora had begun to call it—attempting to coax life back into the ground. As the afternoon wore on, Cora's energy felt as depleted as the soil itself.

The sky overhead was dark with thunderclouds and a breeze that promised rain swept around them, filling the air with the tension that only comes right before the sky breaks open. Cora recalled what Javid had said about the bad storms in this area, and she shivered.

It wasn't long before thick, fat rain droplets began to pelt Cora's face and arms. Swiping at the moisture in her eyes and tossing her wet braid over her shoulder, she let out a huff. "It's no use," she shouted to Alaric over the sound of the now heavy rain falling. "I can't see a thing and it's hard to concentrate like this."

"I agree. Perhaps we should stop for the day."

"Sounds good to me," Cora replied, shivering a bit as a chill from her damp clothes went down her back. Going back to Tamsin's and rustling up a cup of hot coffee sounded like just what she needed.

Unfortunately, the sky chose that particular moment to crack open and unleash itself on the lands. The rain turned pelting and slivers of white-hot lightning sliced across the sky, followed by ear-splitting booms that echoed across what remained of the forest.

Instead of flying directly into the storm in order to head back to Tamsin's house, Alaric headed even further north, hoping to stay ahead of the worst of it. Cora clung to his back, keeping her head low, so as not to be hit in the face by the biting rain. Below, the forest and the valleys were unfamiliar—they had never traveled this far north before. It turned her stomach to see that several more blights appeared along the way, carving through the forest like a disease that was spreading, but she could hardly dwell on it with the thunderstorm growing more fiercely over their heads.

I cannot fly like this, Alaric said a few moments later. *It is much too dangerous for us both. I can hardly see where I am going, and it's getting to be more challenging to dodge the lightning bolts. I do not think it safe to continue.*

Cora's entire body was shivering from the chill and her knuckles ached from how hard she was gripping the leather straps of the saddle. *Let's look for some shelter, some place to ride out the storm.*

Alaric quickly agreed, flying a bit lower in order to scope out the land and look for a place to take cover. At first it was hard to make out exactly what she was seeing, but as she blinked rapidly, trying to clear the rain from her eyes, Cora gasped as she saw a terrifying sight. Nearby, a river cut through the landscape, its banks nearly breeched from the excess water from the storm. But the problem was a stretch of blighted land, the earth bare and unprotected—and taking on way too much water. Without dense tree roots to help absorb the rainwater, and thick-bodied trees to slow the flow of water, a heaving mass of it was sloping downward towards the river, which had already started to overflow.

If the rain continued on that bare ground that no longer had any roots to hold the soil in place, a landslide was imminent.

This wouldn't be a problem in a more remote location, but even the blinding rainwater couldn't stop Cora's ability to read the area—and she could sense a village about a mile downwind with dozens of people who were likely unaware of the danger.

Alaric! she shouted through their bond, alarm firing to life inside her.

I see it! he yelled back, as he focused on keeping them airborne. *How long do you think the ground will hold?*

Not long at all. We have to warn the villagers before—

A rushing sound wrenched through the air and before Cora could say another word, the shelf of land came loose, cascading down into the river and knocking it off its course and sending water, earth, rocks, and debris on a collision course with the town. There was no time to warn the villagers, Cora realized. No time for anyone to try to escape. The landslide was moving faster than any human ever could.

But not faster than a dragon.

Without hesitation, Alaric dove towards the river, flapping his wings as hard as he could against the force of the wind. Cora didn't even have to ask what he was thinking—it was the same thing she was thinking. And it wasn't a choice at all, it was simply what had to be done. They had to save the village.

Reaching deep inside of herself, Cora reached for the energy of her magic. It hummed underneath her skin, much like her bond with Alaric, and she pooled as much of it as she could. She took a single breath to be deeply, profoundly grateful for Tamsin's training, which had made her ready for this moment. A calm certainty washed over her, centering her, and sharpening her focus. They could do this—she knew it beyond a shadow of a doubt. As they raced to stop the river, Cora's magic swirled inside her, ready to be put to use.

We're only going to get one shot at this, she said, her eyes narrowing on the rushing waters. *Are you ready?*

I am ready, Alaric replied, his own body shuddering from both exertion and the hum of his magic.

Up ahead, the outskirts of the village were drawing closer, and Cora knew that they had to work even faster than she'd anticipated.

Lifting her hands for both focus and balance, Cora unleashed her magic, sending it spiraling towards the landslide like an arrow whistling through the air.

Gasping, Cora ground her teeth as the magic poured out of her, pulling at every reserve of strength and concentration she had. Alaric was there, lending his strength and adding his own magic to hers, blending the energy of the two until it felt stronger than steel.

She knew the instant her and Alaric's magic collided with the water because there was a booming sound that echoed across the valley. It was as if a massive wall had been dropped from the sky, preventing the water from careening along in its current course. Instead, the enormous stream of water and debris split into two, rushing both east and west of the village.

We're doing it, Alaric's voice was encouraging. *Keep going.*

Yes, keep going, Cora responded, feeling the pull of the magic so keenly it was as if it were linked to each of her individual heartbeats.

When Tamsin had first tasked her and Alaric with splitting the pile of dirt into two separate piles, the task had felt impossible. But now, weeks later, here they were splitting the oncoming landslide and flood and saving the village from complete destruction.

The onslaught continued, hammering into the barrier that she had created. Cora felt as if every drop of water, every pebble, was hammering directly against her aching head, but she gritted her teeth and held on as the gushing finally, finally started to slow. From a torrent to a rush, to a flow, to a stream, to a trickle, and then slowing…slowing…slowing to a stop. When the danger had passed, Cora pulled back her magic, her entire body sagging from exhaustion.

We did it, she said, her voice soft.

We did it, Alaric repeated, his own voice just as quiet as the aftereffects of using their magic swept over them both. Despite all the training and practice they'd had, they still hadn't quite built up their magical stamina enough to handle something that major and to Cora, it felt like she could sleep a hundred years. She knew Alaric felt the same.

The worst of the storm had passed—the lightning bursts and fierce winds moving on—but the rain itself continued. Flying conditions still weren't ideal and with Alaric's strength dwindling, Cora could feel him struggling to keep them in the air.

Maybe we should land, she suggested. *We can ride out the rest of the storm and then head back to Tamsin's after we've gotten some of our strength back.*

Relief flooded towards Cora through the bond and rather than reply, Alaric simply swooped even lower to the ground, making a hasty landing on the outskirts of the village. As soon as his feet hit the dirt, Alaric tucked in his wings and nearly fell over, exhaustion sweeping through him.

Cora told herself that she needed to move, to dismount and make sure Alaric was okay, but she too was so exhausted she could barely move. She didn't even seem to notice the rain from the storm anymore. All she wanted was to close her eyelids, which felt as though they weighed a ton, and sleep for as long as possible.

She was tempted to curl up right there in the saddle and do just that when an orb of golden light popped up a few feet away. Blinking, she rubbed at her eyes, trying to make sense of the light until her exhausted mind finally realized that it was actually the glow of a lantern, a lantern being held in the hands of a very-wide-eyed villager.

"By the stars," the man breathed, taking in the sight of Alaric and Cora. "I knew I wasn't seeing things!" He hurried over to them. "Are you all right?"

"No," Cora managed to answer. "We're exhausted and the weather is unforgiving."

"Right, of course," the man replied. "I have a barn not too far from here. It's large enough for you and your…your dragon to rest until the storm is over. It's not much—but at least it's dry."

The idea sounded like heaven to Cora, but as she eyed the man, she wondered if he could be trusted. His face was kind and there was no indication of a hidden agenda or deception in his eyes—at least none that she could see.

This man has offered to shelter us in his barn. What do you think? she asked Alaric. *Is it worth the risk? Do you think he truly means to help us?*

It is hard to say, but I do not think I have it in me to fly any more tonight. And if our plan is to shelter and ride out the rest of the storm, then this man is providing the means for us to do that somewhere markedly more comfortable than out here in the rain.

And if he isn't trustworthy?

Well, then I shall eat him for a snack.

Cora snorted a little at that. Dragons did not eat humans, of course. But the exhaustion was clear in Alaric's tone, and the idea of resting in a warm, dry barn was too good to pass up. If trouble came, hopefully it would wait until they'd had a chance to get some rest. She nodded to the villager. "Lead the way, sir."

The man waved them forward and together they trekked through the sodden landscape until the barn in question came into view. The structure was exactly as the man had claimed it would be, large and airy, but warm and with a sturdy roof to keep out the elements. Inside, there were several massive piles of hay. Several horses and goats were being housed within. Thankfully, the animals were asleep and didn't stir when they entered the barn. Cora wasn't very interested in finding out what their reaction would be to a large predator entering their space. That would be a problem to deal with *after* she had gotten some rest. Alaric headed right for one of the hay piles and plopped himself down on it, curling up immediately with his eyes closed.

Cora wanted to do the same, but she turned to the villager instead. "Thank you, sir. We appreciate your kindness."

The man pulled his cap from his head and twisted it in his hands. "Oh no, it is I who should be thanking you. I saw what the two of you did out there, how you kept the landslide from destroying my village." He paused, as though a little choked up. "I thought I was seeing things, but no, there you were, like miracles sent from the stars to save us all."

The words made tears well up in Cora's eyes. "We're not miracles, but I'm glad we were able to help. As soon as we saw what was happening, we knew we couldn't let the river destroy your home."

"And all of us who dwell in this valley owe you a life debt."

Cora shook her head, indicating the barn around her. "You are more than repaying us right now. We'll wait till the storm passes and then be on our way. What's your name?"

He smiled. "My name is Jameson. And you are?"

"I am Cora," she answered him. "And the dragon is Alaric." Cora paused, trying to decide how best to articulate what she needed to say next. "Jameson, I need you to do something for me. I need you to promise me that you won't speak of what you saw today. Alaric and I…well, it's best that other people don't know about us. We could be in danger if others find out. Do you understand?" It was an extremely minimal version of the truth, but Cora didn't feel like going into specifics would help the situation. All she needed the man to know was that it would be prudent for him to keep his mouth shut about what he had seen.

"Oh, absolutely, Miss Cora. I will not tell a soul about you." Jameson's reply was earnest, his eyes wide with sincerity. "After what you've done for me and for my whole village, it's the least I can do." His eyes flitted over to Alaric. "But would you mind if I ask one thing?"

The curiosity written across his face made Cora smile. "You want to know our story?"

Jameson nodded eagerly. "I never thought I'd ever see magic like that. I never thought magic like that *existed* outside of fairy tales for children. And I certainly never expected to see a human and a dragon working together. I was told all my life that dragons were dangerous creatures who would sooner eat our children than actually lift a claw to save us."

Cora couldn't help laughing at that, and when she conveyed it to Alaric, he snorted as well.

Jameson jumped, startled. "Can he understand me?"

"No—not any more than you can understand him. But he understands *me*, and I told him what you said."

"Told him?" The man frowned. "But you didn't say anything."

"Not out loud," Cora agreed, and then proceeded to tell him the whole story of how she and Alaric came to be bonded. Or rather, as much of the story as she felt that she could without revealing too many details that might cause problems. She wasn't sure where Jameson's allegiance lay when it came to the king, so she left him out of it as much as possible. And just in case Jameson broke his word and shared her story with others, she left out any details that would help anyone identify her or her father. But there was still more than enough to make a pretty extraordinary tale, if she did say so herself. Certainly, her audience had seemed enraptured by it, hanging on her every word.

"By the stars." Jameson shook his head when she had finished. "A bonded dragon rider like from the stories of old. I never thought I'd live to see such a thing."

"And now you have," Cora said gently, "but of course your silence is most needed."

"I will not say a word, Miss Cora."

"Thank you."

Jameson put his cap back on, preparing to head back out into the storm. "I'll leave you two to rest now, but if there is anything you need, please come to the big house and I will do all that I can to assist you."

Cora waited until Jameson had slipped outside and shut the door to the barn firmly behind him before sinking down into the hay next to Alaric. There was so much she needed to work through in her mind, but her body was demanding rest, so she did her best to still her thoughts and let the warm, dry hay envelop her.

Alaric was already snoring softly, so Cora closed her eyes and let sleep take her.

CHAPTER 22

It felt as if it had only been a moment or two since she closed her eyes when a loud bang jolted Cora awake. She looked up to see Jameson rushing towards where she and Alaric were resting, the doors to the barn having been flung open.

"Miss Cora, Miss Cora!" he called out, wringing his straw hat between his fingers. "You and your dragon need to leave at once. I don't think you're safe here."

Cora, still groggy from exhaustion, scrubbed a hand down her face and struggled to her feet. "What? What's happened?"

"Nothing yet," Jameson said quickly, "but I fear there might be trouble if you two remain here much longer. I went to check on my neighbors earlier, since it seemed the worst of the storm had passed. I was visiting with Neal, who lives down the lane, when Burke came in —and there's where I heard it."

"Heard what?"

"News that had come in from another village—we trade information and stories, ya see? Generals of the king have been canvassing the area, asking everyone about whether there have been any sightings of a dragon accompanied by a girl. It is said that these generals have been traveling through the Meldona region for weeks after a report of someone seeing such a thing."

Cora's heart sank. This was exactly what they had tried so hard to avoid, but yet, it had happened anyway.

"What did the others say?" she asked. "Did anyone see anything earlier?"

"No," Jameson reassured her. "The storm was too wild. Everyone had hunkered down in their cellars, waiting for it to pass. I only saw because my house was the closest, and I happened to look outside the window at the right time when I was fetching a lantern before heading down below. After that, I couldn't look away…but I'm fairly certain I was the only one. The others I spoke to all treated the idea like a big joke. A girl riding a dragon? Impossible. It's what I would have thought myself, just yesterday. But now that I've seen you with my own eyes, seen what you can do…" He trailed off, his eyes wide with wonder as though he still couldn't quite believe the sight of Cora and Alaric standing in front of him. "Well, now things are different, I suppose."

Cora exhaled slowly, trying to figure out their next step. Outside, the rain continued unabated. The storm wasn't wild anymore, but it still wouldn't be pleasant weather for flying. Still, she didn't see that they had any choice in the matter.

"Do you happen to know where the soldiers are now?"

Jameson shook his head. "I'm afraid I don't. Word travels slowly here and by the time it reaches us, things have usually changed or are not quite what was reported."

Cora nodded. She knew this to be true from living in Barcroft. The remote township hardly ever got news that was current—or fully consistent.

Alaric let out a low huff. He hadn't followed the conversation between Cora and Jameson, but it was clear that he'd picked up enough from their tone and expressions to understand the crux of it. *He is telling us that we need to go, is he not?* he said to her through the bond. *We cannot stay here.*

Yes, that's right, she agreed before telling him what Jameson had shared, about the soldiers asking questions.

Shadow generals? Alaric asked.

Probably. Cora shrugged. *If Tamsin were here, she'd tell us to assume they are—better safe than sorry. And that means it wouldn't be wise to linger.* Cora paused for a second, listening to the rain on the roof. *I think the storm has abated some. Do you think it's safe to fly?*

It is safe enough, Alaric confirmed. *Will it be comfortable for you or for me? Likely no, but I think it is our best option at this point. Additionally, if the soldiers are nearby, the storm will provide us with cover. They won't be traveling in this weather, and I doubt they would expect us to either. Dragons do not like being out and about in driving rain any more than humans do.*

Cora stood up and rolled her shoulders, shaking the dust from her clothes. It was decided, then. She and Alaric would need to put as much distance as possible between them and this village—and any other place near the border of the forest where they might be seen. Her body still felt exhausted, but the bone-deep weariness had faded some. The small respite in the barn had done its job.

"Jameson, I want to thank you for your hospitality. We are grateful for your kindness."

Splotches of pink bloomed on Jameson's cheeks. "It was nothing, just my barn."

"It was a kindness, all the same." Cora gave him a smile. "And we appreciate it. But we have to be on our way now. We wouldn't want to cause trouble for you or any of the other villagers."

"I will not speak of what you've done here today," Jameson swore, placing a hand over his heart. "Despite how badly I want to shout it from the rooftops, I will keep it to myself. It is the only way I can repay the debt I owe you for what you've done here today."

"It was nothing," Cora said, waving a hand.

Jameson reached for the same hand, enclosing it in both of his and squeezing lightly. "It was *not* nothing. This village, though it be small and not a lot to look at, is my home. I have spent my entire life here as have so many of the others. That landslide would have destroyed our very way of life, our family history…everything. But you stopped that from happening. You saved us. The others will never know what you've done, so I must be grateful for all of us."

The earnestness in his words and shining in his eyes made Cora's throat ache.

"If the soldiers question me, I will remain silent," Jameson repeated."

"Thank you," Cora replied, not sure what else to say. "For everything."

Alaric dipped his head in thanks as well, and together they said their final goodbye to Jameson before stepping out of the barn, both wincing at the sting of the rain. It wasn't as pelting as it had been before, but Alaric was right, it wasn't going to be a comfortable ride.

Cora clambered up into the saddle, securing herself and then hunkering down as best she could to shield herself from the wind and the rain. Alaric unfurled his massive wings and leaped into the sky.

As Jameson's village disappeared behind them, Cora thought of Jameson and his vow. *You don't think anything will happen to him, do you?* she asked Alaric through the bond. It had occurred to her that somehow word might get back to the soldiers that he had helped her and Alaric flee from the authorities.

I do not know. But I hope, for his sake, that nothing comes to pass.

Cora sighed. *Sometimes I feel like this is all happening too fast. I don't feel ready for what's coming, but still it comes. And we can't stop it.*

No, we cannot. Nor do I think anyone can ever be truly prepared for one's destiny. All we can do is face what comes with an open mind and an open heart and trust that all will be well in the end.

I guess I wish we had more time. But I think we will have to face Onyx much sooner than we'd like. She thought about the news Jameson had reported. *It's strange, though. We've been so careful to avoid being seen. How is it that the soldiers knew where to look for us?*

Is it possible that Onyx himself started the rumors, to try to weed out our actual location?

Yes, I suppose that's possible. And we have been near the borders of the forest a few times. We could have been seen without necessarily noticing anyone was there. But whether we were truly seen or it's just a ruse to find our location, it's not good news. It confirms that Onyx is actively looking for us, and he has soldiers in the area, whether that's by sheer coincidence or not. We need to get back to Tamsin, finish our training, and figure out what we're going to do from here.

A particularly strong gust of wind zoomed past them, effectively cutting off their conversation as Alaric focused his energy on keeping them level and airborne. Cora gripped the leather straps of her saddle, wishing there was something she could do to make this flight easier for Alaric, but there was nothing she could do and the storm was relentless. So, she opted to stay quiet, so as not to distract him.

They flew for a while longer—Cora wasn't sure how long exactly—but long enough that her stomach was grumbling something fierce. She hadn't had anything to eat, and her body was urgently craving some dinner. But as she glanced around to gauge some sense of how much farther they had to go, she realized that she didn't recognize anything. No sooner had the thought formed in her mind than she felt a sense of unease and confusion come through the bond.

What is it? she asked.

I am unsure of the way, Alaric responded, his words laced with worry and also frustration at himself. *Between the storm addling my senses and my exhaustion from all the magic use earlier, I am struggling to navigate. I fear I have lost our way.*

Another emotion popped up. Embarrassment this time, and Cora immediately sent a burst of comfort towards Alaric. *Don't do that,* she chided. *You have nothing to be embarrassed about. I don't think anyone could navigate well in this weather. We'll get back on course, don't worry.*

She could tell that Alaric was still annoyed with himself at having gotten turned around, but she also felt his relief that she wasn't angry about it. Trying to help the situation, Cora reached out with her magic, attempting to read the landscape below for anything familiar that might be a clue to their location.

As she unleashed the magic, closing her eyes so that she could better focus, she was immediately hit with a strong sense of life, a large presence that wasn't like any of the other animals that lived within the forest. *Dragons,* she realized immediately. They must be flying near to Aspen and his herd.

We should warm them, Alaric's voice boomed in her thoughts, also sensing the dragons below. *If there are soldiers in the area, they may try to seek out the dragons to see if they are harboring a bonded pair. If one of the shadow generals is with the soldiers, he or she would be able to sniff out traces of dragon magic—and since we spoke with them using Dragon Tongue, they will bear that scent.*

Cora hadn't thought of this, but she instantly agreed. *Of course, they deserve to know what's going on—and to know what kind of risks they might face. Onyx's soldiers seem to have an attack first, ask questions later mentality. I dread to think of what they might do if they catch a dragon alone—out hunting or exploring. Tamsin told us that the shadow soldiers' tracking abilities are unparalleled—particularly the one called Kadeem.*

So while Cora didn't exactly relish the thought of running into Galio, the pewter dragon again, she knew the herd needed to be warned. *There's a small clearing just beyond that grove of trees. Can you land there?*

Alaric responded by changing directions, making for the clearing. Even with the hounding wind and rain, he still managed to land gracefully.

Cora dismounted quickly, using her magic to read the area and deter-mine which way the herd was. She was surprised to find that the area didn't look familiar. It definitely wasn't the same location in which they had run into Aspen before, but she reasoned that the herd was likely hunting—or perhaps this area provided better shelter against the storm.

They hadn't walked for very long when Cora felt a strong presence. One of the dragons was close, very close, in fact.

"Hello," Cora called out, making her presence known. "It's Cora and Alaric. We met with Elian and Aspen earlier. And we need to pass along a message."

The dragon did not emerge, though she could feel its presence behind a large outcropping of rock several feet away.

"We won't hurt you," she tried again, thinking it might be one of the more timid dragons. "We're here as allies with an important message. Could you take us to Elian?"

Still, the dragon did not step out from behind its stone shelter.

"Let me try," Alaric said, and called out to the dragon behind the rock, the sound low and grumbly.

This time the dragon responded with a low growl. The hairs on the back of Cora's neck stood up, and a layer of gooseflesh popped up on her arms. This wasn't a sound of welcome, nor was it anything that Cora's magic or knowledge of Dragon Tongue could translate. It wasn't a word, it was a warning.

"Alaric?" she whispered, not understanding what was going on.

Alaric didn't respond; his head cocked as he tried to listen for what the other dragon was saying.

"Alaric, I think something's wrong," she whispered again, though a little louder this time.

Alaric tried again to call out to the dragon.

There was a brief pause and then there was movement as a male dragon with dark-colored scales stepped out from behind the outcropping. His ears were lying flat against his head and his top lip was pulled back over a row of sharp, gleaming white teeth.

Cora sucked in a breath, her heart pounding, but she told herself not to be afraid. Of course, the dragon was defensive, maybe even a little aggressive. They were strangers, and dragons had every reason to think of humans as their enemies. She reminded herself that Alaric had reacted the same way when they'd first met.

She took a step forward, holding up her hands in what she hoped was a non-threatening gesture. And then, using everything she knew about Dragon Tongue, she focused on the symbols that she thought would do the best job of conveying her intent as she spoke again.

"My name is Cora," she said slowly. "We won't hurt you. We're here to help." She kept it short and simple, remembering how it had taken some time before she and Alaric had been able to communicate. She hadn't known much about Dragon Tongue then, which had been part of the problem—but the other part of the issue was that Alaric's herd had been isolated from the magic for too long. That might be the issue with this dragon, too. Surely if she had patience and stayed focused and resolute, the Dragon Tongue would connect, and they'd be able to understand each other at last.

The dragon responded by showing even more of its teeth.

Cora stepped backward, inching closer to Alaric. "I don't think this is one of Elian's herd," she said. "If it were, he would already be able to understand me."

"It must be one from the wild herd Elian spoke of, the ones who he said had gone feral. I had not realized that Dragon Tongue would have *no* effect on them. We should go."

Cora shook her head. "If we just keep talking to it, then I think it will unlock the magic. Just because he'd harder to reach doesn't mean he's unreachable. We can bring the magic back to the herd."

Cora tried again, but no matter what she said or how hard she concentrated, the dragon continued to ignore her words—and to make aggressive moves as if preparing to attack.

Then, to make things worse, three more dragons emerged from the shadows.

Now they were faced with four large, predatory dragons, all wild and snarling. Every one of them seemed to be entirely deaf to the Dragon Tongue, and equally aggressive. For the first time in months, Cora found herself genuinely afraid to be in the presence of a dragon.

One lunged forward, snapping its jaws in an attempt to bite Cora's head off. Alaric threw himself in front of Cora and let his own snarl loose, echoing across the trees.

"Please," Cora implored the dragons. "We're not here to hurt you!" But her words meant nothing to the animals as they moved closer, clearly getting ready to pounce.

"Get on my back, Cora," Alaric growled, not taking his eyes off the wild dragons. "Now." The word was a command and Cora followed it, leaping into the saddle and securing herself quickly.

"I don't know what they will do," Alaric admitted, "but I'm going to make a break for it so hold on as tightly as you can."

Cora gripped the leather straps of the saddle and nodded. "I'm ready."

Just as the first dragon made his move, Alaric sprang into action, dodging the strike and whipping around so fast Cora felt as if she had whiplash. Were it not for Alaric's warning to hold on tight, she might have been tossed from his back during the maneuver.

And then Alaric was running, through the trees and back the way they had come, heading for the clearing that would allow them enough open air to take flight once more.

Bracing herself as best she could despite their breakneck pace, Cora turned to look behind them, reading the area they had left with her magic. She could sense the dragons easily—four large, heavy, angry forms…who were charging forward, heading their way.

"Alaric!" Cora cried out. "They're following us!"

Alaric did not respond, only picked up his pace, running as fast as he could. But Cora could tell that it wouldn't be enough. The four dragons were just as fast and just as agile as Alaric—and they weren't exhausted from a huge show of magic followed by a long flight over the forest. The others *would* catch up—and she and Alaric would be heavily outnumbered.

They made it to the clearing and Alaric leaped into the air—only to have the other four dragons immediately take flight as well. One of the dragons, the one in the front, got close enough to make a lunge for Alaric's tail. Cora squealed as its teeth just narrowly missed finding purchase.

"We have to do something," she said, already reaching within her for her magic. She quickly ran through what she had the strength and capacity for, and what would be most effective. Water wouldn't do any good, of course. They were all soaked already from the rain that still hadn't stopped. Air might push them back for a moment, but she doubted it would deter them. Even wild dragons knew how to fly through the wind. Earth wasn't feasible now that they were in the air.

Fire? Alaric suggested.

She grinned. *You read my mind. Ready?*

Ready, he confirmed.

With a deep breath, she settled her mind as best she could, forcing herself to concentrate as she delved deeply into the bond between them and pulled up the power of fire. The ball of glowing flames sat on her palm for a moment, illuminating the area around them, before she hurled it towards the lead dragon.

Just as she had hoped, its eyes widened for a split second before it let out a growl and leaped sideways. The other dragons looked equally startled and fell back, no longer as certain in their pursuit.

Cora pressed a hand to her heaving chest. "It worked," she breathed. "Oh thank stars, it worked." Wild or not, she hadn't wanted to harm the dragons. She had hoped that the threat of the fire would scare them enough to back off.

She still stayed on high alert as Alaric continued soaring through the night sky. Her eyes stayed closed as she focused on the area around them, tracking the other dragons as they got further and further away until they flickered out of her range entirely. Only then did she relax, her eyes drifting back open as her heart finally began to slow.

"That was…close," she breathed.

"And also incredibly risky," Alaric responded. "If that fireball had caught one of the trees, it would have likely caused as much destruction as Onyx's deforestation."

Cora winced. In the moment, she hadn't really been thinking of the damage the fire could have caused. They were lucky it had been raining. That had kept the fireball from causing any damage. She could only hope it also meant that no one had been out and about near the borders of the forest to see the light show she had put on—right at a time when it was doubly important that they not draw any attention to themselves. "We didn't have a choice," Cora said, struggling to defend their actions. "There was no way we could have outrun them all, and we couldn't have fought off all four. If we hadn't had fire to use, I don't think they would have stopped."

"I know," Alaric said. "It was horrible. I know that Elian said that they had gone feral, but I…I had not realized it would look like that."

Cora sighed, thinking about the whole encounter. She'd been so certain that Dragon Tongue would be able to reverse the wildness in any dragon…and she'd been wrong. Nothing she'd said, nothing she'd tried. had gotten through to those dragons. This realization weighed heavily on Cora. Not only was it incredibly sad, but it also meant something far more sinister: Rewilding could be permanent. Some dragons were so far gone that they couldn't be saved. Out of all the dragons out there in Tenegard—how many were lost forever? She had hoped that there would be a new age of dragon riders, a new dawn of Tenegardian magic once Onyx was defeated, but the odds of that seemed far worse now. The number of dragons who could bond with humans was apparently dwindling. Aside from Alaric's herd and Elian's, how many were left who could still be reached? How much of dragon civilization had been lost forever?

How close had Onyx come to his goal of wiping it out for good, until the dragons that remained truly were nothing more than beasts, as he'd always said?

Cora opened her mind, sharing her realizations with Alaric. She could feel his pain at the thought of it, and his worry over his race's uncertain future. The storm had finally abated and without the heavy wind gusts and cloud cover, it was much easier for Alaric to reorient himself and point them in the right direction. But it was with heavy hearts that they headed back to Tamsin's house.

"I don't know what to make of all of this," Cora admitted. "This complicates things."

"Yes," Alaric agreed, his tone full of tension. "Yes, it does."

They were silent as the world passed away below them, though their worries did not diminish.

CHAPTER 23
OCTAVIA

Octavia gripped the notebook in her hand, studying the symbols on the page. She glanced over her shoulder to check the window. The sun had already begun to set and soon it would be night-fall. *Perfect*, she thought to herself, as a burst of excitement swirled through her. The sooner night came, the better, as far as she was concerned. She was eager to get back to the courtyard, and more importantly, back to Raksha.

That was the dragon's name. *Raksha*. Octavia smiled, remembering how shocked she'd been when she'd discovered that she could actu-ally communicate with the dragon. She still couldn't quite believe it, even though she'd been conversing with her nearly every night for the last six weeks. Octavia kept pinching the soft skin of her own arm just to remind herself that she wasn't dreaming.

"There's a dragon in the courtyard and I can talk to her," Octavia said out loud, marveling at the words. She let out a happy sigh and returned to her notebook, careful to observe all the more minute details of the symbol sketched on the page.

According to Raksha, the strange symbols were part of an ancient magic called Dragon Tongue, which was what allowed humans and dragons to communicate. Mastering even one of the symbols was enough to allow some basic communication, but the more symbols someone learned, the more fluent and complex their communication could be. Octavia knew she didn't have a comprehensive list—all she had were the symbols that she'd found on those artifacts, only a few dozen in total when Raksha had told her that the Dragon Tongue symbols numbered in the hundreds—but she had made up her mind to commit all the symbols she had to memory.

After about a half hour of study, Octavia looked up from her notebook and out the window. The last remnants of the sun, the tiniest of orange slivers, were finally sinking below the horizon. Her body instantly began to thrum with excitement, and she snapped the notebook shut and leaped off the bed. "Finally," she murmured. Worried that someone might have taken notice of her visits to the courtyard, Octavia had started planning her visits for after nightfall when everyone typically went to bed. It was much easier to slip in and out of the shadows at that time, and lately, there hadn't been as many guards posted to keep watch over Raksha. Octavia figured that after the chainmail net and muzzle had proven effective in keeping the dragon grounded, the decision had been made that the guards could be put to better use elsewhere. There was still someone posted there during the day—mainly to make sure that no one unauthorized accidentally wandered back there—but at night, the corridor leading to the courtyard was often left vacant. Octavia was grateful for the lax security. The fewer eyes on her, the better.

Pushing open the door to her room, Octavia stepped out into the corridor, checking both ways before hurrying in the direction that would lead her to Raksha. The path to the courtyard was one she had memorized, and her feet carried her there on muscle memory while her brain whirled with all the thoughts spinning inside her head.

Stepping into the courtyard, Octavia let out a deep breath. The moon overhead was full, casting a silver glow that she could catch glimpses of through the chainmail covering. The mail glinted in the moonlight, and so did Raksha's scales as the dragon, who had noticed Octavia's arrival, hurried over.

"Octavia, it is good to see you," the dragon said when she reached her side.

Octavia beamed at Raksha. "You too," she breathed. "I've been counting down the minutes until I could be here."

Raksha cocked her head and Cora realized in an instant that the dragon hadn't understood her chatter. "Slower," Raksha reminded her gently. "Simpler. It will take time before we can discuss more complex ideas."

"Oh!" Octavia nodded, mentally scolding herself for forgetting. "Sorry." She cleared her throat and thought carefully of what she wanted to say. "It's good to see you too."

The dragon nodded in approval, having gotten the message this time, and Octavia sighed. Although she and Raksha *were* able to communicate, it wasn't an easy or seamless process. It took a great deal of concentration, keeping the symbols fixed in her mind as she tried to decide which was the best match for what she was trying to say. It required a lot of trial and error, and frequently, she got it wrong. Octavia could understand Raksha more easily than she could reply, but even understanding was difficult. Raksha often had to repeat herself, and Octavia had to make sure that whenever she responded, that she didn't speak too quickly or use overly complicated phrasing. They managed as best they could and had gone from only being able to share a few words between them to nearly full conversations. Still, it wasn't an easy process, and that continued to frustrate Octavia. Even now, she could feel the frown forming on her lips.

"It will get easier," Raksha said, as if she were reading Octavia's thoughts. "We just have to keep practicing."

"Right." Octavia nodded. "Practice makes perfect, right? I just…want this to be natural."

"It *is* natural," Raksha replied. "This is how it was always meant to be between humans and dragons."

"I remember." Octavia smiled, recalling all that Raksha had shared with her these last few weeks about the history of the dragons and the dragon riders of old. "And will you be telling me more tonight? I'd love another history lesson."

"I do believe I have told you all there is to tell about our history."

"Well, what about *your* history?" Octavia asked.

Raksha tilted her head, looking confused. At first, Octavia thought her words hadn't gotten through, but then Raksha spoke again. "What is it you wish to learn about my history? I fear I have not lived a very interesting life. Until I was brought here, I had stayed all my life in the mountains where I was born. That is where I met my mate, though I have lost him. It is also where I raised my son."

Octavia's eyes widened. "I didn't know you had a son."

Raksha looked sad when she spoke again. "His name is Alaric."

"What is he like?"

"Intelligent, brave, curious, stubborn. He can rile my temper like no one else, but he always knows how to make me smile. He is all I could ever have asked for in a son—and quite a lot more, besides."

Octavia's heart gave a slight pang at the pride in Raksha's tone. It was obvious that she loved her son very much. It was exactly what she would have expected from a mother. For a split second, Octavia thought of her own mother. She had died when Octavia was small and she had nearly no memories of her, just some faint images and flashes that she wasn't even sure were real. But still, she often thought of her parents, of what her life would be like if they were still alive, if she were not orphaned and then chosen to be the king's heir. And that devotion in Raksha's voice? Octavia couldn't help but wish that someone felt that same way about her. King Onyx certainly didn't, and there was no one else that Octavia was close with or had even been allowed the chance to bond with.

"Do you think he is very worried about you?" Octavia asked. She could only imagine how worried *she* would be if someone she loved was in Raksha's position.

"I am certain he is," Raksha said sadly. "I only hope he does not blame himself."

"Why would he?"

Raksha looked at her consideringly, as if trying to make up her mind whether to tell her something. Finally, the dragon seemed to make up her mind. "Because he is—indirectly and through no fault of his own —the reason why I am here."

"He's…what?" Octavia asked, truly taken aback. "How can that be?"

"The soldiers who captured me were attempting to capture him, you see. King Onyx had been warned by a soothsayer that the bonding would take place, so he sent one of his generals to capture the bonded pair and bring them back to him."

"Your son is…is…" Octavia stammered, "…a *bonded dragon*? But I thought they didn't exist anymore—that they were wiped out years ago."

"That is true—they were," Raksha confirmed. "My son and his rider are the first bonded pair in over a century. When the general arrived and tried to track them down, someone must have told him that a human had been seen with a blue dragon, because after years of humans fleeing from me at every encounter, this particular group was very eager to capture me. I am not surprised that they mistook me for my son. Our scales are nearly the same color."

"So that is why you're here? The king wants to find out more about this bond?"

Raksha gave a head tilt that Octavia had learned was roughly the equivalent of a human shrug. "I believe so, but who can say? So far, his efforts have been confined to trying to communicate with me. But as he has been completely unsuccessful, I really have no idea what questions he has been trying to ask."

"The king has been learning Dragon Tongue?" Octavia asked, shocked.

Raksha snorted. "The king has been *attempting* to learn Dragon Tongue. But thus far, he has not mastered even the most basic level of communication, no matter how hard he has tried." Raksha shuddered. "There were even times when I felt as though he was attempting to inflict his own magic on me as a means of forcing communication, but it did not work. We dragons have magic of our own, and I believe mine repelled his. I have always been told that Athelian and Tenegardian magic are not compatible, and that does seem to be true. I am grateful for it in this case, though during his attempted interrogations, I often feared how he might respond to his failure. The more he tried to speak with me, the more obvious it was that he would not succeed, and this made him angry."

This time it was Octavia who shuddered. She had seen King Onyx angry before, and it was not something she cared to witness.

"He tried for several days, but then he stopped coming to visit me."

"That's because he left," Octavia explained. "He said he was traveling westward because he needed more information about whatever—"

She stopped mid-sentence as a realization slammed into her. "He meant you." Her eyes widened. "I just assumed his travel plans were related to troop movements or something like that, but if he was trying to figure out how to force communicate with you, then that must be the information he's attempting to find."

"It's a reasonable conclusion," Raksha agreed. "Let us hope his search takes him a very, very long time."

Octavia couldn't help but smile at the wry humor in the dragon's tone. "If nothing else, I am glad you are spared his interrogations while he is gone."

"*His* interrogations, yes," Raksha said. "But since the king stopped visiting me, there have been others who have tried, two very unsettling figures."

Octavia groaned. She didn't need Raksha to elaborate to know that she meant Lanius and Nedra. "They're two of King Onyx's generals. I don't like them."

Raksha let out a growl. "I do not like them either. In the time that King Onyx has been absent, they have come nearly every day attempting to speak with me, but much like Onyx, they are unsuccessful."

"So they can't use Dragon Tongue either."

"No, it appears they cannot."

"But isn't that strange?" Octavia asked. "If the symbols in my notebook are the key to Dragon Tongue, then Onyx should know of them. After all, it was in his castle that I found the artifacts that included them. And it was sheer luck that I happened to write them down and then brought them here to show them to you. But Onyx has encountered dragon riders before, back when he first came to Tenegard. Not to mention, he is a great scholar with access to all the works of literature in the country. Surely he must have an idea of how Dragon Tongue is meant to work. So why would he struggle to achieve it?"

"I do not know, but I am glad that he cannot. I do not know that I would still be here if he were able to communicate with me freely."

Octavia understood her meaning. Onyx hated the dragons, that much was evident in the way he always talked about them. Raksha's current safety came only from the fact that Onyx needed information from her. Once communication became possible, he would get that information—by any means—and then Raksha would be of no further use for him anymore. The thought made Octavia's stomach churn with nausea.

"I have to get you out of here," Octavia looked Raksha in the eye. "Before he figures it out. I'll do what I can to help you." She reached up and touched the muzzle that still covered Raksha's mouth and jaw. After discussing it with Raksha and describing to the dragon the parts that she wasn't able to see—which included Athelian symbols carved into the material—they had concluded that the magic of the device was designed to weaken Raksha, physically and magically. Not only did it make her less capable of fighting the guards, but it cut off the internal magic that allowed dragons to communicate with one another telepathically. It was a terrible device, and if Octavia could have gotten rid of it altogether, she would have done so gladly. Unfortunately, if she was understanding the symbols correctly, there was a sort of alarm built into the fastener of the muzzle. If it was removed, the one who had set the magic would be notified. They couldn't afford to remove the muzzle until the time came to set Raksha free for good.

"I think I can remove this fairly easily, once everything else is in place —but the chainmail," she pointed overhead, "I think that one might be a bit trickier."

"Are you friendly with any of the guards?" Raksha asked, "Could any of them help you?"

"No," Octavia said, with a shake of her head. "There's no one that I would trust to aid us without turning me in to their superiors, I'm sorry to say. If we do this, we'll have to figure it out on our own."

Raksha lowered her head and eyed Octavia. "Before we go any further, I have to ask, are you sure you want to do this? To help me escape would be treason, would it not?"

Octavia considered the question before answering. "It might be. The king definitely wouldn't be happy with me when he found out." An involuntary shiver cascaded down her spine, and she grimaced. "He would punish me, I'm sure, but I'm his heir. He'd be comparatively lenient for that fact alone." At least, she hoped he would.

"Please, Octavia, I implore you to consider yourself. I would not wish harm upon you, my friend. Nor would I want you to risk your own safety for mine."

Tears welled up in Octavia's eyes. "You think of me as your friend?"

Raksha laughed, gently. "Of course, and I hope that I may call myself one of yours?"

Octavia blinked the tears back as her lips split in a wide grin. "Oh yes, I would like that very much. I've never really had a friend."

"Well, you have one now."

Octavia nodded, certainty filling her heart. "I don't care what Onyx does to me. You deserve to be free from this place and from him. I'll make sure that happens, no matter what the consequences are for me."

Raksha cocked her head. "Perhaps there's another alternative."

"Oh?"

"Yes," the dragon continued. "What if…" She paused, narrowing her eyes and then, "Octavia, I want you to come with me."

"What?" Octavia wasn't sure she had heard the dragon correctly. "You want me to…leave with you?"

"I do. There's nothing here for you if you stay—only punishment or worse. You could come with me. Once we escape, we can search for my son and his bonded rider together."

It was such a lovely thought that it almost made tears fill Octavia's eyes again. Never before had anyone truly *wanted* her with them. And she could see it all so clearly in her head: flying on Raksha's back, soaring across the sky as they left Llys and all that she had ever known behind. Still, something held her back. She sucked her bottom lip between her teeth, trying to sort through her feelings. Life as the king's heir wasn't as glamorous as the rest of the world might think, but it wasn't a bad life. She was, for the most part, left to her own devices and she wanted for nothing. Sure, she was lonely all the time, but she was well cared for. She was safe.

If she went with Raksha, what would that mean? A life on the run, forever a target of the king's wrath? How would she provide for herself? How would she survive? She wasn't sure she was up for that much fear and uncertainty, despite how strongly she felt about her friendship with the dragon. Octavia let out a long sigh. "I don't know," she admitted. "I need to think about it."

Raksha seemed to understand and didn't question her on it. "I hope that you will. I know that what I am asking is no small thing, but if you wish a chance to be free of your own cage, I would like to give it to you."

Octavia's throat ached and she swallowed hard. "Thank you, Raksha. I promise, I will put some serious thought into it. But for now, we need to focus on the chainmail. If I can't figure out a way to remove it, then neither of us will be going anywhere."

They spoke for a while longer before Octavia began to yawn so much that she could hardly get through a single sentence. So she took her leave, promising to return the following evening.

"I look forward to your visit," Raksha said, bidding Octavia good-night. "Sleep well."

"You too," Octavia lifted her hand. "See you tomorrow, my friend."

Turning on her heel, Octavia hurried out of the courtyard and down the corridor that would lead her past the armory and on to her room. Once there, she kicked off her slippers and readied for bed. All the while, her mind whirled and spun, trying to sort through all her jumbled thoughts.

Plopping down on the bed, Octavia eyed the feather pillows. She knew she should lie down and attempt sleep, but she also knew with the way her mind was spinning that sleep wasn't likely to come—not until she had figured things out. So, she snatched up one of her note-books and nestled herself down in one of the lush armchairs next to the hearth.

She quickly scanned through the list of everyone she knew in the fortress, but unfortunately, the list was small and there wasn't a single human on it that she felt she could truly trust. The ladies' maids who helped her get ready in the mornings were the ones she was closest with, Helda especially, but Octavia couldn't imagine that any of them had much knowledge of the chainmail netting nor how to remove it. She also wasn't sure how the maids would react if she started asking questions about it. If they thought she was considering doing some-thing dangerous, they would likely send word to Onyx or inform one of his generals—not out of malice, but in an attempt to protect her from harming herself. The same problem would happen if she approached one of the guards. In fact, her odds were even lower of convincing one of the guards to help because a guard would actually know what the chainmail net was covering, and none of them would risk a dragon being set free. No, she couldn't trust the guards. She couldn't trust anyone, not with this.

And if asking for help was out, the only other alternative was to figure out a way to bring down the netting on her own. It wasn't magical, as far as she and Raksha had been able to tell. When it came to magic, it seemed that the king relied solely on the muzzle to keep the dragon in check. So, in Octavia's mind, the best way to deal with the chainmail netting was to simply cut through it, creating a hole big enough for Raksha to fly through. But that was easier said than done. Chainmail was incredibly durable. She would need a special tool to cut through it —and locating such a tool would not be easy. There might be something suitable in the armory, but she wouldn't know what she was looking for, which meant she'd have to ask for help…and asking questions would draw too much unwanted attention. She would need to get the tool some other way.

Suddenly, she remembered arriving at the fortress all those weeks ago. When the carriage had pulled up to the gates, she'd noticed a square full of shops. While she couldn't be sure, she felt pretty confident that she had seen the sign indicating a blacksmith's shop. She had enough money to commission a custom piece from a blacksmith. King Onyx had told her to stay within the walls of the fortress while he was away, but Octavia had been dying to explore the city and this gave her the perfect excuse.

Now, she had to come up with some sort of design or plan for what she needed.

Sketching in her notebook, Octavia drew out the specs for what seemed to her to be the type of tool she needed—two sharp, curved blades that were attached to two handles with compound hinges in order to maximize the force behind each cut. The cutters would hopefully be strong enough to slice through the chainmail netting.

Satisfied with her drawing, Octavia closed her notebook and returned it to the bedside table before climbing back into bed and finally snuggling down under the duvet cover. With her mind somewhat assuaged, sleep began to fall on her and she closed her eyes, inhaling deeply.

I'll find the blacksmith and have the special cutters made. And then I'll free Raksha. Whether I'll join her...well, I have until then to decide.

With the plan set, Octavia rolled over and allowed herself to sink into a deep, dreamless sleep.

CHAPTER 24

The sun had already long since risen by the time Alaric finally crested the patch of forest that housed Tamsin's residence. They had gotten so turned around that it had taken them hours to get back. As tired as she was, part of Cora was grateful for the time it had given her to think. The night had been so chaotic—the storm, the landslide, the news that soldiers were nearby and looking for them, and finally the realization that some dragons were incurably feral, beyond the point of saving. It was a lot to process. And she still didn't know what conclusion she should reach.

I am here if you want to talk about it, Alaric said softly. *I don't want you to feel as if you have to sit in this alone.*

It's not that, Cora replied. *I know you understand, it's just that I don't even know how to sort through it all. It's a lot.*

Then let me share in your burdens, Cora. That is the nature of our bond, that neither of us faces battles alone.

So Cora began to tell him of the doubts that had taken root in her thoughts. *Onyx seems to be moving in on us from all sides. I thought we'd hide out here and get through our training safe from his scrutiny, but he managed to track us even here. It feels as though he's already two steps ahead of us. And we aren't the only ones in danger. Every day we let him go unchallenged, he does more damage to Tenegard.* The words tumbled down their shared connection like water. *He's destroying the landscape to mine it for resources. He's tearing villagers away from their homes or leaving them in harm's way when his deforestation causes landslides. And then there's the dragons. He forced them into wildness and now…* Cora broke off, choked up.

And now we cannot save them from it, Alaric finished for her, sadness exuding from him through the bond.

It's just a lot, Cora said, after swallowing hard. *Everything he's done. I know the plan is for us to face him eventually, but what have we actually accomplished so far?*

Please do not diminish what we have achieved during our time here, Cora, Alaric said gently. *While I know that both of us have been frustrated with the timeline, every day has been spent training and learning new skills—skills that we will be able to use to fight Onyx when the time comes.*

Cora sighed. *I know. Deep down, I know that our being here was the exact right thing to do, but it just feels like Onyx has done so much, and we just stood by and let it happen instead of standing up to fight.*

What about what we did with the landslide? That would not have been possible before. And if we had been off in Llys, confronting Onyx, we would not have been here to help those people.

I know, and I'm glad we were there for them, but that feat says to me that we've gained enough control over our magic that we don't need to stay here any longer. Maybe it's time for that confrontation after all. I know training was important but with everything piling up—the danger in staying here if soldiers are already looking for us, and all the terrible things happening that we should be doing more to stop—I just don't think we can stay here any longer. I think if it were up to Tamsin, we would stay for an entire year or more to keep training, but the world will not wait for that. Neither will Onyx.

As she said the words, a sense of rightness filled her. *We have to go back to Llys and make a move to free our parents. I don't think either of us will be able to focus on what's coming if we are still worried about them being used as pawns against us. The word came through that Onyx left the fortress, so we don't have to worry about facing him right away. I believe that you and I are more than a match for the ordinary forces. We've trained enough for that and more. It's time we freed them."*

Solidarity and agreement flooded the bond. *Tamsin won't like it, nor do I think she will approve, but I could not agree with you more. I lay awake at night wondering about my mother, what conditions they have her in and if she is all right. If she is lonely or worried...or if she knows that we will come for her. I fear what will occur if she should lose hope.*

"That won't happen, Alaric. We won't let it. Besides, your mother is far from weak. She is a force to be reckoned with, and I know in my bones that she's doing okay. I also know that she knows that we're coming for her. Because we *are* coming for her, Alaric. I won't rest until your mother and my father are free."

Then I think we are in agreement. There is only one thing left to do.

Cora winced. "Tell Tamsin."

Alaric shuddered at the prospect, and so did Cora. They were both grateful to Tamsin for all that she had taught them, but they couldn't allow her to dictate their actions—or inaction—anymore. The longer they waited to act, the more time it gave Onyx to strengthen his position against them. If the shadow soldiers were already looking for them nearby, it would only be a matter of time before news of their increased powers got back to the king, especially after the incident with the landslide.

Cora thought of Jameson and his vow to keep quiet. She knew him to be honorable, but how long could even an honorable man hold out against shadow soldiers? And the soldiers *would* come to that village and *would* question every man, woman, and child until they learned what everyone knew. Even if only Jameson witnessed what they did, when the sun came up, everyone would see how the landscape had changed in a way that couldn't possibly be natural. The villagers might not realize what had truly happened—but Onyx would know. And when he realized the extent of what they were capable of, who's to say that wouldn't prompt him to up the security at the fortress, knowing that Raksha was connected to them and that they would come for her? No, this was the right decision. They needed to leave the forest of Meldona and head back to Llys. If they did not perform their rescue attempt now, the task would become exponentially harder.

Alaric landed in the small field they used for training, and Cora scanned the area, looking for Tamsin. She spotted her on the side of the house, performing her usual morning agility exercises.

"Well," Cora said to Alaric. "Here goes nothing."

Together, they crossed the field. Tamsin saw them coming and lifted a hand in greeting. "I was wondering when you two were going to make it back," she said in the way of greeting. "I assume the storm waylaid you?"

Cora nodded. "That among other things."

This caught Tamsin's attention, her brows lifting. "Oh?"

Swallowing, Cora cleared her throat. "We need to talk, Tamsin. There have been some developments."

Cora launched into her tale, and together with Alaric, summarized all that had occurred, including their time with the forest dragons, the storm, the landslide, all that Jameson had told them, and finally their encounter with the wild dragons.

"It was…a lot," Cora finished, feeling as though she had just run through the forest, given the way her heart was pounding.

Tamsin clasped her hands in front of her. "Yes, I can see that." She paused, as though needing a few moments to process the information. Cora wanted to give it to her, but the biggest bit of news, the one that would cause the most contention, was still to come. After stewing over it for hours, she couldn't bring herself to keep silent about it any longer.

"And there's one more thing," she said, wishing her voice sounded stronger. As certain as she was of her decision, she hated the thought of disappointing the first person to encourage and support her and Alaric. "We have made the decision to leave. We're going back to Llys to rescue our parents."

There, the words were out like a breath that she couldn't suck back in.

Tamsin's face didn't change, but Cora could tell from the way the light in her eyes darkened that she wasn't exactly thrilled by the news.

When she spoke, her voice was soft, but resolute. "I understand that you've been through a lot in this last day, but I remain firm in my stance where your training is concerned," Tamsin said slowly, punctuating her words. "You are still nowhere near prepared to face Onyx and his shadow generals. You still have weeks of training you need to undertake in order to fully master your powers—and if you go up against Onyx too soon, the only thing you'll accomplish will be landing in Onyx's trap. We have spoken about this before, and I thought I made my opinions on the matter very plain. We decided that you would stay here and complete your training and—"

"No, *you* decided that!" Cora had wanted to be respectful, wanted to leave without fracturing her relationship with her mentor—but couldn't help herself, and the words exploded from her body. "Alaric and I agreed to go along with your training schedule because we both believed it was the right thing to do, but that's not the case anymore. You can't ignore what's happening around us, Tamsin. Onyx is closer than any of us want to realize. It's no longer safe for us here. We have to move now."

"I agree that the soldiers are getting too close. This location is compromised—yes. But that doesn't mean you should go back to Llys. I'll contact the rebels, find somewhere else where we can go and continue your training."

"And keep running?" Cora shot back. "With Onyx and his men always on our tail? With them learning more and more about us along the way, catching signs of our training, seeing evidence of what we've done? What happens when his men get to that village and see how Alaric and I stopped the landslide from destroying the town? Once he realizes who we are and what we're capable of, the security around our parents will get ten times stronger, and we'll never be able to set them free. If we want to rescue them, the time has to be now.

"And if you leave now to go charging in Llys, you could jeopardize your lives *and* your parents' safety when Onyx takes retaliation against you after your attack fails," Tamsin fired back. "Because it *will* fail. There is a bigger picture to consider here. You are being reckless and foolish—which is exactly what makes me so certain that your training is not complete. This is what you do during our sparring sessions as well, you know. You rush in with no plan, no course of action, believing that sheer determination will be enough to win the day for you. Trust a battle veteran who has seen more than you can ever imagine: determination will not be enough to save you or your dragon. Not when you're up against a foe like Onyx."

"Then what should I do?" Cora yelled, throwing her hands in exasperation. "Should I just give up and declare defeat? Onyx has the upper hand—I know that. But waiting and training will not do anything to change that. He is *always* going to have the upper hand. He is always going to have armies and resources and power and experience that I am never going to be able to match. If I wait until I can meet him as an equal, then I will *always be waiting* because there isn't any way to catch up. He has what he has, and I have what I have—and that's going to have to be enough."

"I'm not saying you should wait forever," Tamsin insisted. "I'm just saying that you should wait for now—for a little while longer. You're right that he has many advantages, but every new skill you master is another weapon you can use against him, and don't you want to have access to every weapon possible? Your training is the most important thing. There is still so much for you to learn."

"I'm beginning to think that will always be the case," Cora groaned. "There will always be new skills to master and practice, things that we could work harder at, but Tamsin, I'm also beginning to think that no matter how hard we train or how long, it will never be enough for you. Why is that?"

Tamsin's nostrils had flared at Cora's words and a pink flush had crept up her throat. "That is not true. I just want to help you."

"You keep saying that, but right now, you're holding us back. And honestly, it's getting to the point where I'm starting to think you have ulterior motives—that you're hiding something from me."

At that, Tamsin looked shaken for a moment before anger took over. "Hiding something? How dare you?" Tamsin leaned forward, her face inches from Cora's. "You have no idea what you're talking about. All I have ever done has been in the name of trying to help you. I brought you to my home—I gave you my sword! I've devoted weeks to training you, and I'm prepared to devote months more, if that's what it takes. I'm doing all of this for you!"

"I never asked you to," Cora shot back.

"You didn't have to! I saw what you were stumbling into—I knew the danger you were putting yourself in, even if you were blind to it. I've been trying to save you from yourself since that first meeting in Barcroft!"

"You told me to stay away from the dragons," she said.

"Yes, because I knew what would happen if you didn't," Tamsin said. "I know what it means to have a dragon bond. You didn't, and I wanted to protect you from that if I could."

"Who are you to decide that? You didn't know anything about me. I'd wager you still don't. This is about more than just me and Alaric. I don't know…maybe it's about control. Maybe it's about something else. Maybe you're scared of Onyx and that's why you're hiding out here, in the middle of nowhere. Maybe you don't want Alaric and me to attack the fortress because you're afraid to rock the boat."

"Rock the boat?" Tamsin's face lost all traces of calm stoicism. Instead, her features morphed into angry lines and harsh angles, her eyes flashing. "You foolish girl! You have no idea what you're talking about, no understanding at all of what happens when you 'rock the boat' in Onyx's Tenegard. You think you know it all; you think you know what's best? Then fine. Leave. But when it all comes crashing down on you, don't say that I didn't warn you."

She made to leave, to shove past Cora and keep going, but Cora was feeling too riled up to let this drop, and she reached out to grab Tamsin's arm.

A strong sensation knocked into Cora, and she gasped as she felt herself drop into one of Tamsin's memories.

The memory showed Tamsin visiting the body of her dragon—the same one Cora had seen when Tamsin had shared a memory with her previously. It was lying in some kind of mausoleum—the kind that Cora knew the larger cities used for their dead. At the realization that *this* was what Tamsin had been thinking about during their argument, Cora felt remorse flood over her for the way she'd yelled. Of course Tamsin was sensitive to the idea of anyone running up against Onyx. She might be overprotective, but it was just because she wanted to spare Cora and Alaric the pain she had experienced, losing her bonded partner. Cora was just about to release her hand and apologize to Tamsin when she realized something.

The dragon in the memory she was seeing…it was lying in a mausoleum, but it wasn't completely still. Its large abdomen was moving and up and down in the rhythm of a deep sleep. Not dead, *sleeping.*

What in the world? Cora thought, her mind automatically reaching for Alaric's and sharing what she was seeing. He seemed equally stunned.

Tamsin's dragon is alive? How could that be? It was my understanding that all the bonded dragons were executed.

Cora could feel Tamsin's consciousness pushing back, trying to break the connection that had accidentally formed between them, but Cora just tightened her grip and poured more energy into the connection, drawing strength from Alaric. They needed answers, and this seemed to be the only way they would get them.

Cora pushed further into Tamsin's mind, trying to trace backward from the memory with the dragon to see what had led up to it. She touched on what seemed to be an earlier memory—a public execution with dozens of people lined up on a scaffold. Cora's blood ran cold.

Is this the execution of the dragon riders? She asked Alaric.

I think it must be, he agreed. Together, the two of them let the memory play out. They heard the pleas of the dragon riders, calling out that they were the defenders of Tenegard, begging for the citizens to come to their aid. They watched the jeering from the people, mocking their former heroes as the moment of execution drew nearer. They saw Tamsin in the memory, hiding in the crowd. She didn't join in the jeers and taunts. If anything, she looked heartbroken as she stared up at the others. But she made not a single move to defend them or free them. She just stood there, watching in silence, as the floor fell out below them and they were all hanged.

Cora felt as if she would be sick, but she continued to hold on, continued to press forward in Tamsin's mind. She needed to know *why.* What had happened? What had divided Tamsin from the other dragon riders? Why had she lived when the rest of them died?

There was another memory, almost buried in the back of Tamsin's mind. It was clear that the older rider had tried her best to hide this memory, to never think of it again, and she fought when Cora tried to pull it forward. But Cora was determined—and she had her dragon at her back, lending her strength and resolve to pull on the magic and bend it to her will. Slowly, despite Tamsin's struggles, the memory became clear.

"Please," Tamsin in the memory begged. *"I've tried everything, gone to every healer, but no one has been able to help. My dragon is dying, and Athelian magic is my last hope."*

Pain and shock raced through Cora's body as she realized what she was seeing. Tamsin was prostrating herself, pleading for help…at Onyx's feet.

"I could," Onyx said. *"Her illness is not beyond my abilities. If you turn her over to my care, she will live. But in exchange for your drag-on's life, what will you give to me?"*

"Anything," Tamsin swore.

"And if I was to demand your service to my cause? Would you give me that?"

"Yes."

"And your knowledge of the battle plans of your comrades—would you give me those?"

"Yes."

"And if I were to demand that you help me incapacitate the other bonded dragons? If my price was the defeat of the dragon riders so that I could rule uncontested, would you give me that?"

"I..." Tamsin hesitated for a long beat. But then, slowly, she nodded. *"Yes."*

As shock, horror, and an onslaught of other emotions ricocheted inside Cora, she allowed Tamsin to finally break the connection.

CHAPTER 25

When the images cleared from Cora's eyes, returning her to Tamsin's house in the Meldona Forest, the emotions were so strong that Cora stumbled backward. Alaric, who stood behind her, caught her, keeping her upright, but an overwhelming sense of sorrow and anger spiraled towards Cora through their bond and when she looked up at Alaric and saw the haunted look in his eyes, she knew he'd been just as affected as she by what they'd seen.

For a moment, no one said a word. Cora and Alaric were too stunned to speak, while Tamsin seemed stoic and almost resigned.

Finally, Cora broke the silence. "Tamsin." the name tasted like ash on her tongue. "You know what we saw, right? You saw those memories, too, as we replayed them in your mind." Tamsin nodded silently. "But you and Onyx…please, Tamsin. Tell me it isn't true."

Tamsin stayed silent.

"You…you betrayed them, the other dragon riders, didn't you?" The words came out broken, the mix between a cry and a yell, and it felt as if Cora's heart might burst. Pain and sorrow and anger and betrayal flared so strongly inside Cora that she thought they might tear her apart. "Didn't you?" she screamed, her fists clenching at her sides.

Tamsin's face lost all traces of color, and the cool mask she had been wearing slipped away, revealing eyes that were full of pain and regret. "You don't understand," she said, her voice hoarse. "I had to save her. I would've done anything to save Rivka."

Behind her, Alaric jumped as if he had been struck and an emotion that Cora couldn't quite place shot down the bond. But Cora remained focused on Tamsin.

"He promised to heal her," Tamsin continued, her tone desperate. "I didn't want to betray the others, but there was no one else I could turn to for help—and it was the only deal he would agree to make. I had to save her. I *did* save her."

"You…wait, is that why you still have your magic?" Cora demanded. "I thought the bond lived on even after the dragon died, but that's not true, is it?"

"I never actually said that," Tamsin hedged.

"No, but you let me believe it. Your dragon is alive. I don't know how or in what form, but she's not dead, is she?"

"No," Tamsin confirmed, "she's not.

"And you sold out the other dragon riders to save her."

Tamsin's lips pressed into a line, her silence confirming what was already clear.

Bile rose in Cora's throat, and she pressed a hand to her stomach as it pitched and rolled and threatened to empty its contents.

"I can't believe this." Cora stared at Tamsin. "I can't believe you. And this whole training thing…what was the angle behind that? Were you setting me up so you could betray me to Onyx too? Is that why you wanted to keep me here?"

"No!" Tamsin held up her hand beseechingly. "There was no angle behind it. I have only ever wanted to help you and Alaric reach your potential so that you'll be able to take on Onyx. No one wants his defeat more than I do."

"You know we can't believe a single word out of your mouth, right?"

"Please, Cora. I know what all of this looks and sounds like, but you have to trust me."

"Trust you? Trust you? You mean like the other dragon riders did before you sold them out to Onyx?" Cora shuddered. "No, I can't ever trust you again. You're a traitor. After what you did…I can't even look at you anymore. We'll be leaving now."

Tamsin looked downright desperate. "Please, Cora. Don't go. You have to understand, if you go against Onyx or the shadow soldiers now, you won't make it. Your training isn't complete. You're not ready, and if you don't heed my warning, you and Alaric are going to die."

"Well, at least we won't die as traitors like you." And with that, Cora shoved past Tamsin and stormed off.

Tamsin made to follow, but Alaric stepped into her path and growled, baring his teeth.

It took Cora only a few minutes to gather their things and even less to throw herself into the saddle on Alaric's back.

Without pause, Alaric unfurled his wings and launched himself into the air. Cora's heart was still pounding and her head ached from the thoughts and emotions still wreaking havoc on her, but she allowed herself one quick look back.

Tamsin stood in the same spot where Cora had left her. Her posture was slumped, deflated, and her arms hung loose at her sides. There was much too much distance between them for her to be sure, but Tamsin's eyes were locked on the sky, and Cora could swear that their eyes met just for a brief moment. Cora quickly turned away, a fresh wave of anger surging through her.

I don't even know what I should be feeling more of, she admitted to Alaric. *Anger, sadness, betrayal… I feel all of it, with each emotion fighting the others for dominance.* She rubbed at her pounding temples. *I just can't believe it. I cannot believe she would do that. She betrayed them.*

I do not pretend to even halfway understand, Alaric replied, his voice gruff. *To kill one's own kind like that…it's unfathomable.*

Cora agreed, yet Tamsin's broken words seemed to ring in her head. *I had to save her. I would have done anything to save Rivka.* It wasn't a good enough reason…nothing could ever justify doing what Tamsin had done, but there was a tiny part of Cora, the tiniest sliver of understanding that sprang up within her.

I can understand being desperate to protect your dragon, Cora said slowly, still working her thoughts out, *but Alaric, she betrayed all the other dragon riders. She watched them die. And she's been dishonest with us from the beginning. I just don't know how to make sense of that.*

A low sound rumbled in Alaric's throat. *I am not sure that you can make sense of it either. The thought of all those dragons being forcibly separated from their riders, knowing that they would be killed…* He shuddered. *When you were being held captive by the antiroyalists in Llys, I could hardly stand it. Imagining the worst kept me awake at night and made the daytime hours utterly unbearable. I cannot even fathom what those poor dragons must have gone through, suffering from poison and unable to defend their riders.*

Cora's chest throbbed and she pressed a palm against the aching spot. *I know, it's awful. I understand that Tamsin did what she did because she was desperate to save her own dragon, but I just can't see how she could willingly sacrifice so many others.*

Desperation can cloud one's mind.

Yes, but what of her heart? So many of her lessons to me told me not to get swept away in my feelings—to keep my thoughts clear. Is that what she did? Did she turn off her heart completely? Because I can't see any other way she could justify causing that much suffering, betraying everyone who trusted her. Is that what she was teaching me to do?

It was the question that haunted Cora the most. She had trusted Tamsin, and now all the time they had spent together, everything she and Alaric had learned from her, felt tainted. It made her feel like something was wrong with her.

There is nothing wrong with you. Alaric spoke up, picking up on Cora's thoughts. *You are nothing like her.*

But so much of who I am as a rider now is because of her. And I don't know what to do with that.

Nothing. You take what you've learned and you move on, do something good with it. We cannot often control our circumstances in this life, but we do get to make choices. And your choices are what set you and Tamsin apart. You can choose not to be like her. And I have faith that her choices are ones you would never make. You would not decide to save my life at the cost of everything I hold dear—you would never show my values and integrity that kind of disrespect. Do not let her past trouble you. It is she who must live with the realities of what she's done.

Cora exhaled long and slow. *Thank you,* she said. *I think I needed to hear that.*

I know, Alaric replied, laughter in his voice. *It is why I said it.*

Hot tears welled up in Cora's eyes. So much of her life had been turned upside down in the past few months. She was, understandably, afraid of what the future might hold. And yet, the one thing she was certain of was that she wasn't alone. Whatever she had to face, Alaric would face it with her. And that meant everything to her. *He* meant everything to her.

Which reminded her—back during the argument, Alaric had reacted strangely to something. Cora had been too upset in the moment to follow-up on it, but they had all the time in the world to discuss it now.

You don't have to answer this if you don't want to, but back there when Tamsin was telling us the truth, I felt something from you. A reaction or a feeling or something when she talked about her dragon. What was it?

Alaric let out a deep throat sigh. *I was reacting to the dragon's name. We have never heard it before. Or at least, I have never heard the name from* her. *Rivka is the name of my mother's sister.*

Cora's mouth dropped open as she recalled what Raksha had said about her sister, the memory sharp and clear in Cora's mind. She had said that her sister had been a bonded rider, but that after the other dragons were poisoned—killing many of them and leaving the riders vulnerable to capture from Onyx's forces—Raksha's sister had never been seen again. It had been clear that Raksha believed her sister to be dead.

Cora's mind whirled. "So that means…"

Yes, Alaric confirmed. *Tamsin's dragon, the one that lies in a coma, is the dragon I have heard so much about, the one my mother has always assumed died. She is my aunt.*

Gods above, Cora thought, trying to process this. *What will we tell your mother?*

I have no idea. But we will deal with that as the situation arises. Perhaps once we are with her and she is free, she can help us discover whether anything can be done for Rivka. In the vision we saw...my aunt still lives, but only in the barest sense of the word. It is not a life any dragon would choose.

Do you think Tamsin knew that that was what would happen to her when Onyx said he would help?

Likely not. Onyx seems the sort to pull a low trick like that—to keep Rivka alive, as he'd promised, but keep her mind and her spirit locked away so that she and Tamsin would present no threat to him in the future.

It did make sense. And now that she was aware of more of the picture, she could understand the hatred that had been in Tamsin's eyes and voice every time she spoke of the king. The root of her hatred was more personal and more bitter than Cora had realized—to the point where she wondered if Tamsin hated the king so much because it gave her an outlet to keep from hating herself. She shook the thought away. Now was not the time to preoccupy herself with that—not when there were more important things to focus on. Like rescuing Raksha and her father.

Scanning the horizon, Cora used her magic to read the area. *I think the herd has moved northward a bit.*

Yes, I sense that as well. No matter, we'll find them.

Cora nodded, trying not to let the nerves about what they were about to do get to her. She and Alaric had decided they needed some assistance, some allies to stand with them when they returned to Llys. And the forest dragons were their best option. She knew that many within the herd like Aspen and Elian would be open to helping them, but the naysayers like Galio would be harder to convince—and she wasn't sure how much sway they had over the herd as a whole.

They found the herd near a stream and were greeted warmly by Elian.

"Cora, Alaric, I am surprised to see you again so soon," Elian said, his eyes bright. "But, of course, you are welcome to visit us anytime."

"Thank you, Elian," Cora said politely, "but I'm afraid we're not here just for a visit. We need your help."

"Not just your help," Alaric added. "We've come to ask a favor of your entire herd."

Elian's eyes widened. "That sounds rather serious."

Cora nodded. "I'm afraid it is."

"Right, well then, let us gather together the herd so that you may address them."

It took several minutes, but soon Elian was able to pull all of the adult dragons together, gathering them so that Cora and Alaric could plead their case.

She started with the part that she figured would be most familiar to them—the danger that Onyx represented to Tenegard. They knew the truth of what had happened to the dragon riders—some of them had kin who had been among the dragons. And they knew the more recent damage caused by Onyx's reign, having seen the devastation he was causing to wide swathes of the forest. "As the first bonded dragon rider pair in over a century, Alaric and I feel a sense of personal responsibility to make sure King Onyx's despotism is challenged."

"You wish to take him on directly?" Aspen asked, sounding skeptical. "I have heard that his palace is all but impenetrable."

"It is not the palace that we will be targeting at first," Cora explained. "You see, before we can challenge him, we must make sure our families are safe. And right now, he is holding my father and Alaric's mother in the fortress in Llys. Before we move against Onyx, thus officially revealing our identities to him and the rest of the world, it is imperative that we free our parents."

"And that," one of the dragons called out, "is the favor you ask of us, isn't it?"

Cora recognized the voice, narrowing in on Galio, the pewter dragon. "Yes," she replied. "We cannot allow our parents to be used as pawns against us once we begin opposing Onyx openly. And to break them out of the fortress will require help."

Galio harrumphed and opened his mouth, likely to argue or refuse, but Cora beat him to it, continuing with her plea. "Please, I know what we're asking and trust me, the decision to come here and request this of you was not one that we made lightly. But we know how important it is—to you, specifically," she added sweetly, "to take an open stand against Onyx. The last time that we met, you accused us of hiding away in the forest, right? Well, this is the first step in coming out into the light. And you were so in favor of us doing exactly that, we knew you would want to join us…right?"

Galio scowled at Cora, but it appeared she had rendered him silent for the moment. She hoped that was a good sign.

Alaric cleared his throat, drawing all eyes to him. "I do not believe that my rider could have stated it more plainly. We need your help. I know this seems like a personal quest, but it would strike a serious blow to Onyx if we could overcome one of his strongholds—and it will show a country that has forgotten about the might of dragonkind. They think us beasts, as wild and lost to civilization as our brethren north of here, but we can show them that they are wrong. That not all are lost."

It was Elian who asked. "What of our brethren?"

Alaric and Cora exchanged glances. *So they don't know how bad it is?* Cora asked.

Apparently not. "We ran into them," Alaric explained. "And they attacked us."

"Attacked you?" The crowd of gathered dragons began to murmur unhappily.

"It's true," Cora said. "I'm afraid they've gone completely wild."

"They appear to have reverted back to our most primitive state," Alaric added before proceeding to detail their encounter with the other herd. The more he said about what it had been like trying to communicate with them, how they'd attempted to re-ignite the magic of Dragon Tongue to no avail, the more disconcerted the dragons became.

The murmured conversation among the dragons had grown in volume and now several voices spoke loudly, blending over one another as the dragons tried to wrap their heads around all that Alaric and Cora had shared.

"It is only a matter of time," Alaric called out, raising his voice to be heard over the din. "Before Onyx comes for all of us. Right now, his focus is on Cora and me, but if he realizes that your herd has retained your intelligence and self-awareness, then he will come for you as well. And whether to kill us or strip us of our will, we cannot allow that fate to befall a single dragon without standing up to fight back. Will you help us?"

"Say that we do," Galio's voice rose to match Alaric's. "What benefit is there for us?"

Cora fought back the urge to roll her eyes. Alaric had made the stakes plain enough, still, it seemed the pewter dragon was thickskulled—or perhaps just very self-centered.

"If your herd agrees to help us, then we will do everything we can to bring Dragon Tongue back to all the dragons of Tenegard," Cora stated. "To restore all the dragon herds to what they used to be before Onyx came here. We will remove Onyx from power and give the dragons the freedom to live beyond the forests and the mountaintops again, to live alongside and in harmony with the humans, as you were always meant to do."

"So decide," Alaric added. "We await your decision."

And with that, he and Cora stepped aside and allowed the forest dragons to confer among themselves.

"Well," Cora said to Alaric as they watched from several feet away. "That went better than I thought it would."

"Yes," Alaric added, "I, too, expected more resistance. But even Galio cannot argue with reason. He was the one who said that we needed to stand up to Onyx. Now, we are giving him the chance to do exactly that. Galio is old and stuck in his ways, but even he will not be able to argue that."

Cora nodded. "Well, given his personality, I bet he'll argue about plenty, but hopefully he'll still agree."

The discussion among the dragons did not last but a few more minutes. "We have reached a decision," Elian said, as he approached Cora and Alaric. "We believe you and we want our kind to live in a world where we are entirely free. We will help you free your parents from the fortress in Llys, and then we will stand beside you for whatever action against Onyx may come after that."

Cora's face lifted in a wide grin, and Alaric let out what sounded like the dragon equivalent of a whoop. The other dragons rushed over then, all of them eager and ready. Instead of nervous energy or fear churning in the air, the atmosphere resonated with something infinitely lighter and much brighter.

It was hope.

"So." Aspen turned to Cora. "What now?"

Cora grinned at him. "Now, we come up with a plan."

CHAPTER 26

OCTAVIA

I t was market day in the square and nearly every square inch of standing space was occupied by people either selling or eager to buy. Octavia's eyes were wide as they scanned her surroundings, and her mind felt as though it might overload as she tried to take in all the sights and smells of the square.

She wanted so badly just to wander from booth to booth, sampling the delicious offerings of fruits and meats and sweets and running her fingers along the luxurious bolts of fabrics, hand-blown glassware, intricately crafted jewelry, and more. She wanted to watch the street performers and haggle with the vendors over the prices of their wares, but time wasn't a luxury she had. Her business was pressing, and she needed to attend to it as quickly as possible. Hopefully, before anyone realized that she'd left the fortress at all.

It had been a pure matter of luck that the very day she'd snuck out was also a market day. She was grateful for the throngs of people that crowded the square, screening her from the possibility that someone would see her or take notice of her in any way. She had no idea if anyone outside of the palace or the fortress knew enough about her appearance to recognize her on sight—she was, after all, a far less public and familiar presence than the king, particularly in a town this far from the capital—but she didn't want to take the chance. She pulled the cap she'd stolen from one of the soldiers lower over her ears, looking around self-consciously. She felt rather silly in her clothing—black trousers that she'd only ever worn for comfort in the privacy of her own room, and a thick linen long-sleeved shirt that she had nicked from the laundress' basket. It likely belonged to one of the soldiers, and it was a bit large on her petite frame. Still, she'd felt it was better to don a disguise. Men attracted less attention than women. It was strange to be walking around in public without her full skirts and designer fabrics, but it was also rather freeing in a way. There was something really wonderful about the ability to blend into a crowd—without anyone knowing you or your business or even caring. That was something Octavia could definitely get used to.

Doing her best to move through the crowd, she was relieved when she spotted the blacksmith's on the edge of the square. No sooner had she taken a step in that direction, though, when loud shouting erupted throughout the air. Octavia's head snapped towards the noise, as did everyone else's in the crowd, but it was unclear from her vantage point what it was that was causing all the commotion. Soon, several voices were yelling, their words blending together as the people in the crowd began to push forward, eager to watch whatever was unfolding.

Just go to the blacksmith, the logical side of her brain urged. *Whatever it is, it does not concern you. This is not why you came to the market. You need to get to the blacksmith so you can help free Raksha.*

But her curiosity was too strong to be repressed. Something was happening, and she felt driven to find out what it was, her questions causing a nagging deep within that had her pushing through the throng of people to get close enough to see.

"This is probably a bad idea," she murmured as she squeezed her way to the front, but that did not stop her feet from moving. The voices had grown louder, and she leaned in to listen closely to their words.

"Our people deserve better!" a booming voice shouted. "We deserve a leader who actually cares for the people he rules over, a king who shares the bounty of our beautiful country with his people. King Onyx isn't fit for the crown that sits on his head!"

Octavia gasped, staring at the shouter: a man with thick brown hair and bright eyes who stood in the clearing everyone had formed around him, several men standing cross-armed at his back. All of them wore dark strips of cloth across their faces, concealing everything but their eyes. Disguises to help protect their identities. And with good reason too—for the words they were shouting were treasonous.

Octavia stared, slack-jawed, as another of the men stepped forward, rallying the crowd with cheers and taunts, much like the first man's, all about Onyx and his poor leadership.

"He has seized our lands!" the man continued. "He has claimed the crops from our farmers, all for the price of a pittance, claiming it is needed for the war effort. But what of the *home* effort? What of our families who go hungry? What of our homes that we cannot sustain? The woods have no lumber for us. The fields have no food for us. The stores have no goods for us, even if we had money to buy them. Everything is drained away into the army. And for what? So our children can be sent to fight a war we never wanted? Will he end up taking our sons from us, too, leaving them in Athelian graves?"

It's a protest, Octavia realized, unable to pull her eyes away from the masked men. She had heard about the antiroyalists—she had been present when some of the reports of their activities had been given to Onyx—but the king had made it seem as if these people were merely a handful of disgruntled citizens with chips on their shoulders. Irrational, petty individuals who everyone knew better than to listen to or believe. The majority of citizens, she had always been told, viewed Onyx as their savior for rescuing the country from the historic famine and leading them into health and prosperity. The antiroyalists were just troublemakers, speaking only for themselves and ignored by everyone else.

But that wasn't what she was seeing here.

"I have heard news from the village of Ravenshook," one of the other men called out. "A village that is already struggling to survive under the heavy burden of Onyx's taxation. A village that sent emissaries to the crown, pleading for help, only to have those pleas fall on deaf ears. And now the king has taken away even the protection of the trees that kept the town from flooding with every storm. It is only by some unexplained miracle that the town was spared from the latest deluge. I fear that the next news we get from that town will be that they have finally been swept away. And what does the king say? Nothing. When it comes to the war he wants, he is full of words. When it comes to the well-being of his citizens? He is silent."

The passionate conviction that these men spoke with didn't sound like pettiness at all. Their words rang with a truth that even Octavia, as sheltered as she was by palace life, could pick up on. And far from being ignored by the others, who supposedly loved Onyx, the crowd around her was hanging on their every word. She saw many nodding along.

Octavia's heart pounded in her chest, and she wasn't sure if it was fear that coursed through her or exhilaration. *Think of Raksha,* the logical side of her brain tried again. *You need to get to the blacksmith before someone notices that you are gone. Nothing good will come from staying to listen to these speeches. Better not to get swept up in it. Or caught.*

This time, Octavia heeded her own voice of reason. She was already turning towards the forge when the next of the rebels spoke up, his words stopping her in her tracks.

"King Onyx has painted himself as the great rescuer, a man who came into our country when its people were desperate for assistance. He wants us to believe that he cares for us, for Tenegard, but it is nothing but a farce, an image he throws up for the world to see. If he cared for us, he would show his care. Instead," the speaker paused a moment for dramatic effect, "his actions show that he cares for no one but himself!"

The words shot through Octavia like an arrow. The parallels between what the speaker claimed and her own relationship with Onyx were uncanny. She'd often wondered if the king cared about her at all, as his heir or even as a person. He never took much of an interest in her other than to give her instructions or admonish her.

It was strange to hear that the people of Tenegard felt the same way.

The rebel speakers continued, their words filling both the square and Octavia's thoughts as they detailed all the ways Onyx had been draining Tenegard's resources just to take even more power for himself.

The crowd seemed to be growing more and more frenzied as the rebels' speeches became more impassioned, their cries like fuel to a flame. Some of the details jabbed at Octavia, sending panic spiraling through her. Because the numbers were more than a little familiar. She was the one who had compiled the numbers for Onyx, listing the resources so that he would know how much of this or that a certain region produced. Apparently, he'd used that as a guide for how much of this or that he could *seize,* leaving nothing for the people.

Bile rose in Octavia's throat as she realized with horror that people had lost their livelihoods because of her, had gone hungry because of the reports she wrote.

Before she could even begin to unpack the weight of that, a loud sound erupted from the opposite end of the square. Soldiers from the fortress were spilling into the square. It seemed they had been dispatched to break up the protest.

Octavia knew that she should leave, but her feet felt rooted to the ground. The rebels began to shout back, urging people to stay and stand their ground even as the soldiers ordered the crowd to disperse or be arrested.

And that was when things turned violent. Swords were drawn and fights erupted all across the square. What started as a two-sided fight quickly dissolved into a melee. It wasn't until a man, nearly thrice her size, heaved into her, knocking her over, that she finally unfroze from her spot. She shoved all the thoughts ricocheting inside her head to the side, focusing on getting out of the way before she was trampled.

Just across the square, she could make out the sign for the forge. *Now's my chance. I have to get to the blacksmith.*

But just as she took a step in that direction, a hand wrapped around her upper arm and yanked her sideways. Octavia yelped, losing her footing and likely would have crumpled in a heap were it not for the strong hand holding her upright.

"Princess Octavia! Are you all right?" It was one of the younger soldiers from the fortress—a boy by the name of Phillipe. Octavia had seen him in passing several times. And apparently, he had noticed her as well—had taken note closely enough to recognize her, even in her unusual attire.

"Oh, I'm…I'm fine," Octavia replied, letting the soldier help her to her feet. She appeared to have lost her cap in the struggle and she swiped at the errant strand of hair that had come from the braid she'd pinned at the nape of her neck.

"What are you doing out here?" Phillipe pulled her closer to his side, steering her back towards the fortress. "You could be hurt or worse out here by yourself."

"I didn't know the protest was going to happen," Octavia tried to explain, "I went in the square to…to visit the market. I got in my head that I needed some new skirts and I wanted to pick out the fabric."

"Well, you shouldn't have come alone, Princess. Next time, please take a guard. If you had been recognized by any of the rabble, it might have gone poorly for you. There are many among the citizens who do not approve of the king's rule."

"Yes," Octavia said dryly, as the noises from the fighting behind them continued. "I've gathered that."

"Well, I'm here now," Phillipe said, keeping one hand on his sword as he led her back to the main gates. "And I will make sure no harm comes to you."

"Thank you," Octavia told him. She knew he was only being kind and chivalrous, but the voice inside her head was screaming. *It's not me that needs to be protected! It's them!* Still, she kept her face as neutral as possible. Arguing that the rebels had a point would not go over well with a member of the royal army.

Phillipe went the extra mile of not only escorting Octavia back to the fortress, but also up to her rooms, where he bowed low at the waist and bid her farewell. Inside, Helda was making up her bed with fresh linens. When she saw Octavia, her eyes went wide, and she rushed over.

"Lady Octavia! There you are! I was worried when you did not show for breakfast."

"Sorry." Octavia patted the older woman's hands. "I left my rooms early this morning. I wanted to visit the market." Given that Phillipe had found her, it would only be a matter of time before the entire fortress knew that she'd been caught up in the protest outside. She might as well do her best to control the narrative.

"The market! So you were out in the square?" Helda's hand clutched at her heart. "By the stars! I heard there was a massive riot out there. Some sort of protest by the antiroyalists."

"Yes," Octavia confirmed. "There was. It was peaceful at first, but then the soldiers showed up and demanded that everyone leave. That's when things got ugly."

"My word, and you were caught up in that? Were you hurt?"

"No, I'm fine," Octavia was quick to reassure her. *But there are many who are not fine, and I think it's my fault.*

Octavia let Helda fuss over her for several more minutes before declaring that she had a headache and needed to rest.

Once alone, Octavia fell back on her pillow and tried to make sense of all that she had seen and heard. Her heart felt heavy with guilt.

She needed to talk to Raksha.

CHAPTER 27

OCTAVIA

Raksha was the only one who might be able to help Octavia feel better. She wanted to leap to her feet and rush to the courtyard right away, but she couldn't risk being caught again someplace that she wasn't supposed to be. So even though she was incredibly impatient, Octavia spent the remainder of the afternoon in her rooms, counting down the hours until it was late enough for her to visit the courtyard and her dragon friend unseen.

Then, using the cover of nightfall as she had always done, Octavia hurried from her rooms and down to the courtyard.

Raksha's head lifted at the sound of Octavia's feet on the stone walkway, and she immediately moved to greet her. "Octavia! I'm so glad —" She stopped when she saw the look on Octavia's face. "What is it? What's happened?"

Octavia had intended to tell her everything—but the concern in Raksha's voice seemed to open the floodgates, and her words were washed away in a flood of tears.

"Oh, child," Raksha cooed. "Whatever it is, I am sure there is a way to make it all better."

"But that's just it," Octavia cried, wiping at her face. "I don't think there is. Not this."

Raksha lowered her head, eyeing Octavia closely. "I know that you are troubled and there is very little that I can do to help you, but I can listen to anything you wish to say."

Octavia smiled. "That's all I've wanted to do all day." Taking a deep breath, she seated herself on one of the stone benches facing Raksha. "I ventured out into the square today. I had intended to visit a blacksmith to commission a special tool that I believe will help us deal with this." She pointed upward to the chainmail netting. "It was market day, and the square was flooded with people. I believe it was for that reason that the antiroyalists chose today to stage a protest."

Raksha made a chuffing sound. "Antiroyalists?"

"Yes. They oppose King Onyx and his rule. The ones in the square today were quite persuasive. Even I felt swayed by them."

"The dragons have never held much fondness for Onyx, but I am surprised to hear that there are humans who are willing to stand against him. What is the basis of their protests?"

"They say that he is stealing from the people, that he is stripping the continent of all its resources to fund a war that nobody wants except for him—that he had forgotten the people and does not care for their well-being. And…and the thing is, I think they are right. Listening to their stories, I recognized the man they described. The disinterest he shows his citizens is the same disinterest he shows to me. I've known for quite some time now that he does not care for me. I believed myself to be resigned to it…but I think, before today, there was still a part of me that held out hope that one day the king, my sole guardian, would see me, really see me, and demonstrate some sort of affection for me. I wanted to believe that if I did all that he asked, if I rose to his impossible standards and expectations, that he might grow to care for me. But I don't think that's possible anymore." Octavia's voice broke. "He does not care for me, for the people of Tenegard—or for anyone but himself. The rest of us are all nothing more than pawns in a larger game. And that's not even the worst part."

Octavia took a moment to swallow down the massive lump that had risen in her throat.

Raksha scooted in closer, leaning into Octavia's shoulder as a means of comfort and support. "Go on, little one," she said soothingly. "What was the worst part?"

"I think I helped him harm everyone else," Octavia whispered, her voice trembling. "I wanted so badly to please him. He put me in charge of compiling reports of the resources in Tenegard. I provided him with all the information he needed to know exactly how to drain this country dry. Those people are suffering because of me."

"No," Raksha said fiercely. "No, Octavia. Whatever has befallen those people is not your fault. It is Onyx who chose to act against his own citizens. He is the one who put a plan into action that cost the people of Tenegard. Not you."

"Yes, but his plan was based on the information I gave him, so I don't see how that is any different."

"Would you have compiled the reports if you had known what Onyx planned to do with them?"

Octavia considered this. "I don't think he would have allowed me to tell him no. But if I had realized what he would use it for, I would've completed them in a way so that no one would suffer because of it. As best I could anyway."

"You see?" Raksha said. "That makes all the difference in the world. Onyx's choice is to use people until he has taken everything possible. Yours is to protect them as much as you are able. You are nothing alike, do you understand? Onyx's sins are not yours."

Octavia's shoulders sagged as Raksha's words swept over her. "You have no idea how much I needed to hear that."

"I will always tell you the truth, Octavia." Raksha nudged Octavia's shoulder with her snout. "You can trust me in that."

"I know." Octavia gave the dragon a small smile. "I think you're the only one in my life that I can actually trust." She blew out a long breath. "Which is why when we get you out of here and you leave this place behind, I'm…I'm coming with you."

The words felt so right—and in that single moment, all the hesitation Octavia had been feeling when Raksha first mentioned them leaving together disappeared.

"You'll come with me? You're sure?"

Octavia nodded. "Yes. I want to be where you are. And anyway, after what happened today, I don't think I can stay and be heir to a king who treats his people so callously. I don't want a single part in that."

"The path ahead of us will not be easy," Raksha warned. "As much as I want you to come with me, I think it only fair to remind you of the hardship we will likely face."

"I don't need easy," Octavia said, her mind made up. "I just need possible." She eyed the chainmail netting. "And the first step is getting rid of the netting. I didn't make it to the blacksmith today, but I will try again. I'll get the tool we need."

"You should probably wait a day or two," Raksha suggested. "If there is unrest among the people after the riot today, it may not be safe for you to venture out again. Certainly, I would expect the guards to be more zealous in ensuring your safety, so I do not believe you would be able to visit the blacksmith without them accompanying you."

"And even if I sneak away, there will be extra soldiers in the square," Octavia realized. "I'll be spotted, and I can't risk being seen out of the fortress again." She sighed. "I'll wait until I think it's safe and then I'll get what we need. And after that, we fly away from here."

Raksha let out a low, throaty sound of affirmation. "Together."

Octavia smiled. "Together."

The knocking on her door was loud and obtrusive. Octavia's mind registered it, but her body, still deep in the throes of sleep, made no move to rise from her bed. Warm, golden light beams peeked through the window, but it was early still and all she wanted to do was pull the covers over her head and go back to sleep. She'd spent most of the night in the courtyard talking to Raksha and had only just fallen into bed an hour or two ago. Octavia planned to spend the majority of the morning sleeping. But whoever was on the other side of the door was rather insistent.

Bam! Bam! Bam!

The knocking had morphed into more of a banging or pounding sound, and Octavia's eyes flew open. "Who is it?" she called out, annoyed at the lack of decorum the knocker was showing. She was heir to the king after all. She doubted the person would do the same were it Onyx instead of her asleep in the bed.

When the only response was another short series of pounds, Octavia groaned, throwing the covers off her body and reaching for her dressing gown.

She shuffled over to the door with a yawn and flung it open, her eyes already narrowed. But when she saw who was standing on the other side, her pulse sped up and she felt a jolt of disconcertment shoot through her body.

Nedra—the king's spymaster—stood before her, her cold, unfeeling eyes focused on Octavia's face. Octavia always felt unsettled when pinned under the woman's icy, assessing stare, but she tried not to show her discomfort, not wanting to give Nedra the satisfaction. So, she straightened her shoulders and let out an annoyed sigh.

"Yes?" she snapped. "Is there a reason why you're out here, pounding on my door?"

Nedra sneered down at Octavia. "I have word from the king. He wishes for us to return to the capital city."

It wasn't at all what she had been expecting. "Back to the capital? When?"

"As soon as possible. There is…cargo that must be prepared, but as soon as it is secure, we will be on our way."

Octavia didn't miss the small pause that Nedra had let slip, the way she had almost slipped up. Despite Nedra's discretion, Octavia knew exactly what cargo she was referring to.

"Well, how long will that take?" she fired back, playing up the spoiled princess act for all it was worth, knowing that it annoyed Nedra. It was the best way to ensure the woman underestimated her.

"Soon. Gather your things." And without anything further, Nedra turned on her heels and walked back down the corridor.

Octavia watched her go for a moment before dashing back into her room and slamming the door behind her. She'd managed to keep her cool in front of Nedra, but now that she was alone, she gave herself over to the panic that was building in her chest.

"No, no, no," she murmured, wringing her hands as she paced back and forth. "We need more time." But even as she said the words, she knew whether she was ready or not, there was no way to stop this wheel now that it was in motion.

Ripping her nightclothes from her body, Octavia dressed quickly in the first day dress her fingers touched and yanked her shoes on. Her hair hung down her back in the braid she slept in, but she didn't bother to do anything with it. She didn't have the time to dally over her hair—she needed to see Raksha.

Rushing down the hallway, Octavia did her best to move quickly without drawing any unnecessary attention to herself. There was a lot more activity than usual within the fortress, and it seemed that she was not the only one scurrying about after the king's order.

She made it to the courtyard in record time and was surprised to see that there were no guards on duty.

"Raksha!" she called out, running towards the center of the courtyard where the dragon lay in the sun.

"Octavia!" Raksha's voice was full of worry. "Something's happening."

"I know," Octavia said. "It's Onyx. He's ordered me back to the capital. Nedra came by a few moments ago. She said that we would be leaving as soon as possible, once some special 'cargo' is prepared. I can only assume she meant you."

Raksha growled. "I believe so, yes. I heard a great deal of chaos in the corridor. I believe the guards who are usually stationed there were summoned about an hour ago."

Octavia grimaced, understanding now why no guards were on duty. All available hands must have been called in—most likely to prepare whatever they had used to transport Raksha to the fortress in the first place. "They're preparing to take you to the capital."

Something flashed in Raksha's eyes, and she asked, "And do you know what the king has planned for me once I get there?"

Dread pooled in Octavia's gut. "No, but I think we both know it's probably not good."

There was a moment of tension-filled silence before Raksha lowered her head, leveling her gaze with Octavia's. "I need you to do something for me," the dragon began, urgency filling her tone. "Octavia, I need you to run. Do it now while everyone is distracted preparing for the journey."

Octavia jerked back. "What?"

"You have to go. If you are ever going to be free, this is your opportunity. I do not think you will get another."

Octavia shook her head. "I can't go without you."

"You must," Raksha said gently. "I will be well enough. But you deserve your freedom. Go and claim it."

Tears welled up in Octavia's eyes. She knew what the dragon was offering, but that freedom would mean nothing if she were alone.

"I can't do that," Octavia replied, her tone resolute. "I can't leave you behind. I *won't* leave you behind."

"Octavia—" Raksha began, but Octavia rushed to cut her off.

"No, please. Don't ask me to run and leave you to face whatever awful thing the king has planned for you next all on your own. I won't do it, Raksha. I won't. You are my first and only friend, and I won't abandon you like that."

"But your freedom—"

"Won't mean anything if you're not also free," Octavia finished for her. "We're in this together, remember?"

Raksha let out a sigh, but it wasn't one of disappointment. It was relief. "I remember."

"Good. We'll just have to figure out a new plan, that's all. We'll return to the capital and once we're there, we'll determine our next step."

"I fear what may come next," Raksha admitted, her body trembling just a little.

Octavia wrapped her arms around the dragon's torso as far as she could. "Don't worry. I'll do everything I can to free you. And together, we will build a new life away from all of this."

"I hope you are right, child."

Octavia let the warmth of Raksha's scales seep into her body.

"Me too," she whispered.

Me too.

CHAPTER 28

Cora's heart beat in time to the rhythmic pounding of Alaric's wings. She pressed a hand to her chest, letting the feel of her own blood pumping remind her of their purpose.

Are you all right? Alaric asked through the bond. *You seem unsettled.*

Cora let out a long breath before she answered. *I'm certain of our course,* she said. *I know this is the right move to make, but I guess I'm still nervous.* She glanced over her shoulder. Dozens of dragons flew behind her and Alaric, the various colors of their scales glinting in the sun like a rainbow. It was a truly magnificent sight, and every time Cora's eyes scanned the legion of dragons, tremendous joy and pride flooded through her body. But at the same time, she was plagued by worry too. And the weight of responsibility sat heavily upon her shoulders.

Nerves are expected on the eve of battle, I think. Alaric's voice was smooth and soothing.

That's just it. I never expected to be here. I never imagined that the path of my life would land me atop my bonded dragon, leading an entire army of dragons into the first conflict of a civil war. Cora's next breath hitched a little in her throat. *I don't know if I'm the right person for this.* And there it was, the truth that had been wrapped around her throat all morning, threatening to squeeze all the air from her body. *I'm afraid, Alaric.*

A warm burst of both affection and concern spiraled down the bond, filling Cora with a thousand tingles that felt like a hug. *Oh, Cora, my dear friend,* Alaric said, gently. *That is exactly why you* are *the right person for this. Courage does not come from the absence of fear. It comes from facing the unknown and doing whatever is necessary, even when it fills you with fear. If I were to give you the option of turning around, of flying far away from here and leaving Tenegard behind, would you do it?*

Cora thought for a moment, considering the idea. But she already knew the answer, deep down in her bones.

No, she said, with more confidence this time. *No, I wouldn't. Running from this problem wouldn't do anything to solve it—and the guilt I would face if I did that would be much worse than the fear I'm experiencing now. I cannot abandon our parents, the dragons, and the people of Tenegard. Onyx needs to be removed from power. He is like the blight we saw back there in the Meldona Forest—his greed is eating away at everything good in our country, and if we do not stop him, he will take from this country until there is nothing left. I cannot run from that. Not when I have the chance to stop it.*

You see? Alaric replied. *This is what makes you a leader. In the face of fear, you choose to put others before yourself.*

How did you become so wise? Cora teased, feeling some of the tension ease from her shoulders.

Alaric snorted. *Oh, I have always been this wise. I have just held back so as not to make you feel insignificant.*

His response made Cora throw her head back and laugh, a deep rumbling belly laugh that shook her whole body. From the vibrations coming from Alaric's body, she knew that he was laughing too. And that made the joy inside of Cora double. He always knew exactly what she needed.

Can I ask you something?

Of course.

Are you afraid at all?

The dragon's response was instantaneous. *Yes. But I am with you.*

Cora's heart swelled and she pressed her lips together to keep the tears in her eyes from slipping out. She inhaled deeply and waited until her turbulent emotions settled. She glanced over her shoulder again, eying the dragons flying behind them.

Okay, let's go over the plan one more time. We should be getting close, right?

Yes, Alaric confirmed. *We should begin to see the outskirts of the city in an hour's time or so.*

Just think, in an hour or two, your mother and my father will finally be free.

Alaric let out a happy hum. *I cannot begin to tell you how much relief that idea brings me.*

But Cora didn't need Alaric to tell her. She already understood it completely. The worry about her father had grown exponentially in the last few weeks. She was nearly desperate to see him again and know that he was safe.

Okay, so as soon as we get close, the other dragons will move in and create a diversion, drawing all the attention away from the back side of the fortress where the prisoners and Raksha are being held.

All the attention and hopefully all the military power, Alaric added. *And then while the soldiers are focused on the other dragons, we will swoop in and rescue our parents.*

Cora nodded. That was the crux of the plan. She just hoped it was enough.

A comfortable silence settled between Cora and Alaric, but soon, familiar sights began to dot the horizon.

We are on the edge of the city now, Alaric told her. *I am going to reach out to the other dragons and tell them to get into position.*

Cora gripped the leather straps of the saddle a little tighter and swallowed. "And so it begins," she murmured under her breath.

A few minutes later, Alaric fell back in the formation, allowing about half a dozen dragons to take the point position. In each of their talons were heavy stones that had been gathered from the forest. Their mission was simple: drop the rocks and debris from the forest on top of the fortress and create as much chaos as possible.

As the sprawling city of Llys began to whiz by beneath them, adrenaline and anticipation began to pump through Cora's body. Her fingers itched to reach for the sword strapped to her back, but it wasn't quite time. Not yet.

Below, she could hear shouts and cries coming from the shocked city dwellers. While it was common for the people of Tenegard to see an errant dragon or two in the distance, particularly in more remote regions, it was another matter seeing an entire colorful legion flying together in a battle formation towards the center of a bustling city. There was no going back now, no way to disguise what they were doing. This was a calculated and coordinated plan of attack against the fortress and King Onyx, and everyone was going to see it.

All they could do now was hope everything went according to plan.

Loud booms erupted across the sky ahead, and Cora watched with wide eyes as the first wave of dragons attacked the fortress, releasing their burdens onto the battlements below. Shrieks and shouted commands from the soldiers below mixed with the discordant growls and roars coming from the dragons.

The second wave of dragons shot forward, passing her and Alaric with their talons laden with more large stones and debris.

Aspen was among this group, and he opened his mouth and let out a mighty roar as he whizzed past Alaric, his wings pounding so hard the vibration made Cora's eardrums twinge.

The last of the dragons broke off, fanning left and right to provide coverage for any retaliation from the soldiers against the first two waves of dragons, while also doing what they could to keep anyone from the city from coming to aid the fortress.

And then there was only Alaric left, his wings still pumping in the slow, rhythmic pattern of their flight. But Cora could feel the tension building in his body as he steadied himself. She did the same.

It is time. Are you ready? he asked, his voice calm, but laced with the same adrenaline Cora felt expanding through her own limbs.

I'm ready, she replied, without a single ounce of hesitation.

Alaric immediately picked up speed, his wings beating fast as they hurtled across the sky. Below, the fortress was in chaos as people ran in all directions.

As directed, the dragons were focusing their attack on the northern parts of the fortress, leaving the southern side of the structure untouched. Soldiers scrambled to the battlements, their cries and shouts of instructions jumbling together as they tried to organize some response to the sudden and unexpected attack.

Alaric flew parallel to the fortress, searching for a safe place to drop Cora off. He found a side street that was empty, thanks to everyone fleeing in the other direction. Alaric touched down, and Cora leaped out of the saddle and off Alaric's back. "Okay," she said, slightly out of breath. "It shouldn't take me more than a few minutes to get to the gate."

"Be safe," Alaric replied, already lifting himself back into the air.

Without another glance at him, Cora raced down the street, heading for the fortress's entrance. When she got to the gates, Cora found that the few soldiers that had been left as guards were so distracted by craning to see what was happening that they barely paid attention to anything on the ground at all. Cora smiled. This was exactly what they had hoped for.

I'm in position, she reached out to Alaric through the bond.

And so am I, Alaric responded, only a second before his massive shape emerged overhead, heading directly for the gate.

The soldiers began to scream. Two of them fired some arrows in an attempt to ward Alaric off, but their shots did not even come close to hitting their mark, and as Alaric dropped a massive boulder on top of the gate, the soldiers stopped fighting and scattered.

Cora raced forward as soon as it was clear, slipping inside the fortress and down one of the stone corridors.

Inside, the fortress was a whirlwind of activity. Soldiers raced around, loud voices echoing off the walls. No one paid her any attention as she raced along the hallways. With so much going on, a strange girl in travel-worn clothing hardly seemed worth their attention compared to the assault the dragons were laying outside. Yet, just as Cora passed by the steps heading up to the ramparts, she saw someone who stole the breath right out of her lungs. He wasn't a foot soldier, and there was an air about him that made the hair on her neck stand up. He reminded Cora of General Secare, and Tamsin's warning about the shadow soldiers flitted to the forefront of her thoughts. The large build, the leashed violence in his moments…if she were to guess, she would think this was Lanius, the king's executioner that Tamsin had warned her about. But she couldn't say for sure, and she had no interest in waiting around to try to identify the man further. Still as she ran, she couldn't help but feel as though a pair of eyes were boring into her back.

Cora made her way to the dungeons where Faron had indicated the prisoners were kept when they weren't working. Cora skidded to a stop, trying not to let the dank air or the dim light throw her off. Before her were two long rows of cells. As expected, they were full. She imagined the prisoners had been locked away almost immediately after the attack began.

"Papa?" she called out, rushing down the center aisle, her eyes frantically scanning the cells, trying to peer through the gloom to make out who was locked within. "Viren Hart? Are you here? Papa?"

There was movement within the cells as her voice echoed through the cell block. Grimy fingers appeared out of the shadows, gripping the bars of the cells, and even grimier faces stared back at Cora as she continued her search.

"Viren Hart!" Cora called out, louder this time, refusing to let herself get distracted. "Are you here?"

"Cora?" The voice was familiar though huskier than she was used to. It came from a cell nearly at the end of the row. Cora ran towards it, her hands already outstretched as hands she would know from anywhere appeared, reaching for her right back.

"Papa!" Cora squeaked, tears of relief welling up in her eyes. "By the stars, I've been so worried about you." She quickly moved her eyes up and down his frame, taking inventory of his condition as best she could in the dim light. It did not escape her that her father was even thinner than he had been the last time she'd seen him, and his shoulders were hunched, but he was standing on his own two feet and his eyes were clear. It was better than she had hoped for.

"Cora?" Viren wheezed. "What are you doing here?"

"I'm here to rescue you, Papa," Cora replied, already reaching deep within in for her magic. She didn't offer any more explanation before she concentrated on the metal lock of his cell door. In spite of everything, she felt a fierce burst of gratitude towards Tamsin for teaching her this.

"Cora, what—" Viren's words died in his throat at the metal lock began to glow orange as though it were being heated in the flames of a forge.

Cora's magic thrummed through her as the lock turned to molten steel that dripped away, leaving the cell door slightly ajar. Several of the other prisoners who were watching began murmuring under their breaths, clearly amazed by what they had just witnessed. Viren, however, looked as if he'd seen a ghost. "How…how is…" he stuttered, thoroughly shocked by the display of magic.

"I promise I'll explain everything once we're far away from here, okay?" Cora rushed inside the cell and immediately set her sights on the shackles wrapped around her father's wrists and ankles. "But there's no time for explanations right now. Hold still." Pulling from her magic again, she made quick work of the shackles. Melting them was too dangerous, given how they were pressed against her father's skin, but she was able to manipulate the metal to make it brittle, and the shackles crumbled away.

"Can you walk?" Cora asked him as he rubbed at his wrists. "Are you injured?"

Viren shook his head as a rasping cough erupted from his chest, shaking his entire body. Cora paled. The cough sounded so much worse than it ever had before. She gently but firmly pounded her father on the back to help him clear the phlegm from his lungs.

"I'm well enough," Viren wheezed, stepping out of her reach. He straightened as best he could and nodded. "I am well enough," he repeated. This time his voice was clear, and he wore an expression of fierce determination. It was enough for Cora.

"Come on," she said, leading him out of the cell. "We don't have much time."

Moving to the cell next to Viren's, Cora immediately got to work melting the lock and cracking open the shackles of the prisoner within. Before the man, weeping from relief, could even thank her, she was off to the next cell and the next and the next, until every prisoner had been freed from their restraints and their cells.

"The fortress is under attack," she called out, projecting her voice to be heard over the prisoners. "If you wish to escape, you can probably slip away in the chaos. If you wish to stay and wreak havoc on the people who put you here, that option is available as well. The choice is yours."

Loud cheers rose from the prisoners as they rushed for the door. Cora wrapped a hand around her father's arm to keep him close as they made their way out of the prison wing.

Back in the main corridor, Cora faced her father. "Papa, do you know where they're keeping the dragon—the one that arrived with you? I know she's being held captive somewhere here, but I don't know exactly where."

Viren's eyebrows scrunched together and for a moment, Cora thought he would scold her for trying to rescue the dragon. Thanks to Onyx's magic, her father's opinion of the creatures was horribly askew—an issue that Cora hoped to remedy as soon as possible. But they didn't have time for that now. Thankfully, Viren just blew out a breath and shook his head.

"No, I'm afraid I don't know where the dragon is being held," he answered, his voice hoarse. "I never saw it again after arriving here."

"I was told she was being held in one of the larger courtyards, with a chainmail covering to keep her from flying away. Do you know where the courtyard is? Did anyone mention it?" Unfortunately, Viren shook his head to that, as well.

Cora's heart sank a bit. She and Alaric had hoped that Viren might have some intel about Raksha's whereabouts. No matter, the plan did not change—it just got a bit more complicated.

Although she could feel a bit of weariness already hanging on her from having used her magic to free all the prisoners, she closed her eyes and reached for it again, letting her senses take over as she pulled on her reading ability, hoping to get a sense for Raksha nearby. And yet, no matter how far she reached out through the fortress, none of what she was sensing could be Raksha. There were dragons around by the dozen—but none were Raksha. She was certain of that.

Squeezing her eyes even tighter, Cora concentrated, trying to find that cool focus she needed to really read an area. She managed to feel a thread of something that could be Raksha on a path near the armory, but it felt...old somehow, stale even. Which didn't make sense to Cora.

It wasn't much at all to go on, but at least it was a start.

Leading her father, Cora made her way towards the armory, which was bustling with people. Skirting around it and doing their best not to draw attention to the two of them, she and her father followed the faint sense of Raksha down a long, narrow hallway. No matter how she tried, though, Cora still couldn't sense more than just a shadow of Raksha, like the afterimage of a bright light after you close your eyes.

When the corridor opened and Cora saw the courtyard before them, she ran the last few steps, her eyes frantically scanning the area for Alaric's mother. But there was no one there. There were no soldiers standing guard, and definitely no dragon. The only indicator that this was indeed the courtyard she'd been told about was the massive chainmail netting that had been rigged up to block the open sky.

"No," Cora moaned, gripping the sides of her head. "She's supposed to be here." She scanned again, praying to the stars that she had missed something, but the courtyard was as empty as a tomb. Oddly enough, it felt that way too. A cool shiver skipped down Cora's spine.

"There is no dragon here," Viren spoke up, his voice soft as he spoke the obvious.

"So it seems," Cora replied, her brain whirling as she tried to figure out their next move. "But she must be around here somewhere. We just have to find her." She inhaled deeply and let the breath back out. "Right, okay," Cora said to her father. "Follow me, then." There was only one way to get answers. She would have to attempt to get the information out of one of the soldiers. It wasn't ideal and the risk of capture was great—for her and her father—but there was no other choice. She wasn't leaving without answers about where she could find Raksha.

Together, Cora and her father made their way back to the armory, where dozens of soldiers ran in all directions, carrying heavy looking swords and various other weapons. The arms master stood barking orders at his harried-looking assistants.

"Stay here," she ordered her father, tucking him into one of the shadowy alcoves along the wall. "If I'm not back in five minutes, I want you to head for the gates and run. If you see a dragon, do not be afraid of it. It will help you, okay? Just trust me."

"No, Cora. I will not leave you here. I—"

"If I'm not back in five minutes, you must," Cora said firmly, gripping her father's shoulders firmly. She wasn't sure what her face looked like, but her determination must have been clear enough because her father shook his head, resigned.

"Five minutes," Cora repeated and then dashed back out into the chaos. Dipping behind several racks of equipment in the armory, she eyed the apprentices for whoever looked most likely to be intimidated by her. One of them, a doe-eyed boy that looked no more than twelve, was making his way towards the racks. In his hands was an empty wooden box that looked like it had been used to carry daggers and smaller hand weapons.

As the boy placed the box near the shelf, he turned to hurry back over to the arms master, but before he could take more than a step, Cora snatched him up, her hand covering his mouth.

He shrieked against her fingers, his eyes wide, but Cora quickly shushed him. "I'm not going to hurt you," she hissed in his ears. "I'm running an errand for one of the officers, that's all. So are you going to help me or not?"

The boy relaxed a little, giving her a quick nod. Cora released him and let him catch his breath for a moment before she spoke.

"He wanted me to ask," she said, keeping her voice low but urgent. "Where is the dragon that was being held captive in the south courtyard? Do you know where they took her?"

The boy's brows lifted slightly in confusion. "But why would an officer need you to ask about that? Wouldn't he know that they moved it?"

"Moved? Moved where?" Worry and a bit of panic spiked through Cora.

The boy lifted one shoulder and then let it drop again. "To the capital, I believe. It happened yesterday afternoon. The king's entire entourage left with it. Is…is that it? Because I'm supposed to be gathering—"

Cora's mouth was bone dry, so she swallowed hard before managing to say, "It's fine, go," as she waved the boy off.

Yesterday afternoon. They had missed the opportunity to save Raksha by a day. A single day. And now, she was being taken to the capital.

No, no, no. Cora's heart began to race, and her entire body shook as she struggled to absorb the news. She reached out to Alaric.

What's wrong? he demanded, having felt Cora's despair through the bond.

It's your mother. Cora's braced a hand on the metal rack to steady herself. *Alaric, we were too late. She's already been moved. It happened yesterday. She's on her way to the capital by now.*

Half a heartbeat passed as the words sank in. Then there was such an overwhelming sense of sorrow that spiraled down the bond, it knocked into Cora and stole the breath right from her lungs.

At the exact same time, a mighty roar sounded outside the fortress. It was so loud, so achingly raw with devastation and anger that she imagined everyone within a mile of the fortress could hear it. Cora's heart felt as if it would burst and she gasped, sagging against the rack as guilt ignited within her chest and spread through her body.

"Oh, Alaric," she whispered, fighting against the tears that threatened to spill over. "I'm so sorry." She wanted to offer the dragon some words of comfort or hope even, but anything she could say would ring hollow. They both knew that once Raksha was within the borders of the capital, the likelihood of them being able to free her was slim.

Pushing past the racks of equipment, Cora stumbled her way back through the armory, her mind and heart swimming with emotion. But then she saw something that stopped her in her tracks. She jerked back so sharply that she nearly lost her balance as she blinked, her eyes focusing on the scene before her.

There was a group of soldiers rushing past her, heavy weaponry clutched in their hands. But it wasn't swords or bow and arrows that they were carrying. No, the weapons they had were harpoons.

Cora's stomach flipped over. As a blacksmith's daughter, she knew that the long, sharp metal spears were incredibly effective when shot across great distances or, as Cora realized in horror, great *heights.*

Rushing into action, she sprinted towards the alcove where her father was, still waiting and anxiously wringing his hands. "Cora, I—" he began, but stopped when he saw the stricken look on her face. "What is it?"

"The dragons," Cora breathed, her heart in her throat. "I have to warn the dragons."

CHAPTER 29

Reaching for her father's hand, Cora pulled him alongside her and began hurrying towards the fortress's gate. "Come on," she said, trying to sound calmer than she felt. "We have to get out of here right now."

Viren immediately fell into step beside her, his eyes wide though he didn't say much. Cora knew he probably had a dozen questions, but for now, she was grateful for his silence. There was no time to explain anything. With the fortress soldiers preparing to use the harpoons against the dragons, mounting a credible defense against them, she needed to make sure they got out of harm's way.

Alaric! she called out through the bond. *You have to tell the dragons to retreat! The soldiers are planning to use harpoons and—*

Where are you? Alaric's voice boomed in Cora's mind.

We're still in the fortress, but we're making our way towards the gate now. But Alaric, you have to listen to me. You and the other dragons are in danger. The soldiers have harpoons. We need to get everyone out of here now!

The others are already retreating. The soldiers mobilized much quicker than we expected—and it appears that several of those harpoon machines were already mounted to the battlements. The soldiers you saw must have been sent to the armory for additional supplies when they used up the ones already in place. We've had casualties.

Cora gasped. *How many?*

Alaric's voice was strained as he answered. *I do not know the final number. One or two at least. I saw one of them go down in the square outside the fortress. I tried to get to him, but I could not reach him in time.* There was anger and pain in the dragon's voice as he relayed the information.

It's not your fault, Cora was quick to say. *The forest dragons knew there was a risk involved with helping us, and they chose to come anyway.*

Yes, but that does not make me feel better.

Cora sighed. It didn't make her feel better either. Losing even one dragon in the battle was nearly more than she could stand. Her brain immediately began to supply her with "what-if" scenarios, and she picked up her pace, dragging her father along for the ride. *I want you to fly as high as you can,* she instructed Alaric. *I don't want you anywhere in range of those harpoons, okay?*

I'm circling around now to pick you and your father up, and then we will all get as far away from here as we can.

No! Cora practically screeched, suddenly overcome with worry for the dragon. *It's not safe for you to stay within range, not with the battlements armed to the teeth with harpoons.*

Alaric scoffed. *I cannot leave you behind, Cora.*

You need to get out of here while you can, Alaric. Papa and I will find another way out of the fortress and out of the city. We'll meet back up once it's safe again.

I do not like this plan.

I don't either. Cora sighed. *But I can't stand the thought of you being speared like a kabob either, so humor me, okay? Get out of here and make sure the other dragons do the same.*

I won't go far. I will come for you once the melee dies down.

I know, just be careful.

With her conversation with Alaric over, Cora focused on her father and the path that would lead them outside. But there was a slight problem. With the dragons retreating, things within the walls of the fortress were settling down slightly. The chaos seemed a bit more organized, and as more and more eyes landed on Cora and her father, it was obvious that blending into the chaos and hoping to go unnoticed was no longer an option.

"Hey!" a loud voice called out. "You there! Stop in the name of the king!"

The man's booming voice was intimidating enough, but after one look at his uniform, which signified him as the prison block warden, Cora knew there was only one thing they could do. She tightened her grip on her father and then whispered, "Run!"

She and her father darted down the hallway. The warden's voice bellowed after them, but Cora did not stop running. Beside her, Viren's face had turned a frightening shade of purple and his shoulders shook with a rasping cough that he was trying quite desperately to keep inside his throat, but he did his best to keep pace with her, clearly not wanting to slow her down, even if it meant straining himself past the breaking point. Cora took one look at his lips pressed together so tightly they disappeared entirely and knew that time was running out.

Hurry, hurry, hurry, she urged herself, darting haphazardly through a few more corridors until she was finally certain that there were no running footsteps pursuing them. She let out a breath of relief, but then cringed when she looked around and realized that she had no idea where they were. She'd only been in the fortress once before today, and it was hardly like she'd gotten a full tour back then. This was definitely not a part of the fortress she'd been in before.

Cora spun around, trying to decide what to do. Her senses were still active, allowing her to read the space around her. She'd left it in place because it didn't use much energy and it would allow her to know if there was an enemy lying in wait behind any corner. But now, as she looked around her and read the space with her magic, she got an odd sense from somewhere that was just ahead and to the left. It felt... well, it almost felt as if there was a dragon in there—but not. The sense was strong and yet not cohesive, the way she'd expect it to be if there was one dragon in there. Instead, it felt as if there were multiple dragons...in small pieces. She needed to figure out what was going on.

"We'll rest here for a second, Papa," Cora said, helping her father to a worn looking stool near the wall. "Take some deep breaths if you can. I'm going to look around, see if there's anything that might help us."

Following the thread of magic, Cora let her senses lead her down the passageway to the very last room. As she stepped inside the room, Cora's mouth dropped open. The entire storeroom was filled nearly floor to ceiling with dragon scales. The hoard was absolutely massive, with dragon scales of every hue imaginable.

As Cora gaped at the sight before her eyes, the conversation she'd had with Tamsin about the scavenged scales echoed in her thoughts. She remembered Tamsin's theory that Onyx didn't have any use for the scales at all—that his quotas for scale scavengers and the high salaries paid to them were solely for the purpose of creating dissent between humans and dragons. Tamsin had even believed that Onyx destroyed all the scales as soon as they reached him. But clearly, that wasn't the case.

What exactly was going on here? Cora knew that his Athelian magic wasn't compatible with the magic within the scales. So what possible use could he have for them? The scales were radiating with…*something*. Something more than just the normal dragon magic she would have expected to find.

So many questions, Cora thought to herself, as she picked up a large, turquoise-colored scale. *But no time in which to find the answers. Not now, at least.*

Pocketing the scale, she hurried back out of the storeroom and over to her father, whose color had shifted slightly to an angry red. "Okay, Papa, let's—"

She cut out as the sound of boots resonated down the hallway, heading towards them. Cora whipped around, eyeing the other end of the hallway, already reaching for the sword at her hip.

"Cora, you need to go," Viren urged, clutching her arm. "Leave me here. I'm their prisoner; it's me they want. You need to leave or you'll end up occupying the cell next to mine. Please, little lark, I beg of you. Go now, before it's too late."

"Hush, Papa," Cora said, though not harshly. She drew her sword and adjusted her feet, positioning herself in a battle stance. "I'm not going to leave you. I just got you back."

A shadow emerged first, followed by a tall figure in a soldier's uniform.

Cora squared her hips and drew in a deep, steadying breath.

"Cora!" The solider lifted his hand, hurrying forward, and Cora realized with a start that it was Faron. The breath she'd been holding whooshed from her lungs as she lowered her sword.

"Faron! What are you doing here?" Ignoring the spark of relief—and maybe something more—that sparked in her chest, Cora sheathed her weapon and narrowed her eyes at the rebel guard.

"I'm here to help," Faron said, holding up a hand in a placating gesture. "I saw you run past with your father, and I realized you must have returned to break him out. A pretty brilliant plan, if you don't mind me saying so, though I don't know how you could have guessed that those dragons would show up today."

Cora blinked, remembering that Faron didn't know that she was a dragon rider. She didn't bother to correct him. No one ever seemed to believe her, anyway.

Faron turned to Viren and extended a hand. "And how are you, Viren?"

Cora's mouth dropped open a little when her father smiled at the young guard and shook his hand firmly. "Well enough, thanks to you, Faron. Well enough."

"You two know each other?"

Viren nodded. "This young man has been looking after me and some of the other prisoners. I would not be in near as good of shape as I am today were it not for him."

Cora ran an eye down her father's frame, thinking that "good shape" was the last descriptor she would use to describe his condition. She shuddered to think about how bad his physical state would have been otherwise.

"You kept your promise," she said to Faron, feeling something like butterflies in her stomach.

He gave her a small half smile. "I told you I would."

For a split second, Cora allowed herself to get lost in the depths of Faron's dark blue eyes, but the second quickly passed and she inhaled sharply. "I was trying to get us to an exit, but I took a wrong turn. We need to leave the city as soon as possible."

"I can help you get out of the fortress," Faron answered, "but getting out of the city might be difficult. They're getting ready to close the city gates to make sure that none of the escaped prisoners can get away."

Cora's stomach sank. If the city gates were closed, she and her father would be stuck inside until they reopened them—if they weren't discovered and imprisoned first.

"We have to get out before they shut the gates," she cried out suddenly, unable to hide her desperation. "Can you help us?"

"Of course," Faron responded quickly. "As I said before, any friend of the Crow's is a friend of the rebels. We'll get you out of the city. Come on, follow me."

Cora bristled slightly at the mention of Tamsin, but she was too grateful for Faron's help to dwell on it for long.

"We'll need to play this just right," Faron said. "Can you follow my lead?" He lifted a brow at Cora, who nodded.

"Of course."

"Good." Faron turned to Viren. "Mr. Hart, I'm going to put your hands behind your back so that I can pretend that I'm escorting you back to the prisoner cell block. But I won't hurt you, okay?"

"Do what you must," Viren answered, lifting his chin. "I'm tougher than I look."

Back in the main area of the fortress, the hallways and corridors were full of soldiers returning to their posts. Thankfully, they all seemed to see nothing suspicious in Faron escorting a prisoner, even if there was an unknown girl by his side. No one stopped or questioned them as Faron led Cora and her father through the fortress and towards the main gate. But as they neared the front, the loud chatter of a group of soldiers came towards them.

"Do you think it will hold the dragons off?" one of them asked another.

"No, but it'll make it easier to round up those prisoners—and it'll give us a chance to fortify the city. We'll need to..." The rest of their conversation was lost as they continued down the hallway. Cora, however, had stopped.

"We need to keep moving," Faron hissed at her, trying to look bored and unconcerned.

"It's too late," Cora said back, trying to ignore the pounding of her heart. "They've already closed the gates."

Faron hissed again, but this time out of frustration.

"So what do we do?" Viren asked. "Is there somewhere else we can go within the city and still be protected from the guards?"

"We can make for the rebel safe house," Faron suggested, looking to Cora. "You and your father should be safe there."

Before Cora could respond, Alaric's voice came through the bond. *I am out of harm's way. So are the rest of the dragons. Once the soldiers realized we were moving out of range, they stopped shooting at us. Probably a good thing for them, given the weak spot in their defense.*

Weak spot?

Yes, over where they've been doing construction. The harpoons and the other projectile weapons all point outwards from the battlements, and they're bolted in place with a limited range of motion. Which would be fine if they had weapons covering each direction—but they don't. On the wall nearest to where they are performing renovations, they seem to have taken down their harpoons so as to keep them from getting in the way of the scaffolding.

So that means no harpoons in that section, Cora finished, catching on.

Exactly. But enough of that, where are you? Did you make it out?

Cora quickly relayed the situation to him. *They've already shut the city's gates. Faron said we could hide in the rebel safe house, but I don't like the thought of being shut up in the city when the guards will be out in force, looking for any escaped prisoners like my father. And I don't like the idea of being separated from you either.*

Nor I, Alaric added. *We are stronger together. We need to get you and your father out of the city.*

Yes, well, if you have any thoughts on how to do that, I'm— An idea struck Cora sharply. *Actually, I think I have an idea.* She quickly detailed her plan to Alaric, who wholeheartedly agreed. Now, she just had to get Viren and Faron to agree as well.

She turned her attention back to Faron and her father, both of whom were staring at her, looking bewildered after the way she'd essentially left them hanging while she communicated telepathically with Alaric.

"Okay," she said, not bothering to explain. "I've got a plan to get us out of here. But you're both going to have to trust me. Can you do that?"

"Of course."

"Good. Faron, I need you to lead us to the section of the fortress with all the construction."

Faron pointed down the hall. "It's this way."

Hurrying, they headed away from the gates and back into the confines of the fortress.

"So," Faron said, speaking to Cora under his breath. "Are you going to fill me in on this plan of yours?"

Cora considered it, but with their window of opportunity to escape closing rapidly, there just wasn't time. Besides, she wasn't sure Faron or her father would believe her if she tried to explain the telepathic link she had with Alaric, much less the bond. Better to show them.

"You'll see," she answered. "We just have to be quick about it."

They made it to the construction zone, which was still deserted. The soldiers in this part of the fortress had yet to return to their posts.

Cora headed over to the scaffolding and began to climb.

"What are you doing?" Faron called out at the same time her father cried, "Lark! You must come down from there."

Resisting the urge to roll her eyes, Cora simply waved her hand. "Come on. You said you could trust me. So *trust me*. We need to climb to the top."

Faron moved first, followed by Viren, who moved slower than the rest, though he was able to make it to the top unassisted—even if he was wheezing and looked like he was going to pass out by the time the climb was complete.

Cora eyed the sky above them. A layer of low-hanging clouds had moved in, blocking much of the sun and casting the day in a layer of gloom.

"And what exactly are we doing up here?" Faron asked, clearly still skeptical of Cora's plan.

One second later, Alaric dropped down from where he was hiding in the clouds, coming down to hover by the battlements at the harpoons' blind spot.

Cora beamed as Faron's eyes grew wide. "We're catching a ride," she said, gently pushing her father forward. Viren seemed as shocked as Faron, but he allowed Cora to help him atop Alaric's back.

"Now you," Cora said to Faron, "Come on, we're running out of time."

"Uh…that's a dragon." Faron's voice was full of both shock and awe.

"It is. Now come on," She held out her hand to Faron, who hesitated for only half a second more before gripping her hand tightly and allowing her to tow him forward and onto Alaric's back.

As soon as they were seated, Alaric pushed away from the scaffolding and made to turn around and take off. Cora's heart started to lift, thinking they were actually going to be able to get away…

But all her hopes were dashed in an instant when a strange whooshing sound rent the air a second before a massive net wrapped around the dragon, tangling in his wings.

Alaric let out a shriek of both panic and surprise. Faron and Viren were yelling as well as they gripped the leather straps of the saddle, trying to stay on the dragon's back while he thrashed.

Cora, who was a bit more balanced thanks to training and experience, quickly scanned the area for the threat. Below, the shadow soldier she'd seen earlier grinned up at her. He stood next to a trebuchet, and she understood instantly what had happened. She and Alaric had been so worried about the harpoons, they hadn't considered other weaponry. The net launcher covered half the distance of the harpoons, but it was more responsive and easier to maneuver—easier to adjust over the area they'd thought was a blind spot—which made it the perfect weapon for trapping an unsuspecting dragon.

With his wings tangled in the net and nearly pinned tight against his body, Alaric's attitude began to decrease and soon he began to plummet, like a stone.

Cora only had time to let out a shrill squeak as the ground rushed up to meet them.

CHAPTER 30

A cting on instinct, Cora reached for her magic, forming it into a cushion of air that she hurled into place between Alaric and the ground at the last second before he crashed. It worked to keep him from getting injured, but it didn't change the predicament they were in: trapped and at the mercy of a shadow general.

As Alaric slid to a stop in the square outside the back of the fortress, Cora jumped free of the saddle. Out of the corner of her eye, she saw her father and Faron scramble off of Alaric's back as well, but her focus was on her dragon.

"Alaric," Cora called out, hurrying over to where the dragon lay struggling against the thick netting that was still wrapped around his torso. "Are you okay?"

"I'm fine," Alaric growled, "Except for this stars-blasted netting."

"Don't worry," Cora said, ripping her sword from the sheath across her back. "I'll free you."

She began to hack at the net. The rope it was made of was thick, so progress was slow. "I need help," she called out to Faron and her father, who stood watching, their faces still lined with shock.

Faron reacted first, hurrying over and unsheathing his own blade. He immediately got to work, reaching out with his free hand to pass a dagger from his belt over to Viren, who moved to work on Alaric's other side.

"So um…you have a dragon," Faron's voice floated towards Cora. If the circumstances were different, she might have laughed at the phrasing, but instead she just nodded.

"Yes, we're bonded."

"Bonded?" Faron's voice seemed to jump up an octave, and again Cora felt the urge to laugh.

"Yes," she confirmed again. "I'm a dragon rider." She gave him a quick glance. "Surprise."

Faron opened his mouth, but no sound came out. A moment later, he shut it and returned his attention to the netting. Cora was certain there would be more questions later—and later, she would be happy to answer them. But freeing Alaric was the only thing that mattered.

"Just a little bit more," she called out to Alaric, who was squirming uncomfortably, "Just sit tight. I think we've almost got it."

"Cora," Faron said, lifting his sword to point to the other side of the square. "We've got company."

Cora whirled around as the sound of boots marching on the street filled her ears and forty or so soldiers poured into the open space, effectively blocking off their exit.

Swearing under her breath, Cora sliced the last of the netting away from Alaric's body and then positioned herself in a fighting stance, just as Tamsin had taught her. "Guard my father," she yelled at Faron. "Whatever you do, don't let anyone near him."

For a moment, the contingent of soldiers stood there staring as if they were waiting for something, but then, moving as one, they parted, and a cloak-clad figure stepped forward, his face twisted in a cold sneer.

A shadow soldier. Cora could feel the *wrongness* of him, just as she had with Secare. Now that they were outside and not in the middle of a battle, Cora could see his features more clearly. *Definitely Lanius*, she realized. The one who gloried in brutality, who killed for the pleasure of it. A shudder ran through her spine, but she refused to back down. She was the only thing standing between this monster and the two beings she loved most. She could not afford to falter.

For a moment, their eyes met and then with a predatory smirk, Lanius charged forward, heading straight for Cora, with the soldiers right behind him

Acting on instinct, Cora darted forward, not even hesitating as she lifted her sword, swinging it with all of her might.

Lanius's cold, calculating stare met hers as his own blade slammed into hers, the clash of steel so loud that it made Cora's ears hurt.

Pulling back, Cora stepped sideways out of reach and twisted around, sending her blade slicing through the air. Once again, Lanius's blade met her own and the force of the blow nearly strong enough to make her arms go numb. In terms of sheer strength, he had her entirely outmatched. Forget blocking his blows—she needed to work on dodging them. Otherwise, she was going to end up dislocating her shoulder.

Shoving against his blade with all her might, Cora yanked back her own sword, and threw herself sideways as Lanius struck again—this time, she only narrowly missed the *slink* of the sword as it passed only millimeters away from her throat.

Careful! Alaric roared, from where he was battling a group of soldiers across the square. Now free of the netting, he was using his tail to knock over any who dared try to get close to him. But it was obvious he was keeping tabs on Cora as well, ready to rush to her side, should she need help.

Lanius struck again and Cora yelped, jumping backward to dodge the strike. Despite all the training she'd done with Tamsin, this fight with the shadow soldier was unlike anything she'd ever imagined. It became painfully obvious that she was outmatched—in physical strength and in skill. Lanius knew it too. He could have defeated her —she got the sense that he was drawing things out because he enjoyed toying with her. As if he guessed the direction of her thoughts, he threw back his head and laughed.

"This is absolutely rich," he purred, pulling his sword back. "The new dragon rider is just a little girl, a girl who has practically gift wrapped all of her weaknesses for me." He waved a hand towards Alaric, Viren, and Faron. "Do you really think you can protect them? Silly little fool. I'll make sure you live long enough to see them suffer." He shot his arm out, slicing his sword through the air. "You're just a stupid little girl who will watch all that she loves be destroyed."

The words rocketed through Cora as she scrambled out of the way of Lanius's blade. She knew he was taunting her to throw her off her game…but that didn't stop it from working.

"Do you honestly think you have a chance?" Lanius asked, his voice deep and calm, as though he were making commentary on the weather. "If you were smart, you'd be jumping *towards* my sword, hoping I'll grant you the mercy of a quick death. It would be a kind-ness compared to what the king has planned for you. Well, for you *and* that beast of yours." On the word "beast," Lanius's upper lip pulled back in a sneer.

Don't listen to him, she tried to tell herself as she reached inside for her magic. It was obvious that Lanius had the upper hand when it came to swordplay, but perhaps she could even the playing field by casting as they fought. It hadn't usually gone well with Tamsin, but she knew she had to try something.

Before she had the chance, though, Lanius went on the attack—she found herself dodging blow after blow, each one more forceful than the last.

"You know," he said, practically beaming as he held his sword out and pointed it at Cora. "I think I'll ask the king if I can keep your dragon's hide as a trophy—once he'd squeezed everything useful out of the two of you and there's nothing left but carcasses. I'll tack it to my wall and every time I look at it, I will be reminded of this moment." He laughed again and anger erupted inside of Cora, spiraling through her so fast there was little she could do to control it. Swinging her sword, she launched herself at Lanius, using every ounce of strength she had to attack. But the harder she tried, the angrier she became, shattering her focus and making it nearly impossible for her to cast.

You cannot let him goad you, Alaric reminded her, his tail swishing through the air as he bared his teeth at the soldiers coming towards him. *Calm focus is the only way.*

But even though she knew Alaric was right, Cora could not manage to heed his words. Her rage at Lanius only grew as he continued to spit out terrible threats against her, Alaric, Faron, and Viren.

And with every poisonous word out of his mouth, Lanius attacked.

Strike.

Strike.

Strike.

Cora managed to avoid serious injuries, but she was bruised and nicked in a dozen different places, and blocking the blows had left her arms aching so badly that she could barely manage to hold up her sword. Across the courtyard, Faron let out a cry of pain as two soldiers attacked him at once, one of them managing to slip past his guard and catch his sword in Faron's arm. Stumbling backward, Faron nearly dropped his weapon and lost his footing, stumbling before he managed to steady himself. The soldier who had wounded him seized the small opening and darted around Faron to get to Viren, who had his back turned. Faron tried to intervene, but the other soldiers laid in against him, keeping him from coming to Viren's aid.

Something cracked open inside of Cora's chest, unlike anything she'd ever felt before. She darted out from under Lanius's next blow, leaping over the body of a fallen soldier as she raced to intercept her father's attacker.

With a wild cry, Cora threw herself and her sword in front of Viren, the clang of steel loud as she parried the blow that likely would have killed her father.

In that moment, with all of her rage and fury nearly at its peak, she looked into the face of the soldier—and froze. He was just a boy. Younger than her by at least a year, maybe more. This was likely the first real danger he'd ever seen…and he looked terrified.

The sight of the fear in the boy's eyes doused Cora's temper, and she staggered back. Was this what Tamsin meant when she talked about people not knowing what they'd gotten themselves into? Tamsin, after all, had found herself on the wrong side, despite all her beliefs and values. Perhaps, the same was true of the soldiers.

"Fool!" Lanius appeared next to the boy, knocking him out of the way. "Never hesitate," he snapped, leveling his gaze with Cora's as he once again lifted his sword. Like a viper, he struck, moving so fast the steel of his blade blurred as it whizzed through the air.

Cora spun out of range, the wells of her anger refilling at the sight of Lanius's face, sneering at her. And suddenly, like a dam that had burst, every ounce of rage that Cora had been holding back came rushing forward in a deluge. She thought of everything Onyx had stolen from the people of Tenegard, of the dragon riders he had slaughtered, and the dragons he had condemned to feral mindlessness by eliminating every trace of Dragon Tongue. She thought of the famine that Onyx had created and the restricted laws that practically forced the genante to forget their own history and culture. Opening her mouth to let out a furious scream, she moved to offense, darting forward to land a strike of her own.

In her fury, Cora successfully managed to put Lanius on the back foot, his sword moving to parry her strikes, and for a second, she saw the mocking mask on his face slip.

Fueled by her rage, Cora continued to attack with a ferocity that she hadn't known she was capable of.

Cora! Alaric shouted through the bond.

His voice was like a soothing balm, washing over Cora and quelling some of her anger. She stopped advancing. As Cora glanced around the courtyard, surveying the mayhem, she suddenly realized what just happened. She had let the heat of the moment and the intensity of her anger distract her from the bigger picture. Lanius's taunts had made her want to hurt the man—to strike at him until he regretted all those vivid threats he'd levied against the people she loved. But she wasn't there to teach a vicious man a lesson he would likely never learn. She came to the city to free her father and Raksha. Her purpose was to rescue, not to destroy, maim, or kill. The longer the battle continued in the square, the more likely it was that they would be captured—or, if they managed to fight their way out, that innocent people would get hurt.

She couldn't deny the anger she felt towards Lanius, but that wasn't the most important thing to her. Hurting her enemy mattered less to her than protecting those who she loved.

I'm okay, she said to Alaric. *I lost myself there for a second, but I have found myself again, and I know what I need to do.* She reached for the magic, finding it easily this time. With her focus on those who she loved, it became easy to center herself and control her power.

Alaric, sensing that Cora had finally found her focus, let out a deep breath. *What are you going to cast? Fire? It might be dangerous— there are people all around us and the buildings will go up rather fast.*

No, not fire, Cora assured him. *Something else.* Instead of Dragon Fire, Cora lifted her hands, conjuring up a massive gust of wind that whipped around her like a cyclone.

"Hold on to something," she shouted over her shoulder at her father and Faron. And then she released the magic, sending a wall of wind across the square. It slammed into Lanius as well as most of the soldiers, sending them flying in all directions.

Maintaining the spell to keep anyone from getting too close, Cora shuffled over to Faron, shouting over the whipping wind. "Faron, do you know of somewhere we can go outside the city? Somewhere where we'll be safe? I don't think the safe house here in Llys will be enough to protect us."

Faron's hair was blowing across his eyes, so she couldn't make out his expression very well, but he nodded. "I know a place!" he shouted back.

"Let's go, then!" Cora reached for her father and helped pull him towards Alaric, who was hunched low, bracing himself against her spell. It only took a second to get Viren and Faron settled atop Alaric's back and as Cora dropped the magic of her spell, she threw herself into the saddle.

Alaric whipped his wings out, launching himself into the sky with a mighty *boom!*

And as the clouds swallowed them whole, the city of Llys disappeared below them.

CHAPTER 31

It took nearly ten minutes for Cora's heart to slow back down to a normal rate. As all the adrenaline and energy from the conflict at Llys faded away, her eyelids seemed to grow heavier than they'd ever been before. Cora was pretty sure, if given the chance, that she could sleep for a solid week. But she had the sneaking suspicion that an abundance of peaceful sleep was off the table.

She glanced over at Faron, who sat stiffly next to her father, his back ramrod straight. "It's more fun if you relax," she told him, offering a small half smile. "Alaric won't let you fall off or anything, if that's what you're worried about."

Faron dropped his shoulders slightly as he relaxed a tiny bit. "It's not that," he said, his voice low. "I just never thought I'd ever experience something like this. It's a bit hard to wrap my head around."

"I know exactly what you mean." Cora chuckled. "I often feel the same way. But it's more fun if you relax." She leaned over and nudged Faron's shoulder with her fingertips. The smile he flashed her in return made her stomach flip over and her cheeks burn, so she searched for a new topic. Her father, who appeared to be dozing where he sat, breathing deeply, the air rattling in his lungs. Cora frowned at the sound.

"We have healers where we're going," Faron said, looking from Cora to her father. "If there's anything that can be done for him, I can assure you that they will do it. I only wish I could have done more for him at the fortress."

"Thank you," Cora said earnestly. "For everything you did for him while he was a prisoner and for helping us escape. I owe you so much."

"You owe me nothing. It was the right thing to do."

"Yes, but not everyone does the right thing when given the chance."

Faron considered this. "You're right. They don't."

Sighing, she eyed the horizon. "So, what is this place we're going to?"

Faron had directed Alaric through Cora to fly beyond the city limits of Llys and head east. "It's a village," he answered, "full of people who are sympathetic to our cause. We'll be safe there."

Cora waited for the usual spike of suspicion to spring up, but there was none. As she studied Faron's face, she realized that she…*trusted* him. How could she not after everything he'd done for her, Alaric, and her father? It was both exhilarating and surprising to realize that this stranger, this malhos soldier, was someone she trusted. *What a strange world,* she thought to herself.

Viren stirred then, a coughing fit waking him from his nap. Cora tried not to worry about how much worse he sounded now than he had back in Barcroft. He had been sick even back then, when they were still at home, but now it was exponentially worse.

"How are you, Papa?" Cora asked, digging into the saddlebag for a canteen of water and a leather pouch of dried beef strips. "Are you thirsty? Hungry? I have something for you, if you need refreshment."

Viren nodded gratefully and Cora quickly handed over the canteen and the strips. Viren sipped the water and then began in on the beef.

"It is so strange," he said after a few long moments, "that I used to think dragons were dangerous. But they're not dangerous at all, are they?"

"They can be, Papa. But not all of them are. Many of them are wise and kind and honorable. Grandma Livi tried to tell you."

Viren sobered a bit at the mention of her. "Yes, I know, but I didn't believe her. I do not know why."

It was a little confusing for Cora as well. She had never understood her father's dismissiveness of Nana Livi's stories about dragon riders —especially given how fond he was of his mother-in-law and how much he seemed to appreciate her good sense in every other respect. But for some reason, he'd always had a peculiar stubbornness when it came to the dragon issue. She could only hope they had well and truly broken past it now.

"I have a question, lark," Viren spoke up in between bites of beef strips. "Where did you learn to fight like that? I have seen you with a sword in your hand at the forge, of course, or when you were making a delivery for me, but I have never seen you wield one in such a way. Where did you acquire such skills?"

Faron, who had been looking out over Alaric's side at the passing landscape, swiveled around to face her, eager to hear this story for himself.

"Um…" Cora thought about telling them both everything that had happened with Tamsin, but even though there was newfound trust between her and Faron, she wasn't sure if she was ready to share the full story. As angry as she was at Tamsin, it had been obvious that Faron and the other rebels liked and respected her. Cora didn't want to ruin their illusions. Besides, her story was hers alone to tell.

"I'll tell you everything later," she assured her father. "For now, I think we could all use a bit of rest."

The rest of the flight was relatively quiet. Cora conversed with Alaric through the bond, but she kept her word and said nothing aloud to let both Faron and Viren rest.

As the sun began its slow descent towards the horizon, Faron sat up a little straighter and pointed. "There," he said, indicating a midsize but fairly remote village tucked away among some cliffs. "It existed long before the rebels," Faron explained, "the village, I mean. I'm not sure when the rebel base moved there, but at this time, all who live within the confines of the village are sympathetic to the antiroyalist cause. They provide a safe haven for all who are involved in the movement."

"And what will they think about dragons?" Cora asked, a little unsure of how to approach the village. "What do you think their reaction will be when you show up with a dragon rider in tow?"

"I do not know," Faron answered honestly. "I imagine they will be quite surprised."

Still, as a safety precaution, Cora had Alaric land further up the shoreline rather than having him touch down directly in the village. "Until we know it's safe, I don't want to reveal Alaric or the nature of my relationship with him to the others. Given what happened today, it won't be long before people find out that there's a newly bonded dragon rider, but until then, I have to do all that I can to protect him."

"You can trust the rebels," Faron assured her.

Yes, and I will simply eat anyone who tries to harm you or me, Alaric added with a wicked gleam in his eyes. Cora responded with an eye roll.

That threat would carry more weight if you actually did eat humans for a snack, you know.

Well, it is never too late to pick up a new habit, Alaric teased. To which Cora gave another eye roll.

"I know *you* trust the rebels," she said to Faron. "I want to as well. But the last time I had a run-in with them, I was a prisoner for several days. I don't think you can blame me for being more cautious. Until I'm sure they don't present a threat, I won't risk Alaric."

"I understand," Faron replied. "I promise that I will not reveal any information that is not mine to share. It is up to you to determine what, if any, details you share with the rebels."

"Thank you. And just remember, if you break your oath, I'll let Alaric eat you for breakfast."

An hour or so later, Cora's stomach felt as if it were in knots as she, Faron, and her father neared the edge of the village. *You have nothing to be nervous about,* Alaric said through the bond, reading her emotions. *You're a dragon rider. With a wave of your hand, you could blow them off the mountainside.*

Yes, that's true, Cora admitted, *but I've never been very good with people.*

Faron led the way and as soon as they entered the village, there was an explosion of activity. People came pouring out of the small buildings that made up the village center in droves. There were more of them than Cora had expected. She did her best to remember everyone's names, but after what felt like a hundred introductions, Cora stopped trying and just smiled at everyone she passed.

But then, a familiar face appeared in the middle of the crowd. Cora's eyes widened as she took in the girl's features. "Strida?" Cora exclaimed, stunned to see the scale scavenger from her village who had befriended her not long before she met Alaric. In response, the older girl shoved through the mass of villagers and nearly tackled her in a hug. "It is really you?"

Strida pulled back from the hug, grinning. "It's me all right."

"Oh, it's so good to see you, but what are you doing here?"

Strida's face fell at that. "Things in Barcroft have gotten much worse. Captain Daggett has been more than insufferable, and he's taken nearly every shipment of supplies that's come in and claimed it for himself and his men. The people are starving. We can't get the food we need, and he seems to get more and more cruel each day. I couldn't stay there—not when I know the truth." She smiled then, the light returning to her eyes. "I joined up with the rebels a few weeks ago after following the instructions you gave. About the cave."

Cora swallowed. "And these rebels, do you trust them?" She didn't know anyone who was a better judge of character than Strida. "I mean, do you *really* trust them?"

Strida pressed a hand to her heart and nodded solemnly. "I do. These are good people, Cora. And they're calling for real change."

The earnestness in Strida's words was irresistible. It was the exact same as what she'd heard in Faron's voice. And if the two of them felt the rebels were trustworthy enough, then perhaps it was time to extend some trust of her own.

Alaric, stand by. I think I want you to come to the village and meet everyone today after all.

So soon? I thought you said you wanted me to stay out of sight until you had a chance to make sure things were safe.

I did. And I did. So be ready.

Alaric chuckled, but through the bond, Cora could tell that he had already lifted himself in the air, ready to fly into the village and make a grand entrance. Dragons were such show-offs.

With Strida and Faron's help, Cora gathered all the rebels together and sat them down. "Thank you so much for providing us with sanctuary," she began. "My name is Cora Hart, and I have a lot of news to share. But first…"

She smiled as Alaric's shadow rushed over them from above.

"I have something I want to show you."

There was something incredibly peaceful about the sea. As Cora walked along the waterline, listening to the crash of the waves against the shore, she felt some of the tension that had been lodged in her shoulder blades finally loosen up just a bit.

It was early still, but already the day was shaping up to be warm. Cora licked her lips, tasting the salt in the air. It had only been a day since she and Alaric had arrived at the rebel village, but already she was more comfortable there than she had been in a while. Her father was being looked after by an incredibly kind and talented healer named Blue, and every single person in the village had accepted both her story and Alaric himself with alacrity.

It felt as if everything was falling into place—with the exception of Raksha, of course. At the thought of her, pain spiked through Cora's chest, laced with guilt. Alaric hadn't said anything to her, but there had been multiple times she had caught him looking back and forth between her and her father, and she had been able to sense his sadness. Cora understood well enough. Though she knew he was happy for her that she'd been able to have her long-sought reunion, it hurt that he hadn't been able to have the same kind of moment with his mother.

She'd gotten up with the dawn, determined to spend the morning clearing her head and strategizing ways they could get to Raksha. Cora didn't care what it took, she would free Alaric's mother.

Sticking her hand in the pocket of her tunic, her fingertips brushed across the hard edge of the dragon scale she had taken from the store-room in the fortress at Llys. For what felt like the hundredth time since they'd arrived at the village, Cora turned it over in her hand, trying to make sense of the strange discoloration that ringed the edge of the scale. The dark edges had not been there when Cora pocketed the scale, but something had happened to it—she just didn't know what. Whatever it was, though, Cora didn't have a good feeling about it.

Tamsin had said that scales had memories, but whether this particular scale remembered anything useful, Cora couldn't figure out how to access it. She walked up and down the beach for a while, mulling it over, until she had an idea. Dragon Tongue seemed to be the key to a lot of things pertaining to the dragons, so perhaps it was the key to unlocking this mystery as well. Pulling on the familiar symbols she'd traced so many times in her mind, Cora focused on the scale in her hand, opening herself up to the magic and the possibility of something unexplainable. She felt a thread of energy within the scale, and she reached for it, much like she did when she was trying to read an area for signs of life.

And her efforts paid off. All of a sudden, several different images popped up in her mind: Images of riders dissolving into nothingness; dragons in battle armor fading away; human hands, bleeding and covered in scales. Along with the images, Cora felt something unexpected, something strange and slightly sinister. It felt as if the magic within the scale was being turned in on itself, twisting like a taut thread until it seemed to sever the memory rather than sustain it.

"By the stars," she murmured, trying to make sense of it all. "What does this mean?"

She didn't know and the more she tried to sort it out, the more confusing it seemed. So she kept walking, listening to the waves as she pondered what it could mean.

When an idea began to grow, she pushed it aside, too shocked to accept that it might be true. "No! That can't be it. Can it?"

She jumped when the water lapped at her feet not realizing that she had stopped walking. Dancing back to keep her shoes from getting soaked by the incoming tide, she froze again, midstep.

"That has to be it," she realized, her heart beating faster. "It is."

Hurrying back towards the village, she found Alaric where he was resting in the shade of two trees. "Alaric," she breathed out, needing to share her discovery. "I think I know what Onyx is using the scales for. He's using them to keep everyone from remembering."

Alaric sat up as Cora explained the magic she had sensed from the scales. "It's as if certain memories are simply disappearing," she told him.

"But how can this be?" Alaric asked her.

"Tamsin had said that Athelian magic would allow the user to work on the mind of a target."

"Yes, but they would need direct access to that person. Athelian magic doesn't have the kind of range that Tenegardian dragon magic has," he reminded her.

Cora nodded. "Correct. But with the dragon scales, Onyx could tap into the ability of dragons to communicate from mind to mind, even across long distances. Somehow, Onyx has managed to combine the magic of two extremely different cultures into an incredibly powerful magic spell."

Her eyes widened as she came to another realization. "This is why Viren always refused to listen when Nana Livi or I talked about dragons. This is how Onyx managed to stamp out any belief in the dragon rider legends even though the riders themselves had lived only a handful of generations ago."

It hadn't just been propaganda and censorship of books and newspapers and schoolrooms. Onyx had reached into everyone's minds and simply…taken that knowledge away.

Alaric stared at Cora, the look on his face equal parts shock and horror. He rose up and shook himself off as if he could shake off this entire conversation. "He's using our own scales against us?"

"Yes," she replied, "but there is good news. If it's just a spell, just a twist on the magic already within the scales, then I don't think it's permanent." As Cora said the words, determination filled her and a sense of rightness so strong it was almost tangible.

"After all, any spell can be broken, right?"

CHAPTER 32

OCTAVIA

The road to Kerlin, the capital city, was long, but Octavia didn't mind the length of the journey. It gave her plenty of time to ponder her next move. She assumed Raksha was being taken there to make her captivity more secure, which was going to make things much harder. While she knew breaking her out of the fortress would have been difficult, helping her friend escape from the palace was going to be a far more daunting task. Straightening her spine where she sat, Octavia knew that she was up to the challenge. She would use everything in her arsenal to free Raksha before anything bad could happen to her. The alternative…was unthinkable.

Patting the front pocket of her skirt, she felt a little hum of satisfaction when she heard the crinkle of parchment from within. Her drawing, the one she'd crafted for the blacksmith in Llys. She had no idea what sort of restraints Raksha would be confined by in the palace, but she knew they'd be strong enough to prevent a dragon from escaping, so she'd need something equally strong enough to release her. There were blacksmiths in the capital, just like there were back in Llys. It would simply be a matter of finding one willing to do the job and not ask too many questions. She'd also have to *not* get caught. After what happened in Llys, she'd need to work harder to make sure she could sneak around without anyone reporting her to King Onyx or one of his generals. She couldn't hold back the small shiver at the thought of what might happen if she got caught.

I'm going to figure this out, she thought to herself, as the carriage bumped along. *I'm going to free her somehow, and then we'll begin a new life far away from here.*

It was that thought that kept Octavia from giving into despair whenever her thoughts turned back to the dragon. Raksha was being pulled in a cage behind one of the carriages, and Octavia couldn't stand the thought of her being locked up like that. She ached to speak with her, to ask if she was all right. It felt as if her mind was reaching out to Raksha, stretching out to check on her friend.

No sooner had the thought completed in her mind, did something strange happen. It was as if the thread that connected her and Raksha, the feeling of connection she'd felt since she'd learned the first symbol of Dragon Tongue, intensified. The thread began to heat up, to shift into something more substantial. Soon it wasn't a fraying thread anymore, but a piece of steel. Strong and durable.

What just happened? Octavia mused, not sure how to process the strange sensation. Wrapping her arms around herself, she thought of Raksha again, and this time, her whole body began to tingle with awareness.

What's going on? Octavia thought. She nearly fell off her seat when Raksha's voice sounded in her mind.

Octavia? Raksha sounded as surprised as Octavia felt. *Can you hear me?*

Yes! Octavia clenched her hands into fists, driving her fingernails into her palms to keep herself from showing a visible reaction to the others in her carriage. *I can hear you. I don't know how, but I can hear you.*

337

How is it that you are speaking to me in my mind. Is that normal with Dragon Tongue once your skill at it reaches a certain level?

No, Raksha replied. *Only bonded pairs can speak using the telepathic link.*

Oh so... Octavia froze as the words sank in. Had Raksha really said "bonded pairs"? *Wait...are you saying what I think you're saying?*

There was joy in Raksha's voice as she answered. *Yes, Octavia. The bond between us has snapped into place. You are my rider, and I am your dragon.*

Covering her mouth with her hand, Octavia faked a cough to hide the squeal that she wanted to release. Her mind was spinning. She knew this revelation was big and it was going to change everything, but for the moment all she wanted was one thing. *Say it again.*

And Raksha's voice was there, the connection between them stronger than ever.

You are my rider, and I am your dragon.

END OF DRAGON SCALES
RISE OF THE DRAGON RIDERS BOOK TWO

Dragon Tongue, December 28, 2022

Dragon Scales, January 25, 2023

Dragon Fire, February 22, 2023

Dragon Plague, June 28, 2023

Dragon Crystals, July 26, 2023

Dragon Wars, August 30, 2023

PS: Keep reading for exclusive extracts from ***Dragon Fire, The Dragon King's Egg*** and ***Dragon Connection.***

THANK YOU!

I hope you enjoyed **Dragon Scales**. Please don't forget to leave a review.

Receive free books, exclusive excerpts and be kept up to date on all of my new releases, when you sign up to my mailing list at AvaRichardsonBooks.com/mailing-list.

ABOUT AVA

Ava Richardson writes epic page-turning Young Adult Fantasy books with lovable characters and intricate worlds that are barely contained within your eReader.

She grew up on a steady diet of fantasy and science fiction books handed down from her two big brothers – and despite being dog-eared and missing pages, she loved escaping into the magical worlds that authors created. Her favorites were the ones about dragons, where they'd swoop, dive and soar through the skies of these enchanted lands.

Stay in touch! You can contact Ava on:

facebook.com/AvaRichardsonBooks

amazon.com/author/avarichardson

goodreads.com/avarichardson

bookbub.com/authors/ava-richardson

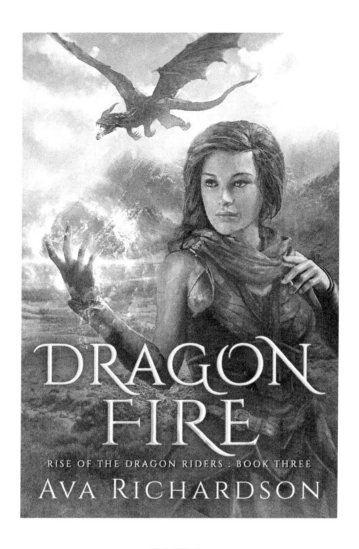

BLURB

A young woman and her dragon must free their kingdom from evil magic…

King Onyx has kept Tenegard ensorcelled for too long. Dragon rider Cora, along with her dragon, Alaric, are determined to free the kingdom from his sinister grasp. With the aid of rebel forces, they're training a new wave of dragon riders—the first the country has seen in a century—but will their forces be enough to combat King Onyx's dark magic? In his quest for power and immortality, there's no line he won't cross and nothing he won't risk. With the nation on the brink of war, the stakes have never been higher.

The rebels must do whatever it takes to cut off the sorcerer king from his source of power, before it's too late. If they fail to stop him, his corrupting reach will extend far beyond Tenegard.

And all hope will be lost…

Get your copy of ***Dragon Fire***
Available February 22, 2023
(Available for Pre-Order Now!)
AvaRichardsonBooks.com

EXCERPT

Chapter One

Slivers of bright morning sunlight glinted against the steel edge of Cora Hart's blade as she spun around, whirling like a wraith, the movements of her feet practiced and precise.

She thrust her sword forward until the tip pierced the pocket of air right in front of her. She then pulled her arm back and turned to face the handful of rebels she was instructing. "The blade should feel like a natural extension of your body. In combat, you must be able to move quickly whether you are dodging a strike from your opponent or taking advantage of an enemy's exposed blind spot. You'll need to be light on your feet, adaptable, and quick to respond."

Cora paused for a moment, pressing her lips together as she tried not to chuckle at the looks of bewilderment on the faces of her students. For a split second, her mind took her to a very different moment in time, one not so very long ago, when *she* had been the one first learning how to fight with a sword. Had she looked as awed and baffled? Probably. Her grandmother Livi had frequently remarked that life was cyclical and that it always came back around on itself. This training session was a prime example of that.

"I know it sounds a little odd," she said to her trainees, "but you and your weapon must move as one, as if each of you does not exist without the other. Every movement should feel natural, so natural that in battle you do not have to think, only act."

"Yes, but how?" One of the rebels, a young man named Fischer, took a step towards her, his wooden practice sword hanging limply at his side. "You make it look rather easy. Yet, when I try…" He grimaced. "Well, my results are not the same as yours."

Cora snorted. "Trust me, I wasn't very good at all when I was first beginning. Learning how to use a sword in combat *isn't* easy, not at first anyway. But it is possible for you to learn to be comfortable handling a sword. And it won't take as long as you think. A year ago, I was exactly like you. While I spent my life in a forge around weaponry, I never had cause to wield one. But that changed, and I had to learn just as you do now. I'm not an expert, and there's still plenty I have to learn, but I *am* capable with a sword—enough that I can at least defend myself in battle if I had to. And you can learn what I know the same way I did." She pointed at the wooden sword. "With practice."

"Practice?" Fischer repeated, doubt still furrowing his brow.

"Yes, practice. Lots and lots of practice," Cora confirmed. "The first thing you have to do is get comfortable with the weight of your sword, how it impacts the movement of your arm, how it affects your reaction speed. From there it's about anticipating your enemy's movements and thinking on your feet." She repositioned herself in a fighting stance and ran through the sequence again, slower this time.

"Muscle memory is your friend. The more you practice, the more your body will get used to the movements."

Fischer and the other trainees mimicked her. Cora smiled as they seemed to be grasping things a bit more this time around. "Good, just make sure that you follow through with your thrust. The last thing you want is to leave your enemy even an inch they can use to escape. In truth, the key to surviving in combat is not hesitating. You don't have to have exact precision or be the strongest, though that would help— you just have to follow through. Don't think, just act. If you hesitate at all, even for a split second, you could die. That one second means the difference between life or death."

Fischer blanched slightly at her words, but gripped his sword a little tighter, holding it out in front of him. "So don't hesitate," he said, putting emphasis on the words.

Cora nodded. "Exactly. Now, let's do a few more movement drills, and then we'll practice sparring."

It had been three weeks since Cora and her dragon, Alaric, had led an attack on the fortress in Llys, and three weeks since arriving at the rebel stronghold following the battle. The rebels, many of whom had never seen a dragon up close before, were a wiry, determined group, all intent on bringing Tenegard out from under Onyx's thumb. They had immediately welcomed Cora and Alaric into their ranks, and it had been decided that Cora should begin helping the experienced fighters train the rebels for both combat on dragonback and the use of Dragon Tongue. And so, Cora had spent most of her time on a training ground in the Calavair Mountains, a range of low-lying mountains about half a day's ride from the ocean-side rebel stronghold.

"Okay, I think that's enough of that for today," she called out a while later, clapping her hands together. "It's not quite time for lunch, but what do you say to breaking a little early?"

The rebel trainees, red-faced and sweaty from their sparring practice, all let out various iterations of agreement. Cora chuckled as Fischer dropped his wooden sword on a fluffy patch of green grass and then plopped down beside it, chest heaving. Several others followed suit.

"Don't forget to drink plenty of water," Cora told them as she passed by. "You'll need to be hydrated for this afternoon's practice." The only response was a chorus of groans from the rebels, which made Cora grin. She knew exactly how exhausting such training could be. It was pretty fun being on the other side of it.

Trudging through the trees, Cora headed to find Alaric. She hadn't seen him all morning, and she was eager to speak with him. Ever since they'd bonded, Cora had found herself most at ease when she was next to the dragon. Despite everything that was going on around them, there was a sense of peace that came from her connection with Alaric—and after a grueling morning of training, she could use a bit of that peace.

Alaric wasn't hard to find. He sat on his haunches in the middle of a small clearing. Ten or so rebels sat in front of him, their faces screwed up in concentration and focus. Alaric, by contrast, looked less focused and more annoyed than anything else.

I take it it's going well, then? she asked through their telepathic bond.

Alaric's eyes snapped to her face, and she felt relief rush towards her from the dragon. *Please tell me that you are here to announce it is time to break for lunch.*

Well, yes, that's why I'm here. But how are they doing, really?

See for yourself, Alaric said, as one of the trainees stood up and took a step towards Alaric.

The woman put her hands on her hips and looked the dragon square in the eye. "Hello," she said slowly. "My name is Peony. Can you understand me at all?"

Cora could hear the earnestness in the woman's voice, her hope that her efforts were working, but she could tell from looking at Alaric that he had not understood a word.

"No, nothing," Alaric said.

Peony's face fell when she realized she still could not understand him.

"Lunch time!" Cora called out, drawing all the attention away from Alaric. The rebels didn't have to be told twice. They leapt to their feet and hurried towards where the mess tent had been erected.

I repel them, Alaric said glumly. *I am doing what I can for them, but I do not think our sessions are doing anything other than frustrating all parties.*

Cora nodded. *It does seem that progress has been slow. I think it's because the rebels aren't fully grasping the concept of the symbols. Dragon Tongue is very complex. Perhaps our instructions are not clear enough.*

I can definitely vouch for them not understanding. I've been working with this particular group of trainees for several days now, and we are getting nowhere.

Cora chewed on her bottom lip for a moment, thinking. *I'll talk to Strida after lunch. Maybe she can help?* It still surprised Cora that Strida, the scale scavenger from her home village of Barcroft, had ended up at the rebel stronghold. She was grateful for it, though— before she and Alaric had left, Cora and Strida had started to become friends, and she knew the older girl was someone she could trust. Cora had spent nearly her entire life feeling like an outcast, a misfit with no friends and no community to call her own. That had all changed once Alaric came into the picture, of course, but her bond with the dragon had led to dangers she never could have imagined. When the situation became truly desperate, Strida and the other scavengers had come to Cora's aid, helping her when there was no one else to turn to. That wasn't something she would ever forget.

And Strida had managed to learn a bit of Dragon Tongue on her own and without a dragon, thanks to Cora's instruction to visit the caves her grandmother had shown her as a child. That had led to Strida eventually leaving Barcroft and ultimately finding her way to the rebels—which, of course, had led her to meeting up with Cora again after she and Alaric had arrived at the stronghold. It seemed yet another example of the cyclical nature of life Nana Livi had so often spoke of. Everything truly did seem to have a way of coming back around.

It is worth a shot, Alaric agreed. *At this point, I think we need to consider all options. The rebels just are not progressing like they should be at this point.*

Cora sighed. *I know. And I worry that we don't have much time to get everyone ready. Our escape from Llys to the stronghold will have Onyx searching the area for their base. It's essential that we get the rebels trained—and, ideally, ready to bond with dragons of their own —so that they will be ready to defend themselves if Onyx comes pounding on their front door.*

Alaric snorted. *It will be quite difficult for them to reach that point if they can't even achieve the basics of Dragon Tongue.*

Agreed. Let's just hope Strida has some ideas for us.

Get your copy of **Dragon Fire**
Available February 22, 2023
(Available for Pre-Order Now!)
AvaRichardsonBooks.com

The Dragon King's Egg

BLURB

A new hope for dragons. A new danger for the world…

Ophelia, High Queen of the Fae, is ecstatic when Sunny, her bonded dragon, announces that he and his mate are expecting a new egg. After all their trials and tribulations, a dragonling is more than welcome in the realm of Charassi…until a prophecy reveals that the new hatchling may bring about the end of the world.

Other dragons demand that the egg be destroyed. And some within the fae kingdom agree, including a mysterious sect determined to capture the egg at any cost. When they succeed, Ophelia will do anything to get it back. Even if it means putting her safety on the line by infiltrating the Wild Hunt.

But Ophelia's fierce determination puts her at odds with her co-ruler, King Corrin. And their relationship is not the only thing showing cracks. A sinister power is rising that threatens to tear a rift in magic itself. With enemies and disaster looming on all sides, can Ophelia protect both her friends and her kingdom, before it's too late?

Grab your copy of *The Dragon King's Egg*
Available March 29, 2023
(Available for Pre-Order Now!)
AvaRichardsonBooks.com

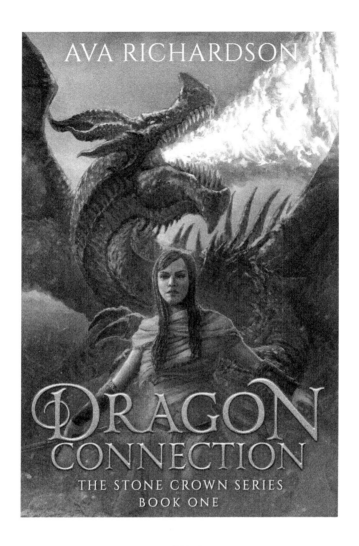

BLURB

One crown can unite them—or destroy them all.

The three kingdoms lie splintered, their aging dragon riders content with stories of glorious battle victories. But a new evil creeps across the land. Inyene, a powerful noblewoman of the Northern Kingdom, plunders valuable resources to power mechanical dragons in her quest to gain a foothold in the Middle Kingdom. From there she will ascend the High Throne, once again uniting the realms under a single crown.

For the wearer of the Stone Crown can wield unlimited power—*if* it can be found.

Narissea has spent a quarter of her sixteen years slaving away in the mines, accused of a crime she didn't commit. When word reaches her of the horrors assailing her village, Narissea knows she must act despite the risk. Already her arm is scarred with four brands signifying previous escape attempts. If she's unsuccessful in her fifth, it will mean death.

But her life forever changes when she stumbles upon an injured dragon, discovers an ancient shrine, and learns the true purpose behind Lady Inyene's mechanical abominations.

Now, Narissea has only one choice: gain Inyene's trust and find a way to thwart her plans, even if it means sacrificing that which she desires most of all.

Her freedom.

Get your copy of **Dragon Connection** at
AvaRichardsonBooks.com

EXCERPT

Chapter One
Wind & Bread

I'm going to remember this day for the rest of my life, I thought to myself.

This was the day that I could no longer remember the gentle caress of the Soussa winds when I closed my eyes. Instead, as I blinked back the tears, all I could feel was the oppressive heat of the tunnel that I was trapped in, and the bite of the unyielding rocks.

And Dagan's latest gift to me.

My lip curled in disgust and hatred at the thick mark of the brand on my upper right forearm. The three others before it had faded from an ugly red to a darker brown. They had stopped hurting. Sorta. Four branding marks for four failed attempts at escape from my prison beneath the world. There was space for just one more at the very top of my arm – but that would also be my last, wouldn't it?

Dagan Mar was the 'Chief' as he liked to call himself – which was just a fancy term for slave master. All of the others here called him much more colorful names behind his back. I didn't even think that Tozut, which was Daza for horse-dung, was a good enough term for him. He wasn't a tall man, but he was wiry and strong. Fair-skinned like the rest of those Middle Kingdomers, and he seemed to like inflicting punishments on all of us tribespeople brought here to the mines of Masaka.

And what for? I bit my bottom lip to stop myself from screaming in rage. Sometimes the overseers and the Chief waved papers and said things like 'Bonds' or 'Crimes' – although I never committed any crime or signed any bit of Torvald paper!

I had been twelve when I had been brought here. Old enough to remember my mother, Yala, her rough sense of humor that hid a gentle heart. *I wish I could hear you make jokes about the old men of the tribe again,* I thought with a sudden hunger. She was the Imanu, or wise-woman, of the Souda tribe – which meant the Daza of the Western Winds. I was old enough to come here remembering the plains. The smell of the grasses. The caress of the Soussa winds. Bright-colored bolts of cloth rippling in an endless sky.

But all of those memories were starting to fade, weren't they? I tried not to cry as I sat in the dark. The colors weren't as bright in my mind as they used to be, and the scents of the grassland flowers not so strong.

And now I couldn't even remember the Soussa winds anymore. I wondered how long it would take me to forget everything else that came before this place, as well.

"Narissea!" my name went down the line, passed from one Daza mouth to the next. Each of us were spread out along the narrow tunnel that was barely taller than we could crouch, and each of us were working at the holes we had painstakingly driven into the hard rocks.

"Nari?" My name changed, becoming smaller as it came out of the lips of my neighbor. That was broad-shouldered Oleer of the Metchoda tribe – the Daza of the Open Places. He was a few years older than me, and had been taken when he had been older, perhaps fifteen? We didn't get much time to talk given the back-breaking work, but he sometimes told me stories of the plains.

"They call them the Empty Plains, but they were never empty, were they," he would chuckle. "I've seen horses, deer, gazelle, wild lion, condors. I even saw a flight of dragons heading westwards, once!" He had been trying to cheer me up, I think. I told him he was making it up. Dragons were rare.

"Nari – the overseer wants you," Oleer was saying, and in the flickering light of the stub of our tallow candles I could see his grimace.

"What does that fat old toad want?" I muttered back. I was in a foul mood today. Hardly surprising, given that my hands were raw from trying to hack and prod at the rock in front of me with my iron bar and my arm was still oozing and sore.

"It's only the overseer," Oleer offered gently. For all his size, he had a soft voice. "At least it's not Dagan."

"Tozut," the next Daza slave up from Oleer spat just at hearing our 'chief's' name. That would be Rebec, smaller than me. She had a scar running from her temple to her jaw from when West Tunnel Two had collapsed. She was one of the Daza who had been here the longest and was well into her twenties.

"Ore Count!" This time, I could hear the guttural bark of the overseer from somewhere beyond me in the dark. I'd never bothered to learn his name, if he had ever shared it with any of us. "Ore Count for Narissea!"

"Oh great," I muttered, as Oleer shared a sympathetic look. "What's that, third time today?"

They were picking on me of course, their next favorite past time after branding me.

"It's because you tried to escape this moon just gone," Rebec called down the line. "You get a brand and an Ore count, and *we* all get half rations!" She was like that. She didn't mean to be nasty but being down here for so long must have done something to her heart.

I can't let myself end up like her, I promised myself. *I have to remember the Soussa wind on my face.* If I could just hold on to one memory – just one – then I might be alright. I might be able to keep my heart beating in my chest.

"Narissea! Get out and get up here!" The overseer bellowed down our small tunnel, and his words echoed and repeated. "Get out. Get out. Get out."

"I'm coming!" I shouted, then, quieter, "Tell him I'm coming, will you?" I told Oleer, who passed on my message as I gave one last crack with my iron bar, slid it out of the hole, and shoved my arm in its place. My carry-basket beside me was woefully light – the seam we were working on was tough as it was, and with all of these Ore Counts I'd already had this shift I'd barely managed to make any headway.

But there, at the end, was a chunk of rock that was loose in my hand. *Aha!* It wouldn't be much, but it would help avoid any further troubles. I yanked my arm backwards—

For it not to move at all.

"Oh, come on!" I hissed. I was stuck, my arm pinned down in the hole, wedged between the teeth of the protruding rocks. I pulled again, but my arm only gave a little, and I hissed as my skin scraped.

"Nari! What are you doing?" Oleer turned back to face me, and then saw the predicament I was in. "Oh, wait," he shuffled forward to my spot, reaching out to grab ahold of my branded arm.

"No! I don't want to break my arm, thank you very much!" I snarled in pain and saw Oleer's face look as though I had just slapped it. I was going to have to apologize to him for that, I berated myself.

"Narissea! Are you disobeying me!" the words of the overseer barked and echoed down the tunnel towards me. "Disobey. Disobey. Disobey." I heard a snicker from Rebec, which only made me feel worse.

"I can do it, just everyone give me a moment," I said, wedging my cloth-bound foot against the wall and pulling. "Argh!" It felt like my shoulder was going to pop out of its socket, but I was rewarded with a *shlooop* as my arm scraped backwards, before getting caught again.

Only this time it was my fist that was causing the blockage, hanging onto that big bit of ore.

"Nari!" Oleer said in alarm.

I had a choice. It would take too long to try and break it down with my iron bar, so I had to get it out by hand. But with the overseer shouting, I had to either drop the rock and leave it or try and break my fingers to get it out of the hole. *Drat.* It was no choice really. Even if I broke my fingers the overseer and Dagan Mar would still expect me to work. That was the kind of people they were, after all. *And* they would probably give me extra shifts or dock my food rations just for having the temerity to get injured.

"Fine. Whatever." I grumbled, dropping the ore and removing my shaking and battered arm back to grab my carry-basket with its tiny number of rocks sitting at the bottom. Oleer must have seen my look of misery, as he quickly dipped into his own woven carry-basket and deposited a heavy lump into the bottom of mine.

"Here. Just don't tell anyone," he said, not waiting for my thanks as he turned back to the rock face and resumed work.

"Thanks," I muttered anyway as I clambered and squeezed past the line of my fellow prisoners, back towards the waiting ire of the overseer. When I got back, I would have to give him the rock I'd left behind and hope it would repay his kindness.

"Hm," the overseer said. He was a large, older man, easily twice my size in every direction, with a balding head and a thick set of leather and glass goggles over his eyes. We stood in one of the main avenues that speared down through the mines of Masaka, where it was wide enough to stand up straight and walk three or four abreast. I relished the moment of luxury as I stretched out my fingers and arms.

"Not bad, I suppose," he had to mutter as he hefted my haul in one hand. "But not any good, either!" he ended with a snap as he dumped my woven and frayed basket onto the cart next to several others, before pulling on the rope that extended from the iron ring of the cart up the passageway. There was an answering jangle of a distant bell, and the cart slowly started to creak forward on wooden wheels. There was a treadmill up there, where a couple of my fellow tribespeople would be endlessly walking as they pulled or lowered the carts up and down the length of this place.

And why all this effort? It was for a woman called Inyene, we had been told – although I had never met her, nor known any slave who had. No one except Dagan Mar, if he was to be believed. He said Inyene owned this patch of highlands – although I didn't understand how anyone could own a mountain at all, that was as absurd as saying that you owned the air you breathed!

Whatever. This woman Inyene wanted iron brought up and out of *her* mountain, and so here I was.

But that wasn't all that she wanted.

"You're to go Up." The overseer jerked a callused thumb after the cart. "Special orders from the Chief himself."

"What?" I said, appalled. Every one of us knew precisely what 'going Up the mountain' meant. It was possibly the most dangerous work that any of us could do. "But our shift must be ending soon, by the time I get up there." I started to protest. I could see a few meters away the large collection of cylinders that made up the Work Clock. It had something to do with bags of sand and ticking rings of metal, but I didn't understand it. Anyway – I could clearly see under the light of the oil lamps that the large bronze pointer hand was *definitely* not far off a full circle.

That meant that the bell would ring, and the shift would change over.

"It's not ending for you though, is it?" the overseer croaked with an almost-laugh. "Special orders I said. Now go on, get!" He aimed a smack for the top of my head, but even in my exhausted state I was too quick for him and I jumped back. I didn't even bat an eyelid at his attempt to hit me – this was just another daily occurrence for those of us unlucky enough to find ourselves down here.

"But what if I collapse up there without any dinner?" I called to him as I backed away. It was true. I would miss my next scheduled meal.

"For goodness' sake!" the overseer growled, but he plucked a skin of fresh water from one of the stationary carts and threw it at me, then tore a chunk off the round of bread and lobbed it at my face. I managed to duck that one too, and when I recovered the dusty bit of loaf, I realized that he had 'given' me the bit that was dusted with white and green mold.

"Wow, thank you so much, toad," I muttered under my breath.

"What did you say to me, you little—" the overseer shouted.

"Gotta go sir, special orders!" I called back and jogged up the tunnel after the creaking cart before he could decide to throw any bits of rock at me this time.

Get your copy of **Dragon Connection** at
AvaRichardsonBooks.com

Printed in Great Britain
by Amazon

20956030R00220